Coconuts
and
Wonderbras

A romantic comedy adventure by
Lynda Renham

ISBN 978-0-9571372-2-6

first edition

Cover Illustration by Gracie Klumpp
www.gracieklumpp.com

Printed in Great Britain by the MPG Books Group,
Bodmin and King's Lynn

Chapter One

Don't you just hate diets? Well maybe you don't. You're probably one of those people who never need to go on a diet. Generally I couldn't care less about dieting, but now that I am on a diet it is a completely different matter. After struggling to zip up my best pair of jeans this morning, and painfully pinching my naval in the process, I've decided it's time for drastic action. The problem is I keep changing my mind about which diet to be on. I never realised there was so much dieting paraphernalia. You know the kind of thing, watching everything you eat, counting calories or counting points, measuring food in those colourful measuring pots and trying to get as much out of them as you can. Not to mention those embarrassing weekly weigh-ins. Then there is the awful food. Eating salads instead of proper food and making your own vegetable soup. Talking of soup, I did try the Cabbage Soup diet. It seemed so easy, but the stink in my kitchen and the amount of time I spent in the loo put me off that one. Then, of course, there are the wonderful diets. Chef-made meals diet, homemade meals diet, and tiny portion diet, eat all you like diet, not to mention the low carb or high carb diet. I rather liked the sound of the 'Ducan' diet, but I seemed to end up with the 'Ducant' diet.

Then there are the marvellous magazine articles with headings like 'Eat Yourself Slim'. Oh yes, I like the sound of that. You can choose whether to diet online or offline, or you could just have a milkshake and forget about food altogether. It's all so confusing. And why do we do it? I don't know why you do it, but I'm doing it to keep the man in my life because I am sure my boyfriend is seeing someone else, and the someone else is far skinnier than me. I know, of course, I should be doing it for myself. But, starting a diet three weeks before Christmas is not only very bad timing but sheer stupidity. I'm Libby by the way, and I like to think of myself as slightly curvy rather than fat, although some days I must admit to feeling huge. My best friend Issy is blessed with a metabolism that allows her to eat anything, and I could gladly kill her. I only have to think marshmallow and I look like one. She, on the other hand, is one of those women who can polish off a plate of fish and chips with a bread roll on the side and still manage to lose a pound. However, it doesn't seem to improve her temperament.

'Sod off.'

It's Saturday night and three weeks before Christmas and Issy, somewhat inebriated, shares some Christmas spirit with the carol singers outside my cottage. I am mortified and tell her so. After all, you just don't tell the Salvation Army to sling their hook do you, especially when they are singing 'Onward Christian Soldiers'.

'That's my bloody point. If they are the Salvation Army then I'll eat my Christmas hat. And if they are going to sing outside your front door they should at least sing carols. Since when has Onward Christian Soldiers been a carol? Hark, I do believe they have now turned into Mariah Carey,' she says scathingly.

Embarrassed beyond belief, I attempt to inject some Christmas cheer by offering mulled wine and homemade mince pies. After all, one of us should show some Christmas spirit, especially to the Salvation Army. I open the door to be met by three youths and a ghetto blaster. They hungrily devour my offerings while I stand shivering. Honestly, it's Christmas, what happened to goodwill to all men? I love Christmas, and the lovely warm cosy feeling you get at this time of the year. I also adore Christmas shopping and the crowds, and I happen to love those garish houses that seem to be hopelessly devoured by Christmas lights and huge reindeers. Oh yes, Christmas isn't really Christmas without all that tacky stuff. And I like carol singers, real carol singers, that is. I am more than happy to give them my mince pies but fake carol singers are something else.

'Now you can sod off. I don't want to hear this rubbish. If you have to play rubbish at least play sodding traditional rubbish, then go and find your mince pies somewhere else,' Issy, queen of tact, shouts from the living room.

The three youths and ghetto blaster trudge off into the snow. I return gratefully to the warm living room, where Issy is breathing fire down the phone to some poor assistant at Domino Pizza.

'I know it is Christmas. What has that got to do with the price of cod? We ordered it over an hour ago, or are you telling me that you have to deliver to Santa and his reindeers first?'

'Price of fish,' I correct under my breath.

'What the bollocks.'

Issy, my best friend and women's journalist agony aunt, likes to say bollocks a lot. Frankly, she is a crap agony aunt and the last person I would ask advice from. If you feel depressed she is likely to agree that jumping off a cliff is the best option. Issy spends bucket loads on clothes and cosmetics, and always emerges from a dress shop looking like a million dollars, whereas I come out feeling like I have spent a million dollars but never looking it. I can never grow fingernails like Issy, and when I do, her bright purple nail polish makes me look more like a witch than tantalising seductress. Issy is confident where I am not and oh yes, she is slim. Like I have said, I am just a little bit fat. Did I say a little bit? Okay, a slight correction needed. A fair bit fat I suppose would be nearer the truth. Although, Issy assures me I am nowhere near as fat as I think. Okay, I am one stone ten pounds over my normal weight, or 10.88 kilograms overweight to be precise. Whichever way you convert it I still come out fat. So, what the arsing head and hole has possessed me to eat a Domino's pizza you're thinking. Well, it is almost Christmas, and I am convinced my boyfriend, Toby, is seeing someone else. Of course, I have no real evidence for this belief except he seems to smell very sweetly of Lancôme Trésor perfume these days. I can't exactly confront him with that can I? After all, he is a highly respected journalist who writes not only for our local rag here in Fross but also for *The Political Times*, which means he works with lots of women, many of whom I am sure wear Trésor. I can't very well accuse him of sleeping with all of them can I? The thing is, they are all slim and trendy whereas I am neither. Don't you just hate the word 'trendy'? In fact, according to him these women are bloody perfect, whereas I am just bloody useless. Not that Toby has ever told me that I am useless. I just feel I am. So, a few weeks before Christmas I have decided it is time to do something drastic about the weight problem. I need to turn myself into a slim, trendy and somewhat perfect woman by Christmas Eve. I decide to call in Issy for diet advice. She suggests we discuss it over a Domino pizza and a bottle of wine. Good start. Like I said, I should never take advice from Issy.

'Obviously you should diet darling, after all, no one likes a fat person, not that you are terribly fat, but don't do it for that little fart Toby, and stop baking sodding cakes. Nigella Lawson you're not!'

As you can see, Issy is as tactful as a sledgehammer. Although I have to agree, I am probably more Delia Smith than Nigella Lawson. I love baking cakes you see. Cupcakes, fairy cakes, fruit cakes, Christmas cakes, sponge cakes, you name it and I bake it. Toby loves my cakes. His favourite is my Victoria sandwich and I have made one for him today along with the mince pies and sausage rolls for the office. The problem is my hobby does tend to end up touching my lips and of course lands on my hips resulting in an insult from Toby's lips... *Have you gained more weight Libby? Your hips look bigger, and that dress used to look nicer on you.*

So, after exhausting every slimming pill on the market and still managing to eat like a horse I have decided drastic measures are needed.

'A gastric band, have you gone insane? Do you really think that little sod is worth it?' Issy gasps when I voice my plan.

I actually think the little sod *is* worth it.

'I'm thinking it would be beneficial to my health and besides...'

'Bloody hell Libs, you could die under the knife, or even worse, have your spine severed.'

Yes, that is my kind of luck.

'Isn't that one and the same thing?'

'What?'

'If they sever my spine, I will die won't I?'

'Whatever, anyway they're bound to perforate something. It's par for the course.'

'It's unlikely.'

'God, you do think the little shit is worth it don't you?'

I'm wondering how many more derogatory words Issy will find to describe Toby before the evening is over. I am actually thinking the little shit/sod/fart is actually worth it, although I don't imagine anyone else would think so. I sometimes even wonder why I think so.

'Right now, the little fart/sod/shit is the only boyfriend I have,' I moan.

'And that's the way it will stay if your spine is severed.'

The truth is I'm not very confident, and even less so when it comes to men. I was so flattered when Toby asked me out a year ago. He is good looking, successful and confident. I can't imagine what he saw in me.

With raised eyebrows, Issy says I should dump the little bugger.

'Stop thinking you can't find anyone better,' she sighs.

With perfect timing the Domino Pizza man rings the doorbell, and I am saved from admitting that I really don't want to dump the little bugger and that I actually do love him. I have to wonder how much I love him, however, when five minutes later I am stuffing myself full of 'Chilli Surprise' deep pan pizza and potato wedges, not to mention the garlic bread. I am proud to say that when Issy opens a tub of Ben and Jerry's ice cream for dessert I actually do reign myself in. After all, there is the Christmas party tomorrow night, and I will doubtless eat heaps. Maybe I should start the diet after the party. Yes, that's the best thing. I'll start my diet on Monday. I'll make the party my final indulgence. After all, publishers lay on fab parties, and Hobsons are no exception. Did I mention that I work for a publishing house? I probably didn't. I work as an agent at Randal and Hobson's publishing house aka Hobnobs. Not that I have anyone famous on my account but I live in hope. My real ambition is to be a journalist like Toby, and although I have written tons of stuff, I just can't get anyone to actually read it. Toby says it is pretty amateurish, but I'm sure with practice I could get better. I actually have this crazy idea that maybe tomorrow night, at the party, I could propose to Toby. Yes, you heard me, propose. I am twenty-nine after all and I really should get married. I know one shouldn't rush into marriage just because one is almost thirty, but can you imagine still being on the shelf in your thirties? Oh God, it is enough to make me reach for the Ben and Jerry's. Well, I have already eaten the pizza so let's face it the damage has been done.

'Oh, I really can't face the thought of being single for another year and Toby is so lovely, he makes me feel...' I say with my mouth full of ice cream.

Issy leans towards me and grabs the spoon.

'Makes you feel sick I shouldn't wonder,' she hiccups. 'He certainly has that effect on me.'

'Special. He makes me feel special,' I say lamely, knowing full well that he doesn't.

'Oh please. By the way, did you hear that radio interview with the luscious Alex Bryant? Oh, that voice. He trashed Toby's article on the Cambodian uprising unmercifully,' she says gleefully. 'But what a dreamboat. Talk about fabalicious. Did you see him on the *Morning Show*? He's just back from America and has signed with a publisher here. Wouldn't it be fab if you had him as a client? He is as close to an Adonis as any man can be. Imagine working twenty-four-seven with him. I bet he has a penis so large that...'

'Issy, please, I have just eaten,' I snap and try to get the image of a huge penis out of my head.

'Anyway, I'm not in the least interested in the *Oh look at me, I'm an ex-SAS super hero, call me when the world needs saving* arsehole. I thought that radio interview was pathetic as it happens,' I say scathingly. 'He is so arrogant, I'm so glad we didn't sign him last year. That is the second time he has trashed Toby's work.'

'He is ultra-gorgeous though, you have to admit that.'

'I wouldn't even know what he looks like.'

'You're the only woman who doesn't then,' she scoffs, flouncing off to the bathroom.

I take the opportunity to see if Toby has sent me a text. Disappointedly I throw my Blackberry back into my bag and clear the dishes.

'Bastard,' slurs Issy sneaking up behind me. 'He hasn't texted you has he?'

'He's probably busy at work,' I mumble, splashing soapy water over the plates and crashing them onto the drainer.

'Where is Toby taking you for New Year's Eve?' she asks, taking a tea towel from a drawer.

'Not sure. I have mentioned the party at the Glass Dome. It seems everyone is going there this year.'

'I've promised myself I will only go if I have someone special to go with,' she sighs.

She throws down the tea towel and gleefully hands me an envelope tied with a red ribbon.

'This will cheer you up. Happy Christmas,' she says nodding excitedly.

'But it isn't Christmas for three weeks. Blimey, you're organised.'

I turn the envelope around in my hands and then place it beside my row of cookery books.

'I'll stick it on the tree as soon as it goes up.'

'No,' blurts Issy retrieving the envelope and sending a Gordon Ramsay cook book flying. 'You have to open it now.'

'Can you please mind Gordon. He is the closest thing I have to male company most days.'

She rolls her eyes and thrusts the envelope at me. I raise my eyebrows. Aren't you just highly distrustful of presents that have to be opened weeks before Christmas?

'Why?' I ask suspiciously.

'Because you have to use it by the end of next week,' she sighs.

Ah, one of Issy's second-hand presents. I open the envelope with trepidation. Please don't let it be anything life affirming or God forbid, dangerous. I am still quivering from the hand-me-down bungee jump that she gave me for my birthday. Please let it be a cookery lesson or something equally as safe.

'A makeover and photo shoot!'

'It expires next Friday,' she cries delightedly. 'I've had the thing hanging around for a year, and then I thought of you. I really don't need it, but you do, and I thought it would be a great present.'

Bloody cheek, what does she mean I need it? I try not to look crestfallen.

'Come on; we are going to Madam Zigana's after all.' She throws my coat and gloves at me.

Oh no, not the psychic. I had hoped that the pizza and the Ben and Jerry's would have made her forget all about that.

'I can't hobnob with the dead. I have nothing suitable to wear, and anyway Toby might phone and I would hate to miss his call,' I protest.

'God, you're starting to obsess. Come on, grab a shroud and let's go.'

'But it's snowing,' I complain.

'Grab a fur shroud then. Come on. She is doing a Christmas special and you are getting so maudlin these days, verging on depressing in fact.'

A Christmas special... God, it sounds more harrowing by the minute. I think a hand-me-down bungee jump would be less vexing. I would much rather snuggle up with a mug of hot chocolate and dream about Mr Right.

Chapter Two

'This can't be right,' I whisper, although there is nobody around to hear us.

Madam Zigana's is situated in a sex shop in the sleazy part of town.

'Shit, it's a bit seedy I agree?' Issy squints at the steamed up window.

I dread to think what is going on in there. I find myself visualising streams of mysterious smoke spiralling up from Tarot cards and encircling vibrators and sleazy books while videos of feverish coupling can be heard in the background.

'A bit seedy, that's an understatement,' I mutter, keeping my head down.

God, what if someone sees us here, like my mother, or Toby or even worse, the vicar. Not that I know the vicar, of course. I swear my nose is turning blue, and I can barely feel my feet. I'm relieved to see that Madam Zigana's fortune-telling parlour is actually in the basement of the sex shop.

Okay, so it wasn't so bad. It was actually a relief to get away from my own thoughts. Shame the whole thing cost us sixty quid. Thirty quid each that is. Correction, it cost me sixty quid. Did I mention that Issy doesn't carry money?

'I never carry cash darling, so common.'

Good job I'm common then. Madam Zigana offered to get her crystal ball if we stayed another ten minutes and paid another fifteen quid. What a rip-off. I almost asked Madam Zigana if, along with her Christmas special, which by the way we never heard any more of, did she by any chance have a two for one offer. You can't blame a girl for trying, can you? The trouble is I am already broke, what with it being Christmas and everything. I had spent a small fortune on dieting food and other bits that Weight Watchers and Rosemary Conley swear are important if weight loss is to be achieved. You know the kind of thing, weighing scales, tape measure, pedometer, skin-firming cream, not to mention the exercise DVDs and packs of special diet food, which are half the size but twice the price of normal stuff. My bathroom looks like a miniature gym. Anyway, back to Madam Zigana who failed to conjure up any dead people, or if she did I failed to notice. In fact, it was so dark and cold in there I failed to notice very much at all. I could barely see the Tarot cards. My future as told by a Manchurian fortune teller and based on some accidentally dropped Tarot cards and for the amazing price of sixty quid is, hold your breath... By the end of the week I will make plans to travel. I will meet a dashing man whose name begins with B or T, *'you will fall at his feet, my lovely'* and have an opportunity to change my whole appearance. I also need to gain more confidence. My mother could have told me that for the cost of a lemon drizzle cake and a ten minute 'how to use your mobile phone' tutorial.

'*Time*, my lovely,' she had pounced on me as we reached the door and grabbed my arm with her bony hand. 'I'm getting a message to warn you that *time* is important. Should I get the crystal ball?'

Tell me something I don't know. I'm late for everything.

'Look to the clock dearie. Don't forget that. A few minutes can change the path of your destiny. A few minutes can make all the difference.'

Fifteen pounds difference in your case if you get your crystal ball. What a load of rubbish. I don't know anybody whose name begins with a B and considering Issy let it slip that my boyfriend's name is Toby was not surprised the initial T came up. I have no plans to travel, unless of course it's for my honeymoon, and the last time I thought about changing my appearance was, good Lord, it was about an hour ago when Issy gave me her present. Oh well, one out of three is not bad for sixty quid is it? Issy is told she will meet her soul mate in the most unusual circumstances. Considering Issy finds herself in unusual circumstances much of the time I assure her that she will meet her Mr Right long before I do.

Issy hails a taxi and I lurch toward it and by lurch I mean, literally. My eye catches something familiar and I lose my footing. My feet skid on some ice and I fly arse over tit and land on my bum with legs flayed, and would you believe it, right at Toby's feet. Good heavens, Madam Zigana truly is prophetic. I try to speak, but the breath is knocked out of me. Not from the fall, you understand, but from seeing Toby, and not just from seeing him but seeing him emerge from the sex shop. What is my boyfriend doing in a sex shop when he is supposed to be working? And what is that in the brown paper bag he is holding? And why does he smell very distinctly of Trésor? Oh God, my boyfriend is a pervert. This could only happen to me.

'Libby,' he exclaims, as though it had been us and not him that had waltzed out of the sleazy sex shop with suspicious brown paper bags in our hands. He doesn't even attempt to help me up.

Issy takes my hand and with one strong pull, yanks me onto my feet.

'Toby,' she exclaims back, 'fancy, bumping into you here.'

'Yes,' I say in a hoity-toity voice, 'fancy seeing you here.'

'Small world isn't it?' giggles Issy, and I shoot her my best dirty look.

Toby coughs, sounding like a strangled choke.

'It is, isn't it? I mean, who would ever have thought I'd see you here. What were the chances of that happening?'

Yes, Toby, what were the chances of your girlfriend catching you coming out of a sex shop?

'I mean, what a coincidence,' he continues, his voice rising by an octave.

Good Lord what is he on? He is talking out of his arse. Speaking of arses, mine is beginning to feel like it has frostbite.

'It's not so odd,' I say flatly, while at the same time thinking how sexy he looks.

'No, I know, but...'

'I suppose the chances of us all being here at the same time...' butts in Issy.

What is Issy saying? Is there something in the air which hasn't hit me yet? Issy swishes back her long blonde hair in an elegant fashion and shakes her head in the direction of the taxi. I shrug and lower my eyes to the brown bag. Maybe he has bought me some sexy underwear for Christmas. Yes, that will be it. Good God, we will be romping for England all over Christmas. Well, that can't be bad seeing as we haven't romped at all in the past few months, well, not much anyway. The truth is, my old rusty vibrator has seen more action than Toby. I swear the quality time I spend with my vibrator is unhealthy. An uncomfortable silence is broken by the ringing of Toby's mobile. We all stand freezing our bollocks off waiting for him to answer, but he just stands there with a foolish grin on his face.

'Aren't you going to answer that?' I ask through chattering teeth. It is freezing. I swear if we don't all move soon they will be digging us out with a snowplough.

'No, I don't think so,' he answers stupidly.

'It might be work,' I suggest.

'I don't think it is.'

What a lying, shagging, deceiving, two-faced little shit. He knows damn well it isn't work. To think I made the two-timing little runt a cake too and stupidly considered having a gastric band fitted and a possible spine severing. Now what do I do? Of course, I should march off all defiantly but pride before a fall, as my mother would say. She says a lot of rubbish to be honest but right now keeping my pride seems a good idea. Anyway, I can't possibly go to the Christmas party alone tomorrow can I? I know Issy will, but she has the kind of confidence to carry it off, whereas I have, well I have no confidence to carry anything off. So, right there, right then, with my nipples turning to ice I decide to stop wearing sturdy pants and roll on girdles that make me heave each time I breath in and finally go on a diet that works. I also decide to chuck Toby after the Christmas party. A few seconds after these great decisions are made he leans across and plonks his frozen lips onto mine, and I melt, that is my frozen heart melts. I find myself saying breathlessly,

'I'll see you tomorrow.'

'I love you Libby. You do trust me don't you?'

I nod. Issy sucks in her breath and mumbles something which sounds very much like 'prick' before bundling me into the taxi. Maybe I can give Toby another chance. After all, not answering his phone is not concrete proof he is seeing someone else is it? I really should stop jumping to conclusions all the time. Issy tells me the answer to all my problems is a good shag, and I don't think she necessarily means with Toby either.

'You're not getting enough,' she says knowingly.

How Issy ever got a job as an agony aunt is beyond me. I shake my head in despair.

'Right, I'm taking you to *Dirty Doug's*,' she announces.

Don't panic, it isn't anywhere near as disgusting as it sounds. Issy is a bad advice columnist but not that bad a friend. Dirty Doug's is the new 'in' place in town and not a male prostitute about to give me the shag of my life. I really don't want to go, but all that awaits me back home is Gordon Ramsay and my rusty old vibrator, affectionately known as *Orlando Broom*. How sad is my life? So with that thought in mind, I agree. We fight our way through the throng to the bar. So here we are. A typical Saturday night where the girls are slinging back their Smirnoffs and Appletinis, while doing quick mirror touch-ups.

'What do you want?' Issy shouts above the deafening Christmas music.

To leave seems the best choice.

'A red wine,' I scream back, thinking I really should say 'diet coke'.

I step back onto someone's foot.

'Shit,' mumbles the man behind me, 'and a Happy Christmas to you too.'

'Sorry,' I mumble.

'Plenty of talent here,' Issy observes, slamming the drinks down and flopping into a chair.

I sip from my glass and watch as droplets fall carelessly onto my white top. I watch Issy shove cheese and onion crisps into her mouth without any fear of retribution. I crunch a cashew nut and look for the toilets.

'I'm going to find the loo,' I shout above Wham's *Last Christmas*. After trudging up two flights of steps and along a narrow corridor I finally find it. Christ, no wonder no one else is about. It's freezing up here. I quickly pee and dash straight out only to collide with the most handsome man. I feel like I have been hit by a truck, in more ways than one. I attempt to steady myself, fail miserably and rely on his strong arms to save me, which they do.

'I'm so sorry, I didn't see you.'

God, there's enough of me. Which bit of me didn't he see? He speaks in one of those clipped upper-crust voices. You know, public schoolboy type although I can assure you, he is not in the least schoolboyish. His voice is deep and as smooth as silk. He seems to have muscles where I didn't know you could have muscles. It's like he came out of nowhere and I'm beginning to wonder if I have come face to face with God himself, he is so perfect. Maybe I am having one of those epiphanies. Good Lord, and I practically fell at his feet. Madam Zigana gets more impressive by the minute. Dishes like this don't come my way very often, at least not the human kind. This dark haired, blue eyed one seems to have dropped from heaven. He hangs his jacket over one shoulder and his starched white shirt dazzles me, making me wonder if he has shares in Daz. I thought Toby was attractive in a white shirt, but this vision in front of me is irresistible. It's all I can do to stop myself from ripping the dazzling shirt off him. What am I thinking of? I'm in love with Toby, aren't I? He looks questioningly at me, and I realise I am staring unashamedly.

'I'm a little shook up,' I say finally.

That's the understatement of this year. God, did I sound flirtatious? He smiles, and I feel my knees go weak.

'Would you like me to escort you back?' God, how does he manage to make it sound like an indecent proposal?

If you mean back to your place, I'm game. After all, a cupcake and an overused Orlando is all that awaits me at mine. I decide to go with the flow. Mother would like him very much. What am I thinking now? Mother will never meet him. It is Toby I am to marry, providing he says yes when I propose, of course. I nod and meekly follow and find myself desperately wishing I was three times slimmer, twice as tall and at least twenty times prettier. His voice is so deep and manly. He must be overdosing on testosterone. Every time he speaks it feels like a caress. There is a throaty sound to his voice and he has eyes only for me. Silly me, I must pull myself together. How stupid to think for one minute that this perfect specimen of a man came here alone. There is probably an equally perfect female specimen somewhere in the building and they probably go together like jelly and blancmange at a party. Trust me to think of food at a time like this. We seem to descend the stairs in record time. Blimey that was quick. He opens the door and we are back within the bosom of the heaving throng. Christmas music blares at me and I hesitate for a second, wanting to stay a little bit longer in his company. He does not move but waits patiently for me to go ahead of him. He holds out his hand and I take it with my sweaty one. His hand is cool and soft, and I savour the moment.

'It was nice to meet you...' he begins when another man equally posh and full of muscle but not as handsome approaches.

'Hey, Ace, same again? I'm getting another round.'

Ace? What an odd name. I can't even imagine what that is short for.

'I'll be with you in a sec, Harry,' he replies while looking at me.

'I'm Libby,' I say quickly in case he disappears in a puff of smoke. I debate whether I should slip him my phone number. I don't imagine it would occur to him to slip me one, his phone number that is. Although I would be happy with whatever he wants to slip me.

Goodness, what is wrong with me? It's as though I have swallowed a love drug.

'Nice to meet you, for the second time,' he smiles. 'I'm…'

'Ace,' I say, tasting his name on my lips.

He smiles, and I nearly say *I'll do whatever*. God, does he have this effect on every woman he meets?

'So, what do you do Libby?'

I'll do whatever.

'I'm a literary agent for a publisher,' I shout above the music.

'You're Libby Holmes?' he says in astonishment.

Blimey, I am more famous than I thought. Maybe there is another Libby Holmes. It is not possible that he can know of me.

'Mmm,' I say, wondering if I should commit myself.

'You work for Randal and Hobson right?'

Heavens, I actually am famous. Maybe I should ask for a pay rise.

'Sorry, I'm confusing you,' he smiles and lays his hand on my arm in such an over familiar way that I blush immediately and feel my legs turn to jelly.

'I've just signed with Randal and Hobson. I do believe you're my agent.'

I must have misheard him surely. I never have luck like this. There is so much noise that I am tempted to ask if he wants to go somewhere quieter. After all, there doesn't seem to be a blancmange in sight. I can't believe he is available. At that moment a very flushed Issy pushes between us.

'Well I never, a celebrity in our midst I see,' she says loudly, handing me my glass.

She obviously doesn't mean me. Ace looks slightly embarrassed but flattered at the same time. God, don't tell me, I just pulled the new Brad Pitt. Just as well I started the diet if I am to become the new Angelina Jolie.

'So, what is a top journalist and world hero doing in this part of the country?' yells an ever bold Issy.

I smile apologetically at him. Maybe now is a good time to invite him back for coffee. Get him away from the fans and all that. I wish I had tidied the cottage before leaving.

'I was stationed here some time ago. I've been meeting up with some old friends and getting to know my new agent.' He smiles at me.

Stationed? What is he, a soldier or something? I raise my eyebrows at Issy as the penny drops.

'Why didn't you say you were representing Alex Bryant?' quips Issy excitedly. 'Were you keeping it a secret or something? You never said a word earlier.'

Because, I'm sodding not, that's why. How dare he deceive me into thinking his name was Ace. I can't believe this. I really can't. How could this gorgeous, lovely man be that awful Alex Bryant?

'You're Alex Bryant, the journalist? The stuck-up arse who thinks he can criticise and slaughter other people's work without even discussing it with them first?' I shout.

Issy cringes. The music stops and I feel all eyes on me.

'Don't do anything rash,' hisses Issy.

What on earth does she mean? So this is Alex Bryant, the Alex Bryant with the huge penis. Don't think about that. Too late and before I can stop myself, my eyes are lowered to his crotch where I can just make out a small bulge.

'Do you want to be a bit more specific in your accusations,' he responds, his tone hardening.

Well, as long as it only his tone that is hardening. I pull my eyes away and blush.

'Is Toby Mitchell specific enough for you? Toby Mitchell, my fiancé to be more specific,' I spit angrily.

Issy attempts to manoeuvre me towards the door.

'Ah, that Toby,' he says nonchalantly, taking a swig of the beer that Harry has just handed him. 'I didn't realise you were intimately connected.'

'Nor did I,' says a shocked Issy. 'Engaged? Shit, you only went to the loo.'

'Hello ladies, can I get you both a drink?' asks Harry.

'This is my agent, Libby,' smiles Alex Bryant.

Issy looks at me expectantly. I roll my eyes. She surely isn't expecting me to introduce her.

'Oh, thank you,' replies Issy. 'I'll have...'

'No thank you,' I snap giving Issy a piercing look.

I really didn't believe I could fume any more.

'Toby is an excellent writer,' I persist turning back to Bryant.

'Bollocks. You're getting carried away now,' chips in Issy.

'We'll have to agree to differ on that one,' he says, seemingly disinterested.

'Absolutely,' agrees Issy. Honestly, she is supposed to be my friend.

'I would never work with you, never. Anyone who offends Toby offends me. Never insult an alligator until you've crossed the river,' I snap.

'Jesus, what did you do, swallow the *Guinness Book of Quotes*?' quips Issy.

I ignore her and march out of the pub. What was I thinking? I should have known someone like him was too good to be true. I've got a good mind to go back to Madam Zigana to demand a refund.

Chapter Three

'You have to help me,' I cry down the phone, while frantically searching for tissues. Such was my dedication to Rosemary Conley, that when I went to Tesco I was so focused on cottage cheese and tuna that I clean forgot the basic essentials needed for wiping one's arse and nose. How did I get to this point? I don't mean out of tissues and loo rolls. How did I get to be single, fat and alone at twenty-nine? Well, not strictly alone of course, if you count Toby. That's my whole point, can I count Toby? I don't know what came over me last night, being so forgiving to him and yet so unforgiving with Alex Bryant. Still, Bryant did make me look something of a fool. If he thinks I am representing him, he can think again.

'I thought you were wearing that thing you bought at Jigsaw,' replies Issy.

'Thing?' I object. 'I paid fifty quid for that *thing*, and now it won't go over my sodding hips. What am I going to do? I haven't got time to buy something new, and I haven't even done my hair yet. What am I going to do? I can't go.'

'Not go to Hobnobs party, are you mad?'

I do wish Issy wouldn't call it Hobnobs. It always makes me think of food. This is terrible. Whenever I get stressed I want to eat, and so far I have consumed three tangerines and two apples and trust me, they just do not work the same way as a Yorkie bar. I find myself staring longingly at the freshly iced anniversary cake I'd made for my neighbour. No, I must not, what on earth am I thinking? I exhale and bite into a carrot.

'What about that black shirty wots-it-thing that you wore for your parents thingy? You know, what I call an all-rounder.'

Christ, was that English? I fly upstairs and scramble through my wardrobe punctuating the air with 'bollocks' and 'balls'. Finally, I pull out the black shirty wots-it-thing. Actually, it's not too bad. I check the clock. I had whipped myself up into such a state of panic that I am now exhausted. Two hours to go.

'Calm down and get ready, slowly. I'll see you later,' says Issy mildly.

Thank God she is coming. Every year we get to invite one guest, and this year Issy is mine. Toby gets an automatic invite as a local reporter. I get the best of both worlds. I let out a long breath, flop onto the couch and plug in the heated rollers. There is a loud *crack*, a blue spark and the little red power light goes out. I begin to sob and dab at my tears with a reindeer tea towel. It isn't mine you understand. That is I didn't buy it. I wouldn't be seen dead with a reindeer tea towel. Mother bought it when she went to Eastbourne with the WI and palmed it off onto me. Ten minutes later with red-rimmed eyes, I pop the kettle on and grab a cupcake scoffing the whole thing in one go. Well, that's the diet buggered. Still, I wasn't really starting it properly until after the party. It has been impossible to start the diet this week. I can start seriously dieting tomorrow once the Hobnobs party is over. I grab some kitchen towel and find myself staring at the cooker. For goodness sake, what am I thinking of? I can't gas myself for Christ's sake. Sylvia Plath, I certainly am not. Her death might have been somewhat macabre, romantic enough for a film, but mine would just be plain macabre and wouldn't even make the local paper. I sigh and decide that gas would be very unfair on the cat. Not that I have a cat of course, but there is a stray that comes in sometimes and it would be just awful to gas the poor thing. No, I can't do that, most certainly not. Besides, things aren't *that* bad are they? So, all thoughts of suicide put to one side I attempt to make myself look as glamorous as possible. It doesn't help, of course, that I have wild crazy hair and red swollen eyes, and feel ancient. I grab another cupcake, as I really need a sugar rush, and trundle upstairs to dress my ample frame. Well, my even more ample frame now that I have eaten the cupcake. I will soon be shopping for clothes in 'Big Girls Only'. I want to weep.

***

Toby is pacing up and down outside the hotel when I pull up in the taxi. He is wearing a big, heavy coat, but I spy his bow tie and feel my knees go all wobbly. There is something about a bow tie, don't you think? Well, it certainly does something to my loins. Not just the bow tie, obviously. It has to be wrapped around someone's throat. Of course, in my case, the preferable someone has to be Toby. I picture his starched white shirt and feel myself go all weak. It will, of course, be a new shirt. Toby is very fussy about shirts. They always have to be crisp and expertly ironed. In fact, he is so fussy about his clothes that I very much doubt he will let me get up close and personal tonight just in case my lipstick should land on his shirt. Did I mention that Toby is ultra-pernickety when it comes to his appearance? I probably didn't. It drives me mad some days. He never dresses casually. Issy once joked that he puts on a tie to take a dump. He even wears his suit to take me to the cinema, I mean, how embarrassing is that? But tonight, he really does look gorgeous. His hair is freshly washed and his deep green eyes twinkle at me from under their heavy lids. I almost wish we didn't have to go in and could just go back to his place, or my place come to that. Actually come to think of it any place would do. God, how powerful is a bow tie. He is smiling at me, and I feel sure that everything that took place last night outside the sex shop was perfectly innocent.

'I'm not late am I?' I ask, knowing full well that we are both early.

He appraises me and then says we should go inside in a tone that sounds like he is not happy. Obviously, the smile I thought I saw must have been wind or something because he certainly doesn't have it now. I follow miserably feeling pathetic, all sexual longing driven from my loins. It doesn't help that my new corset is cracking my ribs with my every breath. Honestly, all the trouble I went to and he can't even tell me that I look nice.

'What's the matter?' I ask.

'Nothing, I just thought you were going to wear that new dress.'

Oh dear. Best not to tell him it doesn't quite fit. An usher requests our invitations and, with a sinking stomach, I remember mine is still stuck to the fridge door. I fumble busily in my handbag in the vain hope he will wave us through. Toby fidgets as people bustle past us.

'Now what's wrong?' he asks irritably.

I am saved from answering by my boss, Jamie. A nice guy, thirty-something and a queer of course. He stands camp as Christmas and throws one arm around Toby. Toby hates gays. I mean, seriously. He is as homophobic as they come and Jamie knows it and is outrageously flamboyant whenever Toby is around.

'Toby, darling, you look gorgeous. Libby sweetie, why are you fumbling around?'

I open my mouth to explain.

'Come on, darlings, let's go in and get a drink. I could murder a champagne cocktail.'

He takes my arm and leads me into the functions room without a murmur from the usher or Toby. What a great entrance, gliding in without showing the invitation. Except of course, I am so busy looking around at everybody that I don't notice the step and trip, falling flat onto my face. Toby gasps and Jamie laughs while helping me up. Why is it that everyone else helps me up except Toby? He shakes his head despairingly, and I fight back my tears. Why does everything go wrong when I am with him? I feel like a thousand eyes are on me and excuse myself to find the loo to tidy myself up. God, how embarrassing was that. I give myself a quick face check, spray some Rive Gauche onto my neck and brush my hair before walking out of the loo and would you believe it, straight into Alex Bryant. Is this déjà vu or does Alex Bryant spent a lot of time loitering outside women's loos?

'Well, hello again,' he says with a wink.

'Hi,' I say, forcing a smile.

I should be banned from black-tie dos. I could easily rip the shirt off him too. I'm either seriously sex-starved, or my hormones have gone crazy. I assure you that I don't normally spend my life wanting to rip shirts off men.

'We must find somewhere less salubrious to meet,' he jokes and my heart flutters, much against my will. What is he doing here? I then remember that he is a client and what's worse, one of mine it seems.

This time he is with what is obviously the blancmange to his jelly. She is exactly how I would have imagined. A size ten and with legs up to her armpits, blonde hair, flawless porcelain skin, and wearing a backless little black dress that clings to her shapely hips. Clearly, no corset needed here. Smokey grey eyes lock onto mine for a second and then travel critically over my black shirty wots-it. I feel like I must be wearing sackcloth and ashes. She goes to smile, but her thin lips seem to struggle.

'Penny, let me introduce you to Libby, my agent,' he says, raising his eyebrows at me.

'Hello, Libby, nice to meet you,' she says in a stiff voice and reluctantly holds out a limp hand. I go to take it but she moves away leaving my hand hovering in the air. I look like the Queen waving to the nation.

'Gerald, how are you?' she calls and dismisses me with a half-hearted wave. I find myself walking backwards nodding stupidly. It's a wonder I don't curtsey. Alex Bryant gives an apologetic smile. I take a final step and bump into Miles, Hobnobs accountant.

'Throwing yourself at me, are you old girl? I say, you are looking sophisticated tonight.' He burps, and champagne fumes waft into my face.

'Less of the *old girl* please, Miles,' I say, wrinkling my nose.
I try to see Toby amidst the throng, but he is nowhere to be seen.

'What, no drink? Good heavens girl it's bloody Christmas. If you can't get off your face tonight then when can you?'
I am dragged to the bar to join the others who are determined to get off their faces. Miles reluctantly orders me an orange juice, attempts to make me laugh with his jokes, fails miserably and finally directs me to our table. I spot Issy, gesturing with her head to the seat next to her. I gasp. Oh no, not Alex Bryant. I see Toby approaching, aka my fiancé, at least, that is what I had said. He reaches the table and leans towards me. I think it is for a kiss but instead his lips whisper into my ear.

'Where have you been? I've been lumbered with that bloody shirt-lifter for the past fifteen minutes.'
Is that the distinctive smell of Trésor that is wafting up my nostrils? I turn to Toby and see he is staring at Bryant.

'Oh for God's sake, what is he doing here? Did you arrange the seating?'
Before I can answer Jamie glides up and drapes an arm around Alex.

'Let me introduce you,' he says gaily, oblivious to our shocked faces. I spin round to grab a glass of champagne from the waiter. I do believe now is the time to get off my face.

'Thanks very much Libby,' mumbles Toby.
Why is he blaming me? Christ, this is turning into a fun evening. I should have gassed myself while I had the chance. Anyway, the introductions that followed should have gone something like this...

'Libby, this is Alex Bryant. You've heard of Alex, of course?'

'Yes, of course. What an honour to meet you Mr Bryant.'

'Alex, this is my fab assistant Libby and her lovely, soon to be fiancé Toby, whose work you have read of course.'

'Of course. I found your article on the Cambodian revolt fascinating Toby.'

Then there are lots of cheek kisses that aren't quite kisses, and we all sit down and smile at each other.

It actually went like this:

'Libby, this is Alex Bryant, the famous war correspondent who you've heard about of course, and this is his lovely fiancée Penny. Alex has recently joined Randal and Hobson.'

Now Jamie tells me. So, she's his fiancée. I should have known someone like him would have been taken. Not that I care of course. I avoid eye contact and clasp Toby's hand under the table. He squeezes it gently and I feel a little bit better.

'Hello,' I respond nonchalantly and blow my nose noisily to release the Trésor odour.

There is a tiny cough from Jamie and he continues,

'Of course, you know of Toby Mitchell don't you Alex?'

An uncomfortable silence follows. Issy burps and I respond with,

'Bless you.'

Alex Bryant, who shall be known as *The Bastard* from here on in, looks only slightly embarrassed.

'And this is Issy,' I throw in casually. 'Writes for the agony column and burps for England but not necessarily in that order. You've heard of her surely?'

Issy drops the olive that she was about to pop into her mouth. The olive rolls towards Blonde Blancmange who stands up haughtily, swings her shoulder-length bob over her shoulder, sighs heavily and declares,

'How rude, I don't have to listen to this.' She makes to leave the table. Bryant gently takes her hand and pulls her back down.

Toby looks thunderous, and with knuckles clenched he gives Jamie a disparaging look while Issy stares wide-eyed. Alex Bryant, correction, The Bastard is the only cool one amongst us and why am I not surprised. Issy hands me another glass of champagne which I knock back in one hit. The only way to be in difficult social situations is drunk.

'Libby, what is wrong with you?' whispers Issy.

Alex leans across the table with an outstretched hand.

'Nice to meet you Libby,' he says softly. I ignore the little flutter in my stomach and put it down to flatulence. Why isn't he mentioning that we have met already? I touch his hand and a tingle runs through my body. Toby snatches my hand roughly.

'Right, that's enough. You have already tarnished my name, so keep your hands off my girlfriend,' he snaps.

I'm quite impressed. Shame his voice has a shake though. Although after reading what the bastard Bryant has done to some people, armed with only a cheese grater, it is enough to make anyone shake.

'Blimey,' says an astonished and rather tipsy Miles.

'Criticism should always be taken in a constructive manner Toby, that was exactly how I meant it,' croons The Bastard.

What a patronising sod, I think. Oh no, I didn't think it, I actually said it. There is silence. Alex Bryant and I lock eyes across the table.

'I can see it is going to be quite a challenge working with you Libby,' he says finally.

I look at Jamie with daggers in my eyes.

'Don't do anything rash,' hisses Issy as I stand up.

Why does she always think I am going to do something rash?

'Jamie...' I begin.

'Constructive,' explodes Toby, making me jump as I reach for an olive and accidentally knock over Blancmange's champagne glass. A foaming tsunami rushes towards her and spills onto her legs. Oh shit. She lets out a squeal and Issy quickly dabs at her with a serviette. It is quite gross to watch. I am relieved when Jamie pulls her off. There is a loud screeching sound from the PA and a booming voice silences us all.

'Ladies and gentlemen, dinner is about to be served.'

'Bloody marvellous,' groans Toby, elbowing me in the ribs as he shuffles in his seat. Great, food is all I bloody need right now. I always eat more when I am angry or upset. Just as well I am starting my diet properly on Monday. Miles squeezes himself into the seat the other side of me.

'That was bloody exciting,' he whispers. 'I wouldn't fancy taking on old Bryant myself, what? He'd slice your tongue out before you could say Bruce Lee.'

Why do these things happen to me? And who does this Alex Bryant think he is that he can go around patronising everyone? Okay, not everyone, but he did patronise Toby. I see him burst out laughing at something Jamie has said. Blancmange follows suit, and I feel dead miserable.

'Bloody poof,' says Toby sulkily. 'And I can't believe you are going to work with that arrogant prick.'

23

'It's the first I have heard of it,' I protest feebly and hate myself for thinking what nice even teeth Alex Bryant is displaying.

'It feels like treachery,' moans Toby in a pained voice.

'Treachery,' I echo.

'Salmon with salad madam, or turkey with roast potatoes?' trills the waiter hovering beside me with a plate of each. I suppose I had better have the salmon and salad. I watch enviously as skinny Blonde Blancmange accepts only the salad. Show off.

'You and Jamie conspiring against me, that's what it is.'

'Conspiring?'

Christ, I'm turning into a parrot.

'Why do you keep repeating everything I say?' he snaps.

'Everything you say?' I question.

I find I am pointing to the turkey. This is so wrong. Redirect finger Libby, redirect. But it is too late. Four lovely, crispy roast potatoes are placed in front of me and then covered with lovely fragrant gravy. Oh, heaven.

'That looks good,' comments Bryant with a smile that both Toby and I return with icy stares. Blancmange looks at my plate in distaste, while Issy points greedily at it and requests the same.

'I couldn't possibly eat a dead bird,' says Blancmange pompously.

I stab the turkey viciously with my knife.

'Just checking,' I smile. 'Yes, it's definitely dead. I couldn't possibly eat a live one.'

Issy giggles and good Lord, is that a sly grin on Bryant's face? He catches my eye, and I quickly turn away. He leans across Blancmange and her slim arm with its row of silver bracelets jangles around his neck. Why is it that I now feel fat, clumsy and ugly in my black shirty wots-it thing?

'Why, it's Alex Bryant, how wonderful,' bellows a high-pitched voice followed by a highly fragrant, over made-up woman who is wearing what appears to be my mother's living room curtains. She leans across and plonks a wet kiss on Alex Bryant's cheek.

'Lucy Parker Smythe, thrilled to meet you,' she says, wiping the lipstick stain from his cheek with her thumb.

'Oh, may I join you,' she squeals excitedly.

Before any of us has the chance to object she has plonked her wobbly bum onto a chair and begins spouting a load of bollocks.

'I mean, this situation in Cambodia is just dire isn't it? Personally I think we should round up all those rebels and be done with it. Give the peasants more rice and everyone will be happy. Our WI is going to be doing something on it this month.'

Oh well, that's the Cambodian problem solved then. Maybe the WI after bringing world peace can help me with my weight problem.

'I'm afraid it is a little more complicated than that. The rebels aren't all bad actually. The politics are very confusing,' says Alex Bryant with that irritating smile.

'Well, that is certainly a matter of opinion,' argues Toby. 'I would say rounding up the rebels is not such a bad idea. They are clearly thugs.'

Oh dear, not again.

'Actually, it was quite clear from your article that you wrote it with the minimum of research. You haven't been to Cambodia have you?' replies Bryant, calmly.

'These things are black and white if you ask me.'

I roll my eyes, tuck into my roast potatoes and nod at Issy who is replenishing everyone's glasses.

'I wonder Alex,' coos Lucy Parker Smythe, leaning closer to him so that her breast wobbles very near to his nose. 'If you could come and have a little chat with our ladies and advise them what to put in their shoe boxes.'

'Nothing in Cambodia right now is black and white Toby,' responds Alex Bryant, manoeuvring his nostrils from Lucy Parker Smyth's nipple and depositing her into a chair in one motion.

'Smooth,' I remark to Issy.

'Oh, he is that,' she replies, fluttering her eyelashes at him.

'I thought Toby's piece had some interesting points,' butts in Jamie, pouring gravy onto his turkey.

'Thank you Jamie, but I really don't need you to stand up for me,' snaps Toby.

Alex passes a dish across the table towards me.

'Stuffing,' he says flatly and the colour rises to my cheeks.

'Ooh,' Issy whispers into my ear and the burning spreads throughout my body. I lift my eyes to Alex Bryant to see him looking at me with that arrogant smile on his face. He really manages to make me feel quite ridiculous, and feeling ridiculous is something I do very well without anyone helping me thank you.

'That's fattening,' remarks Toby, snatching the dish from Alex.

He is quite right of course. In fact, the whole dinner is full of sodding calories, but did he have to really make the point in front of everyone? I wish I could crawl home to my little cottage with a cheap bottle of wine and a box of Toblerone and not be a part of this debacle.

'How about fifty quid,' bellows Miles. There is silence and all eyes are on Miles. Well, it makes a change from all eyes on me.

'In the shoebox, put fifty quid in each one. Surely dosh is the best thing. You can't send over a shoebox of rice, what!'

What, indeed.

'Honestly, how naïve,' mumbles Toby, but Alex Bryant, who evidently has bionic ears, hears him.

'With all due respect, it is no more naïve than your article, which apart from the outstanding paragraph on the futility of war, was really very lame and lacked substance.'

'Didn't you write that bit Libby?' chips in Issy gaily.

Toby shoots me a murderous look.

'She just tidied up some errors,' snarls Toby.

Alex squints at me. Oh dear, now my life will not be worth living.

'I wasn't aware you contributed to the article,' says Bryant, studying me.

'Why did you have to open your big mouth,' Toby snaps at Issy.

I feel quite inclined to ask Bryant the same question. It is at this point in the proceedings that I decide to take up smoking. Not literally you understand. I just need to make my escape and get out of the hall.

'Just going out for a ciggie,' I mumble, scraping back my chair.

'What!' Issy exclaims.

Instead of fresh air, I find myself swallowed up in a whirlpool of blue haze as smokers indulge their habit by the French doors. *Driving home for Christmas* assaults my ears. I grab two Quality Street from the sweet dish at the doorway. This is turning into the Christmas from hell. How on earth can I propose to Toby in this atmosphere? I cough and splutter my way through the haze until I reach fresh air. I smooth down my dress and see to my horror that my tights have ripped. That's about right. Why is Toby snapping at me so much? Is it my fault Alex sodding Bryant is on our table? I sit on the courtyard bench for a while and compose myself. I turn to head back and then I see *them*. How I didn't hear *them* before is beyond me as *she* has a laugh like a foghorn. I am frozen to the spot and stare at them as if hypnotised. As if in slow motion, she turns, flicking her hair from her face and leans back so he has to hold her tighter. She throws herself forward and kisses him passionately on the lips before she sees me. It is Serena Lambert, the daughter of Toby's boss, and she is kissing my boyfriend by the Christmas tree in his new starched shirt. Stop thinking about his starched shirt, you mad bitch. Jesus, this is the worst moment of my life and I'm worried about his new shirt. Christ. Serena's shocked expression must reflect my own. If there had been a knife nearby I swear I don't know who I would have stabbed first. Okay, I am probably hysterical, and don't know what the hell I am thinking. Serena Lambert and my boyfriend kissing, surely I should stab him first. Oh damn it, it is probably easier to stab myself and be done with it.

'Libby,' squeals Serena pushing past the Christmas tree and plonking herself in front of me. Sparkly tinsel from the tree is now attached to her static lacquered hair making her look a bit like a Christmas Barbie doll. All the same, she is a slim Barbie doll. Compared to her I look like a fat Womble.

'Isn't it just a fantabulous party? I was just saying to Toby, isn't it a fantabulous party.' She squeaks much too shrilly while seemingly popping her breasts back into her dress. I feel nauseous.

'Yes, it certainly is a fantabulous party indeed,' says a cool voice behind us and we all turn to see Alex Bryant. 'This fell from your bag,' he says holding out my Blackberry.
A very flustered Toby looks from Serena to Alex and then back to me.

'Libby, it isn't what you think,' he says.
I mustn't cry. Whatever happens I mustn't cry in front of them all. Alex gives Toby a hard stare before turning to me.

'Let's get you a drink,' he says softly and before I can speak he is taking my hand and leading me past Toby and towards the bar.

'What's your poison?'
I look at him. My head is spinning. How could Toby humiliate me like that?

'What?'

'What would you like to drink?'
Oh God, this is awful. Is Penelope watching us?

'I should get back to the table,' I say weakly.

'I think you need a drink,' he tells me smiling, 'unless of course you are very hungry?'

The truth is I have totally lost my appetite. I feel such a fool. Did Alex Bryant see them kissing as well? Oh, it is just too awful for words. I shake my head. The smell of Trésor seems to be all around us and I wonder if he can smell it too. God, I hope he doesn't think it's my perfume. I hate the stuff.

'I'll have a whisky and coke,' I say.

A whisky and coke, what am I saying? I never drink whisky and coke. I must be in shock. I'm also wondering what the hell I am doing drinking with Alex Bryant. Of course, had the circumstances been different, it would have been rather nice. I notice several women at the bar are looking at me enviously. Now that is a first.

'Why were you there?' I ask in an accusatory tone.

'There?' he questions, handing me the drink which I throw back in one hit. The burning liquid hits my throat with such force that I immediately cough and feel my eyes water.

'In the courtyard,' I say throatily and dab at my eyes with a tissue.

'I came to give you your phone, but also to apologise for my rudeness the other evening in Dirty Doug's.'

His eyes are twinkling.

'Oh,' I stammer. I know I should apologise too, but somehow my pride won't allow me.

'Are you okay,' he asks gently.

I nod, although I'm not really.

'Would you like me to take you home?'

Now, there's an offer I wouldn't have refused when we were at Dirty Doug's. Before I have time to answer Miles joins us at the bar.

'Bottoms up old girl,' he bellows, handing me a glass of wine. Oh, don't tell me Miles saw everything too.

'We haven't been introduced properly,' he says leaning drunkenly towards Alex. 'But I'm a great admirer of your work.' He shakes Alex's hand vigorously, and Alex winks at me.

Good heavens.

'Down the hatch,' I say gulping down some wine.

'Here's mud in your eye,' chips in the waiter as Toby rushes up to the bar with a pained expression on his face. I gulp down the wine and hold out my glass for more, which Alex gladly refills.

'Libby, for Christ's sake, let me explain.'

I give him a scathing look and lift the glass to my lips.

'Down in one,' shouts Miles.

I giggle.

'Get that doon yer gullet,' laughs the waiter.

'Over the lips, past the gums, watch out tummy here it comes!' I hiccup and giggle at the guilty look on Toby's face.

'Don't tell me Toby, she had something in her eye. Am I right?' Toby's face colours and Miles laughs. Although, I don't think he is sure what is going on. Alex looks scathingly at Toby.

'Up your bum,' Miles shouts and throws back his drink. Alex takes my arm.

'Let's get you home,' he says softly.

Toby pushes his hand off my arm roughly.

'Take your fucking hands off her, you arrogant prick.'

'Let's not have a scene, Toby,' Bryant responds quietly but there is the undercurrent of a challenge in his voice.

'How could you Toby? You've made a fool of me. I've only ever tried to be a good girlfriend to you. I hate you,' I say and before I know what I'm doing I have emptied the glass over his head.

Issy pulls me gently by the arm.

'Thank you Alex, I'll take care of her. Come on Libby, we're going home.'

I give Toby a two finger salute as I am dragged from the 'fantabulous' party. I look to Alex Bryant who is watching us with a serious expression on his face. The last words I hear are Toby's.

'At least she doesn't belittle me... and she isn't fat.'

What a bastard. And you know what; I think I still love him. There must be something seriously wrong with me.

Lynda Renham

Chapter Four

It is seven-thirty the morning after the party, and my brain is in turmoil. Okay, I am suffering from a mild hangover, and to make matters worse I have started my period, and all I have in the house is one measly panty liner. Why did Hobnobs have their 'fantabulous' party on a Sunday night? It's all I can do to get out of bed, let alone go to work. You remember the fantabulous party, the one where I dumped Toby.

I fly out of the cottage, coat flapping and tights slipping to the bottom of my buttocks. I get that uncomfortable feeling that my sanitary towel is creeping upwards and will soon be residing between the crack in my bottom. Don't you just hate panty liners? They never stay where you put them. How could I forget to buy tampons? I know diets are important and all that, but hell, did I forget all things hygienic at Tesco? I turn to lock the door and realise I don't have my keys. A quick fumbling in my handbag just produces a four letter word and an apology to the milkman. If only he sold tampons. He sells everything else. I notice his flies are undone and turn away to fumble in my handbag again. A quick thrill from the milkman is the last thing I need. I rush back inside and dash from room to room looking for my keys. I punch Hobnobs number into my Blackberry while crawling under the bed.

'Good morning, Jamie Murray's office,' says a cheery voice.

Christ, how does Jane manage to sound so chirpy at seven-thirty in the morning? More importantly, what does she swallow with her Weetabix that propels her there at such an unearthly hour? And how can she sound so bright and breezy the morning after the fantabulous party?

I pull the keys from under the bed along with a solitary contraceptive pill. Ah, that's what happened to Wednesday.

'It's me,' I mumble while banging my head. 'Shit.'

'Right,' responds Jane somewhat dully.

'Running late...' I mutter.

God, I am appalled at the layer of dust under the bed. How did that get there?

'You don't say?'

'I have a meeting with Jamie...'

'I will tell him the bad news myself.'

I blow a raspberry, hang up and fly out of the door knocking over a bottle of milk.

'Shit.'

'Not what you wanted?' asks the milkman with a broad smile on his face.

'Leave me skimmed in future. Don't make me smash another.' I smile and run to my car, where I skid and bump into it. The sanitary towel rises up and lands in the middle of my back. I sigh and limp round to the driver's side.

'You make my mornings,' he laughs. 'Where's that ginger cake you promised me?'

A vision of the ginger cake sitting on my kitchen counter flashes in front of my eyes. Damn it.

'Tomorrow, remind me,' I call back before driving off with a wave in the manner of a celebrity. Twenty minutes later I mount the kerb and park on a double yellow line by the cash machine in a manner very unlike a celebrity. I wonder what Madam Zigana is spending my money on. I check my balance and gasp. Two hundred pounds overdrawn! That can't be right. I print out a balance sheet and cringe. Debenhams £98. I struggle to remember what it was that I had bought in Debenhams. Oh yes, the shoes I had treated myself to for the party. What a waste of money that was. Eighty quid to that bitch Rosemary Conley for the pleasure of starving me. Well, not her personally of course. Then there had been the fortune I had spent in Tesco. Oh, and yes, the low fat cookbook. I had forgotten about that. But, hang on, this can't be right, two hundred and fifty pounds taken by the electricity board. How can that be right? I live in a little cottage not a bloody nuclear station. I know I have been using the vibrator a bit more but bloody hell. Good job I didn't have a multiple orgasm, it may have blown the entire electrical network. I make a mental note to query the bill and quickly withdraw thirty pounds before I change my mind. The rent hasn't even been paid yet. My heart sinks at the thought of asking Jamie for an advance, again. Shivering, I clamber back into my little old Nissan and drive to work, steering with one hand while attempting to yank the sanitary towel back round to where it belongs with the other. I arrive at Hobnobs almost thirty minutes late and oh, who the arsing head and hole has parked in my space? There is a big sign saying 'STAFF', for Christ's sake. I spend the next ten minutes trying to find a space and eventually have to park so close to a wall that I have to get out on the passenger side. I climb over the seat inelegantly and rip my tights in the process. Jesus, I am getting through tights like nobody's business, I'd do well to take out shares in Marks and Spencer.

Once I finally get inside the building I storm past Jane and head towards Jamie's office, yanking at the sanitary towel.

'Morning... oh Libby...' calls Jane.

I wave while struggling with Jamie's door, applying a hefty kick to the part that always gets stuck.

'Shit. This door drives me mad. Sorry I'm late Jamie, it's been an eventful few hours. It seems my vibrator almost caused a total power wipe out, and some wanker parked their Range Rover in my space would you believe?' I say, while fingering the hole in my tights.

'I'm sorry, was that your space? I apologise.' I recognise the posh voice and my heart sinks.

I look up and see that I am standing in front of Alex Bryant. Oh, for goodness sake. I feel myself blush. Hot liquid floats into my knickers and I want to die. I must look a tramp. I attempt to straighten everything up and avoid Jamie's disapproving look.

'Ah, you're the wanker,' I say.

'It would seem so.' He is smiling, and his laughing eyes seem to mock me. 'And if my memory serves me correctly, don't vibrators run off batteries?'

Smart Alec.

'Mine is a turbo-powered one.'

That puts him in his place. He is annoyingly good looking, I really can't deny that. Jamie coughs, lowers his eyes to my tights and then looks me in the eye. He looks so young and fresh faced, and I feel old and very weary. He looks at his watch and then back at me.

'Is everything okay?' he asks, nodding strangely.

I nod dumbly.

'Okay if we start the meeting?'

Surely he doesn't mean with Alex Bryant still here? Before I can reply he clicks the button on his intercom.

'Can we have some coffee please Jane? Thanks.'

Obviously, he does mean with Alex Bryant still here. Jamie smiles at me, and I relax my shoulders slightly.

'Alex tells me that you and Toby got engaged. Congratulations.'
Whoops.

'Erm, yeah, thanks.'

Alex looks closely at me. The sanitary towel is now dangling dangerously outside my knickers. I consider excusing myself and think better of it when Alex the creep pulls a chair out for me. I move slowly towards it and sit down. What the hell is Alex Bryant doing here? Why didn't Jamie tell me that he would be sitting in on our meeting this morning? I find I cannot even look at him. Not that there is anything wrong with him you understand. Issy, for instance, thinks he is drop-dead gorgeous. I suppose he is if you like the dark, brooding type, with dark wavy hair and come-to-bed eyes. There is certainly something animalistic about him, but that is probably the war correspondent in him.

'Libby, you met Alex last night.'

'Briefly,' I answer and stupidly feel myself blush again when Alex winks at me.

'A definite brief encounter,' he acknowledges. Whatever the hell that means.

'Alex's book has done very well in the States,' says Jamie.
Is that an accusing tone I hear? Okay Libby, don't get defensive. You need an advance don't forget. Did I mention that Alex Bryant sent his first book to us? No, I probably didn't. I rejected it you see. I always thought him a pompous arse. Nothing has changed there then.

'Really, I hadn't heard,' I lie, shifting in my seat in a vain effort to propel the sanitary towel back upwards only to send the slimy sucker towards my thigh.
Jamie gives me a quizzical look.

'The book is number one in the *New York Times* bestseller list,' he persists.
For Christ's sake, what does he want me to do? Lick Alex Bryant's shoes or something?

'Oh, *that* book,' I say in a bored tone.
Alex chuckles.

'Yes, *that* book,' says Jamie impatiently, opening a folder.

'Yes, of course. They obviously like that kind of stuff in America,' I say sarcastically.

'That stuff?' asks Alex raising his eyebrows and giving me a sardonic smile.

'You know. If a door is closed karate chop it open. Use your light sabre to hack the concrete to pieces should you be trapped underneath some debris. You know the kind of thing. How to fight off terrorism single handed. I am surprised, in fact, that you managed to find time to attend this meeting. Can you put saving the world on hold?'

Jane glides in at that moment. She takes the time to give Alex Bryant an admiring 'you are my hero' look and then offers to pour him coffee.

'That's fine. We have it, thank you Jane.' Jamie escorts her to the door while shooting me a dirty look.

Alex Bryant's eyes seem to bore right through me.

'Yes, I did read your review of *Life in a War Zone.*'

He did?

'I had hoped you may have changed your opinion of my book,' he says lazily, seeming not in the least interested in my opinion.

'No. I still think it is a useless piece of journalistic crap,' I say, standing up and feeling the sanitary towel slide even further. I immediately cross my legs and feel sure I resemble a constipated duck or something. Jamie slams a coffee cup onto the table.

'Randal and Hobson disagrees with you Libby. We are picking up Alex's contract and will be handling his new book. The fact you rejected *Life in a War Zone* is history and Alex would very much like you to handle things from here on. After all, there are no mistakes in life, only lessons,' Jamie says profoundly and looks quite pleased with his little speech.

'Ooh, can I stitch that onto a pillow or something Jamie? Or do you have bookmarks already?'

Honestly, this is just too much. Having just split from Toby, I feel I cannot take much more.

'Excuse me. There is so much testosterone in this room that I fear for my genitals.'

I am rewarded with another dirty look from Jamie. I really must go to the loo to sort out my sanitary towel. I shuffle to the door in the manner of John Wayne. I slam it behind me and rush to the loo. The sanitary towel falls limply to the floor and I feel like following it. Oh God, please don't make me have to work with him. I was right to reject that book. I know I was. Why doesn't Jamie support me? What does he mean *Alex would very much like me to handle things*. The truth is I have done nothing but ridicule his book, and he has done nothing but ridicule Toby's work. Honestly, just because he is an award-winning journalist doesn't mean he can dictate who handles his books. I bundle a wad of loo paper into my knickers and pull up my tights. I really should go back. A quick glance in the mirror confirms my fears. I look gross. I twist my hair up into a messy bun and pinch my cheeks to give them some colour. My lips have cracked from the cold, and the bottom one not only feels sore but looks it. Why can't I look all sophisticated like Alex's fiancée Penny? Honestly, couldn't Jamie have given me some warning that Bryant was coming in today? I'm tempted to phone Issy for advice and then remind myself how disastrous Issy's advice can sometimes be. No, it is best to follow my instincts on this one. There is no way I can work with Alex Bryant. I give my tights another tug and open the loo door, only to come face to face with him. What is it with this guy and the ladies loo?

'Is this a hobby of yours, or just a bad habit you're trying to break?' I say, without thinking.

'I'm having counselling, and I think it's getting better,' he replies, grinning at me.

'I'm pleased to hear it,' I say, feeling myself blush.
I turn and begin walking back to the office.

'I wanted to ask if you were okay after last night. I didn't want to ask in front of Jamie.'

'I'm fine,' I say briskly, while feeling stupidly happy to think someone actually does care about my feelings.

'We can have this meeting another day if it helps?' He is scrutinising my face.

'It's fine, really,' I say, wishing he would stop looking at me.

'For what it's worth, I think Toby's an idiot.'
His arm brushes mine as he passes and it's like a hundred volts shoot through me.

'See you in a bit,' he says softly.
I wait a few seconds, take a deep breath and follow him into the office.

Jamie looks unperturbed when I stroll in, and Alex barely glances at me.

'Right, where were we?' says Jamie, looking inside the folder desperately.

'I really don't think I am the right person to represent this particular author. I am sure Mr Bryant would benefit from having an agent that appreciates his work,' I say as tactfully as I can.

Jamie opens his mouth to speak and from the corner of my eye I see Alex lift his hand.

'I'm sure we can put personal issues to one side, Libby. What do you think?' he says looking directly into my eyes.

I gulp.

'I fly back to the States tomorrow to wrap everything up. I'll be back the middle of next week. Why don't you read the book in the meantime?' He places the enormous volume, which makes *War and Peace* look like a novella, onto Jamie's desk. Good God, surely that can't be full of me, me, me, I'm the master of improvisation and how I fought off a grizzly bear with nothing but a cotton wool bud?

'It's a collection of dispatches from the time I spent in Cambodia. See what you think and let me have your decision when I get back. I really want to work with this agency. I've seen what you've done with some of your writers, and I really want you to handle this book and the film rights for *Life in a War Zone*.

He turns to Jamie.

'I'd better run. I'm meeting Penelope for brunch before she flies back. Think about what I said. I really would like Libby to handle things, she has an impressive résumé.'

Surely he cannot be talking about moi. Jamie grins from ear to ear. I nod stupidly while wondering how much one can earn from waitressing. Jamie escorts Bryant to the door and he doesn't even turn to say goodbye. What an arrogant man. I flop down in the chair again and wait for Jamie to return. He bounces back in with a whoop.

'You don't seriously expect me to work with him,' I say petulantly, thumbing through the great tome.

Jamie studies his reflection in the wall mirror. God, what a poof. I have nothing against gays but Jamie takes the biscuit. He strokes his eyebrows several times and finally turns to me.

'You look fab, but I really don't think you're his type,' I say flippantly.

He laughs revealing his well-cared-for teeth.

'Ah, but our next client most certainly is. What the hell was all that about your bloody vibrator by the way?'

I pull a face.

'My electricity bill was huge. I can't think what has shot it up so much.'

'It's your heating darling. It's like the bloody Sahara in your cottage.'

He closes the folder and hands it to me.

'Here is your homework. Everything you need to know about your favourite author. I know you don't want to do it, but he is the biggest client we have ever taken on. He's returning home to England, and we are lucky he wants us. The film will be huge. Just try for Christ's sake. Every other woman is falling at his feet. He is a heart-throb for goodness sake. At least try and...'

'He didn't even say goodbye,' I say crossly, picking up my bag. 'Oh, can you give me an advance, just so I can pay the rent? I'll bake you some rock cakes.'

He shakes his head, and I feel my face crumple.

'Oh, okay, don't start bloody crying. Just do me one favour, please don't walk around my office again like you've got a stick up your arse. He must think you spend all your time sitting on your bloody vibrator.'

'I probably will now. Toby and I broke up last night, so Orlando Broom will be my best friend.'

'I thought you got engaged?'

'Well, I almost did; in fact, I probably would have done if it hadn't been for that arse Alex Bryant.'

Well, let's face it, everything is his fault. If he hadn't had caused such upset I wouldn't have gone outside, and Toby would have stayed at the table with me. The whole Serena thing would not have happened. Damn Alex Bryant. I walk from the office. Jane looks longingly at the book in my hand, and I drop it carelessly onto her desk.

'Here have it. It's easier for me to watch *Superman the Movie*,' I say scornfully.

'Don't you think he is just great?' she says flicking through the pages and licking her lips. 'He is so manly and brave.'

'He is just a journalist,' I reply flatly.

'Matt Rudlin, on his chat show, called him *a modern day hero, a man to inspire*,' she says dreamily.

I take a step back and look at her.

'Inspires you to do what? Fight grizzly bears? Anyway Matt Rudlin is gay. Come to think of it, gay men do seem to like Bryant. I wouldn't be at all surprised if all that macho stuff is just a cover for *his* homosexuality,' I say smugly.

'Oh no, he has a girlfriend. She is lovely.' Her eyes travel down my body before she adds spitefully, 'And she is so slim. Really, she has a figure to die for.'

Don't you just hate women? They are so unbelievably bitchy.

'Really,' I say sharply and grab the book. 'Maybe I will read this after all.'

I ignore her gasp and march to my office deciding that waitressing is, in fact, a very good idea indeed.

Chapter Five

I remember twenty minutes before I am supposed to be there that I had promised to have dinner with my parents. Madam Zigana's words have not had much of an impact because I'm obviously not looking at the clock enough, or my diary come to that. I had just laboured over a chopped salad and prized open a tin of tuna when I remembered. My mother is bound to have made some wonderful dessert, and she will, of course, expect a cake. I grab the ginger cake I had made for the milkman and jump in the car. I speed my way to my parents while my stomach rumbles at the thought of a roast dinner with crispy roast potatoes. I arrive breathless, late and starving.

Mother greets me dressed for a cocktail party. I greet her looking more like I am dressed for a painting party.

'Good Lord, Libby, what are you wearing? And why are you so breathless, you didn't forget did you?' she says grabbing the ginger cake and slamming the front door.

'I'd almost given you up for dead,' she calls over her shoulder as she hurries to the kitchen.

The aroma of roast lamb reaches my nostrils. Guilt punches me in the stomach. I really should be tucking into my chopped salad and 50 grams of tuna and not indulging in a lamb fest. Oh dear, this will mess up the diet but I guess just one non-dieting day will not make much difference, I can start the diet in earnest tomorrow, although since I've split up from Toby there seems little point in dieting now.

'We have some news,' she announces as I approach the kitchen. Dad sits at the table fixing a tangled mass of wires and fairy lights.

'Have you lost weight?' he asks hopefully. 'I must say you are looking jolly good.'

I shake my head miserably.

'You can't expect people to see your weight loss if you insist on wearing those baggy jumpers. You look like a beached whale in that thing,' remarks mother as she delicately slices the lamb. 'Do you have any ideas what you would like us to buy you for Christmas? Your father and I were just discussing it. Would you like one of those fancy weighing scales that do your BMW and stuff? We could also get you a voucher for Debenhams or something. Buy yourself some clothes. I could come shopping with you.'

She gives my jumper a dirty look.

'Don't you mean BMI?' I correct, accepting the glass of wine my dad is offering while wondering if I can ask for fifty quid as an early Christmas present.

'You do know there are about a million calories in a glass of wine?' I say taking a gulp.

'Have one less potato, that's the idea,' he smiles and walks into the lounge.

'Or would you like us to pay for someone to staple your stomach?' asks mother, accepting a small sherry.

Honestly, my parents. I swear someone should have removed me from them when I was five. Still, apart from a bad case of mumps, which mother insisted was a toothache and took me into school every day, I actually came through my childhood surprisingly unscathed.

'What's the news then?' I ask, peeping into the fridge to see what dessert is on offer. 'You haven't drawn up a bucket list have you and are off to the Himalayas or something?'

Dad hovers in the doorway holding a jug of gravy.

'That was a joke,' I say quickly.

'Who told you?' asks mother crossly. I grab the lamb. If food was ever needed then this is the time.

Oh my God. My sodding parents are off to the Himalayas while I sit freezing all alone in my little cottage having myself a very miserable Christmas. Honestly, they could have timed it better.

'You can't go to the Himalayas. It is Christmas. Besides, you should think of the children.' I gulp down my wine and pour some more.

'You're an only child.' Father smiles at me indulgently.

'All the more reason, because I don't have siblings to comfort me.'

Jesus, can things get any worse. Why didn't Madam Zigana predict this? I've a good mind to return and demand my money back.

'Anyway, you can't. Not at your age, it would be obscene.'

I take my plate and help myself to lamb. Mother shakes her head.

'The way you dive at food is obscene. Anyway, we are not going to the Himalayas for Christmas.'

Thank God. I let out a sigh of relief.

'We're going to Kilimanjaro for the *Kilimanjaro Christmas Extravaganza.* We are going mountain climbing.'

I choke on a potato and hold out my glass for dad to top-up. Bloody hell, I need to put myself up for adoption.

'But it's dangerous.'

Dad laughs and squeezes mum's knee. Oh gross. I mean, they are in their fifties for Christ's sake. There is something almost pornographic watching your dad squeeze your mother's body parts. Can't he just peck her on the cheek or something?

'That's not all,' says mother excitedly, getting up. Oh no, what now? Any news I had is going to be a bit mediocre after this. Shuddering with excitement she produces a brochure and drops it at the side of my plate.

'Now don't get upset, it's only for a week.'

I feel the breath knocked out of me. Oh good God, have they gone mad? Their gas fire must be letting out some kind of toxic fume that has totally scrambled their brains. Heavens, they really have no idea what they are doing. I may need to wheel them down to the solicitor to get power of attorney before they go completely gaga.

'A naturist holiday,' I stammer, pushing the brochure away with my little finger. God knows where they got the brochure from, and heaven above knows who may have handled it before them. They are going on holiday with a load of perverts. I wonder if I should call the police.

'Come on darling, do eat. If you have been dieting all week you must be famished.'

Yes, well my mother always was encouraging.

'You can't possibly go on a holiday where people are naked. You'll have to be naked. And won't it be a bit cold, a bunch of nude old people climbing up Mount Kilimanjaro in the middle of winter?'

'Don't be silly darling. It's for when we get home. It's in Weymouth, and we won't be going until later in the year.'

'But you'll be naked,' I say again.

Mother nods and rubs her hands together excitedly. I push my chair back.

'I won't have it. What if the photos get on Facebook and what about Christmas?'

'You said you wanted a quiet romantic Christmas with Toby, so we started to plan our bucket list, didn't we dear?' says mum, leaning seductively across the table and stroking dad's thigh.

Christ, I swear my parents do it more than I do. Although at the moment everyone will be doing it more than I do, considering I am not doing it at all. I down half my glass of wine to drown my sorrows.

'Yes, well we broke up didn't we?'

'What? When did that happen?'

'Last night. I saw him kissing Serena Lambert.'

'What a knob,' says mother angrily.

Yes, a knob indeed.

'I know, a real prick,' I agree miserably.

'Oh dear, and he seemed a jolly nice chap for an architect,' chips in dad in his usual preoccupied way.

'A journalist, you remember? He's a writer.'

'Oh, jolly good.'

Oh jolly hell.

'Let's not get maudlin,' scolds mother. 'Have more vegetables otherwise you'll get constipated, and after dessert I want you to get me onto that bird thing. Everyone at the Health and Beauty club is on it.'

Sounds like a class 'A' drug. Maybe I should get on it too.

'I think you mean *Twitter* don't you?'

'Yes, that's it, and then I can chirp away.'

'Tweet away.'

Good God, are people their age allowed near computers? It really ought to be illegal. Perhaps I should set up some kind of parental control. Otherwise, before I know it, they will have their gross nude bodies all over the Internet. What a thought! I can't believe my parents are jetting off to God knows where, and over Christmas too. I debate telling them about Alex Bryant and his God-awful book when I spot it sitting on the coffee table. Dumbstruck, I point at it and splutter something incoherent, almost choking on my vegetables. My parents are not only abandoning me to go mountain climbing but they have betrayed me and bought the enemy's book.

'Oh yes, I meant to ask you about him,' says dad, leaning forward to retrieve the book.

'George at the bowls club said he heard that Bryant was signing with Randal and Hobson. Jolly good show. He's an ex-military man you know. Excellent book.'

I am stupidly speechless.

'Quite the heart-throb,' says mum, leaning over dad and literally drooling over the photo of Alex Bryant. 'Now, he would be a good catch for you...' she trails off after giving me a fleeting look.

I stand up.

'If only I wasn't so fat, right? Well, Alex Bryant is an egocentric know-it-all and he is not fit to wipe my arse. He is nothing but a wanker,' I fume, remembering the upset he had caused the night before.

I storm from the room.

'I can't think what possessed you to buy his book,' I call over my shoulder.

'Libby dear, we didn't bring you up in Essex you know,' exclaims mother.

'Oh dear,' groans dad.

'They have obviously signed him at Hobsons then,' says mother loudly as I crash around in the kitchen.

I hack at the strawberry pavlova imagining it is his head. I storm back in with three dishes.

'I'm thinking of waitressing,' I state bluntly, slamming the dishes onto the table. Mother winces and dad mumbles, 'Lovely dear, you'll look nice in one of those aprons with the frills.'

'I would think most women would consider Alex Bryant more than fit enough to wipe their arse. In fact, he can wipe my...'

'Mother, please...'

I hand her my dish and watch her pour double cream over the pavlova. I really should ask for yogurt I suppose. Why isn't there a pill that would just magically spirit away the fat, this is the twenty-first century after all. Honestly, of all the places where I felt sure I could forget about the wanker it was at my parents and here is my mother, frothing at the mouth over him. I decide it is best to drop the subject before she orgasms over the After Eight mints. How can I ever be expected to stick to my diet when everyone keeps talking about my love life, or rather the lack of it? I shamelessly help myself to another serving of pavlova and wash it down with more wine. There is silence until dad says,

'You'll need hygiene training, health and safety and all that rot.'

Mother and I stare at him. Surely he's not talking about Alex Bryant and the wiping of my arse?

'If you're going to be a waitress, you'll need hygiene training.'

Ah, yes of course. The thing is, do I really want to waitress? I would most certainly struggle to pay the rent on a waitressing salary. I would have to move into some dingy flat in the worst part of Fross, probably ending up next door to the sex shop. At least I would only have to pop next door for a new Orlando the next time he blows up on me. I groan and broach the subject of rent. I explain about the psychic and how I had forgotten about it being winter and putting money away for heating. Mother is terribly sympathetic and mumbles something about how economical an Aga would be while pushing two fifty-pound notes into my hand, whispering *'don't mention this to your father.'* Of course, I don't, and when he pushes another two into my hand at the front door I take them gratefully. Apart from the jetting off to the back of beyond and leaving me all alone over Christmas, they're not bad parents after all.

Chapter Six

Issy told me in no uncertain terms that I couldn't possibly be a waitress, and she is quite right of course. It would be a dieting nightmare taking orders for wonderful cheesecakes, chocolate fudge cakes, sticky toffee puddings... I am sure that even thinking about these things makes me put on weight. And Hobnobs is not so bad. The pay is quite good, and I do meet some interesting people. Well, most of the time anyway. It has been well over a week since Alex Bryant came to the office. I am starting to wonder if he has changed his mind and that Jamie is too embarrassed to tell me. Mind you, he is besotted with some Filipino poof who parades around in pink braces, has purple streaks in his hair and looks a little like a peacock. Jamie, that is, not Alex Bryant. I can't picture Bryant with anyone who parades around in pink braces and has purple hair. Bryant has obviously decided to go elsewhere and I celebrate by chucking his book in the bin and treating myself to a square of Black and Green's chocolate. I believe it is best to enjoy one or two indulgences now, so that I will not be craving them once my diet properly starts. Did I mention I am starting it tomorrow? It has been a hellish week, and one really shouldn't start a diet when stressed or depressed.

It is the morning of my makeover. Issy is convinced she will meet the man of her dreams during the course of the day.

'Madam Zigana said I will meet someone in the most unusual of places,' she recounts.

'I thought it was in the most unusual circumstances.'

'It's unusual, that's what counts,' argues Issy.

Yes, well, probably the less said about Madam Zigana, the better. I'm wearing a pair of tight fitting leggings to enhance my curves. Mind you, I only discovered this morning that they are actually a size ten and not a fourteen as I at first thought. No wonder I nearly gave myself a hernia when trying them on in the shop.

'Don't you think they are a bit tight?' questions Issy.

'Do you like them? They are Vivienne Westwood's,' I say proudly, twirling around.

'Is that right? I'd give them back to her if I were you, they look bloody painful,' she scoffs.

'You have no appreciation of fashion.'

'Thank God.'

I look past her to the kitchen window and see Toby. He waves. I wave back and blush. Issy looks and widens her eyes.

'Was that Toby?'

'No, was it? Yes, you could be right. On his way to work I expect,' I reply, picking up my handbag.

She peers out of the window and gives a quizzical look.

'Libby, what's going on?'

I shrug.

'Nothing, I've just bumped into him a few times.'

The truth is I have seen Toby more in the past ten days than I did when we were actually going out together. The first time had been a few days after the party. He had been in the sandwich bar near the office. He was even buying the same filling as me. Later that evening he walked past the kitchen window. At first I had thought all this bumping into each other was a coincidence until I bumped into him at the sanitary protection shelf in Waitrose. There I was, rummaging through the Tampax shelf when I spotted him studying the sanitary towels. I happen to know that Toby does not have a use for sanitary towels and there were no condoms in sight. He was obviously there because I was.

'If you want wings, they are on the shelf around the other side,' I had said helpfully, trying not to smile.

He looked me right in the eyes and said wings weren't a priority. My legs had gone all wobbly and I swear there was an ache in my loins like the one they describe in a Mills and Boon novel. In fact, at one point I had to grab my trolley with both hands to steady my trembling legs. We had chatted for almost half an hour. He even said how he missed watching Woody Allen movies with me. I was so tempted to ask him about her, but of course I didn't. I noticed he didn't buy any sanitary towels in the end. In fact he left the shop empty-handed. I am now of course convinced that things with Serena are not working out, and he has finally realised what a sex bomb I am. Well, something along those lines anyway.

'Don't even think about it Libby. Your power lies in making him think you don't need him any more.'

I agree wholeheartedly, while secretly hoping he will pass the kitchen window later this evening, after the makeover. He will find me hard to resist. I decide to make his favourite sponge cake when I get home, just in case. After all, there is no harm in being hospitable and offering him refreshment is there? I visualise myself standing sexily in nothing but a frilly apron and smiling seductively at Toby with my hair perfectly styled and looking for once in my life like a million dollars without having to spend said same amount. It is with these warm happy thoughts drifting through my mind that I answer my mobile to a screaming Jamie.

'Where the fuck are you? Did I say you could have the bloody day off?'

I grimace at Issy.

'Actually, yes you did.'

Don't tell me he has forgotten already.

'What!' He bellows.

Christ, why isn't he having mad passionate fellatio with the Filipino poof instead of screeching at me.

'You said I could take the day off for the photo shoot,' I reply calmly.

'Shit, so I did. Well, get your arse over here as soon as you're done. I need to go over some important stuff with you.'

What can be that important? I meekly agree to pop into the office on my way home after the makeover.

The photo shoot is in the heart of Soho, in a deserted studio, in the basement of a seedy jazz club. Issy is horrified and I am only convinced it will be worth the while when the make-up artist produces touché éclat, to cover 'Those hideous blemishes darling', which are actually my freckles, but never mind. He also has a wonderful array of Chanel cosmetics which I am told I can keep. The place is freezing and smells musty, and Issy spends most of the time jumping up and down to keep warm, or hogging the small two-bar electric heater that the photographer brought in. I feel sure my goose bumps will show in the photos. I'm highly flattered when told I should be modelling as I have all the attributes needed. Feel rather deflated, however, when the Littlewoods catalogue is mentioned as the primary contact if I would like some work. I am even more deflated when the modelling agency's application form must be accompanied with a fifty pound registration fee. Issy's hopes are raised each time the door opens in the hope it will be her mysterious beau. However, apart from a sixty-year-old Brazilian cleaner and a seventeen-year-old pizza delivery man the only other person to enter is the lighting guy, who we both felt sure had to be the ugliest man on earth. We leave the basement and walk hastily through Soho as Issy is concerned we may be approached. I am somewhat insulted that before my makeover she didn't voice any such fears, and now she is worried we may be mistaken for prostitutes. Now, there's a job I hadn't given much thought to.

'You'd have to pay *them*,' giggles Issy.

Not the most flattering of compliments. I let her talk me into finishing the morning off with coffee and cake at Harrods which, amazingly, she pays for.

'This place is so pretentious don't you think?' she giggles.

We both gawp at the statue of Princess Diana and Dodi Fayed for about five minutes. Memories of Paris, car crashes and a highly fragrant London unwittingly enter our heads.

'Christ,' grunts Issy, and we move on.

I would have much preferred Marks and Spencer. At least the women there seem a little more my equal.

'Do you have PG tips?' Issy asks the waitress with a wide smile.

'I'm sure we can acquire some madam,' the waitress replies and I blush.

Following tea, and yes, I am ashamed to admit, cake too, Issy drags me around the women's department and oohs and ahs over the clothes while saying.

'This is only two thousand, five hundred, what a bargain. I'd buy it but the tea wiped me out.'

To which I respond,

'Delightful darling, but you already have two of those and didn't you say the butler found it a bugger to iron?'

'Oh, I've sacked him darling. I have Pudsey now.'

'Oh goodie,' I squeal, while tempted to ask who Pudsey is. 'Is he any good?'

'Marvellous darling, especially when I get the whip out.'

I manage a quick glimpse of myself in the Harrods loo and am quite impressed, even if I say so myself. I could be mistaken for a slightly overweight celebrity. My hair is shiny and my natural curls have been softened and gathered up into a neat chignon, and my lips seem to be in a permanent pout which is very Marilyn Monroe. If only I had a more glamorous looking face. I feel an overwhelming urge to stroll along Oxford Street in the manner of *Pretty Woman* but instead trip and fall into the taxi in the manner of Libby Holmes. Issy convinces me to keep on the Donna Karan dress that was part of the makeover package.

'Let Jamie see what he has got. You look absolutely fab. You know if you made the effort, you could look like this every day.'

Make the effort? What a cheek. It took a ton of touché éclat, a professional make-up artist and a camp hairdresser to achieve this overhaul. Just what kind of effort she expects me to make I do not know, but she can certainly forget it. It will obviously mean losing an hour in bed and let's face it if there is no man in your life it really isn't worth it.

I arrive at the office and attempt to enter the building in the manner of glamorous model and surprise myself by actually succeeding. Feel a little perfect, you know, like Gwyneth Paltrow but without the 'Apple' child. I hit the lift button with the palm of my hand and receive an admiring glance from a handsome man who exits. Oh yes, so it only needs a four-hour make-up overhaul every morning and I can get this attention every day. I give it some thought and then decide bed is the better option. I glide effortlessly up to the second floor and sing happily along to the Christmas music that serenades me. Please God, let Toby walk past the window tonight. I put my head to the side and pout my lips seductively to the lift mirror. Oh yes, I look good. I feel warm inside, knowing that tonight could be the night Toby and I get back together. Maybe, I won't be alone over Christmas after all. That reminds me, I really should do some Christmas shopping. I also need decorations for the tree. Things are looking up. I will pop to the shops after work tomorrow and buy lots of festive goodies. After all, I will be paid soon and there is bound to be a Christmas bonus. I practise inviting Toby in for coffee again and decide to buy one of those negligee things on my way home. Pyjamas just don't have the same appeal do they? The lift doors open and I come face to face with Jane while still practising my pout.

'What on earth happened to you,' she blurts out.

Well, thank you very much, and what does that mean exactly? I manoeuvre my lips back to their normal position.

'I've had plastic surgery, don't you like it?'

I walk past her towards the office, trying to regain my earlier confidence. I take a deep breath and with a kick, fling open Jamie's door.

'Tra-la-la. What do you think?' I say, while posing seductively in the doorway.

I am confronted with Jamie, Alex Bryant and the Blonde Blancmange. How more dire can things get than coming face to face with Miss Glamour on sticks? I take one look at her and am instantly deflated. I slowly untangle myself from the doorway and smile awkwardly. She sits upright looking like a model. Jamie could have warned me.

'You look fab darling,' he exclaims. I really can't tell if he means it or not.

Blancmange surveys me. I decide it is best not to move in case my wobbly bits wobble. I so wish the floor would open up and swallow me.

'Yes, rather amazing, actually,' says Alex, ignoring a sharp look from Blancmange. I meet Bryant's eyes, and find myself flattered by the appreciation in them. I blush and turn away.

'You've already met Penelope Vistor, haven't you Libby. Penny is the advertising executive for Chanel's new ad campaign,' says Jamie, proudly.

She would be wouldn't she?

'Am I missing something? What exactly have you had done?' asks Penelope, in an upper-crust horsey drawl while squinting at me.

'I've had a sex change,' I reply not missing a beat.

Jamie sniggers and Alex seems to bite his lip. Penelope, however, continues to look curiously at me. Good God, she believes it. After a moment of staring, she turns to Alex and kisses him on the cheek.

'Well, I must fly. I've got to pack for Beijing. I'm flying first thing tomorrow. Meetings with Chanel delegates there,' she says flicking back her hair. 'I still have heaps of emails to answer. I'll see you later at the house honey. God, I hope that cleaner woman has managed to tidy up the muddle. Don't you just hate moving countries? And cleaners are a nightmare aren't they?' she says airily, looking at me.

'Oh, yes absolutely,' I say stupidly.

I barely move counties, what would I know? As for cleaners, well I'm more likely to be one than to have one.

She sweeps past without a second glance. There is silence.

'Was it the testosterone from the other day?' asks Alex breaking it and grinning at me.

'Oh sharp, very sharp,' laughs Jamie.

I give them a dismissive look. Jamie makes a show of pulling himself together and sits behind his desk before gesturing to me to sit down.

'Right, glossing over your sex change,' he says and bursts out laughing again.

I sit down and glance at the clock on the wall. I really want to get to the shops before they close. I spot a photo of Jamie with his Filipino boyfriend at a fancy-dress party and let out a snort. Honestly, he has only known him a matter of days.

'So, what are your plans for Christmas?' he asks.

He isn't going to invite me to a gay party is he? Toby will never go to that. We will spend the whole evening with Toby's arse suctioned to a wall. I will rush around fetching drinks and food while he glues himself into a position where his arse cannot be seen. No, I don't think so. I would much rather spend Christmas Eve watching a Christmassy movie cuddled up on the couch.

'I still have loads of Christmas shopping to do. In fact, I have all my Christmas shopping to do. Then there is a tree to buy and...'

Jamie shifts in his seat and looks uncomfortably at Alex. I am starting to get a bad feeling about this.

'Why are you asking me?' I say bluntly.

No point beating about the bush. After all, it will be Christmas soon, and Toby and I will be back together. I must be forgiving about Serena Lambert. Toby obviously isn't in love with her, and he probably just wanted to be seen with a slim woman, and do you blame him? I'll buy a book on the art of forgiveness by the Dalai Lama or someone, and make a determined effort to keep to my diet.

'We have ourselves a bit of a situation,' says Bryant, calmly.

Jamie pushes some papers towards me.

'The rebellion in Cambodia is building momentum. They have the elections soon. Colonel Kuma Pong, the present governor, is hoping to get re-elected.'

Fascinating, but what has this got to do with me?

'Well, I am mighty glad I am not there then,' I laugh nervously, pushing the papers back at him. I really don't like the serious looks on their faces.

'The annual Ventura book fair is being held this January in Cambodia, and Alex will be attending. His new book *The Smiling*

People's Revolution has been chosen for all the major awards. We have a TV interview booked out there and... Well, anyway we've managed to get most things brought forward because of the high security risk. Alex, as you know, has accused Kuma Pong of corruption on more than one occasion, and he isn't going to like Alex being in the country at election time...'

So, he's going to Cambodia again. That's good news.

'Yes, well, that has nothing to do with me,' I break in. I really don't want to hear any more. I just want to plan my Christmas with Toby.

Jamie sighs.

'Janet, the media woman we assigned to go with Alex, has gone down with chickenpox. You're his agent and...'

'No one asked me to be his agent, and I never said I would be,' I say firmly. 'I'm not going to Cambodia. I quit.'

Saying 'I quit' sounds smugly American but saying 'I'm handing in my notice' just doesn't have the same impact does it? I don't really want to leave but what else can I do. I don't want to go to Cambodia. I never wanted to go when it was peaceful so I certainly am not keen to go while there is an uprising. Especially considering Bryant has accused Colonel Pong of corruption. Honestly, fancy even asking me. Let him go alone. I'm sure if we arm him with a toothpick and a cheese grater, he will be able to take care of himself.

'Don't do that Libby. I realise it's a crap thing to ask. But Alex knows of a safe house should there be any difficulties, but I'm sure there won't be. I think you could also write some good stuff out there and...'

'A safe house?' I echo, 'I'm an agent, not a bloody spy, and Toby is the writer not me.'

Why did I bring Toby into the conversation?

'And, yes, it is a crap thing to ask,' I say, feeling hurt that he even did. I pick up my handbag.

'I've got Christmas shopping to do. Excuse me.'

'*The Political Times* thinks your writing is very good as it happens. They are keen to publish anything you write while you are out there.'

I turn to Alex Bryant, who is reclining in his seat, his voice smooth and calm. It is quite hard to picture him as the action man, but I suppose if I ever do consider going to Cambodia, not that I ever would of course, but if I should, which I won't, I imagine Bryant is the safest man to go with. Oh, the thought of being alone with Alex Bryant. I feel the need to fan myself. What is wrong with me?

'How dare you both talk about me to *The Political Times*? Toby writes for them, and I would never upstage him even if I could, which I can't.'

I fling the door open and march to the lift, the whole time wondering how I can possibly afford Christmas now that I have quit my job.

Chapter Seven

'I've fired that bloody woman. I mean, just look at the place.'

Alex Bryant looks around and wonders what the *bloody woman* did to deserve to be fired. The flat seems tidy enough to him. Okay, there are several boxes lying around and a few things still wrapped but overall it looks tidy enough. Penelope flounces past him, swooping down on the flowers he is holding as she does so.

'They're lovely darling but you know Freesias make my mother sneeze terribly. I did tell you that.'

'I bought them for you, not your mother.'

He walks into the kitchen, takes a bottle of water from the fridge and fills a glass. He is about to lift it to his lips when she sighs.

'I do wish you would put things back,' she snaps, picking up the bottle of water and returning it to the fridge.

'We need to hire someone else. Can you phone that agency tomorrow?' she says, busying herself putting the flowers into a vase. He sighs and walks into his office where she follows him.

'Alex, did you hear me?'

When did she become such a nag? he thinks irritably. Things were never like this when we lived in separate apartments.

'You fired the help. You phone the agency and get someone else. I was quite happy with Trudy. I've got to prepare for my trip. You're the one who wants a housekeeper.'

She sits tearfully on his desk and crosses her legs seductively.

'I don't have time now. I can't believe you're going to Cambodia with that silly 'Lilly' woman.'

The image of Libby standing at the door of Jamie's office enters his mind and not for the first time that day.

'Her name is Libby,' he says absently, remembering her excited tra-la-la. She must have felt terrible he thinks, seeing us sitting there.

'You'd think she would lose some weight. What on earth was that all about today?'

'What do you mean?' he asks, pulling his mind away from her image.

'That sex change business, honestly.'

He laughs.

'It was a bit of fun.'

'Well, I don't get it,' she snaps, climbing off the desk. 'She needs to lose some weight if you ask me.'

Alex didn't like to say that nobody had asked her. He thought back to Libby's entrance and realised that he hadn't really noticed her weight. But now he thinks about it, she could lose a few pounds, but what she lacks in that area he feels she certainly makes up for in personality. He can't help wondering what she is doing now. He tries to picture her having dinner with her boyfriend. God, that Toby is an idiot he thinks irritably. What does she see in him? She is obviously still with him. Surely she could do better than that. It annoys him to know that Toby certainly won't change her mind about Cambodia, and in fact, he will probably be doing just the opposite. What a shame, he thinks. She would have been fun company. He hasn't had much fun in the past few weeks. She's got some pluck too. He likes that.

'We need to go over the wedding guest list tonight. I had thought of doing it next week when I got back, but it looks like you're going to be away now,' she calls from the living room.

Ah, yes the wedding. He pulls his own list from his pocket. He has a few things himself to discuss.

'We can discuss it over dinner,' he calls back and feels a sense of dread at the thought.

Alex decides to phone Jamie, and see what they can come up with to convince Libby to come.

Chapter Eight

'Don't you think you overreacted?' Issy asks.

I beat three eggs like a maniac, splattering yolk on everything in the vicinity.

'Libby, calm down for Christ's sake, you're quite lethal when you're like this,' she says picking yolk out of her hair.

I beat in the sugar. I feel so angry. What was Jamie thinking of?

'How can I go to Cambodia? It's a ludicrous thing to ask.'

Issy looks thoughtful as she measures out flour. I've made a sponge cake and am now in the middle of a cheesecake and after that fairy cakes, and if I still feel angry I shall make another sponge. Someone will eat them over Christmas. Talking of which, how can I not be in England over the holiday period?

'Well, your parents won't be here over the holiday, and I'm going to my parents. Frankly, I wouldn't mope about for that little weasel if that's what you're doing.'

'Are you suggesting I go to Cambodia?'

I slap her hand as she goes to stick her finger in the bowl.

'I'm just saying you should think about it. I know I wouldn't have to think twice about going away with Alex Bryant.'

I point a floured finger at her.

'Don't mention penises.'

She shrugs.

'I wasn't going to but you can be sure with a man like him you would never need an Orlando Broom again.'

'Issy, you said you weren't going to.'

She mimics zipping her lips.

'I can't believe they discussed me with *The Political Times*. I would never upstage Toby. I don't believe I could anyway.'

Issy's finger hovers in mid-air before plunging into the mixing bowl.

'What do you mean they *discussed you* with *The Political Times*? You didn't mention anything about that.'

'Didn't I? I probably didn't. Well, it isn't that important is it?'

'Bollocks Libby, of course it bloody is. This is the opportunity you have always wanted isn't it?'

At that moment Toby walks by and my mind freezes as I find myself standing in front of the window with a wooden spoon in my hand instead of a mug. I make a half-hearted attempt to mime '*coffee*' but it looks more like I am offering a lick of the spoon. It all comes across rather obscene actually. Oh, how I hate Alex-*we-have-a-situation*-Bryant. I watch as Toby hovers at the gate and feel my heart jump as he opens it. I drop the spoon and race to the door, patting my hair as I do so. After all, this is my one and only chance to stand on my own front porch looking like a million dollars.

'Oh Christ,' moans Issy, 'I thought we'd seen the back of that loser.'

I open the door to a slightly embarrassed Toby and attempt my best seductive smile.

'Hi, Libs,' he says quietly. 'I was having a walk.'

In his Pierre Cardin suit, is he serious?

'Hi, I thought I'd offer you a quickie,' I say, adding hastily, 'a quick cup of coffee that is.'

I hear Issy giggle.

'Erm, well...' He hesitates and then seems to do a double take. 'I say, you look glamorous, are you going out?'

I fiddle with my top.

'Oh no, I just had a shower,' I lie. 'I've just made some cake, that's if you've got the time to stop.'

He inclines his head towards the kitchen.

'Issy was just leaving, weren't you Issy?' I shout.

'What, oh yes. I've got to go home and wash some egg out of my hair.'

'Well, I suppose I could...' says Toby hesitantly.

'I made a sponge cake.'

His face lights up with the mention of cake. It's just a pity that the mention of my sponge cake did it rather than the sight of me. He nods and I open the door wider. At that moment the top pocket of his jacket begins to vibrate. There is an awkward tension as Toby seems unable to move.

'Aren't you going to answer that?' I ask sweetly.

Why am I getting that strange déjà vu feeling?

'No, I don't think so.'

Issy comes bounding towards us and from the coat rack I take her long shawl which she deliberately swings wide so it slaps Toby in the face.

'I see you've gone for the casual look Toby,' she says mockingly.

'Aren't you going to answer that?' she echoes pointing to his vibrating pocket.

I push her towards the front door where the heat I can't afford is drifting down the street and give her a little shove. She shrugs, pecks me on the cheek and pushes past Toby.

'Ciao.'

I close the door and usher Toby and his vibrating phone into the kitchen. I try to ignore the continual vibration but it really is all I can do not to snatch the phone from his pocket and throw it down the loo. It finally stops and I feel the atmosphere relax only for the phone to start vibrating again. I click on the kettle, and as I am about to cut the cake I hear the gate squeak and look out of the window to see Jamie walking up the drive. Why do these things happen to me? Toby tenses further at the sight of him and raises his eyebrows when I reach for another mug.

'You're surely not letting him into the cottage,' he says appalled, like I am about to let in Fred West.

'I can't make him stand on the doorstep. I am sure he won't be here long.'

'But he's gay.'

Oh Toby you don't say. It occurs to me that should Toby and I marry he may well say I cannot work for Jamie any more so maybe it is just as well that I have quit. I open the door before Jamie has time to knock.

'Toby is here,' I say immediately.

'Oh God, I'm so scared. Homophobic creeps don't bother me darling. I can't stay long anyway.' He looks over my shoulder and raises his voice. 'I have left Philippe tied to the bedposts. I only popped out for strawberry flavoured condoms.'

'Pervert,' calls Toby.

'I'm as queer as fuck, darling, live with it.'

I exhale and pull a face. Not the sort of conversation I want my lovely elderly neighbours to hear.

'Look, sweetie, if you want to quit, that's up to you. But this is not just about Randal and Hobson the publishers, it's also about you. This opportunity to get some great stories may never happen again and to practically be commissioned to do it and with someone like Alex to show you around. It really is a God-given opportunity darling. Besides you're a bloody good agent and to get Alex as a client is classic, so at least give it a bit of thought. Alex really wants you to go.'

Like I care what he thinks. I incline my head to remind him Toby is in the kitchen.

'Yes, well you know our feelings on him. Issy has given you the best advice there. But, really darling, if he loves you, surely he will support you.'

I know Jamie is right but it really is not good for a relationship if a woman upstages her man. Anyway, why on earth would I want to go to Cambodia where the water is poisonous, not to mention the food, and where there is an uprising and everyone wants to kill you. Does he think I am mad? To suggest that Alex Bryant is a good person to go with confirms my worst fears that Jamie isn't thinking clearly. I peck him on the cheek and tell him firmly that I will not change my mind. What I will do I have no clear idea but flying to Cambodia is definitely not it. Toby is busy talking on his mobile and doesn't hear me return to the kitchen. I am quite grateful for as soon as I hear him say Serena's name and call her 'honey' I burst into tears and dash to the bathroom. What a two-timing shagging prick. I was a fool to put my misplaced loyalty in Toby and sacrifice my career for him, and right now I want to be as far away from Toby as I can, and as the furthest place I can think of is Cambodia I guess I will be going after all.

Chapter Nine

'Mother, what *are* you wearing?' I gasp.

I had tried to phone my parents all day but with no luck. Issy suggested we drop in on them after we had finished making my travel arrangements. After struggling to find a parking space outside their house we trudged through the first sprinklings of snow and were accosted by an inflatable snowman that lurched at us as we approached the house. Fairy lights twinkled over the door, which was adorned with a note saying *IT'S HAPPENING HERE*.

Oh Lord, my heart sinks. Just what is happening at my parents?

I already have an acidic headache from too much wine the night before, so the music that now blares forth is a very unwelcome sound. Raucous laughter reaches my ears and after falling over numerous wellington boots and an assortment of coats, I come face to face with my mother. She is wearing what looks like a dead pig, or rather, several dead pigs. I never know what to expect from my parents and I am never too surprised with what I find but seeing my mother wearing what appears to be a dead animal is not something I had ever anticipated in my wildest dreams. Oh God, from the smell I am beginning to think that maybe it doesn't look like a dead pig but actually is one. Issy taps my chin and I close my open mouth. My mother is wearing a dress made from pork and lamb chops. It is at this point that I begin to wonder if I could actually divorce my parents on the grounds of unreasonable behaviour.

'It's a meat dress. You know, like the one Madam Gaga wore. What do you think? I had it made especially.'

She twirls and I grimace. The overpowering smell of Madam Rochas perfume coupled with the sight of the chops makes me feel nauseous.

'It looks… amazing,' stammers Issy giving me a sidelong glance.

'Are they real chops?' I ask hesitantly, feeling an obsessive need to touch them.

'Of course, that Madam Gaga is ingenious.'

'You can't wear dead animals, and it's *Lady* Gaga, not Madam,' I protest.

'Why not, people do it all the time.'

'No, they don't. When did you last see someone popping to their local in their lamb chop dress?'

There is no point telling my mother that wearing leather shoes is slightly different to draping oneself in raw pork chop.

'Are you having a party?' I ask stupidly.

Issy, deciding to make the most of things, grabs a plate and heads for the buffet. Although the food smells tempting I decide not to follow. After the debacle with Toby the other night, I must have gained a few pounds. That night alone I consumed five cupcakes, half a sponge, a pizza, a packet of Bourbons, a bottle of wine and two bars of Cadbury's Fruit and Nut. I was depressed. I know that's no excuse and I am now fatter than ever. Of course, a second bottle of wine last night hasn't helped. This weather makes thing worse, of course. Everyone knows you eat more in the winter. I console myself that there will be very little food to eat in Cambodia. I doubt you can get pizza there, right? Dieting in Cambodia will be a piece of cake, and I will start my diet as soon as I arrive in the country. The shock of seeing my mother looking like an advert for the local butchers has taken away my appetite for tonight. I dread to think what she has dressed my father as. I am about to ask when, as if on cue, he appears. I want to go home. He is wearing an abundance of bird feathers which drop off him as he comes laughing towards me. My father is a duck. I am speechless and mouth 'help' to Issy who duly ignores me and stuffs more cocktail sausages into her mouth. The room is full of people wearing a colourful array of outfits and a shocking amount of make-up.

'What do you think of my Boy George outfit?' he shouts above the music.

Boy George! I shake my head in disbelief and edge towards the drinks table. Of course, now that I notice the bowler hat and the colourful plaits that hang around his face, I suppose there is something of a resemblance.

'I thought you were a duck,' I say flatly.

'Quack quack,' guffaws someone behind me.

It's a madhouse. I should sue them for emotional distress. I accept a glass of wine from Basil, their neighbour, who I assume is supposed to be a transvestite.

'Who have you come as?' he asks seriously.

I shrug.

'I'm Libby in a track suit, actually.'

He nods earnestly.

'Ah, yes, very good. Did you spot who I am?'

Oh dear.

'Well, actually...'

Dare I say, *Lily Savage*?

'Flash Gordon,' he roars.

Yes of course. Beam me up Scottie before I see someone I actually know and have to admit that these people are my parent's friends and that the most outrageous couple here are, in fact, my parents. I manage to manoeuvre mum to the loo and shove her inside.

'Darling, what on earth is going on?' she asks, tripping over the loo brush stand and landing on the toilet seat, sending several lamb chops flying off her.

'I need to tell you something. I'm flying to Cambodia tonight,' I say narrowly avoiding an airborne chop.

She gasps and then claps her hands.

'Ooh how exciting. That is very daring of you darling, but why? Don't they have drug barons and things like that there?'

Drug barons? I didn't know about them.

'I made up with Toby, but then broke up with him again,' I say miserably.

She clucks.

'Really, Libby, most women can keep a boyfriend for twenty-four hours. I do wonder if you should see one of those counsellors. Robin, you know, daddy's golf friend, he has been marvellous after seeing that doctor in Reading.'

'He's on lithium.'

'Well perhaps you should get some. It has done marvels for him.'

'I'll just pop to Boots shall I?'

'Just trying to help darling,' she replies in a hurt voice. 'It helped him.'

'He's a recovering alcoholic and total nutcase.'

I shriek as I accidentally touch the dead animal that hugs her hips. God, I'm sure it moved. This is the grossest thing I have seen at my parent's house, and let me tell you, I have seen some gross things.

'Don't raise your voice to your mother,' says father pushing open the door. Thank God neither of us is perched on the toilet. Things are getting a little cramped in the smallest room now.

'I just thought you should know that I am flying to Cambodia, where there is an uprising and the rebels are completely out of control. Just so you know I could be killed,' I say dramatically.

'Perhaps you'll meet someone there,' says mother calmly, 'and maybe even lose some weight. I certainly think you have gained some more.'

She suddenly jumps up and grabs me by the hands.

'Are you going with that dashing brawny heart-throb, Alex Bryant?' she says breathlessly.

Dad holds his breath.

'Yes, I am.'

Next she'll be telling me to shag him in the plane's loo.

'You should join that mile club,' she giggles.

What did I tell you?

'Are we members?' asks my dad curiously, collecting wayward feathers out of the bathroom sink.

God, I bloody hope not.

'No you're not and it's the Mile High Club,' I snap. 'And he is the last man on earth I would shag on a plane,' I say loudly, walking out of the loo to curious eyes.

Not that I would ever shag any man on a plane, of course, let alone Alex Bryant. After all, I do have principles. Issy rolls her eyes and pops another olive.

'Darling, you must visit this divine village that your father and I saw on telly. We had thought about going there ourselves but it is pretty dire out there right now, what with the political situation and all that,' says mother, trying to rearrange her meat dress.

Oh, I see. It's too dangerous for my parents to visit but perfectly okay for me.

'But you're going with Alex Bryant darling. You'll be fine with him.'

She makes him sound like Indiana Jones. I am handed a scrap of paper with an almost illegible address on it.

'It's in Cambodian language. Give it to one of the taxi drivers, they'll know. You must go darling, it looked fabulous, and it has a beautiful temple with a huge bell. Apparently, when the monks sound the bell all of the villagers go to the temple. How amazing is that? You must bring back a silk shawl from there. And try and lose some weight while away, darling.'

'You mean *Khmer* don't you, there is no such thing as Cambodian language.'

'Do I? Well, whatever they speak out there, it certainly isn't English is it?'

Lady Gaga sings loudly in the background and mother is encouraged by her friends to impersonate her. This is all I need. I look at Issy who winks. I rack my brain to think of some excuse to escape.

'Anyway, I'm not fat as such. I'm a bit curvy, that's all,' I say, kissing mother on the cheek and moving towards the door. 'I only need to lose a few pounds.'

'A healthy lifestyle is what you need. Lots of sex and rock and roll,' yells Flash Gordon, rolling his hips towards my mother. Someone hand me a bucket.

'Curvy is just another word for *fat* darling and don't forget, we are off to Kilimanjaro,' calls mother, excitedly.

Thanks mother, as if I could forget that they are off to Kilimanjaro. I make a quick exit with Issy and rush out into the now heavy falling snow.

'What a cheek. I do live a healthy life style. I don't smoke, I don't drink and I don't exercise, how much healthier can I be,' I say, skidding on the snow.

'I wish I was coming with you,' says Issy sadly. 'You make me laugh.'

I hug her tightly, wishing so very much she could come with me too. I really don't want to go out there with just Alex-*I-can-save-the-sodding-world*-Bryant. In fact, I don't actually want to go at all. It had all happened on impulse. I'd walked back into the kitchen to find Toby talking all soppy to Serena on his mobile and had seen red. How dare he come into my kitchen for tea and cake and talk to her. Jamie had just reached his car when I had called him back and said with more confidence than I felt,

'Book my flight. I am going to Cambodia. How soon can I leave?'

Of course Jamie's face had lit up while Toby's had dropped. I instantly regretted it. Maybe I should have given Toby a chance to explain himself. Instead, I demanded that he leave and threw the sponge cake at him. To give him his due he had attempted to explain but I wouldn't listen. What am I doing flying to Cambodia and just before Christmas too? Someone is bound to blow up the plane. They do that sort of thing at Christmas time don't they? That would be just my luck.

'Can't you fly out after Christmas? Maybe do a story on the fashion of Cambodia? After all, I imagine it is very exotic there,' I ask hopefully, feeling my own tears well up.

'What sodding fashion. Libs, you are a clown. Oh fuck a duck, I wish you weren't going. I will miss you.' She leans towards me awkwardly and we hug tightly.

I tuck my arm into Issy's and shiver. At least I will get some sunshine and who knows maybe I will meet someone. After all, stranger things have happened.

Chapter Ten

Alex walks towards me and for some stupid reason I blush. I quickly recheck the hotel address and pop it into my bag along with the address of the village that mother had said must be visited.

'It sounds glorious, and the silk shawls they make are astounding. Promise to bring me one back and take lots of photos. It's in the middle of nowhere so you can escape old Bryant although God knows why you would want to,' she had said on the phone.

Looking at his stiff arrogant back as he speaks to a security guard, I can think of a hundred reasons why I would want to escape him. I watch as he finally extradites himself from several admirers and strolls towards me, or should I say swaggers. This man brings out the worst in me. He drops a rucksack at my feet and stares wide-eyed at my two large suitcases. He lifts his steely blue eyes to meet mine.

'Hello,' I say.

'It really is sensible when visiting a country like Cambodia to travel light,' he says in a cool voice.

Here we go.

'A country like what exactly?' I snap, revealing my hand luggage from behind my back.

He sighs.

'We're entering a country where there is an uprising. I'm not popular with the government there and there may be situations where we may have to move quickly. We won't have hours for you to pack each time we do.'

He watches as I struggle and heave to get the cases up to the counter. After minutes of panting and heaving and giving myself a hernia, he gently lifts them for me. Without effort he plonks them onto the conveyer belt.

'Now, if this were a life and death situation you wouldn't get away would you?' he says in that arrogant voice which I am growing to detest. 'In a hostile conflict situation you would never make it.'

Is he intense or what? He moves closer to hand over his passport and I feel my heart quicken as the fresh clean smell of him reaches my nostrils.

'Well thank God I put my machine guns in there then,' I snap. 'I'll just shoot everyone if they get in my way.'

The check-in clerk stares at me with her hand hovering over my cases. Oh shit. I hand her my passport with my sweetest smile.

'Did you pack your suitcases yourself?' she asks suspiciously.

I nod. It's all going well so far I don't think.

'Yes, even the machine guns,' I say jokingly, attempting to ease some tension.

Bryant sighs. Her expression doesn't change but her eyes flick from me to Alex Bryant, where it hovers for longer than it should and then back again.

'I will need to get security to check your bags madam.'

'No really, there is no need. It was just a joke. Of course there aren't machine guns in there,' I protest.

Damn, they will mess up my neatly folded clothes. I turn angrily to Alex-*courage-under-fire*-Bryant and am about to let rip, when mother calls me and Michael Jackson's *Thriller* blares from my Blackberry, almost as if I had choreographed the music to add effect to the increasingly tense situation. Alex Bryant gives me a despairing look. I click it off and turn to the clerk.

'It really isn't appropriate to joke about machine guns in this present climate,' she says in a solemn voice and manages to get her face to match. A quick glance at my ticket gives her more ammunition.

'I see you're going to Cambodia,' she says, raising her eyebrows.

'Miss Holmes is accompanying me,' says Alex in a hot sexy voice while giving her a smile that is enough to melt any woman's heart. It certainly makes mine flip which makes me angrier than ever.

'What flight is she on?' calls someone from the waiting queue. 'I hope you're going to check those bags. I don't want to get on a plane that may be hijacked.'

For heaven's sake, do I look like someone who would hijack a plane?

'Really, you only have to look at me to see I'm not a hijacker,' I say, forcing a laugh and wishing it sounded more authentic.

No one else laughs. Not even sodding Alex Bryant, to whom I now look at pleadingly.

'We're travelling together,' he says, draping an arm around me, 'and I think you can rest assured that I would not travel with a terrorist.'

I shrug his arm off me.

'Excuse me, I'm a hijacker,' I correct. 'They think I am a hijacker, not a terrorist.'

'It is the same thing isn't it?' he says dismissively turning to the clerk with a wide grin. How dare he make me look foolish?

'It's quite different actually. I might hijack the plane but may not necessarily want to blow it up.'

What am I saying?

He turns from the clerk and gives me an odd look. His mouth moves but he doesn't speak. I wait expectantly as does the clerk. After what seems to be something of an internal struggle his steely blue eyes bore into mine, and he says in a smug voice,

'And your point is?'

That is just the kind of question he would ask isn't it. You know the kind that you just find impossible to answer.

'My point is that I would never ever consider being a terrorist because they blow people up whereas a hijacker just hijacks and doesn't actually kill people...'

Christ, I'm just getting in deeper and deeper. Why do I feel this overwhelming need to somehow get the better of Alex-*always-right*-Bryant?

'Lady, you are killing me right now. Just how long do you intend to hijack that counter? Some of us would actually like to get on our flight,' yells another passenger.

'Merry Christmas to you too,' I snap.

'So, what you are saying is you wouldn't consider being a terrorist, but you would consider being a hijacker?' says a smug Alex leaning close to me. I blush furiously and hate him for it.

'No of course not,' I say defensively. 'What I meant was if I had to choose, I would obviously choose to be a hijacker and not a terrorist...'

He nods knowingly.

'That is what I just said.'

What a smug irritating arsehole.

'This is when they do it isn't it, at Christmas time. They are such bastards. Someone arrest her. I don't want to be on a plane that is going to be hijacked,' shouts a woman from the queue.

'I'm not going to hijack the plane, have you all gone mad?'
Jesus Christ, all I did was crack a silly joke about machine guns and now all eyes are on me and everyone has gone nuts.

'I think you would be wise to stay quiet,' whispers Alex.
He leans forward and says something to the check-in clerk which I can't hear. I really do not know what I am doing here. It is almost Christmas and Toby is probably all cosy round a tree with Serena, and chestnuts roasting on an open fire, while mum and dad are preparing for their Kilimanjaro Christmas extravaganza. Issy will be late-night Christmas shopping, while Jamie is probably shagging for England with his Filipino lover. And me, well I am attempting to convince people I am neither a hijacker nor a terrorist and that I really don't have machine guns in my suitcase. To make matters worse my sodding button just popped on my skirt and I can feel the zipper slowly creeping undone. I see my suitcases gliding through a curtain like two little coffins on their way to cremation. That means I am stuck with this skirt for the duration of the journey. Alex hands me my hand luggage and with a tilt of his head indicates that I should follow him to the departure lounge. He gives me my boarding pass, in case we get separated. Honestly, anyone would think I was five years old. I ring mother fearing my plane, or God forbid, hers, may crash and we may never speak again. She instructs me to buy Imodium for my stomach as 'You never know,' and asks casually if I have packed condoms.

'You might get lucky, as long as it isn't some Cambodian man with a leg missing.'

'What?'

'You know all those land mines and everything.'
My mother is a national embarrassment with zero political correctness. I suppress my gasp and wish her a good flight. I am about to hang up when she says,

'By the way, your father read they don't have toilet paper out there. Can you imagine?'

'In Kilimanjaro?'

'No silly, in Cambodia. You had better get some.'
I blink rapidly. I will never get a toilet roll into my hand luggage.

'But they must use something,' I say, not really wanting to know what.

'Apparently they use their hands darling. Oh, your father's calling, must dash. Have a super time.'

I shudder and look at Alex. My God, surely he doesn't? A graphic picture of Alex Bryant wiping his bum enters my head and I quickly shake the thought away. Holding my skirt together I amble into Boots for some safety pins. I take another sneaky look at him. He is extraordinarily good looking. Don't get me wrong, I could never fancy such an arrogant man but I can see the attraction, and there is something safe about him. If only he wasn't such an arsehole. Admittedly Toby's articles haven't always been as well researched as they could have been but nevertheless they are powerful and well written. My mind wanders to Toby, and I wonder if he is thinking about me. This would have been our first Christmas together and I was so looking forward to it. Instead I'm flying to Cambodia and won't really have a Christmas at all. After dropping safety pins and a box of Imodium into my basket I find myself hovering around the toilet roll section. *'Have yourself a merry little Christmas'* screeches into my ears from a nearby speaker as I stare longingly at the rolls. How can they not have any in Cambodia? I see the security guard looking at me strangely and move onto the tissues and throw several packs into my basket. That should do it. I am about to edge my way into the queue when a scruffy young man blocks my way. I attempt to edge round him. He makes no effort to move and I am about to kindly ask him if he would when he leans forward, his alcohol breath wafting into my face.

'Listen up fatty, if you're on my flight and try anything stupid I'll knock you're fucking head off, got it?' he spits.

Before I can spit anything back he is escorted outside the shop by Alex Bryant. I quickly follow. I can hear shouting behind me but am oblivious to it. The only thing reverberating in my head is the word *fatty*. Did he really call me that? God, I must be really fat if people are starting to call me names. I stare bewildered as Alex leans close to him.

'You're going to apologise now aren't you, because if you don't I will come after you when it's dark and slice your tongue out,' says Alex-*don't-mess-with-me*-Bryant in an evil voice.

Okay, he didn't quite say that, but from the tight mean look on his face you could easily be forgiven in thinking that he had. He is quite frightening when angry. I must admit to feeling a small thrill at having him stand up for me.

'Both you and I know that is no way to talk to a lady. I want you to apologise right now.' Is what he actually says.

'And you'll do fucking what if I don't,' spits the youth, struggling to free himself from Alex's tight grasp.

'Let's just say you don't want to refuse my request.'

Good Lord, he sounds like 'The Godfather'. He will be making him an offer he can't refuse next which will be a bit extreme to say the least. Although, it is nice to have someone protect me. I can't remember Toby being protective.

'He's fucking ex-SAS,' squeals the man's friend, making Alex sound more terrifying than he already is.

I see the Boots security guard pointing at me and I realise I have rushed from the store with the goods still in the basket, and the basket still in my hand.

'I'm not fucking apologising to that fat terrorist cow.'

Does he really have to shout so loudly? And honestly, he really doesn't have to have such a look of disgust on his face. Even I know I am not *that* fat. Of course everyone looks at the fat cow and I just want the floor to open up and swallow me. In a moment of quick thinking I unashamedly look behind me for the fat cow myself. It is all very well having a few people think you're fat, like your mother and your boyfriend, but when a whole bloody airport does it is something else.

'Perhaps you just need a bit of convincing,' says Alex evenly.

Oh my God, he really is going to slice up his tongue.

'No,' I shout

Alex gives me a *don't interfere* look. This trip is turning into a nightmare, and we haven't even got to the departure lounge yet.

'Fucking apologise Mick, else this maniac will kill you. You don't want to mess with him,' shouts the friend.

'Alex Bryant is a hero. Don't you bloody insult him, you little whippersnapper,' calls someone else.

Meanwhile, the security guard is attempting to escort me back into the store.

'You sort the young sod out,' screams an elderly woman standing beside me.

The youth is squealing to be released. Oh dear, it really is quite unpleasant. Everyone else is getting very excited and they all seem to hold their breath when the scruffy youth looks towards me.

'Very sorry for my comment Miss,' he says lamely, while struggling to get out of Alex's grip. I nod my gratitude and Alex releases him. He wobbles slightly before rushing off to join his friends. Everyone cheers and begins to surround Alex, who is smiling at me. I attempt a thank you nod and then allow myself to be escorted back into the store where I come face to face with a stern looking woman.

'Are you with Mr Alex Bryant?' she asks.

There is obviously a right answer to this. The question is what is it?

'Yes, we are travelling to Cambodia together to attend a book fair,' I say truthfully.

She snatches my basket. I am about to tell her that I really need those things when she puts them into a carrier bag and hands it to me.

'There you are madam, compliments of the store. Have a good flight.'

Blimey. It seems Alex the hero has his uses after all. I debate asking for some loo roll but change my mind. After all, I don't want to be seen to be taking advantage. I return to Alex to find him busy signing autographs and surrounded by several paparazzi. I'm a bit taken aback. Of course, I am aware he is well known, I just hadn't realised how well known. Groups of people are standing around, each holding a copy of his book. I approach slowly and hope no one points me out as the fat cow. After a few minutes the groups disperse and he smiles at me.

'Thank you for...' I stammer. 'Although I think you were rather hard on him.'

'Not as hard as I could have been. You, no doubt, would have preferred I threatened to step on his toes,' he responds sharply.

'That is far better than slicing out someone's tongue,' I say angrily and wonder where Miles got that from.

'Obviously, it hadn't occurred to me to threaten slicing up his tongue,' he says calmly, picking up his bag. 'Although that wouldn't have been a bad idea.'

'Oh, I am sure it did cross your mind.'

'What were you going to do then, after he insulted you?' he asks, his handsome features hardening.

'Not threaten to slice out his tongue, obviously.'

'No one threatened his tongue in any way shape or form, as far as I can remember.'

I can tell by his face he is offended. Honestly, men and their egos.

'It's just I'm not used to men standing up for me, that's all.'

I try to imagine Toby threatening to remove someone's tongue but it doesn't work. No matter how hard I try. In fact, I don't think he has ever stood up for me.

'Perhaps you have never been with a real man before.'
What a cheek.

'Thank you all the same,' I add quickly.

'Not a problem. We've been offered an upgrade, but I declined. Seeing as we're going to a poverty-stricken country it really didn't seem appropriate.'

I feel sure he must be joking with me. Is this guy a complete moron? Who turns down an upgrade? What kind of upgrade are we talking about anyway and how does declining help a poverty-stricken country. It's not like we are declining an eight-course meal for Christ's sake.

'Offered an upgrade to where?' I ask, feeling my voice falter.

'Business Class. Of course if you want to and feel it's appropriate, I could...' He is studying me closely.

'No no, it's fine.'

What a horrid man, he did that on purpose. Now, not only do I feel fat but unreasonable too. He gives me a smug smile and suggests we should make our way to our departure gate. I feel inclined to tell him to make his way to the gate that goes to hell, but of course I decline. Cambodia here I come and very reluctantly at that.

Chapter Eleven

A twelve-hour flight in economy with Alex Bryant is my personal hell. To make matters worse, many on the plane recognised him or had overheard the altercation (his word, not mine), between him and the youth. It wouldn't be so bad if they didn't keep mistaking me for his girlfriend. One man approached us to see if I really was fat.

'She's got a bit of meat on her bones.' I, and rows sixteen to twenty-six, could hear him tell his wife later.

'She's a bit on the plump side, but I wouldn't call her fat.'

Oh well, that's a comfort.

I can't help thinking about the Business Class seat I could be reclining in. Instead, I am sandwiched between Alex and a tattooed bald man, who, on sitting down, tells me,

'I fucking hate flying, and it's a long fucking flight ahead so I'm going to fucking kip the whole fucking way. I'll probably take a fucking pill and fucking die.'

I fight an overwhelming desire to respond with.

'Can you *fucking* take the *fucking* pill now and die *fucking* soon please?' But of course, I don't. Instead, I say.

'That's nice.'

He mumbles something which sounds very much like 'fucking posh bitch.' Mother would be pleased.

I'm hoping he will fall into a coma very soon. Who seriously declines an upgrade on a principle? Only Alex-*I-am-so-altruistic*-Bryant. Really, as if whether I fly in comfort or misery is actually going to have any effect on the poverty in Cambodia.

So, here we are, or at least here I am, stuck in the middle of Alex-*it's-a-matter-of-principle*-Bryant and Mr-*I-hate-fucking-flying-tattoo*-an. It doesn't get worse than this. I debate whether to ask if Alex would swap his window seat but decide against it. I really would prefer he didn't do me any favours. Knowing him, he would throw it in my face at a later date. He has headphones on and is acting like I don't exist. I pull my Blackberry from my bag and see I have a text from Toby.

My heart skips a beat. I turn the screen away from Alex and read it. I then read it again and again.

'Hope you have a good flight Libs. Christmas won't be the same without you. I'll give you your present when you get back. Take care of yourself and stay in touch.'

He misses me and he has bought me a present. It is all I can do not to whoop aloud. It's obvious he still loves me or he wouldn't miss me at all. I shudder with excitement. I reply and say how Christmas will not be the same without him also, and that I will give him his present when I return. Not that I have him a present but I can buy him something special in Cambodia, maybe a nice silk shirt. He will like that. I try not to think of him with Serena. I turn my phone off and feel happier than I have for a long time. Even Mr-*I-hate-fucking-flying* can't alter my mood. Perhaps it will be good for us to have some time away from each other. In fact, the longer I am away the more he is likely to miss me. Maybe coming to Cambodia wasn't such a bad idea after all. Alex glances over at me and then pulls out his own phone with such flourish that for a terrifying moment I think he is going for a gun. Talk about a vivid imagination. He's an ex-SAS officer I remind myself, not an ex-Mafia gangster. I glance at his screen saver and see a photo of him with Blancmange. I really cannot imagine what he sees in her. I give him a weak smile.

'How long have you and Blanc... Penelope, been together?' I say, attempting to make conversation.

He gives me a warm smile and removes the headphones. He has taken off the thick woollen jumper he was wearing and his face looks softer in the pastel blue short-sleeved shirt he is wearing. His hair is tousled and he looks younger. God, he is as hairy as an ape. I don't recall ever seeing that much hair on Toby. In fact, I don't recall seeing that much hair on anyone apart from a gorilla in the zoo. Okay, a slight exaggeration.

'Sorry, did you say something?'

He looks right at me and I drown in his warm blue eyes. He has a way of looking at you that makes you feel he only has eyes for you. He is a born flirt I tell myself. Already the air hostess has glanced at him more times than necessary.

'I just wondered how long you and Penelope have been together.'

I find my eyes going to his crotch. What is wrong with me? And why am I blushing? I asked how long they had been together not how often they have sex. He raises his eyebrows and wrinkles his nose slightly.

'Too long,' he replies and I can't tell if he is serious or not.

The plane races down the runway and I feel my shoulders tense. I am pressed back into my economy seat and feel my stomach turn upside down like being on a ride at Alton Towers. I force myself to think of Toby and in moments we are in the air. I'm on my way to sodding Cambodia. The man on my right has fallen asleep and Alex has retrieved a Kindle from his hand luggage. Why am I not surprised? He certainly meant it when he said he travelled light. I lean back and think about my future with Toby. In a few weeks all the Serena business will be forgotten and we can get back to normal. Of course, part of me knows I am being a bit naïve. How can I really forgive him for seeing her behind my back? It really is my own fault though. If I wasn't so fat Toby would love me. It really is rubbish that a man will love you just the way you are. Only in silly romantic comedies like Bridget Jones do you get that and although I may have the figure of Bridget Jones, Toby is not a Darcy. Trust me, when emerging from water, he looks more like a drowned rat than heart-throb. Alex Bryant, on the other hand, probably looks... What am I thinking? Alex Bryant is a pain in the arse and I would be wise to remember that. Besides, he obviously thinks I am a fool. What am I doing travelling with this man? In fact, what am I doing with my life period? Is Jamie right? Should I be focusing more on my own writing rather than defending Toby's all the time? The bald tattoo man is snoring for England and I glance at Alex, who seemingly cannot hear a thing through his headphones. Any attempt I make at sleep is thwarted by the snoring. I so hate Bryant for declining an upgrade. What sensible person does that? To make matters worse we hit turbulence and the 'fasten seat belts' sign bongs and I can't get up and go for a wander. Imprisoned in seat 22B, I wonder what on earth mother was thinking of when she spoke so excitedly of shagging on the plane. It's clear she always flies Business Class isn't it? There is something quite decadent about flying Business Class and I am sure the loos are much better equipped for shagging. I feel somewhat inadequate in economy. Come to think of it, I always feel inadequate, period. Just going to the loo in economy is like running the gauntlet. Let's face it, getting out of an economy aeroplane seat should be essential national curriculum training or part of the Duke of Edinburgh Award scheme. Seeing as I have no other choice but to stay strapped in I might as well look at the films and get my mind off the loo. Sleep is obviously out of the question unless I can steal one of bald tattoo's pills and 'fucking die'. It's just my luck that all the films are sodding disaster movies. What airline shows *Final Destination* as the in-flight video? And as if I am going to happily watch *United 93* after being accused of being a terrorist. This is just plain awful. I shove my headphones on and plug into the music channel. I can still hear tattoo's snoring. I am seriously beginning to wish he *would* bloody die. Flying brings out the worst in people don't you think? When else would you seriously wish someone dead? In fact, if I don't get some sleep soon, I imagine I will be very close to killing him myself. It's well known that long flights are detrimental to your health. I will probably get deep vein thrombosis. Come to think of it my left calf is a bit tingly. That will teach Alex-*tight-fisted*-Bryant to decline an upgrade. To think there are two empty seats in Business Class. I wonder if I can just stroll down there and plonk myself in one. I guess not. Sod Alex Bryant. What an idiot. I probably won't get any decent medical help for my blood clot while in Cambodia either and will most certainly die. In an effort to relax I tune into the meditation channel and before I know where I am I have dozed off. Not for long, however, for the desire to go to the loo is overpowering. I wake with a start to see Mr Tattoo is sprawled partway over my seat. I untangle my foot from his and shake my leg. Now I have a dilemma... Do I wake tattoo and get him to move so I can go to the loo? Or climb over him as he sleeps? If I wake him it means I may well have him talking instead of snoring. Is having him snoring preferable to having him 'fucking' for the next eight hours? Not literally fucking, obviously. Mother would be appalled at his language. I imagine she would be appalled at Alex's refusal of Business Class seats too. The space for me to manoeuvre is about one inch. It's in moments like these that I very much wish I were slim. In fact, it is moments like these when I make firm decisions to diet. Meanwhile, however, I am still fat and have to somehow squeeze past Mr Tattoo without waking him, having decided that snoring is better than fucking. First I have got to untangle myself from all the paraphernalia surrounding me. Why do airlines bombard you with so much stuff while you are sitting in such a confined area? I don't have this much stuff in my living room. I shove my blanket, headphones, goody bag and pillow as far under my seat as I can. I also push my sodding shoes under there with them. Oh well, nothing for it but to head to the loo barefoot then. I throw my handbag into the aisle and then contemplate how I can climb over Mr Tattoo and avoid contact with his body. Alex is seemingly deep into whatever he is reading and does not seem to notice me fidgeting. After a great deal of calculation I conclude it would be safer to climb over Mr Tattoo while facing him. Would you aim your bum at a stranger? Exactly. I rest my case. After much panting and heaving I manage to get one leg over him. It is as I am attempting to retrieve my other leg that Alex asks,

'What are you doing?'

I shush with my finger on my lips but all is lost. I lose my balance and have to grasp Mr Tattoo by the shoulders to steady myself. He wakes with a start and looks straight into my eyes and his arms wrap around my waist.

'What the fuck?' he mumbles.

Yes, what the fuck indeed. Remove your hands sir.

'Just popping to the loo,' I say quickly and pull my other leg free. God, is the whole journey going to be like this? Thankfully, I do manage to doze off, as does Alex and am gratefully relieved when we finally reach Bangkok. Just another hour and we will be in Cambodia. Me in Asia, can you believe it? I know I can't.

Chapter Twelve

Alex Bryant is a control freak. He has taken total command of my luggage, my passport and my visa. In fact, I am beginning to think he has taken control of my life.

'Right, we are all sorted. You need to go through passport control yourself,' he says in an authoritative voice handing me my passport.

'I think I can manage that.'

'Smile, the Cambodians are very pleasant people and use the proper greeting. You'll offend them if you don't smile back. And as a sign of respect to someone bow your head slightly with your hands together.'

God, he's so bossy. A woman behind us visibly swoons and pushing me to one side thrusts her face towards his.

'It's a thrill to meet you,' she says breathlessly, edging even closer so her breasts touch his chest. 'I've admired you forever.'

Her push unbalances me and I wobble for a few seconds before regaining my balance. God forbid I should stand in the way of sexual magnetism which I really can't deny he has, after all, I felt it in the pub didn't I? Fortunately I am a professional and don't let personal feelings interfere with my work. Even if Alex Bryant were interested in me I would not allow myself to respond. All right, we all know that someone like Alex Bryant would never look twice at someone like me, hence why he is with model lookalike Penelope who has neat breasts, a flat stomach, not to mention permanently tanned legs that go on forever and teeth like a horse, while I have... Well, best not to go there.

I am still wearing my thick jumper, not to mention tights underneath my leggings. I am dressed for cold wintry England and it must be 30 degrees in here. Stepping off the plane is like walking into an oven. My head aches from tiredness. I cannot help wondering what Toby is doing, or rather where Toby is. With my hand luggage bulging with boxes of tissues and my hair a straggly mess, I trudge towards passport control. The officer is not smiling. I scrape my hair back and tie it into a scrunch and attempt to give him my most winning smile. He does not respond. He is most certainly not one happy Cambodian is he? He barks at me and I look at Alex who is pointing at the floor. I move slightly so my feet are on the sign that reads 'STAND HERE.' I sigh and the officer gives me a dirty look. I continue smiling until my face aches. For goodness sake, I'm doing my very best not to offend him but he doesn't seem to give a fig if he offends me.

'Hond, hond,' he shouts.

What does *hond* mean?

'Nice to meet you,' I say in my friendliest voice.

He points to my hands and gives me a cross look. Of course, I'd forgotten the 'respect' thing. I clasp my hands together and bow gratefully.

'Thank you so much,' I say warmly.

'Hond,' he shouts again.

Jesus, he is a bit intense. What more does he want? I turn to Alex but there is no sign of him. My God, they haven't arrested him already have they? Perhaps they realised who he was. I hold my hands up in surrender. I'm so hot. I feel sure I will pass out in a minute. He attempts to grab my hand and I step back.

'Look, can you please stop shouting at me,' I hiss, while continuing to smile and feeling sure my mouth will never return to normal. Where is sodding Alex-*slice-your-tongue-out*-Bryant when I need him?

I turn and see him standing behind me. Thank goodness.

'They want to take your fingerprints.'

'But I haven't done anything yet. I'm not a criminal.'

'Nobody said you were. It's standard practice here at passport control.'

'Oh, I thought... I don't really know what I thought,' I say in a whisper.

'You're not a secret agent,' he says dismissively, making me feel stupid. I suddenly hate him very much. I really don't need anybody's help to feel stupid. He talks rapidly in what must be Khmer. Honestly, he thinks he is such a smart bugger. He then ushers me through security and outside into the hot evening air where a driver is waiting with our suitcases. We weave through the sea of taxi drivers, porters and ticket touts each insisting we accept their services. The setting sun paints the airport terminal building a fiery orange. Everyone is shouting and beckoning to us. A row of palm trees line the road where countless motorbikes stream by. The noise from the motorbikes eclipses the shouting of the touts and a smell of hot tarmac and exhaust fumes assaults me.

'As you're tired we'll take a taxi to the hotel but in future it is best to use a tuk-tuk.'

I am starting to detest that 'I know-it-all' voice of his.

'A *tuk-tuk*?' It is more of a statement than a question. Of course I know what a *tuk-tuk* is.

'Don't worry about it,' he responds tersely, making me feel stupid again.

He signals for me to climb into the taxi and I do so gratefully, collapsing onto the back seat. Within moments he has joined me. I fumble in my bag for the hotel's address. After inspecting it the driver says in a flat voice,

'I take you for twenty-five dollar.'

I nod, but know-it-all Bryant perks up.

'That seems a lot. There are plenty of taxi drivers, is that the best you can do?' he argues.

For pity's sake, I am knackered and he wants to argue over a few dollars?

'It's fine, I'll pay. I'm not going to look for another taxi,' I say forcefully.

'It's your money but he's ripping you off,' he says dismissively.

I let my head flop back. The air conditioning wafts over me and after a cursory glance at Alex, who has also dropped his head back, I allow myself to fall asleep. I figure I can see the sights another night.

Something jolts me awake and for a second I am unsure where I am. I check my Blackberry to see we have been travelling for several hours. Alex's head is resting on my shoulder and he is sound asleep. His hand is lying on my knee. I take a quick peek at his sleeping face. His superhero guise has taken on a childlike quality. I imagine all that will change when he wakes up. I try to imagine what I must look like and gently remove a mirror from my bag. God, I look like a member of the Addams family. My eyes are black and smudgy. I knew I shouldn't have worn mascara. The corners of my mouth are crusty and horrid and there is a distinct odour coming from my armpits, or is it Alex Bryant's arm pit? Stupid Libby as if Alex-*call-me-Indiana*-Bryant actually perspires. His mobile dangles precariously from his other hand and I gently remove it. It vibrates as I do so and a text pops up onto the screen.

'I am so wishing we could have talked more honey. I'm missing you so much already. You must be at the hotel. Can't imagine how you are coping with that Lily woman. At least I don't have any need to be jealous. We're wrapping everything up here in Beijing tonight. Speak soon. Love you Pen. X'

What a cheek. She can't even get my name right. I suppose she thinks I am too fat for Alex Bryant to fancy. I stupidly feel tears prick the back of my eyelids. This is ridiculous. I must pull myself together. I am so tired and the hotel seems miles away. We must surely get there soon.

'Hotel?' queries the driver suddenly.

'Oh good, are we near?' I ask, attempting to speak as clearly as I can.

'Hotel?' he asks again.

'Yes please. We are very tired.'

He shrugs and turns the taxi onto a dirt track where we swerve and bump dangerously along. Alex stirs and his hand wanders up my thigh. Surely he is still asleep, or is he pretending to be asleep and making a pass at me? With me looking like I do? I don't think so. Or he is mistaking me for someone else. My hand brushes his off roughly. He jumps with a start, shouts something incoherent and looks at me like I have just dropped from the sky.

'Ah,' he says on recognising me.

He stretches lazily and I spy a tiny bit of chest as his shirt rises. God, he is hairy all over. He gives his phone a cursory glance and looks curiously out of the window. The taxi bumps down an even narrower dirt road and finally stops. Alex yawns and strains to see out of the window.

'This isn't Siem Reap,' he says casually.

It isn't? I look out of the window and see nothing but darkness.

'Right, let's make the best of things, dump our luggage and get some sleep,' says a bossy Bryant.

The driver helps with the luggage and leads us down a dark road to a building. Jamie could have booked a hotel nearer the town. I expect the rebels are more prominent there though. Best to be safe I suppose. I pull my jumper off and quickly put it back on when I realise the odour is most certainly mine. God it is so hot. We climb a flight of steps and finally enter the foyer of the hotel and any attempt to suppress my gasp is lost. This can't be right. I turn to ask the taxi driver if we are in the right place but he is already climbing back into his car. Before I even have time to beckon to him he has gone in a cloud of dust. He has dumped us in the middle of nowhere.

Chapter Thirteen

I enter the dark inertia only to have Alex pull me back.

'It's respectful to remove ones shoes.'

I dutifully do so, not wishing to offend anyone. The reception area is a tiny room with deafening air conditioning. Two rickety chairs sit in one corner and a large sink in the other. The floor consists of rough bare boards with a thin scattering of straw. Ahead of us a wrinkled old man stands behind a counter. Tiny chicks scramble around my feet. Oh God, they are pecking me. I'm going to get rabies or something equally as bad. I am so tired I can't remember what vaccinations I had. A fully grown hen makes clucking noises at me and I let out a tiny sob. Jamie said we were staying in a five star hotel. I can't imagine what star hotel this is. Minus three I imagine. I want to protest but am speechless. The wrinkled man bows and smiles widely at us as he retrieves our luggage which the taxi driver had dumped outside. With perspiration running down his face, he fills two glasses with water from the rusty tap in the corner of the room, handing one to me and the other to Alex. I watch as Alex throws the liquid back eagerly and then talks in fluent Khmer to the man. What an arrogant arse. I am so thirsty but surely it is dangerous to drink the water here, even more so from a rusty tap. The old man thrusts the glass unmercifully at me, smiling the whole time. Please don't let me get rabies and cholera my first day. I wonder if Toby will fly out for my funeral. I imagine they will have to bury me right away. They wouldn't want a cholera epidemic. Toby would be devastated and write a moving obituary. How romantic. Alex will blame himself and vow never to return to Cambodia, and will dedicate his next book to me.

Alex's weary voice pulls me out of my fantasy.

'He wants to prepare some food for us. I have agreed. It would be disrespectful not to.'

He points to the water.

'I'd drink that if I were you. For some reason they don't have any bottled water here. I need to phone Jamie as soon as possible. This is not the right hotel, but I'm too tired to do anything now.'

'But I'll get cholera,' I protest. 'Surely the food here won't be safe?'

'I very much doubt you'll get cholera.'

'But I...'

'You are the most argumentative woman I have ever had the displeasure of meeting,' he snaps, his eyes cold and hard.

I gulp and frantically think of a suitable response, but am too tired to do anything but cry. Bugger it. He blinks rapidly and shakes his head.

'I'm sorry, I shouldn't have said that. I'm very tired. I'll contact Jamie. In the meantime let's make the best of things. This chap here is very happy to have us to stay.'

He briefly touches my arm with his hand. I grudgingly accept his apology and swallow some of the water. The old man beckons us to follow him through a doorway and up a rickety ladder. I hesitate for a second and then gingerly make my way up. The last thing I can cope with is Alex snapping at me again. Just wait until I get my hands on Jamie. The man continues to talk incessantly to Alex who answers him fluently. I have to admit I am impressed, but I try not to let my admiration show. I cannot suppress my gasp, however, when we reach the top of the staircase I find myself standing in what can only be described as a run-down attic. It houses a bed with a sheet and pillow on it. The dusty floor is part covered with a coloured rug and in the far corner is a wash basin with a neatly folded towel at the side of it. I stare in horror at the bucket which sits beside it. What is that?

'I see you have the en suite,' smiles Alex and I fight a desire to push him back down the rickety steps. I attempt to hide my appalled look and with a permanent smile attached to my face I turn to face him.

'Surely, he has a better room than this?'

'Actually, this is his best room, and he is really proud to be giving it to you.'

Christ, I wouldn't want the worst room in this joint. The old man grins and nods at me. Alex places his hands together and bows gratefully. I follow suit, feeling neither grateful nor happy. He then takes Alex through a beaded curtain and they disappear presumably to Alex's room. I am having trouble holding back my tears. I am hungry having not eaten much on the plane. I had envisaged a lovely hotel, a hot bath and a dinner with a cool glass of white wine. Okay, I know wine is fattening, but I have barely eaten. Instead, I am contemplating drinking a glass of rust-infested water and a dinner made of God knows what. I have no malaria tablets because I am not supposed to be in a high-risk area but I somehow think I am. What on earth was Jamie thinking of, sending me to Cambodia with a man who seems to have no sense of responsibility whatsoever? I must speak with Jamie tomorrow and impress on him that I cannot possibly stay here with Alex Bryant. It is seriously putting my health at risk. I stare longingly at the water and then with eyes closed and a hand over my nose I throw it back and drink greedily. Oh God, please don't let me die. Alex dumps my bags in the room and disappears again but not before promising to fetch me for the late dinner. I study the wash basin and am about to call Alex to ask where I go for the water when he returns with a bucket and empties it into the basin.

'I'm going to wash downstairs. Dinner will be ready in about ten minutes. Cover yourself in insect repellent. You do have insect repellent don't you?'

He is grinning at me again in that mocking way that I hate so much.

'Of course,' I snap.

I would rather be bitten to pieces and die an ugly and painful death than admit to not having any. As soon as he leaves I pull off my clothes and rummage through my toiletries for soap and body lotion. The water is cool and clean and within minutes I am feeling a hundred times better. From my suitcase I take one of my favourite summer dresses that I had bought from Jigsaw. I think it looks okay on me, but without a mirror I can't be sure. I feel fine, so maybe I haven't caught cholera after all, although I imagine it will be hours before I know for sure. Dinner is served in a small room off the foyer. Alex and I are seated opposite each other and an old woman, who I presume is the hotel owner's wife, brings in plates of hot steaming food. It smells delicious but let's face it, even poison can smell great. Alex piles rice onto a plate followed by small round pieces of meat.

'It looks good. Try and eat some. They consider it an honour to be feeding us.'

'Don't tell me, even they know who you are. Your reputation as saviour of the world must precede you.'

What am I saying? He hasn't even been rude and I am insulting him. He certainly brings out the worst in me. He gives me a quizzical look and bites into the meat. I fork some rice into my mouth.

'The rice is good isn't it? Aren't you going to eat your meat?' he challenges.

Why is he so horrid? He deliberately stabs two more pieces of meat and makes a big show of eating them. The old woman smiles at me as she pours what looks like wine into glasses. Thank God, I need something alcoholic. I spoon two pieces of meat into my mouth and chew slowly. Actually it isn't too bad, a bit chewy but quite nice considering. In fact, it tastes very much like chicken and I suddenly remember the little chicks that were pecking around my feet earlier. Oh no, surely not. I point to the meat and look around for the chicks. They are nowhere to be seen.

'The baby chicks and their mother, this isn't them is it? We're not eating the babies are we?' I ask.

I feel sick.

'Of course not, it's water snake. What do you think of it?' laughs Alex.

I think I am going to be ill is what I think. I wind my hand around my glass of wine and take a long gulp and almost fall off my chair.

'It's palm-sap wine. I'd go easy on that if I were you,' he advises in that know-it-all voice.

'You can go off people,' I mumble.

He smiles, and I stupidly feel my heart do a little flutter. He does have a nice smile. I can't deny that and he is very good looking. In fact he seems quite approachable at the moment and less of the macho man. His hair is slightly damp from his earlier wash and he has that fresh clean smell about him that is uniquely his. In fact, now I think about it, I don't recall him ever smelling of aftershave, unlike Toby who pongs of it, so I find it quite amazing that I ever picked up the smell of 'Trésor' on him.

'Does Penelope eat the food out here?' I find myself asking, recalling her disgust at the party when I tucked into the turkey.

'God no, she barely eats food in England. Hot countries aren't her thing.'

I wonder what her thing is but say nothing. So, I am taken by surprise when he asks,

'I take it a country like Cambodia isn't Toby's thing either? Or am I wrong and he has been here and just got his facts all wrong.'

Immediately, I find myself feeling defensive on Toby's behalf.

'He actually spends a great deal of time on his research, but no, he hasn't been to Cambodia and neither have I come to that.'

He looks at me over his forkful of rice but doesn't comment. I lower my eyes and fiddle with my meat. The dessert is much more palatable. We finish with water melon and sweet sticky rice, and I eat more than I should. Alex chats in a relaxed manner to the owner and doesn't bother to translate. I sit drinking the palm-sap wine until I feel a little tipsy. By this time I had completely forgotten that my room is several rickety steps up a ladder, however, I am rudely reminded of that when Alex quips,

'Right, I think you and I should go to bed.'

'Not together I hope.'

God, did I say that? I have drunk too much. He either didn't hear or conveniently ignores my comment. He thanks our host by bowing gratefully. I attempt to bow but am so giddy that I almost topple forward. Thankfully Alex escorts me up the ladder. After bidding me goodnight he disappears through the curtain to his own room. I fall onto the bed and take my Blackberry from my bag. It is late afternoon in England and even though it is the weekend I decide to phone Jamie. It clicks straight into voice mail.

'Jamie, it's me. Can you please phone me? The hotel is absolute crap. It has a bucket for the loo and Alex know-it-all Bryant is no help at all. He is so arrogant, and I am sure I will catch cholera, or something worse, and he couldn't care less. Please phone me.'

I hang up and feel an overriding anger towards Alex Bryant. After washing my face in cold water and giving my teeth a cursory brush I attempt to negotiate the toilet. Surely, Bryant could have explained to the owner that this wasn't suitable and found another hotel? No, it's no good. No matter how desperate my bladder is to be relieved I can't go. I strain and strain but nothing happens. I visualise running water but still nothing happens.

'Oh, come on, it's just a bucket. You've done a wee in a bucket before,' I reprimand myself. Although, actually, I have never had a wee in a bucket, I mean, why would I?

'Bloody know-it-all,' I say loudly. 'Who does he think he is, talking in blooming Khmer? *It's water snake, what do you think?* Up yours, fancy pants Bryant. If I get cholera you'll be sorry. Honestly, all that stuff about knowing the customs and stuff, what a show off. I hate you Alex-*know-it-all*-Bryant. Maybe half the women in the country would go to bed with you but I certainly wouldn't, not even if you asked me, so there, and you could at least have got me some air conditioning, you horrible man.'

My bladder, seemingly hearing my rant and obviously in agreement with me, decides to let my urine flow free. What a relief. At that moment there is a strange tapping sound and I practically fall off the bucket.

'Who's that, who's there,' I call frantically. Can't I pee in peace, for Christ's sake?

'Alex. My room is literally the other side of the curtain. Can I come through?'

Oh no.

'What do you mean?'

'My room is next door,' he whispers, peeking around the curtain just as I am pulling up my knickers.

'Oops, sorry,' he says, but I hear the amused tone in his voice.

'Come on, what is wrong with you?' I say angrily.

'Apparently, I'm arrogant and a show off but I do have air-conditioning fans.' He holds one out to me.

Of course, I now feel terrible.

'Obviously, I didn't really mean it when I said you were arrogant and a show off,' I say, not meeting his eyes.

'Of course not,' he smiles.

He is wearing nothing but a pair of shorts and as much as I try to direct my eyes to his face they just keep strolling to his... well you know how it is.

I grab the fan off him and point to the curtain.

'If you wouldn't mind.'

'Certainly, and if you wouldn't mind keeping the noise down, some of us are trying to sleep. By the way, you looked very nice this evening.'

I am speechless. Before I can respond he is gone. Did he actually say I looked nice? Not fat, or a bit overweight, or even a bit on the plump side but very nice? Blimey, he must be delirious with the heat. I get into the bed and turn the fan on full. I strain my ears but can hear no sound through the curtain. Tomorrow I will make arrangements to return home. Did I really say I wouldn't go to bed with him even if he asked? I embarrass myself, I truly do. With a cringe I pull the sheet over my head.

Chapter Fourteen

I wake up hot, sweaty and with light streaming in through the window. I groan. I groan even louder when I see it is only six o'clock and hear the cockerel. How is a girl supposed to get her beauty sleep around here? I squeeze my eyes shut and attempt to ignore the crowing. After five minutes I irritably climb from the bed. I hear Alex talking to the hotel owner downstairs. So, he is up, which is a bit disconcerting because it means at some point he wandered through my room and past my bed. This is unless, of course, he spirited himself down the rickety staircase which wouldn't surprise me. He would have seen me stark naked as I awoke in the early hours sweating like a Cambodian pig and threw everything off me. I peer out of the window to view the dastardly cockerel. The view is amazing. All I can see are rice fields and blue skies. Not far in the distance is a temple. How lovely to have a temple so near. It can only be about 100 metres away. I must have a look later. Oh no. My mother's words echo in my head,

'It looked fabulous, and it has a beautiful temple with a huge bell. Apparently when the monks sound the bell all of the villagers go to the temple. How amazing is that?'

Please don't let it be that village. I dive into my handbag and pull out the address that Jamie had given me. Sod it. It is neatly written in both English and Khmer and most certainly directs us to Siem Reap. I gave the driver the wrong piece of paper. I'm in the village mother recommended. Oh, wonderful. Now, how do I tell Alex-*never-make-a-mistake*-Bryant what I've done? I really don't want to hear his *I told you so,* especially not at this time of the morning. I head downstairs to reluctantly impart the bad news.

'Ah, good morning,' he greets me brightly, 'did you sleep well?'

'Very well, thank you.'

He is clean shaven, fresh faced and looks disgustingly healthy and fit. I open my mouth to tell him my mistake and close it again when he says.

'I'm waiting for Jamie to call back. I've left a message and told him the name of the village. It's not ideal. I can't understand what went wrong. I covered all the bases to keep us secure.'

Oh dear. This is so not good. How on earth do I break the awful news?

'If I find out who has put us in danger…' he continues.

On second thoughts, maybe it's best not to break the awful news after all.

'Are we really in danger,' I ask, trying to hide the tremor in my voice. I don't want him thinking I am a coward, even if I am.

'At the moment all westerners are good hostage material, if that's what you mean?'

I look around for the other guests.

'We are the only guests,' he says reading my mind. 'There is some fruit for your breakfast and coffee in the pot. The owners have gone into the village.'

I notice he is far too diplomatic to mention last night. He turns from me to take a call on his mobile while I pick up a bowl of watermelon. I have donned the same dress I had on last night and although it is already hot I feel a lot cooler than when we arrived last night. Toby hasn't replied to my text. Come to that, neither has Jamie. I pour myself a cup of coffee and wander outside to the veranda. I step around the baby chicks that I'm pleased to see are still alive and sit on a rickety chair. I can now see that the hotel is nothing but a ramshackle old house which stands on stilts. No wonder there were so many steps when we arrived. Opposite is a never-ending rice field, and the view is breathtaking. The sun shimmers on the water between the tufts of rice plants and a solitary cow grazes by the side of the sandy road. An old cart is propped against the house almost resembling a biblical scene. The terrain is flat, and I can see palm trees in the distance. I sip at my coffee and soak up the tranquillity of the place. The sun bathes my skin with deep warmth. You would never think there was an uprising here. It is so peaceful.

'Ah, you're here. That was Jamie on the phone.'

This morning he is wearing combat trousers and a loose black top. He looks a little more like the superhero, and I find myself viewing him the way I always have. I've never liked him. How could I like someone who has humiliated my boyfriend in public? But, it is hard not to admire his good looks and his obvious bravery.

'It's quite lovely here,' I say wistfully.

'And very unsafe and totally exposed,' he says in that *don't worry, I can take them all single handed* voice I so detest.

He is so intense. This is Cambodia, not the Middle East. I often think he gets his countries muddled up. At that moment my Blackberry blares loudly from my handbag. Thinking it may be Jamie I plunge my hand in to grab it. It's Toby, and I hesitate as I don't want Alex to hear our conversation. I hesitate for too long, and the call goes to voicemail. I'm about to throw it back into my bag when it rings again. God, he is persistent. He must be missing me. I feel so happy I could jump up and dance. I'm beginning to think that coming to Cambodia was a good idea after all. I wait for Alex to go inside but does he? No, he just stands there looking at me. I answer the phone and hope my voice doesn't shake.

'Libby, is that you?'

No, it's the Queen Mother. Who else would it be?

'Yes, of course it's me. Are you...'

'You've got to get out of there. Jamie said you've somehow ended up in Khum Pleeung.'

What is he on about?

'What is the weather like there? I bet it feels Christmassy. What are you doing over... ?' I begin pleasantly.

'Why did that bastard take you there, he should have known better, Jesus Christ, what a wanker...'

I cough slightly but make no comment.

'If anything happens to you I'll never forgive that idiot, or myself for that matter. I wish you were here Libs. I really miss you.'

Blimey, I should go away more often.

'Well...' I begin.

'Why the hell did he take you there when you were booked into a hotel in Siem Reap? I'll have Bryant hung by his balls for this, that's if he's got any, the stupid bastard,' yells Toby.

I imagine he is quite red in the face. This must mean he really loves me. I decide not to tell him, after what I saw of Alex Bryant last night, that he most certainly has balls. Oh yes indeed, of that I have no doubt. I feel my face grow hot and turn it from Alex.

'I don't mind telling you, if I was there I'd make mincemeat of that arrogant bastard.'

'Toby, I'm getting a bit confused. What exactly are you talking about?' I say finally, when sensing he is about to take a breath.

'You're in the heart of it. You're fucking sitting ducks. If you're lucky they will hang, draw and quarter him.'

The truth is I have no idea what on earth he is on about. I know we are not in Siem Reap but he is making it sound like we are in the middle of a drug baron war. All I have managed to ascertain is that Toby is very angry and wants to make mincemeat of Alex, presumably after he has hung him by his balls, and if he has not already been hung, drawn and quartered by someone else. Not that I have the vaguest idea who this 'someone else' may be. I am beginning to wonder if I should mention that we are here because I buggered up the addresses, and not Alex. On reflection maybe not, I really don't think I could cope with them both shouting at me.

'All I can say is it's a bloody good job Alex Bryant isn't standing in front of me,' rambles on Toby.

'Oh my God, it certainly is,' I shriek as Alex pulls out a gun. My God, it really is a gun, with a barrel and everything. Christ, how did he get that through customs? When he collected another bag at the airport I didn't imagine it held his own artillery. He'll be producing a grenade next, and to think I nearly got arrested for being a terrorist. I ask you.

'I'd have his guts for garters. I'm not scared of him,' continues Toby.

Not to mention hanging his balls out to dry. There won't be much left of Alex to make mincemeat of at the rate Toby is going.

'Why don't you just have a word with him, he is right beside me,' I say, finishing on a whimper. I really just want to get away from the damn gun. For the first time since he phoned Toby goes silent.

'Toby, are you still there?'

Is that a smirk on Bryant's face? Oh, if it wasn't for that gun, I would happily wipe it off.

'Well, no, it's okay. I'm not going to get far talking to him on the phone am I? But, I tell you, if I was there, I would...'

I sigh. Really, do I have to listen to this?

'Hang draw and quarter him and then hang him by his balls. Of course, this is after you have had his guts for garters and then you will make mincemeat of him. But, of course, you don't want to tell him what you think of him over the phone.'

I don't know why I say all this in front of Alex Bryant. I actually feel quite let down by Toby. If he really loves me, which surely he must considering he is so worried about me, then why doesn't he tell Alex

Bryant what he thinks of him? Alex pulls me by the arm and leads me back into the house. Obviously I don't argue. The door is slammed shut and Alex shoots the flimsy bolt across. Now, bearing in mind I have no idea what the hell is going on here, I have come to the realisation that it is not good. You don't pull out guns and slam and bolt doors if everything is hunky-dory now do you? Alex is frantically looking around, and I feel an overwhelming urge to throw myself to the floor like people do in the films. Oh my Lord, It seems like I am not going to stay alive long enough to contract cholera. I stare at the gun.

'Don't worry, it isn't loaded. It's just a scare tactic,' mumbles Bryant, pushing a chair against the door.

'What's happening? Is everything okay?' Toby shouts down the phone.

I am now trembling so much that I can barely speak.

'I'm really not sure,' I say in a shaky but I'm attempting to be brave voice.

Alex is pulling things from under the reception counter but by his grunts he obviously isn't finding what he is looking for. He fiddles with a belt for a few seconds and then throws it to one side. He turns and studies me and then seems to make a decision.

'Take your bra off,' he says firmly.

Jesus, someone help me. What the hell is going on?

'For fuck's sake, put that arsehole on the phone now,' screams Toby.

'Libby, take your bra off,' Alex says again, his voice soft but firm.

'Don't you fucking dare,' yells Toby.

I really don't see what right Toby has to tell me who I can or can't take my bra off for. After all, when was the last time he asked me to take off a bra? My bottom lip trembles and my legs suddenly give way, and I quickly grab the reception desk for support.

'We have a situation, we've been compromised,' whispers Alex peering around the curtain.

'Libby, are you there, for Christ's sake answer,' cries Toby.

'I've been compromised,' I reply stupidly.

'What! You mean he took advantage of you? That is the last straw... I...'

'No not Alex.'

'Who then?'

'I don't know,' I say beginning to cry.

How dare Bryant ask me to remove any part of my clothing? Toby is quite right about him, he is indeed a prick. I hand Alex my Blackberry with shaking hands.

'Toby wants to speak to you,' I hiss, tears streaming down my cheeks. 'Toby is very angry with you.'

'I couldn't care what Toby is feeling,' he says, snatching the phone and clicking it off.

'I hate you,' I cry.

'Whatever, just give me your bra woman and do as you're told.'
I can't take my eyes off the gun. I'm not sure I believe him when he said it wasn't loaded. I'm here for a book conference for Christ's sake, not the showdown at the OK Corral. There is a lot of shouting from outside and from the window I can see a group of men angrily waving sticks and heading towards the house. What if they make me watch them hang draw and quarter Alex? I know I hate him but not that much. A stick hits the window and I scream and dive dramatically to the floor, accidentally grabbing Alex Bryant by the leg as I do so. We both fall and Alex collapses on top of me. I feel the heat from his body and his pounding heart vibrates against my chest. His face is so close to mine that his breath seems to caress my neck. I feel a strange tingle deep inside me.

'We really have been compromised, Libby. The rebels are holed up in this village. They think we're a threat or a possible hostage negotiation prospect. I don't want to get too aggressive with them but I need to see them off. There is nothing here I can use. Now, will you please give me your bra? It's better than nothing. Whatever you think of me, I can assure you I am not a rapist.'
His soft whisper sounds like a caress, and if I wasn't so scared I think I might have swooned just a little bit. I wasn't really thinking that he was going to rape me, was I? Okay, yes I suppose I was. What was I supposed to think? He looks into my eyes and we both jump at the sound of shouting and cracks at the window. I really am going to die in Cambodia. I roll over onto my stomach and pull my dress straps down. It takes some manoeuvring to get the top part of my dress down while lying on the floor. Before I have time to lean back to unclasp my bra, Alex has already expertly unclipped it. Without a moment's hesitation he whips it out from under me. His warm body leaves mine and I crawl behind the counter and pull my dress up. I sneak a look around the counter to see Alex outside swinging my bra around his head. Good God, my Wonderbra has become a slingshot.

I know it is the eighth wonder of the world but isn't this taking things just a bit too far? I'm seriously having a Wonderbra moment in that nothing seems entirely what it really is. My phone shrills and I cover my ears to drown out the sound. The shouting is much louder now and more continuous as they seem to be chanting something. I am gripping the corners of the counter so hard that I swear the circulation in my hands has stopped. All I can think about is how good Alex smelt and how warm and delicious his breath felt on my neck. Stop being so stupid Libby. As if a man like Alex Bryant would even give me a second glance.

The temple bell chimes three or four times. I realise that Alex must be using my bra as a slingshot to fire pebbles at the temple bell. The shouting becomes fainter, and I realise the crowd are retreating. They must all be going to the temple. Alex returns and looks at me and seems strangely embarrassed. I quickly look down. It would be just like me to have my bloody tits on show. No, all is well, but I'm not hanging half as well as I was earlier when wearing my Wonderbra. Although that stone infested thing is not getting anywhere near my breasts now, I can assure you.

'Are you okay?' he asks almost shyly.

I attempt to stand up, but my legs give way. How embarrassing. He must think me such a weakling. It isn't every day that armed rebels attack the hotel I am staying in, is it? And it certainly isn't every day I am boldly asked to whip my bra off in order to fight them off. Thank God he didn't ask for my knickers. The only pair I could find this morning was my Spanx panties. Massively embarrassing, of course, but highly useful. Next time we get attacked I shall just strip off and ask him what bit of my underwear is the weapon of choice to fight the enemy.

'I can't think why you didn't use your gun,' I say, accepting his hand and allowing him to pull me up. 'That surely would have been more effective than my bra and easier to get your hands on.'

Oh God, that sounds awful and very wrong. He raises his eyebrows but says nothing. I attempt to put things right and of course things just get worse.

'What I mean is, pulling out your gun surely would have been far easier than taking off my bra. It would have saved you all the trouble.'

'It was no trouble,' he replies in a calm cool, smooth voice that has more of an impact than if he had just made a pass at me.

I feel myself flush red.

'I don't know what you've read or what your boyfriend has told you, but the rebels aren't all they seem. They actually have some very valid arguments. I didn't want us to be a bargaining tool for them. Hopefully they now know that we will defend ourselves, but we're not aggressors. We need to leave here and get to Siem Reap. If you really want to learn what we are dealing with, read my book and not some badly researched article by Toby. You would do well to consider writing some stuff yourself while you're here.'

I realise his hand is still holding mine and I reluctantly slide it away and pat my hair.

'We should pack,' he says in a practical voice and strolls away from me and seems to leap up the rickety stairs. He stops half way and turns.

'We don't have time for you to change, or time to pack all your stuff. I'm taking one rucksack. Get together essentials and then we're going.'

I stare at him.

'Oh yes, very useful,' he smiles and tosses the bra to me.

I can barely breathe and feel an overwhelming urge to phone Issy for advice. Before I can, my Blackberry rings. It is Toby. I hear his booming voice before I even put the phone to my ear.

'What the fuck. Are you okay Libby? He's a bloody maniac...'

'Toby, you are massively overreacting. We were compromised but Alex has everything in hand. We have to move out right away.'

Christ, I am sounding like a female Alex Bryant.

'Libs, I'm coming out there,' he says with a dramatic air of finality in his voice.

'You're what?' I squeal.

'This has made me realise that I really love you Libs, and if you insist on staying in a dangerous country then I want to be with you.'

Stone the crows. Am I hearing him correctly? Toby loves me and is coming to Cambodia to be with me? At last, Toby is doing what I dreamed of, and all I can seem to think about is Alex Bryant, who doesn't even notice I exist until he needs my bra. Christ on a bike, isn't that just typical?

Chapter Fifteen

I look at the rickety boat and my heart sinks. We have walked for miles and I am seriously exhausted. It is stiflingly hot and Bryant keeps saying we can't chance getting a taxi. I think he is paranoid. Any warm feelings I felt for him vanished when he refused to allow me to change before leaving. If that wasn't enough, he also forbade me to bring my hairdryer, face cream and a spare pair of sandals. The only thing I threw on was my bra which, I swear, must still have stones in it as something has been sandpapering my nipple the whole way. I've heard of joggers' nipple but this is ridiculous. Alex Bryant is most definitely bad for my health. This is the most exercise I have had in years, I'm not sure my body can take it.

'There's no time to lose,' he had snapped, his blue eyes hardening.

I have been dragged through rice fields, hurried along dirt tracks and told to turn off my phone in case we are being tracked. If Alex Bryant is Indiana Jones, then I am most certainly Lara Croft. I rather think if I had been allowed to have my hairdryer and face cream I could have looked half like her too. Well, I can dream can't I? I imagine I look more like Nora Batty at present. My feet are filthy, and there are bits of tree in my hair. I have no intention of staying in this God-forsaken country for one minute longer than I have to, and shall phone Jamie as soon as we reach the hotel. I only hope Toby has not got a flight already. I daren't phone him. The last time I had pulled my phone from my dress pocket was about an hour ago and the sharp look I had got from Alex-*hold-it-there*-Bryant was almost enough to kill me on the spot. We have trudged through a thick wood and ahead of us is a rickety boat on the shore of a lake. If he thinks I am getting in that then he has another think coming. Alex surveys me in such a way that I blush from head to toe. He slowly removes the rucksack from his back. I stand mesmerised as I watch him unsheathe his knife. What now? And why is being with Alex Bryant like being on a date with Crocodile Dundee?

'Whatever you do don't move,' he whispers.

I freeze and open my mouth to scream, although I am not sure why. Although you can be sure if Mr Crocodile Dundee is concerned, it must be serious.

'What now?' I groan.

'I'm preparing myself to deal with the cobra that is currently wrapped warmly around your leg, or did you think you had left your socks on?'

'Oh my God', I begin to sweat, and my head starts to thump unmercifully.

'Don't panic, it's important to keep calm,' he whispers.

Don't panic? After just telling me there is a deadly snake wrapped around my ankle? Is he mad? I will panic, in fact, how can I *not* panic? My throat feels dry and I can't seem to swallow. Oh, Jesus, how much more? All I want is a bath and a proper hotel room with loo paper and a suitcase of clothes if at all possible. I have so far managed to escape death from cholera and a lynching by a mob of rebels. But it seems I am destined for a bloody snakebite. Why do these things happen to me?

'Please, hurry up and stab it,' I plead.

'The knife is for you. If the snake bites, which for your information is the worst case scenario, I will need to open the wound to get the poison out quickly.'

Oh, what is he doing to me? What have I ever done to him? A vision of him cutting into my ankle makes me go quite woozy and I feel my body sway.

'Don't move, with a bit of luck it will slither away. It doesn't want to attack you so don't give it any cause. So far it has not reacted to you.'

What! Why is he hesitating? Surely he isn't going to wait until the bugger bites me. Oh Christ. I don't want to be sodding Lara Croft. I mean, seriously, do I look the slightest bit like Lara Croft? I'm fat for Christ's sake. Jesus, that means more meat for the snake to tuck into. Oh Toby, I wish you were here.

'Please, just shoot it or stab it or bloody strangle it before it bites me,' I say hoarsely.

'Shut up talking and keep still. I've got my eye on it.'

What the hell good is his eye? I close mine and feel tears run down my cheeks. Why is he always so horrible to me? I try to swallow and can't. My throat has closed up. My arms ache from clenching my hands. I open my eyes to see Bryant has moved closer to me and in front of him on the ground is a snake which is slowly slinking away. I feel myself wobble and his arms reach out to catch me as I fall.

'It's okay, it's gone,' he whispers softly into my ear.

I pull back sharply and stare angrily at him.

'You would have let it bite me. You are insane, bloody insane. What is wrong with you?' I shout. I'm sounding hysterical and, knowing Bryant, he won't think twice about slapping me across the face. Okay, maybe he isn't that bad but he was seriously going to let that snake bite me. God, my throat is so tight I feel I will choke.

'Do you really think that little of me? It was highly unlikely that it would have bitten you. If I had considered that at all a possibility do you really believe I would have just stood here and watched?' His eyes flash angrily.

I clench my jaw. I am so livid with him it is all I can do not to slap him.

'In a word, yes,' I spit, knowing it is a hateful thing to say but not being able to stop myself. I feel very alone right now.

'Toby would never have put me through that.'

'No, of course not,' he says, looking pained. 'I do know what I'm doing. If I had moved even half an inch, it would have bitten you. I've been around more snakes than you. However, I am always prepared whatever the eventuality. I know exactly what I am doing,' he finishes arrogantly, leaning down to pick up his rucksack.

'Oh purleese,' I scoff, 'you're not James Bond you know. Or do you spend your time electrocuting your enemies with nothing more than a damp towel and a table lamp? No, on reflection don't answer that. I really don't want to know.'

Do shut up Libby, you're making a fool of yourself. He smiles in that patronising way he has about him and for some reason I get that fluttering in my stomach. There are two very good reasons why I must not be attracted to Alex Bryant. The first being he is engaged to someone else, who it must be remembered has legs up to her armpits, tiny neat breasts and not a single blobby bit in sight, and that's not even mentioning her perfect lacquered hair and permanently shaved armpits. The second reason, of course, is that Toby has finally realised he is in love with me. I haven't even mentioned the fact that Bryant is an idiot. I must have been mad coming here with him, stark staring mad.

'We need to get to the other side of this lake,' he responds quietly.

It seems nothing I say or do can ruffle his feathers.

'That's another thing, I really don't believe we are at risk if we get a taxi and you could have let me bring more of my things. There is no way I am getting in that boat, if you can call it a boat. You really don't know what you're talking about. Why on earth would anyone be interested in us?'

He drops the rucksack angrily and his jaw tightens. I must admit he is terribly handsome when angry. Here I go again.

'I do know what I'm talking about. The rebels have valid points, and if I am not mistaken you are very aware of that yourself. The best part of Toby's article was your piece in it. You approve of the Arab Spring, and you said yourself that it is time for the Cambodians to have more freedom in the way their country is run.'

'Toby said that,' I break in.

He shakes his head.

'No he didn't. The rebels know we are high profile and we are good hostage material. We need to get out of the countryside and get to the town. The last taxi driver compromised us. We need to get on the boat now.'

His voice is clear and even and he doesn't take his eyes off me.

'They're not interested in us,' I say forcefully. 'You're just a writer...'

'I'm a journalist and a good one.'

Mr Modesty or what.

'That's a matter of opinion,' I snap nastily.

Good heavens, what has come over me? He sighs and wanders over to the owner of the boat who is bagging up his fish. I hear Alex negotiate a price for use of the boat. If you can call it a boat, it is more a raft with a paddle. Oh, this country is driving me mad. He marches back towards me.

'I got him down to five dollars, let's go,' he orders.

What a bully.

'Five dollars, well I think you have been ripped off, but it's your money,' I say mimicking his comments to me yesterday.

He seems to suppress a smile before pointing again at the boat.

'I'm not getting on that, it's not safe.'

He rolls his eyes and sighs.

'Not again,' he mumbles.

'What does that mean?' I snap.

'Are you going to get on the boat or do I have to drag you on?'
Ooh, I'd like to see him try.

'How dare you, if Toby heard you talking to me like this I
wouldn't like to say what he would do to you.'

'I wouldn't think very much,' he retorts, throwing the rucksack
over his shoulders.

He gives me a mean look and grabs me by the waist. Before I know
what is happening he has lifted me off the ground. It is seriously like
something out of *Gone with the Wind*. I am so shocked that I cannot
speak. He places me gently onto the wooden planks which
constitute the floor of the boat and proceeds to push it out. I am
shaking with anger. How dare he? A paddle is shoved roughly into
my hand.

'How dare you,' I stammer. 'When Toby finds out...'

'Start paddling, I need to push it out further and do stop
threatening me with Toby.'

I swish the so-called 'paddle' lazily through the water while giving
him a dirty look. He jumps aboard and takes the paddle from me.
Within seconds we are cutting through the water, and the cool air
washes over me. My hair is damp with perspiration and my sandals
are thick with dirt. My lips are cracking and my throat is dry. I have
never felt so wretched in my life and I have no means of escape. His
back is to me and I watch as he steers the boat expertly through the
water. I am beginning to believe he is capable of anything and am
finding it difficult not to admire him. He turns at that moment and
tosses a hat to me. I have no idea where it came from but I accept it
gratefully. The sun is hotter now and I lean back on the rickety bench
and attempt to relax and enjoy the views which are spectacularly
beautiful. The sky is a deep blue and the surrounding fields lush and
green. The rhythmic swishing of the paddle through the crystal-clear
water is crisp. I believe I could actually enjoy it here if I could just
relax. The gentle movement of the boat soothes me and I feel my
eyes growing heavy. I really must let Toby know I am okay, he will be
very worried. It occurs to me that it would be quite safe now to use
my phone. I snap my eyes open to see Alex has removed his top. I
drag my eyes from his taut muscular torso. It's hot enough without
the sight of him topless. I pull my phone from my dress pocket. He
doesn't utter a word and then I realise I have no signal. I huff and
begin cleaning my sandals with a tissue that I dip into the lake. I

can't deny the sight of him rather takes my breath away. He leans across me to soak his top in the water and the fragrant smell of him wafts over. I swear he smells faintly of baby talcum powder. You wouldn't think that very sexy but, God, it's turning me on. If I am to be totally truthful, I have fancied Alex Bryant right from the first time I saw him in Dirty Doug's. I imagine he is fanciable because he is unavailable in more ways than one, not mentioning that he would never give me a second look. I watch as he puts the wet top on and smiles at me.

'You've got dirt on your face,' he says softly and leans into the water again with a tissue.

I feel my heart pound like crazy as his hand comes into contact with my cheek. I bite my cracked lips as he dabs at my face and fight the urge to lean forward and kiss his very kissable mouth. What on earth is wrong with me? It must be the heat or something. Then he sits back and smiles cockily at me. He is so close that I swear I can feel his breath on my face. I'm certain he knows the effect he is having on me. I blush furiously and grab the side of the boat for all I am worth. I grab it a bit too firmly and it dips lower into the water.

'Oh God,' I cry, rather weakly.

He laughs and easily manoeuvres it back. I lift my face to his and see he is looking closely at me.

'I can't spend my whole time rescuing you, you know.'

Why not, I almost swoon, but of course I don't. Instead I retort quite haughtily.

'I'm quite capable as it happens.'

'I've noticed,' he laughs, revealing his perfect white teeth.

I lower my hand into the water and stroke the passing lotus flowers. I clasp one in my hand and fix it precariously into my hair.

'Very fetching,' he comments.

'I didn't mean it when I said your being a good journalist was a matter of opinion,' I say, averting my face.

'Ah, so you don't think I'm so bad after all.' His face lights up. 'But you're considering going home?'

He looks at me earnestly. I wish he would stop looking at me in that way. In fact, I wish he would just move his body back by a few inches. I can barely breathe, let alone think of an answer. What is he doing? He's engaged to be married isn't he? What if he is just frustrated? A man like him, well, you know what I mean? He must be full of testosterone and longing.

'I don't really know what I'm thinking.'

Well, isn't that the truth. At that moment his phone rings. We finally have signal. He continues looking at me for a few seconds before turning to answer it. I grab the boat with shaking hands and take deep breaths. Blimey, I don't remember ever feeling like this whenever Toby came close. Obviously I must have done. I just can't quite recall the moment. I'm sure it will come flooding back to me when I can think properly. From the conversation, I gauge the call is from Jamie and listen intently, although a one-sided conversation barely makes much sense. He is quite right though, I am seriously thinking of going home. I don't want to be considered a good hostage or a great negotiating tool thank you very much. I have no ambitions to be a heroine, although I can't deny, now I am over the shock of almost being bitten by a snake, the whole trip is rather exciting. It's probably the most exciting thing that has ever happened to me. How sad is that? I expect this is rather tame for Alex Bryant, who has rescued hostages as an SAS officer and fought off more than a cobra in the Middle East. Okay, so I did read his first book. I suppose it is fairly impressive if you get impressed by men who can survive in the jungle for ten days without food and water and that kind of stuff. I can't say I have read anything of the new book though. But I am aware that he is quite a hero, and if I can't feel safe with him then I won't feel safe with anyone. All I've got to do is get through the book convention, do the TV interview and we can go home. The likelihood of anyone even considering kidnapping me is so slight that it is laughable. I'm here for two weeks. Long enough for Toby to really miss me and decide that he loves me more than he ever imagined he could. On reflection, I should stay and make the most of things. After all, I shall probably never travel like this again. Toby and I will marry and before I know where I am my life will never be the same again. It will be a whirlwind of babies, breast milk, mastitis, and stretch marks. Not an appealing thought. Whatever will I do if Toby does fly out here? How awkward that will be.

'Yes, I'll tell her, of course. Thanks Jamie.'

I look at Alex expectantly. He continues paddling confidently and wipes his forehead with the back of his hand in that 'Indiana Jones' way he has and says in a voice full of authority.

'I need to know if you are staying or if you seriously intend to fly home. Personally, I would like you to stay but obviously it is up to you. If you are planning to stay then we need to go over a few safety techniques, proof of life and so on, as I won't always be with you. Just for precaution you understand. Jamie, however, said to tell you that he fully understands if you want to return home. I will arrange a flight if that is what you want.'

Is it what I want? I try to picture my future if I do marry Toby. I'll eventually be surrounded by bellowing children. Toby once said he wanted four. I'll have to give up work, which means we'll have to buy a fairly cheap house in the worst part of Fross. The children will spend their days charging around the house, and it will be a full-scale military operation just to go to the shops. I will be the haggard wife while Toby is the about-town journalist. I'll be so knackered that I'll hit the sack by eight. As for sex, well, come to think about it I don't suppose it could be any worse than it is now. The highlight of my life will be a Chinese takeaway on a Saturday night. After this vision of my future, I decide to stay. This may be the only excitement I ever get in my life.

So Alex teaches me the safety codes as we drift aimlessly along in the cool water with the sun beating down on us. What a lot of bollocks the codes are. It's a bit like an in-flight safety video. Everyone watches it but let's face it, who remembers it when the plane is about to crash? I have to remember that the code for '*I have a problem*' is '*It's raining cats and dogs*'. I'm really going to remember that aren't I? If Alex should ask me '*Are we friends?*' what he really means is '*Am I in danger?*' Clear as day isn't it? I have to remember to answer *yes* if I am okay and *no* if I am not. That to me is as back to front as anything could be. I didn't dare argue though. He was really quite intense when teaching me and I have to say he looks very appealing when intense. The most important one is '*Are you hurt?*' Which in code is '*Can I get you something?*' If I am perfectly fine I have to request *tampons*. If I am in dire straits I have to request *toothpaste*. You really have to wonder how he came up with this crap. I'll know he is coming to help me when he tells me he will *pick up a takeaway on the way home*. After an hour he considers I know the codes well enough and refuses to let me write them down.

'You have to memorise them,' he insists firmly.

As if I am ever going to have a need for them. He was so animated teaching me the codes that he has relaxed his grip on the paddle and is allowing the boat to drift happily in the current. The views are fantastic and I am finally relaxing. My headache has eased and all I need is a drink for everything to be perfect. Jamie has protested quite strongly, and I don't blame him, that he gave me the correct address for the hotel and has no idea why the driver took us to the village. I attempt to look surprised. I really must own up soon but there never seems to be a right time. Either Bryant is too nice and I don't want to spoil it, or he is being really horrid and I don't want to make things worse. It is becoming tricky, very tricky.

The only thing on my mind right now is my thirst and I voice my desire unwittingly. Without a word he steers the boat to the bank and climbs out. I watch mesmerised as he cuts a coconut from a tree followed by several bananas. Smiling, he throws them at me before climbing back into the boat.

'By your face I'm presuming not something Toby would do then?'

'He'd hope to buy a bottle of Perrier from a nearby stall,' I say, trying not to smile, while feeling quite bad for mocking Toby.

He grins and points the penknife at the coconut.

'For my next trick...' he continues, raising his eyebrows at me.

Good Lord, he actually does have a sense of humour.

'You will slice through the coconut with your penknife?'

He opens the rucksack with a flourish.

'That is not a knife.' He mimics an Australian accent. 'This... is a knife.' And with a flick of his wrist produces a large knife and slashes into the coconut, which he then hands me to drink. I stare at it fussily and after seeing him raise his eyebrows, I lift the rough hairy shell to my lips and drink. The milk is cool and refreshing.

'What would Penelope do then?' I ask hesitantly.

He peels a banana and hands one to me.

'She wouldn't climb from a boat and cut down a coconut if that's what you mean and I would have to fashion a cup out of something. She would never drink straight from the coconut, there might be germs.'

I wrinkle my nose at the coconut shell.

'You're doing well, don't spoil it,' he reprimands.

'I don't need your compliments,' I snap.

Obviously I can't help wondering why someone like him, with such an adventurous spirit, should be engaged to someone as prim and proper as Penelope. They are as different as chalk and cheese. At least they seem it, but of course, I could be wrong. He points to the view. An occasional palm tree gives some relief from the burning sun but not enough. So, when he pulls suntan lotion from what is becoming his very own Mary Poppins rucksack, I sigh with relief. I don't remember ever being anywhere this hot before and I don't have a change of clothing. I let my hand drop into the cool water. It's rather nice being with someone who takes control. I gently rub the lotion onto my arms. It will be so lovely to get to the hotel to have a shower and don some fresh clothes.

'I've arranged for our luggage to be taken to the hotel. It is probably there already,' he says, seemingly reading my mind.

His voice is crisp and clear. I can see why mother likes him. He has all the essential boyfriend qualities according to my mother.

'We just want you to be with someone suitable darling. Toby is nice enough but a little rough-spoken don't you think?' she had commented dryly on meeting Toby. *'Do you not think a military man is more suitable with your education and what not?'*

I mean, seriously, who wants a military man for a husband? It's bad enough having an ex-military man for a father without one for a husband too. As for school, a fat lot of good that did me. The only thing I excelled in was knots. I seriously did. I can tie a good reef knot blindfolded and my half hitch is something to be envied. I was a top Girl Guide and still know the alphabet in semaphore. Apart from that I am plain useless. Be prepared may have been the Girl Guide's motto but being prepared was something I left behind with Brown Owl. I jump as Alex leans towards me and gently takes the suntan lotion. Before I can protest, he has turned me around and is gently smoothing the cream over my back. His hands are cool and I feel myself shiver under his touch. To think Blancmange gets this all the time. Good God, what is happening down in my loins? This is terrible. He is only stroking the top of my back, but oh, the way he is stroking, it is far too sensual for my liking. I must pull myself together. He is just applying suntan lotion. I must not make a fool of myself. What would Blancmange think if she could see her fiancé now?

'Why don't you wear a ring?' he asks in a matter of fact voice.

'What?' My voice sounds all strangled and hoarse.

'Why don't you wear an engagement ring? At the Christmas party you told me you and Toby were engaged.' His deep blue eyes bore into mine.

Now what do I say? I suppose I had better tell the truth and let him see that I can't keep a man for love nor money. I don't have to admit that we never were engaged now do I? And I surely don't have to admit to the horrifying fact that I can't keep a man because I'm fat?

'We sort of ended the engagement,' I say hesitantly. That sounds like I've been dumped.

'That is, I ended it,' I choose not to mention Serena. I'm sure he can put two and two together, after all he saw them kissing at the party.

'But you're still going out with him?'

I simply shrug. He stretches lazily and points at a group of monkeys in a passing tree.

'I love this country,' he says almost wistfully. 'It's mostly like this, calm and peaceful. Damn governments spoil everything.'

He points at some more monkeys further along the bank.

'Isn't that Toby over there?' he asks.

'I mixed up the addresses,' I say quickly, ignoring his comment.

'Mother gave me the address of the village. She saw it on television.'

He laughs.

'And you have a go at me for protecting you, when it was you who put us in danger. You realise I will have to kill you now,' he laughs.

'Aren't you angry?' I say surprised.

He shakes his head and halves a banana, throwing one at me.

'I promise to feed you something better this evening. I'll take you to this really great place. The food is cheap, freshly cooked and it's all outside in the cool evening air.'

This is getting better and better. I am seriously hoping Toby has decided not to fly out after all. Although I really mustn't get any silly ideas about a romance with Alex Bryant, because let's face it, the majority of the time he is a bit of a knob head. Not to mention the fact that he is engaged to a leggy blonde who makes me look like Hatti Jacques. I don't even know much about the guy except that he was an SAS officer and retired three years ago, aged thirty. He came home after rescuing three hostages from an underground rebel cell in Afghanistan and claimed he is now too old for all that malarkey. He then became a journalist in the States and apparently did some undercover work here in Cambodia. Of course, in that time he managed to annihilate several pieces of Toby's work, believing that only he can write accurately, which if I am totally honest, he can. Right now he has forgotten all about Toby and our engagement and seems preoccupied with the side of the boat. My phone shrills and Toby's photo lights up on the screen.

'Has your phone been off? For Christ's sake Libby how can I contact you if you turn it off? Is everything okay now?'

'Signal is bad,' I lie.

'I couldn't get a flight. The weather is bloody diabolical here. Have you seen it on the web? There is fucking snow everywhere. I tell you, it's freezing. I'll go to the airport in the morning. You're well out of it.'

'I haven't had time to go on the web and check the weather,' I say irritably, flapping my hand at a fly.

I hear Alex groan.

'We have a slight technical problem,' he mumbles.

Great timing or what? Why do all the problems happen when Toby is on the other end of my Blackberry?

'No, no of course you haven't had time. Sorry, I wasn't thinking. Jamie said you've got out of that hell hole then. Thank God. I suppose that prick is still with you.'

'I need your bra,' says Alex.

Oh, for Christ's sake.

'What the fuck!' bellows Toby.

'We're sinking and the water is deep here. I need to bale the water out. There is nothing else we can use. It's pretty urgent Libby, can you call him back?'

'Toby, I'll need to call you back...'

'Does he do it on purpose? I swear when I get there...'

I end the call and look around. If anyone had told me that my Wonderbra would be in such demand I would have bought a box load. I find myself thinking of the most sensual way I can remove what is becoming the greatest weapon of our time. I wonder if they will consider using it in the army after all this. Oh yes, most certainly not. I fumble to undo it and manage to slide it down my left arm. Alex grabs it urgently and makes some comment about it still being warm. He then proceeds to scoop the water out of the boat using the cups. I was so engrossed in taking my bra off, that it only now registers that he said the boat was sinking.

I look to the vast expanse of water ahead of us and then to the vast expanse of water behind us and finally at the vast expanse of water that is filling up in the boat. How can there not be another person anywhere in sight?

'But, we're in the middle of a lake and it's really deep,' I say, stating the bloody obvious.

'I'm well aware of that,' he snaps. 'Can you stop stating the obvious and paddle for us? I'm presuming you can swim, should we need to?'

Well, Mr Nice didn't last long. I try to conjure up the music from *Hawaii Five-O* to make us go faster, but that doesn't seem to work.

'Of course I can swim,' I say, insulted.

'Keep your weight central. I don't want to unbalance the boat.'

What a cheek! How dare he? What a horrid thing to say.

'How dare you say I'm fat,' I cry, feeling the threat of tears prick my eyelids.

'I didn't say anything of the kind,' he retorts looking genuinely surprised.

'Keep your weight central, I don't want to unbalance the boat,' I mimic.

As if on cue, my Blackberry shrills. Oh do sod off Toby. Alex gives my phone a filthy look.

'Exactly, at what point, did I say you were fat?'

My Wonderbra is now soaking wet and I could sob. How can I enter a hotel, and a nice one at that, looking like I do? I must look a sight and he obviously thinks so too.

'You know exactly what you said,' I say in a hurt voice. 'You're a rude person.'

'Yes, so you keep saying,' he snaps, and furiously leans over to my phone and clicks the off button. I am about to speak when he gently pushes me onto the seat.

'Sit there and paddle towards the bank. Unless you want to end up in the water stop moaning and do something practical.'

I can't imagine what Toby is thinking and I can't imagine what I was thinking earlier either. I really am so stupid to think Alex-*we-have-a-technical-problem*-Bryant, actually likes me. He is no better than Toby and thinks me fat and stupid. Toby, no doubt, thinks something must be going on. Well, I shall assure him nothing could ever go on with such a rude, arrogant arse. Concentrate on paddling Libby, otherwise you'll only get shouted at again. The boat feels so heavy I can barely pull the paddle through the water, either that or I am getting weak. The water is now rising over my ankles.

'You're doing great,' shouts Alex. 'Not far to go. Your bra is doing a great job too. The cups hold loads of water.'
Now what is he trying to say?

'What does that mean?' I demand, feeling my blood boil.

'I'm just stating a fact. The cups are big and hold plenty of water. Look, I don't have time to deal with your issues of sensitivity.'
He is so loathsome. Finally, we hit the bank and after throwing out the rucksack he climbs into the water and offers to help me out. Reluctantly I take his hand and jump from the boat. I slip on the muddy bank and reach out to him. I feel his arms go round my waist and I cling onto him. His face is close to mine and I feel the beating of his heart. His arms are strong and strangely comforting.

'Are you okay?' he asks. I swear his voice is husky. Surely I am not imagining all this. I'm certainly not imagining that hand on my buttock. Good heavens. I slowly extradite myself and dust the front of my dress. I must look like I have been dragged through a bush backwards. He pulls the boat ashore.

'We don't want to lose our deposit,' he laughs.
A water buffalo surveys us from further along the shore. As if nothing has occurred between us Alex plonks the hat onto my head and walks towards the beast. I hobble behind him. I look down to see one of my flip-flops has well and truly flopped. Isn't that just my luck? I couldn't have been on the beach in Eastbourne, or just walking along Brighton pier. I had to be in the middle of nowhere, in the depths of the Cambodian countryside. Aside from being buried alive I can't think of anything worse. I'm bra-less, shoe-less and the way Alex is staring at me you would think I was brainless. He waves to a man in a nearby rice field. Alex beckons to me and I hobble forward.

'This very fine gentleman with the help of his buffalo is going to give us a ride on his cart to the next village and from there his brother will take us to Siem Reap.'
I bow in gratitude to the rice farmer, who reciprocates and offers me a banana. I accept it gratefully even though I am feeling just a bit overdosed on bananas. Oh well, I guess I won't get fat on bananas and coconut. They both help me into the cart and Alex then sits up front with the rice farmer. I feel quite upset to think that Alex Bryant thinks I am fat. Well, I will show him.

Chapter Sixteen

The hotel is absolute luxury compared to the little bed and breakfast house we had escaped from. It even has a swimming pool and a tea room with a butterfly garden. I am desperately hoping my luggage will be in my room. The reception staff gawp at us and I can't blame them. We must look a dreadful sight. Even with our quick clean up, courtesy of the lake, we still don't look like typical tourists.

'You have booking?' the clerk asks us, doubtfully.

After studying our passports and booking details he hands keys over to Alex. I find myself fascinated by the hustle and bustle outside. I decide to go into the city first and then visit the butterfly garden afterwards. I voice my plans to Alex as we mount the stairs to our rooms. He immediately looks worried.

'I think you should trust my judgement on this. It is safer if we travel together. I'll take you around Siem Reap later when we go for dinner.'

'I can assure you I will be fine,' I argue. 'Besides I have my Blackberry and...'

I realise he has stopped walking. I follow his gaze to see Penelope bounding towards us. Good Lord, what is she doing here?

'Baby, oh honey are you okay? I've been missing you so much,' she screams and leaps into his arms.

'Jamie texted me and said you had some trouble with the rebels.'

It is the first time I have seen him shell-shocked. I have to admit to being a touch shell-shocked myself. In fact, I'm not quite sure how I feel, aside from murderous. Why is she here? More importantly why is she not in Beijing?

He gently pushes her away and I try to ignore the scathing look she is giving me.

'Hello, Lily, how are you?' she says with a smile that doesn't quite reach her eyes. She turns back to Alex before I have time to answer. Clearly she is not interested in how I am at all.

'What are you doing here Pen?' he asks and I pick up a suspicious tone in his voice.

'It's Libby, actually.'

She spins round to look at me.

'What?' she snaps.

'My name is Libby, not Lily,' I repeat.

She blinks and then dismisses me with her hand before turning back to Alex.

'Come on honey, don't be cross. Aren't you pleased to see me? I thought as I was in Beijing, and it was so close, I would join you instead of flying straight home. I've booked us into a fab restaurant in Siem Reap that is owned by Americans. They are going to cook you a good steak. I'm not sure what I will eat in this place but never mind.'

I cannot deny she looks terrific. Even after a flight she still manages to look fantastic. I look down at my dirty broken flip-flop and feel myself hating Alex Bryant all over again. He could at least have allowed me to change before we fled. I would have perhaps looked half decent when seeing Lady Penelope instead of looking like I have just climbed out of a bush, which I guess I have. To make matters worse the button on my dress has popped and my tits are almost hanging out. I swear I look like Nell Gwynne. All I need are a couple of oranges and I'll be all set for a fancy-dress party.

'Well, if you'll excuse me, I really need a shower.' I hold my hand out for my room key. Alex hesitates and turns to Penelope.

'We were actually going to the outdoor restaurant tonight. Libby and I need to talk over the book conference.'

Blimey, that was a bit blunt. Penelope stabs me a look and then smiles warmly at Alex.

'Well, obviously, if you've made plans... I'm sure there will be something there I can eat.'

Penelope is livid and her mouth has turned all tight and her eyes are blazing. Alex seems either not to be noticing or if he has then is untouched by it.

'It's fine. Why don't we discuss the conference over coffee once I've showered? I'm a bit wacked anyway to be honest, I'll probably order room service or something,' I lie.

The last thing I want to do is have dinner with Blancmange. He looks at me gratefully.

'I'll give you a knock in a couple of hours. Have a rest until then.' He smiles but I can see the anger in his eyes and wonder is he angry at me or Penelope. I take the key and walk down the corridor to my room.

To my relief my luggage is there. Oh, what luxury compared to last night. There's a proper loo, toilet paper and a real shower. All the same I can't help wishing we were back in the country where all was peaceful and quiet. Well, apart from when we were attacked, it was quiet and peaceful. It all felt so intimate there. I look out of the window. The place is vibrant. People are shouting and the road below me is a mass of tuk-tuks, motorbikes and people carrying all kinds of wares on their back. Maybe I will pop out later. As long as I keep away from the posh restaurants I am not likely to see Alex and Penelope. I do hope she isn't going to come along to the conferences. I will go mental if she does. Isn't this just so my luck? I check the time on my Blackberry. It's ten in the morning in England. I phone Issy. From the background noise it is clear she is at her sister's.

'Libs, you've got everyone up in arms here, hold on. Barnaby go and play with your sister, like a good boy, if that is at all possible.'
I catch her tell someone she needs to take a call and then hear the clip clop of her heels.

'Shit it's freezing. I bet it is bloody hot where you are. Remind me never to have kids. Rachel is oozing breast milk and cries at the drop of a hat. I presented her with a sodding Ricky Gervais DVD for her birthday and she had a mini breakdown. Hugging and kissing me. It was dead embarrassing. Honestly, bloody hormones. And that bloody Bradley still shits his pants even though there are potties all over the house. I hate sodding families at Christmas time.'

'Penelope just arrived,' I say and burst into tears.
Why am I so upset? This is ridiculous. Alex Bryant is just a big knob who drives me mad isn't he? The truth is in the past few hours he has made me feel more cared for than I have felt in a long time. I felt interesting and worthwhile, even if he did make insensitive comments about my weight. I know that he didn't mean them in the way I took them. He isn't Toby, and if he had something to say about my weight he would have come straight out with it. He thinks I am intelligent and capable, and I was actually looking forward to our

dinner. Now it is all ruined and I feel awful for hating Penelope. After all, she is his fiancée.

'Christ almighty,' groans Issy. 'Why is *she* there? Why are you getting so upset? Did Toby phone and say something to upset you? Honestly him and his big mouth.'

I hiccup and blow my nose.

'It's just Alex is so... I don't know. I thought we were having dinner but she wants to go to the steak place and he didn't, and now we're just having coffee and I feel so fed up. Plus I can't remember the codes and everything is going wrong and my flip-flop is broken...' I take a deep breath.

'I thought she was a vegan...'

'And he used my bra, not once but several times,' I hiccup.

'Bloody hell,' is her response. 'I heard from the ever obnoxious Toby that you hit a spot of bother and that Alex was being a bit of an arsehole, but...'

'No, he isn't, honestly, he has been really nice in a funny way.'

'What a dream hunk. Hate to say I told you so. Are you okay though, seriously? There is no real danger of you being kidnapped and all that crap is there?'

I hear the concern in her voice and panic in case she tells mother. It will be the final straw if mother starts calling me with all her great advice.

'No, of course not and really I am fine. I'm just tired. It's been a hectic day. A nice long shower, room service and an early night and I'll be my old self in no time.'

It takes me some time to convince her that I am fine and after promising to call her the next day, I hang up and turn my phone off. I know I really should leave it on, in case Toby should phone. I really don't feel emotionally capable of dealing with him right now. He only needs to be a bit sharp and I will burst into tears. He will blame Alex and I will argue with him and it will just get worse and worse. I am beginning to learn that the way to Toby's heart is not through his stomach, or sex, or even being slim come to that. The way to his heart is to make him jealous. I seem to have done that and it doesn't feel good. I would much prefer Toby loved me for who I am and not because he feels slighted by someone else and now needs to prove his manliness. It occurs to me that I really should check on my parents and phone my mother in Kilimanjaro, hoping she isn't half way up it. It really doesn't bear thinking about. She answers her phone immediately.

'Darling, I was going to phone you later. What a disaster, a total disaster we're just airlifting daddy to hospital.'

I can feel myself getting all hot, as If I'm not hot enough already, and my heart is beating rapidly. Images of my father swathed in bandages and with an oxygen mask over his face assault me.

'Is he going to be all right? What happened?' I feel all faint.

'We were only a short way up, oh it is so exhilarating darling, far better than sex…'

'Mother,' I yell.

'Oh sorry, I am quite flushed with it all. The instructor was marvellous, quite your type. Speaking of types how is the gorgeous Alex Bryant? Did anything happen on the plane?'

Oh, yes, mother, lots of things but nothing like the things that are going through your head.

'Is daddy going to live?' I ask, hearing the panic in my voice.

'Of course, darling, it's only gout, but what a time to have an attack. We were right in the thick of it all too. I must say your father has really thrown himself into this. It's had an amazing impact on him. He is like a young man. He has become like that Bryant chap, all hormones and action. Trouble is all the action has gone to his foot.'

I don't know how I cope, I really don't. I am just grateful they are not on the nudist holiday. That would have been too much to bear. Just the thought of my naked father being airlifted anywhere is enough to make me shudder. I'm already emotionally bruised, I can't take any more battering.

'I hope you're staying out of the sun Libby and you are shaving aren't you? There is nothing worse than being caught out unshaved.'

Oh God.

'Email us. We bought one of those Blueberries, just like yours, and daddy has worked out how to get emails on it. He is becoming a real little whiz-kid. It's so exciting and as soon as we get to an Internet café I can answer them.'

Is there any point in explaining?

'Blackberry, I think you mean,'

'Well, whatever, it is marvellous.'

My phone pings several times. It is Toby trying to get through. I say goodbye to mother and turn it off. I just can't bear to speak to him. I have a shower and fumble through my suitcase for something suitable. Of course, everything makes me look dumpy. I try on three tops, a dress, and finally chuck a loose and very thin smock top over a pair of cropped leggings. I attempt to be cool and poised and am about to twist my hair into a bun when there is a knock on my door. Surely it isn't that time already. I check my face in the mirror and see it is flushed from crying. Why can't I be the epitome of sophistication and chic like Penelope? With my heart thumping I open the door. A gorgeous fresh-faced Alex stands there and I visibly swoon. My God, how does he manage to look so irresistible? I feel my breath catch in my throat and think it wouldn't be such a terrible thing if I couldn't breathe, at least Alex can perform CPR. Just the thought makes me go all hot. He can pound my chest anytime.

'You look nice,' he says politely.

'Thanks.'

'You look pretty fantastic yourself,' I want to say but obviously I don't. He has a fiancée for goodness sake. I check she is not standing behind him.

'Can I come in?' he asks, his eyes widening.

What am I doing? He must think me so stupid.

'Yes, of course. I'm sorry.'

I find I am touching myself everywhere. What is wrong with me? I can't keep still. I feel so damn self-conscious around him and fatter than I have ever felt. He is holding a thick folder and I pull a face. Surely we haven't got to go through that?

'Penny was a bit of a surprise. I wasn't expecting her,' he says apologetically.

I push a bracelet over my wrist and shake my head dismissively, attempting to look nonchalant. I shake it too much and my earring flies out of my ear. He picks it up and smiles at me.

'All we need is for Toby to come too,' he grins and looks relieved that I am not too upset.

'Yes, party poopers.'

Did I really say that? He points tactfully to the door.

'Shall we head downstairs for coffee?'

Well, we could head for the bedroom, I think shamelessly. Honestly, I really think the heat has affected me. In fact, I think it has affected me more seriously than I had at first thought. I actually find that once we are in the coffee shop I am not in the least tempted by the cake on offer. That's a first. Alex orders drinks and leaps into discussion about the book conference that is in two days' time. I feel

I should remind him that I am somewhat jet-lagged, but before I can say anything he is handing me a detailed list of ideas for articles, and asks if I can manage to cover some of them. I freeze the coffee cup halfway to my lips.

'Me? I can't cover any of those stories,' I say, astonished he should even ask.

He looks tiredly at me.

'There is a lot there you could cover. You can talk to several of the villagers here about life under this regime. You can get a feel for who supports the rebels and who doesn't. You can put your own views across. You have strong opinions.'

What a nerve. How dare he tell me what I do or don't have?

'I don't, actually. I am not in the least interested in the politics of the country.'

'I think you are,' he argues, casually spooning sugar into his coffee. 'I think you are well aware that the government is the problem here.'

'It was the rebels who came after us.'

Why am I arguing with him? It is obvious he will win, he always does, damn him.

'But under whose orders? You know how to write a balanced article, which is more than your boyfriend does.'

Why does he have to keep doing this? Just as I was beginning to like him he criticises Toby all over again.

'Why are you always so negative about Toby's writing?' I snap, trying not to bang my cup down.

'Probably because it is near impossible to be positive about it,' he snaps back.

Right that's it. I really can't be party to this annihilation of Toby's work. I stand up angrily and grab my shawl from the back of the chair.

'Enjoy your dinner this evening. I shall see you in the morning when hopefully you will be in a less critical and damning mood,' I say and march from the coffee shop and back to my room, except I get all the way to my room before I remember I need the key. Sod it. I begin the walk back downstairs and come face to face with him. He is holding my key and smiling. I do not smile back. He is so damn arrogant if he thinks I am over it already.

'You certainly are hot headed,' he says, making it sound like a compliment.

I take the key and turn from him.

'You're more than welcome to join us for dinner this evening. Won't you change your mind?'

Oh, I'm sure Penelope would be thrilled if I did.

'Thank you, but I would much prefer to get room service.'

Like hell I would. He looks concerned for a minute and cocks his head slightly.

'You're not thinking of getting out are you?'

He makes it sound like a prison break out. I simply shrug.

'If you do, and I am not for one minute suggesting that you should, remember the people here will always try to please. They may say they know where you want to go but more often than not they don't.'

'I'm quite happy to have room service,' I repeat.

He shrugs, flashes that wide arrogant grin of his and wanders back down the corridor to his own room. Well, honestly. He could have attempted to change my mind. Now, what the hell am I going to do about dinner? I miserably enter my room and sit by the window staring at my Blackberry, trying to get up the courage to turn it on. In the street below things are getting busy and several tuk-tuk drivers look up at me and wave. The temptation to go into the town and have a look around is overwhelming me. I get a burst of courage and decide I will. I turn on my Blackberry and feel a bit deflated to see Toby has not left a message. He has tried to call but no text or voicemail. God, I hope that doesn't mean he is on a flight. That's all I need. I decide it is time to take the bull by the horns, or in this case, the tuk-tuk. I make an effort to walk confidently from the hotel lobby, making sure my shawl is covering my shoulders, and am mobbed by a group of tuk-tuk drivers. If only it were this easy to get a taxi back home.

'Lady, where you want to go,' asks one, winking at me.

'I take you to temples, good price,' calls another.

'You want to go to Pub Street for nice dinner?' asks the first driver.

Heavens, is he asking me out? I know he isn't, of course and accept his offer of a ride.

'I want to go to Angkor market,' I say climbing up into the tuk-tuk.

The tuk-tuk is an amazing way to travel. Although how the thing can stay upright is beyond me.

'You want hotel?' he asks turning around to look at me.

Didn't I just say the market? Why do I feel I can't go anywhere without Alex Bryant?

'No, I want to go to the market please.'

His face lights up.

'Ah, Hotel Market. That two dollar. You tell me where is Hotel Market?'

Oh dear.

'I'll go to Pub Street,' I say resignedly. Hopefully there will be somewhere to eat there.

It is very humid and I am grateful for the cool breeze that the speed of the tuk-tuk brings. On several occasions I feel sure he is going to collide with other tuk-tuks and cling onto my seat for dear life. I never imagined I would be travelling through a city on a motorised rickshaw. I have to say it is very exciting. We pass a river, a small monastery and several people carting heavy goods on their backs. As we get closer to the city I feel a tremor of excitement. As we enter the busy centre I spy craft shops and several open markets. I see the lovely jewellery and beautiful shawls. I remind myself I must look for something for mother and Issy before going home. Siem Reap is a mass of colour and smells and I feel energised by the vibrancy of the place. I have no idea what 'Pub Street' is, or where it is, but I am deposited in a street full of restaurants, people and music. I feel exhilarated. The colours and smells are evocative. I wander along looking at menus and fighting off tuk-tuk drivers. I find myself glancing sheepishly inside the restaurants to see if Alex is there with Penny but I realise it is probably quite early for them. I push my way past begging children and stroll down a quiet lane where shawls and purses are being sold. I study them for a while and then tire of fighting off the endless demands from an assistant to buy her goods. I enter a small eating establishment and order myself a coffee and a slice of banana cake. I feel quite liberated. A young girl tries to sell me some postcards. I am sorely tempted but refuse after vaguely remembering something Alex had written in a piece for the *New York Times* about street beggars in Asia. Okay, I admit to reading some of his stuff. I am just relaxing over my coffee when my phone rings. It is Toby. I reluctantly answer. I might as well get it over and done with.

'Have you gone out of your mind?' he bellows. 'Your phone has been off for hours. You can't expect me to phone you all the hours God sends.'

'I didn't ask you to phone me at all,' I respond huffily.

I wonder if Penelope is snogging the life out of Alex.

'Libby, don't you love me any more?'

Oh God, now there's a million dollar question.

'Where is Serena?' I say feeling the pain again, as I picture them at the Christmas party.

'I only want you, Libs,' he says in a soppy voice.

He does? Oh, well that's okay then. Honestly, just what kind of a pushover does he think I am?

'I can fly out if you want me to. I can probably get some time off.'

What? Didn't he tell me he was going to the airport? What does he mean he can get some time off?

'I thought you *were* going to the airport this morning.'

There is silence.

'Toby?'

'On the web it advises not to go to Cambodia unless it is absolutely necessary. Obviously, I'll come if you want me to.'

Oh, obviously.

'No, it is fine, Toby. I'll text you tomorrow.'

I hang up and push my sunglasses on so no one can see I am crying and quickly pay. What a bastard. He had no intention of coming at all. Why did I ever believe he would? He's not missing me at all. He just hates the thought of me being with someone else. I am such a fool when it comes to men. I walk angrily down a small deserted alley wondering where the tuk-tuk drivers are now that I want one. I realise I am the only one walking through the narrow pathway and feel a slight panic. Why did I come through here? I walk a bit quicker when I see the opening into the busy streets and lots of tuk-tuks. Oh, thank goodness. I am almost there when a man jumps out of an entrance. I let out a small shriek and wave my arms at him. He smiles at me and walks past. What is wrong with me? It's that bloody Alex-*we-have-a-situation*-Bryant who has put the wind up me, telling me we have been compromised and all that rubbish about being 'good negotiation material' or whatever he called it. I can see a tuk-tuk driver now and decide it may be better to go back and order room service. I feel lonely and tearful. I am almost at the entrance when a lady pops her head out of a side window and calls me.

'Lady, there is a phone call for you.'

A phone call for me, that can't be right.

'No, it can't be for me...' I begin stupidly, but before I have time to think, she has gone, and someone is grabbing me from behind and throwing something over my head. Oh, Jesus, famous last words or what. I am being sodding kidnapped and I am buggered if I can remember any of the codes.

Chapter Seventeen

'Help, help,' I scream but it comes out all muffled and strange. My heart is hammering like mad.

Whoever has grabbed me is being very gentle. I try to calm down. I try to think of what Alex would do. I guess he would slice out their tongues with a penknife. I don't care what he would do I just wish he was here instead of snogging Lady Penelope. Of all the times to get kidnapped, I do it when Alex Bryant is snogging the life out of his fiancée.

'I really am no good to you,' I cry. 'No one will pay the ransom. No one cares enough,' I say feeling very sorry for myself.

'You stay quiet and we not hurt you,' responds a deep voice in broken English.

Okay, whatever you do, don't think about kidnapped journalists. Of course, that makes me think of John McCarthy and Brian Keenan. No, don't think about them. In fact, don't think at all. Oh Lord, I am far too young to be beheaded. I remind myself the Cambodians are Buddhists and beheading is surely against their religion or must at least be bad karma or something. I am gently but firmly pushed into a car, and I wonder if the tuk-tuk drivers saw anything. I hope Alex thinks to ask them. I also hope my parents have enough money to pay the ransom. God, what if they want a million dollars or something? I wonder if Jamie has insurance for this kind of thing. What am I thinking? Alex is his biggest client and I don't imagine he foresaw this. Oh this is so not good. I have a hideous journey in the car with lots of bumps and my nose pressed against a horribly smelly seat. I hear two of them talking in Khmer and wonder how many more of them there are. It is all very frightening and I am trying hard not to cry. What if I never get home? At least I will lose plenty of weight. I am thinking the oddest of things. I must stay positive. Alex will rescue me by using my Wonderbra to break me out and capture the kidnappers in one movement. What on earth am I thinking? This can't be real. I am probably dreaming and will wake up in a minute and find myself back at the hotel room. How wrong can I be? The car stops with a shudder and I am bundled out. I take deep breaths and tell myself all will be well. It will be all over the news and I'll probably be released and back to the hotel in time for breakfast. Trust me to think of food at a time like this. The thing over my head is removed and I blink and see two men standing in front of me. I must say they look fairly harmless. I don't see any guns. I'm in what looks like a barn. It is so hot and perspiration drips down my neck where it runs from my hair. A mobile phone is thrust into my hand.

'Call Mr Alex and you tell him you need him come get you, tell him you lost.'

The man speaking is trying to sound mean but he looks as soft as a teddy bear. He bangs his hand on a table like the bad cop in a low-budget film. They obviously don't know Alex Bryant if they think he will just pop out and find me because I have got myself lost. With shaking hands I call him.

'Alex Bryant.' He answers on the first ring.

I have never been more grateful to hear his voice.

'It's me,' I say in an unnatural high-pitched voice.

I can hear music in the background and the sound of people shouting. He must be out with Penelope. Oh dear, she will not be pleased to be disturbed.

'Libby is that you? Hi, where are you? Are you coming to join us?' he asks cheerfully.

If only I could say yes that I would love to join them.

'I'm lost,' I say flatly. When what I really want to yell is *I've been kidnapped and I'm sure they are going to behead me. You've got to do something...*

'What do you mean? Is everything okay?'

He sounds concerned and I feel all warm inside to think he is worried about me.

'Yes, but I'm lost,' I try to think of a code to let him know I have been compromised. If only I had paid more attention in the boat and taken his crazy codes more seriously.

I hear Penelope say,

'Is that her?'

Oh dear, she sounds cross. I'm feeling guilty for getting kidnapped; I should have taken Alex's advice and been more careful.

'It's just...' I begin and hear myself whimper.

'Libby, what's going on?' There is real concern in his voice now and the firmness I know so well.

'For God's sake, what is it now?' snaps Lady Penelope.

The man leans towards me and whispers,

'Tell him you lost.'

'I'm so lost,' I say, 'can you come and get me?'

Alex is silent.

'Alex, I am getting very wet and I'm lost. I'm getting very wet,' I repeat, placing emphasis on the wet.

Christ, I am sounding like a moronic half-wit. He will think I am either drunk or insane.

'Libby have you been drinking?'

What did I tell you?

'Or are you telling me it was raining cats and dogs last night?'

I knew water was in one of the codes.

'Yes, chucking it down. Can you come and get me, I am very lost.'

'Libby, are we friends?'

'What the hell Alex,' fumes Penelope.

What the hell indeed. Surely his coming to get me doesn't depend on whether we are still friends. Oh, I so hate him and to make matters worse Penelope sounds very cross. Oh dear, this couldn't have come at a worse time. Why couldn't they have kidnapped me after dinner?

'Libby can I get you something?' he asks.

The tone in his voice is more serious now and I suddenly realise this is one of the codes. Oh God, what is the right answer to this? This is worse than *Mastermind*. If I get this wrong it may mean he won't come and rescue me. Stupid, silly codes, it would be far easier to shout help. Everyone knows what that means. This is something to do with tampons isn't it? Oh shit, why can't I remember? They are now holding a small card in front of my face with an address on it.

'You are lost here, tell him.' The man attempts to grunt crossly but it still comes out soft.

'Alex, I am lost at 92 Phelm Tue, and I need tampons.'

I hear Alex snap at Penelope and then he sounds breathless as though he is walking quickly.

'Libby, when I come to the lost place, should I bring tampons or toothpaste. I want to get the right things for you okay?'

Oh God, must get it right, must get it right. Think. I am beginning to realise just what contestants go through on *Who Wants to be a Millionaire*. It's impossible to remember anything while I'm under such stress.

'Toothpaste,' I scream as it all comes back to me. 'It's toothpaste I need.'

'Good, I'll get a takeaway on the way home.'

What, oh no! Any other time that would have been lovely, a curry, or even fish and chips but he has totally misunderstood and thinks things are fine. It must have been tampons. Shit. The phone is snatched and clicked off before I have time to scream down it. I don't believe this. The mobile and my Blackberry are snatched off me and both men walk away. The one with the soft voice stops at the door and mumbles something to the other. He hands me a bottle of water. At least I won't die of thirst. The door is closed and I am alone in the small room with a tatty armchair, an equally tatty couch and a small table. I cannot believe Alex misunderstood me. My only hope now is that when he sees I am not at the hotel he will realise something is wrong and try my Blackberry. Of course, when I don't answer that, he will realise I have been compromised. Although I still find it very hard to believe that anyone could get much money for us, although didn't Alex say we would make good bargaining tools? Maybe they will exchange me for a political prisoner. I really can't believe this. When Jamie talked about the high risk I never for one minute imagined he meant this. I need the loo so badly. I so wish I was home and preparing for Christmas and the New Year like everyone else. Not that I had any plans for New Year's Eve. I wonder what Alex and Penelope have planned. They probably plan to romp in the New Year in their nice apartment. I shall refuse any invite from them as it will just be embarrassing. God, what if I never get to see another year? No, I mustn't think things like that. I wonder what Toby is planning. I couldn't give a fig what anyone is doing to be honest, but it keeps my mind off the kidnappers and my predicament. I must try and remain buoyant and positive. No matter what the kidnappers say or do I must try to be receptive. I'm sure this would be Alex's advice. Of course, in his new book there is a whole chapter on his kidnapping in Afghanistan but I really couldn't face reading about his courageous coping strategies without throwing up. I wish I had now. At least I could have got some pointers. Christ, I don't even know what the time is. One thing is for sure, when Alex does come to rescue me I will look a mess. Although it doesn't really matter does it? I'm well out of Alex Bryant's league aren't I? One only has to look at Penelope to see what I lack and yes, that is just about everything. I expect she stuffs her face full of vegetables and doesn't gain a pound. I only have to look at a carrot cake and you can be sure the weight piles on. She has this knack of looking perfect, whenever, however, and wearing whatever, and it probably only takes her ten minutes. I have hair that goes into a frizz at just the sight of rain. My eyelashes are non-existent and my pain threshold so low that plucking my eyebrows would necessitate a day off work, sick. My best feature is my lips, however, and I have a cute cupid's bow, which even I like, and a small stubby nose which Toby always said was the cutest thing about me. All the same though, I could never compete with Penelope. She has a fantastic job as an advertising executive. I'm just an agent with a small publishing house. She mixes in social circles that are in a different world to mine. Out of Alex Bryant's league I most certainly am. I stretch my legs and look at the door. I wonder if they will let me go to the loo. I must keep positive and work at keeping my spirits up. Alex must surely be coming soon. He must by now, have realised something is wrong.

It must have been an hour if not longer since I phoned. I am just about to call out to my captors when there is a tapping at the window. I turn and see Alex looking in at me. Coming up behind him is one of my captors and I scream and point behind him. But it is too late and I watch as he is dragged away. Oh my God, what will they do to him? Moments later the door is thrown open and Alex pushed in. He falls at my feet and I give him a disdainful look.

'I thought you were going to rescue me,' I say accusingly.

He leaps to his feet and swiftly looks around.

'Well, that's gratitude. I didn't have to come you know. I could have left you here and finished my dinner.'

He's quite right, I mustn't sound ungrateful.

'Oh, and what did you have?' I ask spitefully.

'A fish curry, and very nice it was too, until you phoned.'

What a horrible thing to say. At least it's more than I've had.

'Have they told you their demands?'

I shake my head. He walks around the room, tapping walls. It all looks very impressive but is it going to get us out of here?

'Have they mistreated you?'

'I haven't really been here long enough, but I am sure they were going to.'

He gives me a sharp look.

'I told you not to go out on your own.'

Oh please, is this really the time for a lecture? He stops tapping the walls and listens at the door.

'As far as you know is there just the two of them?'

I nod.

'Do they speak English?'

I nod again.

'I want you to call them and say you need the loo.'

How does he know I need the loo?

'But...'

'I'm not debating,' he says sharply.

Ooh, Mr Masterful or what. I call the guards. One enters and I begin to explain that I need the loo. Before he has time to answer me Alex has lunged towards him and in seconds has him in an arm lock. The other man rushes in and seems to plead with Alex to release his friend. I look on in amazement as they all begin chatting in Khmer. Alex's tone is firm and there is much pointing and gesticulating before Alex releases the man. A map is produced and Alex studies it intently. Honestly, you would think he'd tell me what the hell is going on.

'Where are the car keys?' he demands and they are handed over to him immediately. This is incredible. It is as if he has hypnotised them or something.

'Great, let's go. They're making it very easy for us, which I'd anticipated,' he says pushing the men towards the door.

I have no idea what he is on about and I don't really care. I shall be glad to get to the hotel and from there I shall arrange my flight home. I'm not even going to phone Jamie or Toby. I really couldn't care any more. I just want to get home and back to my normal boring old life. The car I thought I came in is not even a car, I see now, but a small van that has certainly seen better days. Alex bundles the men in the back and gestures me to get into the front passenger seat.

'Now, listen carefully...' he says seriously.

'And I'll begin,' I add, in an attempt to show him I do have a sense of humour.

It just gets me a sharp look.

'You need to hurry into the hotel and grab what things you need. Go to my room and just pack a few essentials. Penelope won't be there. I left her having a massage.'

'But...'

'We can't risk going back there.'

What is he saying? What about Penelope?

'I'm not staying here. I'm getting a flight...'

He brakes hard and we are all thrown forward. The men in the back grunt and I let out a tiny moan.

'You've been kidnapped and so have I. Do you understand?' he snaps coldly.

Now, what is he on about? He just foiled the kidnap attempt didn't he?

'But we've escaped and...'

'We want everyone to think we have been kidnapped, especially the people who organised this.'

I look at him bewildered and point exaggeratedly to our kidnappers.

'Hello...' I cry. 'Here are the kidnappers.'

He starts the engine.

'Don't act so naïve, you're smarter than that. These gentlemen were sent by Colonel Pong to keep us under wraps until after the election. They didn't want to do it but their families have been threatened and they had no choice. For their safety, and ours, everyone must think we have been kidnapped. It is better for us to be in the safe house. That way I get to do all the interviews as planned.'

'I don't want to go to the mattresses,' I say in the manner of the Godfather.

'I rather think I am making you an offer you can't refuse.'

'But...'

'But what?' he snaps crossly.

'What about Penelope?'

He runs his hands tiredly through his hair.

'She's having a massage and tomorrow I've arranged for her to fly back home. She will no doubt alert the authorities that we have gone missing and then fly home. It's stupid putting herself in danger.'

Oh, but it's okay for me to be put in danger. I feel a sudden flutter of excitement in my stomach. It won't be that bad being alone with Alex Bryant for a few days will it? Let's face it, I don't have much choice. Maybe I can make the best of a bad job. Of course, that's if you can consider having the two clowns in the back seat with us as being alone. Honestly, this really is my kind of luck.

Chapter Eighteen

The safe house is magnificent. I want to ask how Alex knows about this place but decide to ask him some other time. We drive down a bumpy dirt track which runs between two rice fields and into a driveway concealed on either side by high bushes. As we turn the bend the house comes into view and I gasp. It looks similar to the pagodas I had seen in the countryside. In the dim lighting from the house I can make out several columns which support a wide veranda. Two comfortable looking wicker chairs sit invitingly. We drive to the back of the house. I see what looks like an allotment where I can make out neat rows of plants and bushes in the light of the silvery moon. Behind the allotment is a wood which casts ghostly shadows over the ground. To think I cannot tell anyone about this. It is just the sort of annoying thing Alex Bryant would do. We are in the middle of nowhere. The house has three bathrooms, six bedrooms, an enormous lounge and an equally enormous kitchen. There is also a small cosy sitting room which houses a music player, a laptop and an assortment of board games. The only thing lacking is air conditioning. Alex-*I-have-everything-under-control*-Bryant has instructed all of us to turn our mobile phones off and give him the batteries. I am very reluctant to do this and stubbornly stand my ground. The two men, whose names I learn are Lucky and Mr Navy, admit they were following orders by the country's Governor, Kuma Pong, and hand their phones over without protest. They are terrified of Pong and his henchmen and seem very agreeable about helping Alex. They are safe for as long as Pong thinks Alex and I are kept under lock and key by the gentle Lucky and Mr Navy. This is all beyond me. I'm a simple publishing agent. I don't go to safe houses and hand over my phone. I don't go to countries that are in the middle of political uprisings. I can barely conduct a simple romance, and it is becoming very annoying to find that everything Alex says is right. It seems that Kuma Pong, stinker by name and stinker by nature, has been terrorising the country for some time with his protection racket.

'He threatened destroy my house if I not kidnap you and lady,' Lucky fumes.

'He has the police under his thumb too. This is why the people are rebelling. They've had enough,' Alex tells me.

'But why is he after you?' I ask while inspecting the kitchen cupboards.

'I've exposed him and he's scared I'll say too much about him on television,' he explains. 'So, he sends someone to kidnap us. And will presumably dispose of us when the time is right.'
I shiver. Does he have to make us sound like a black dustbin bag?

'This is all very well but I have a life to get back to and people who will be worried about me. What about my parents. I really should phone them,' I say firmly while pulling several cake tins out of a drawer. 'Issy is expecting me to phone her tomorrow.'

'I'm afraid both Toby and Penelope will have to think we've been kidnapped. This also applies to your parents and Issy. I will need your phone, Libby. These two fine gentlemen will be at risk if Pong even gets a whiff that we foiled his plans.'

'Holy strawberries Batman! We're in a jam!' I say with a smirk.

'Indeed, Robin. It's sometimes difficult to think clearly when you're strapped to a printing press,' he retorts with a similar smirk on his face. There is also something else in his expression but it's difficult to read. Could it possibly be appreciation?
He does have a sense of humour and God, he is so gorgeous. Good heavens, if I am to be holed up with him for an indefinite period who knows what I will be capable of. Then again, if I walked around naked all day I don't imagine he would even notice me. If only he wasn't so damn irritating. I hand him my phone and walk to the room he has assigned me. It is actually the best room I have seen so far since arriving in Cambodia. I have a huge bed, my own en suite, and, I am pleased to report, plenty of loo paper. However, on the down side, I only have a few things to wear. I hardly took any of our clothes from the hotel because I was so panicked that Penelope would return. Frankly, this whole business seems totally crazy. I really can't believe that anyone would care about Alex and me, well not *me* anyway. There is a soft tap on the door and before I can respond he has walked in. He has changed into a pair of shorts and a

white shirt, and there go my eyes again. Why did Issy have to mention his huge penis?

'Are you okay?' he asks gently.

I force my eyes up.

'What, oh yes. I was just thinking about your pe... predicament,' I stammer, sitting down on the bed. He sits beside me and I think about locking the door and molesting him while I have the chance. I have a vivid imagination. As if I could handle a man like him. He was quite right at the airport of course, when he said *'perhaps you've never been with a real man before.'* I certainly have never been with a man like Alex Bryant before.

'We have someone bringing supplies. Is there anything in particular you would like? I hope you don't mind but I did hint to the guys that you bake cakes and good ones, so Jamie told me. We can get you what you need and you could make some,' he says raising his eyebrows several times at me.

My God, he is serious.

'I suppose I could,' I say hesitantly.

'I'm presuming you can make them without a cookbook.'

What an insult. So, an hour later while Alex prepares dinner I make a cheesecake and a lemon drizzle. Dinner is a lamb curry which is superb with fragrant rice. The meal is a bit uncomfortable. We eat silently, sizing each other up. After all, we are going to be housemates for, I actually don't know how long. I decide to ask Alex later when he thinks we can all go home. Mr Navy washes up and I excuse myself to the small sitting room. The doors are open wide and I feel cool and comfortable and pleasantly weary. I'm quite pleased with myself as I haven't touched the cake at all. Alex strolls in with two mugs of tea and sits on the couch opposite me.

'I made you some camomile tea. So, how goes it Robin?' he asks.

I am beginning to think he isn't so bad after all. Issy would be proud of me if she knew that I had finally seen the light.

'I'm coming to terms with being a wanted woman, in fact, it is quite liberating. It's just a shame I can't share it with my friends on Facebook of course.'

What a great status update, I am almost tempted. *Holed up with the lovely Alex Bryant and just waiting for the Cambodian government to storm the place. Have had a very exciting day so far...* No, I don't think so.

'I'm sorry about the mobile business. I imagine you're desperate to speak to Toby?'

I feel a tingle of excitement when I note it is more of a question than a statement.

'Not really. To tell you the truth we had a bit of a disagreement. He got quite possessive, especially after you used my Wonderbra.'

Annoyingly I feel myself blush. I take a sip from my tea in the hope to hide my embarrassment. Why am I talking about my bra and looking at his crotch? Now, here is a man that mother approves of. He speaks nicely and father would enjoy talking to him. And here is me, overweight, lacking confidence and without the foggiest idea of what is or isn't the right outfit for a posh function. I don't move countries. I don't even move towns. Come to think of it, I simply don't move. I'm as far from the right woman for Alex Bryant as any woman could be, whereas Penelope is most certainly the right woman. She has the right name for a start, and the right 'breeding' no doubt, not to mention the right long legs that come up to her armpits and the marvellous right job. I wonder what Penelope is doing now, is she phoning the British Embassy to report us missing?

'I hadn't realised it was a Wonderbra but that explains a lot. If it can rescue us from rebels and sinking boats think what it could do for you?' He grins at me.

'You should be in advertising,' I say without thinking and immediately regret the remark as it reminds him of Penelope. At least I hope that is the reason his face drops. Oh, that was mean of me.

'You don't think Toby is being a little immature? I'm an ex-SAS officer, I'm trained to improvise and use whatever weapon is available. The rebels wouldn't have hurt us. I just knew that if I hit the bell they would retreat to the temple. My biggest worry was that they would try and kidnap us as, unfortunately, we are perfect bartering material to get some of their colleagues released.'

His voice is so smooth and soft that I find myself mesmerised.

'I was quite happy for you to use my bra,' I say and bite my lip. What a silly thing to say.

'Let me get a jug of the local brew and some of your lemon drizzle,' he says suddenly and leaves the room, giving me time to fan myself. He reappears with two glasses, a jug and a plate of cake.

'Lucky and Navy are playing cards. I said we would be going to bed soon...'

I blush and I see him wince.

'Let's have a drink,' he says quickly, and pours liquid from the jug into the glasses. Good God, he is embarrassed. Have I actually misunderstood his comments and he really does like me? Well, sod a dog, wouldn't mother and Issy be impressed. Sod them, I'm bloody impressed.

'I'm just relieved their names aren't Army and Navy,' I say, laughing, 'or Happy go Lucky'.

He hands me the drink and takes a sip of his own.

'I want you to be prepared. The news will be out tomorrow that we have been kidnapped. The government will blame the rebels and make it sound much worse than it is. Kidnapping us has two purposes, one is to get us out of the way so I, correction *we,* can't appear on TV and secondly, it makes the rebels look bad, which is of course the government's aim. I'm really sorry that I dragged you into this. I really didn't think it would be this dangerous. Things are getting out of hand here but I didn't think...' He stops and thoughtfully sips from his drink. 'I don't know what I thought,' he finishes.

I know I am staring at him. For the first time he seems really vulnerable. He looks up at me and I simply shrug.

'I've hypnotised you,' he smiles.

I think how much mother would like him. Well, she likes him already but she would be so excited to meet him in the flesh. I wonder what she will do when she sees me on the news. Phone all her friends, no doubt. I hope she doesn't worry too much. No doubt, dad will be very pragmatic and keep her calm. With a sigh I take a sip of my drink and immediately choke as the strong rustic-flavoured liquid hits my tongue and burns my throat.

'It's potent,' he laughs, 'palm-sap wine, courtesy of the safe house'.

'Frankly, this is the most exciting thing that has ever happened to me. How many women can say their bras were used as a weapon to fight off the enemy?'

There I go, talking about my bra again. Before I know it I'll be talking about my knickers next. It must be this palm-sap wine, of which I sip some more.

'I really can't believe this is the most exciting thing that has ever happened to you,' he says, relaxing back onto the couch and opening his legs as he does so. Don't look at crotch, I instruct myself. I am unable to speak for a moment.

'What about the time your vibrator blew up the power station?' I snap my head up and see he is smiling at me. I feel the heat travel up my body.

'That was a joke, obviously,' I say quietly. 'I don't think Orlando has anywhere near enough power in him to blow up a power station.'

He laughs and I bite my lip realising what I have just said.

'You really shouldn't give your bra all the credit you know,' he says, leaning forward and refilling my glass. 'I was impressed with the piece you wrote in Toby's article and your review of *Life in a War Zone*, although scathing and painful to read, actually had some valid points, and I took note of them when writing the new book.'

That fresh fragrance that is uniquely his wafts over to me and I feel all atremble.

'You did?' I can't hide my genuine surprise. He actually took note of my review. Good Lord.

'I rather thought you didn't take much notice of anyone,' I say boldly.

'Well, there you're wrong. Why wouldn't I?'

Because you're an arrogant arse I almost say but bite my lip.

'Because you don't make mistakes and always seem totally in control and...' I break off when his eyes lock onto mine.

'Is that what you think, that I am always in control? There have been times when I've made mistakes.'

'Like publicly slagging off writers just because they can write as well as you?'

Here I go again, putting my foot quite squarely into my mouth. He looks thoughtfully at me.

'No, I can safely say I've never made that mistake.'

I feel my blood begin to boil and am about to give a sharp retort when he says softly,

'But I have made serious misjudgements and once almost got a good friend killed in Afghanistan.'

He looks at the floor.

'What happened?' I ask.

'We were on a mission in Helmand, four of us. I was careless and stupid. As an SAS officer we are trained to spot these things but

I just didn't see it. I led my lads into a trap, it was awful. I thought we were all done for'.

He shifts uncomfortably.

'How did you escape?' I ask softly.

'There was another squad in the area, and we owe our lives to them. One of my lads was badly wounded, we got out but he lost his leg. I don't think I will ever forgive myself for that.'

I feel I want to put my arm around him to comfort him. I didn't expect to see him looking so vulnerable.

'By the way you make fabulous cakes,' he says, suddenly changing the subject.

'But you have never tasted my cakes until now,' I object.

'Ah, but I have. You made some for the office, and very nice they were too.'

'Toby tells me that. He also tells me to stop eating them,' I sigh, and realise I have done the one thing I meant not to do. I have drawn attention to my weight.

'Toby seems quite distracted by your weight. Does he not notice your other qualities? I happen to think you're rather appealing.'

His eyes wash over my body and this time I cannot control my blush. Oh my God, he really is coming onto me. What do I do? Don't look at crotch, whatever you do, don't look at crotch. I blush and where do I look? Yes, you've got it. I want the floor to open up and swallow me. I can't even act offended and storm out. Well, of course, I could but there is always the danger of storming out into the arms of Colonel Pong. I drag my eyes from, well you know, and find myself wondering just how huge it actually is. I picture my Facebook status again. *Just seen the intimate side of the lovely Alex Bryant and oh, he really is hung like a horse...* Good grief.

'You are talking about me? You're not getting me mixed up with someone else by any chance.'

He pretends to look thoughtful.

'It was you in Dirty Doug's wasn't it? And it was your bra I used not once but twice and it was you I lifted onto the boat?'

I nod mutely.

'Toby wouldn't lift me anywhere in case he ruptured himself,' I mumble.

He smiles and sips from his drink.

'I'm sorry about your friend,' I say quickly while I have the courage to do so.

He simply nods.

'If you don't mind me saying, and hopefully you won't throw one of your wobbly things when I do...'
I raise my eyebrows.

'Toby talks a lot of crap and frankly writes a lot of crap, whereas you are interesting and good company. There are some things I'd really like to do with you.'
Good heavens, has he swallowed a 'compliment pill' or something, or is he buttering me up for something else.
I'll do whatever.
Well, so much for my consideration of Penelope. But let's face it, surely in times of danger all niceties go out of the window. It isn't like I am going home to Orlando and Gordon any day soon. In fact, let's be morbid, I may never go home to Orlando and Gordon again. In which case, one should grab every opportunity.

'I'll do whatever,' I say. Oh, my goodness, I actually did say that too.

'It's important that while we are here we alert the world to the fact that the government here are corrupt. I know they will spread propaganda that the rebels are bad, violent and dangerous and are trying to topple the government. It is our job to highlight the truth. The people here are suffering under this regime and the rebels are just defending their rights. You can help me expose this.'
That wasn't quite, the whatever, I meant, but I can work with that. He looks thoughtfully at me for a few seconds and then gets up.

'You should get to bed. Here is your phone by the way. The battery is in it. I don't want you to think I don't trust you. For our safety it is better left turned off. I will be setting up some security outside so you needn't be afraid to go to sleep.'
I put my hand out to take the phone and his hand gently strokes mine, sending a shock through my body. I have to fight back my gasp. He clasps my hand and I feel myself being pulled gently from the couch. His face comes closer and I close my eyes and savour the taste of the wine and lemon as his lips linger ever so slightly on mine. It is over so quickly that I almost wonder if it actually happened at all.

'Goodnight, sleep well,' he says, releasing me. Was that a shake I heard in his voice, or did I imagine it? I fall back onto the couch. The door clicks shut and I let out a long breath.

Sleep well. Bugger me, after that kiss I will be lucky if I sleep at all. To think I only had a starter. Penelope gets the whole three course meal. Phew, that must be mind-blowing. I mustn't go over the top. It was just a goodnight kiss after all. Although, thinking about it, he could have kissed me on the cheek couldn't he? In fact he could have simply kissed my hand. Oh dear, I am already going over the top.

Issy

I'd been trying to reach Libby for several days. It just isn't like her to say she will call and then not do so. At first I had just presumed phone signal was bad or she was so fed up that she didn't want to talk to anyone, but when I didn't even receive a text, I finally called Jamie. He told me Penelope had flown back from Cambodia in a right state and it looked like something pretty dire had gone on over there. Along with Libby's parents, I have been summoned to a meeting in Jamie's office and told not to say a word to anyone as it is top secret and all that jazz. We are now all assembled and I really can't believe I'm hearing what I'm hearing.

'Kidnapped, are you sure?' I say doubtfully. 'Who would seriously want to kidnap Libs?'
I'm not too certain who I should direct this question to. We seem to be surrounded by leaders of the CIA, SAS, MI5, Special Branch, USSS and the KGB. This is heavy shit. Who would have thought it of old Libs?

'More importantly, who on earth would want to kidnap them?' I ask, and put a comforting arm around Libby's mother, Fenella, who had flown home from Kilimanjaro the day before.

'I think the ATO should answer that question,' replies one of the men gesturing to another, who steps forward with an arrogant swagger.

'The ATO?' I ask Jamie questioningly, but he just shrugs.

'I'm the Anti-Terrorism Officer and I will brief you the best I can and answer any questions.'

'Oh my goodness, terrorism,' squeals Libby's mother.

'It will be all right,' I say soothingly. I find myself unwittingly flashing my eyelashes at the ATO. He is rather appealing.

'I'm fine, darling. I feel sure Alex Bryant will take good care of her. He's such a hero,' she says with half a swoon.

'Harrumph,' huffs Toby loudly. 'He's done a bloody bad job so far.'

'And you are, Sir?' asks the ATO.

'He's the FA,' I reply sarcastically.

'FA?' Fenella whispers.

'Fucking Arsehole,' I whisper back.

'And FA stands for what?' asks the ATO.

'Fi-ancé,' butts in Jamie, giving me dirty look.

'Well, I'm not, actually,' quivers Toby.

What an arsehole, what did Libby ever see in him? Fenella sways slightly.

'She never said anything about an engagement. When did this happen?' she asks worriedly.

'Don't get in a spin dear. Wait until you get proper intel,' advises Libby's father.

You have to laugh. She isn't in the least upset that Libby has been kidnapped by the rebels but as soon as she thinks her precious daughter might marry that little shit Toby, she comes over all atremble. Way to go Fenella.

'I intend asking her first thing. I love your daughter very much,' Toby asserts.

'Oh dear,' mumbles Fenella.

'Yes, right,' responds the ATO looking confused and wandering around the room. All eyes follow him with bated breath. Mine especially. He is gorgeous.

'Now, the intel is that ex-SAS Officer Bryant was compromised by Ms Holmes...'

'I object,' I interrupt. 'That's absolute bollocks. Libby would never compromise anyone.' He puts his hand up to silence me and I notice he isn't wearing a wedding ring. Ooh this looks promising.

'Not deliberately, no, but unknowingly we think she led the kidnappers to Bryant. The rebels are getting more violent by the day...'

'The bastards,' curses Toby.

'And we are fearful of what they will do. We know Bryant is very capable. He will be aware of everything that is going on and we're hoping he will try and get a message to us...'

'Fine chap is that Bryant. Most likely has everything fully under control, what?' says Libby's dad suddenly.

'He's a fucking pervert. I want him court-martialled or whatever it is you people do. I won't be responsible for my actions if he comes back here,' threatens Toby.

Fenella winces.

'Ooh, you'd better get him some protection,' I say mockingly. 'Bryant won't stand a chance against the mighty Toby.'

'Why don't you zip it,' he snaps.

'So common,' mumbles Fenella.

'What should we do, in the meantime?' Jamie asks, ignoring all of us.

The door is flung open and Penelope waltzes in, dabbing at her eyes with a tissue. Jamie rushes to her and she falls dramatically into his arms before covering her eyes with a pair of Ray Bans.

'There aren't photographers or press here are there?' she asks looking around. Good grief, she is made up to the nines, wearing a Prada dress and Coco Chanel boots not to mention a fabulous Chanel beret.

'No, you're fine,' replies Jamie sympathetically.

'Oh,' she says disappointment evident in her voice. She carefully removes herself from his arms and looks around her.

'Who's in charge?' she asks bluntly.

Everyone seems to look at everyone else before the ATO steps forward.

'When have you arranged the press conference? I'd like to filter the questions.'

He seems unimpressed by her.

'There will not be any press conferences, and you are?'

Jamie steps forward.

'This is Alex Bryant's fiancée. She flew back from Cambodia yesterday.'

'Thank you Jamie, I can speak for myself. What do you mean no press conference? Do you have plans for getting him out of there?'

'And my daughter also,' chips in Fenella.

Penelope spins round and appraises Fenella.

'You're the traitor's mother?'

I step in front of them. I'll soon wipe that Max Factor from her face.

'Now, look here madam,' I say pompously.

She begins to look tearful and Toby, of all people, rushes to her aid.

'She's upset,' the little git says sympathetically.

Upset, my arse.

'Everything was fine, until she phoned him,' she hiccups. 'We were having a lovely dinner and then she phoned. Alex was very cross. I think they may have argued before we left for the restaurant. We hadn't been there very long when she called him...'

'We'll need a statement from you later...'

But Penelope isn't listening. She is centre stage and loving it.

'I could tell he was upset by the call and kept getting irritated. He then said he had to go and fetch her because she had gotten herself lost. She was the decoy to get him there, she...'

'Let's get you some water, shall we?' suggests Toby.

Oh yes, why don't we? Let's get enough to drown her. The ATO whips out a flip chart and I feel like I'm at a bloody board meeting. Penelope sips at her plastic cup of water while Toby makes sympathetic noises. I wonder if I should gently remind him that he is planning on asking Libby to marry him.

'If either of them should contact you let us know immediately,' says the ATO forcefully. Oh, I do like a forceful man.

'Don't try to be a hero or a heroine,' butts in the head of somewhere else.

'It will be featured on the news tonight. Unfortunately we couldn't do anything to stop the news getting out.'

The ATO shoots a glance at Penelope. She sniffs.

'We have the press under control and do not want any of you talking to them. You must stay anonymous.'

'Can we not talk to anyone about it? I have the parish council meeting on Thursday and...' begins Fenella.

'No one,' snaps the ATO. Oh, I say, he is masterful.

'We're having a little slideshow of Kilimanjaro,' she whispers into my ear. 'It would have been so exciting to have told them how Libby is fighting the rebels with Alex Bryant in Cambodia. I will have to say I have news, but it's classified. She's a bit of a prima donna isn't she?' she finishes, nodding towards Penelope.

'Indeed,' I agree.

'If anyone approaches you, the response must always be 'no comment'.'

'Ooh, how thrilling,' trembles Fenella excitedly.

I smile indulgently and feel a small pang in my stomach. Libby will be okay won't she?

'The rebels won't hurt them will they? Alex said they're not as bad as they have been painted,' I ask worriedly.

'They're a force to be reckoned with.'

'My sentiments entirely,' echoes Toby.

'We will all meet here again in two days' time and will continue to do so until this situation is resolved. As their closest friends and allies, you should be prepared to be contacted by anyone at any time. I must reiterate that always your response must be *no comment*. If at any time you suspect you have been contacted by someone inside Cambodia then let us know immediately.'

Meet here every two days? I've seriously got to see that little runt Toby every two days, not to mention Madam Penelope. Oh, I don't think so. I'm owed annual leave.

'I'm going there,' I say. 'If Libs is in trouble I want to be there for her.'

'Oh bravo,' declares Fenella.

'Tally ho, that's the spirit,' cries her dad.

'Are you fucking mad?' asks Toby.

I see Fenella cringe, God he is so coarse.

'I'll come with you. And I'll bring Philippe,' cries Jamie, 'after all, I agreed to the whole trip and I do feel a bit responsible.'

Toby looks decidedly uncomfortable. Meanwhile Fenella claps her hands in glee and looks at Libby's dad.

'Let's do it,' she pleads. Not that I imagine she has ever had to plead for anything.

'Jolly good,' he answers.

We all look to Toby.

'It all seems rather risky,' he mutters.

'I would seriously have to advise against it,' interjects the ATO. 'It is not safe to visit Cambodia right now.'

'Perhaps you should come with us then,' I say, attempting my best come-hither look. 'Some of us may need protecting.'

Penelope jumps up and heads for the door.

'In that case, I shall return. I am not dealing with all the flack here on my own. I will need to be there when they release Alex and arrest Libby. I shall be staying at the Shadow Angkor.'

143

And what's that when it's at home? It's all I can do not to hit her. I give Toby my best evil look.

'What did she say?' asks a puzzled Toby.

'She said you are a shallow wanker.'

'If you are coming, please let me know what flight you're on so I can avoid it,' shouts Penelope as she exits the room.

Fenella titters. I take her by the arm and walk out on the heels of Penelope. Fenella and I watch wide-eyed as she climbs into a waiting taxi.

'Why do you think Alex Bryant is with her?' I ask, shaking my head.

'You're the agony aunt psychologist dear,' winks Fenella.

Toby marches towards us, face like thunder.

'Don't you think it is rather reckless of all of you to go storming out there like the magnificent...' he pauses for a second to count numbers on his fingers. 'Six,' he finishes.

'At least we're not the hesitant magnificent one,' I retort, leading Libby's parents to my car. It isn't that I want Toby to join us. In fact he is the last person on earth I want to come with us, but I can imagine how devastated Libby will be when she discovers we are all there but him. Then again, it will probably devastate her that we are there at all.

Jamie calls out and mimes that he will phone me before diving into his car.

'You could make it the magnificent seven of course,' I call out to Toby from the car window.

'Not if that fucking shirt-lifter is going,' he calls back.

Jesus, I swear Toby would bring back stoning if he could.

'Rest assured Toby, your arse will always be safe.'

Fenella titters and before he can respond I put the car into gear and drive off.

Chapter Nineteen

I have been praying that Alex Bryant will most certainly have a need for my knickers. In fact, I am so prepared for it that I have been washing and wearing the same lace-edged frilly pair for the past two days. But, disappointingly, danger seems to elude us. Isn't it just my luck? I am now quite desperate to remove all and sundry in aid of the so-called 'war effort' and what does he do? He protects me so well that the chances of my having to remove even an earring are looking more and more remote. The goodnight kiss, which seems an age ago now, is seemingly the most intimate I am ever going to get with him. I have to be brutally honest with myself and admit to being something of a scarlet woman, well, in my head anyway. I haven't given a second thought to Penelope or Toby, and it is becoming apparent that a temptress I am not, for apart from the occasional cursory glance, Alex acts as though I do not exist. It is very odd behaviour for someone who said, only forty-eight hours ago, that he found me rather appealing. Obviously, 'appealing' does not mean, 'tear your knickers off'. I am beginning to wonder if I am sex-starved and perhaps I was more dependent on my old friend Orlando Broom than I thought. All I seem able to think about is sex, and not sex with my boyfriend Toby either. I am constantly thinking about sex with Alex Bryant. Although at the moment I would settle for a snog and fondle, but the only thing about me that he seems to find appealing is my cooking.

We are staying in a monastery. Our personal food supplier, named Bourey, proudly showed me around the allotment where everything I could possibly need was growing. I asked if he could bring me some supplies to make a curry. That night I made chicken Thai curry, sticky rice and cupcakes. Before I retired to bed the men were giving me their food preferences. I ask you, I get kidnapped and where do I end up... in the kitchen. And I don't mind telling you, I am feeling quite taken for granted, in a good way. It is nice to be making cakes. It relaxes me and what's more, I feel so content at the moment that I am not even eating them. Who would have thought that somewhere like Cambodia, in the middle of an uprising I would learn to feel contented. The past two evenings I have spent writing using the information I have gleaned from Bourey and his friends and family, although I am still very nervous about showing my articles to Alex.

'Carrots, papaya, onions, coconut and chicken,' Bourey says now, smiling widely as he drops the provisions onto the large battered table.

'Tea, lemons and bags of sugar also,' he adds in good English.

'And flowers for the lovely lady cook,' grins Alex, who comes in behind him. 'Happy Christmas, Libby.'

I had forgotten it was Christmas. There is so little here to remind me. Lucky comes in carrying a huge wreath.

'It's the nearest we could get to a tree,' smiles Alex. 'Where would you like it?'

'Oh, it's lovely,' I gush before I can stop myself and as usual, I blush.

Whenever he so much as looks at me, I flush scarlet. He must think I have Rosacea or something.

'Thank you,' I say, accepting the small bunch of flowers which he had obviously picked from the garden. I mustn't read too much into this.

'We see you later,' says Bourey with a wave of his hand.

Lucky proudly affixes the wreath to the wall. We are cooking dinner for six this evening. Alex has asked Bourey to join us along with Mr Navy and Lucky. It is a special occasion, for we are hosting dinner for Samnang, the head of the rebels. I feel a little nervous having him in the safe house, but Alex said all will be fine. I have a horrible sneaky feeling that Alex may well inform me that we are going home and that is the last thing I want. All that awaits me there is Toby, who I am starting to see as more useless than Orlando and Gordon. I know I am being totally stupid in thinking that Alex might notice me in a romantic way. Let's face it, I am one of those all rounded homely girls and not half as athletic looking as Penelope, who, Alex told me, goes to the gym every afternoon as well as her 15k run at weekends. The only 'K' that I do is 'Special K' and I didn't like to say that I feel people should only run when being chased. I would go to the gym every day, you understand, and even run at weekends, if I was fit. That's the problem; I'm far too unfit to go running. I only have to walk briskly and I am huffing and puffing like a steam train. Yes, I know, you have to work up to these things. The truth is, exercise just doesn't appeal to me that much. I'm also pleased to say that sweet foods don't appeal to me much either at the moment and I can actually feel where I have lost some weight. I imagine, and I must admit to imagining this quite a lot, that a woman who sleeps with Alex Bryant, and I go all hot just thinking about it, would need to be quite athletic to keep up with him. What a thought, it is enough to make me go all atremble. Going to bed with Alex must be a bit like going to bed with James Bond. I would most certainly like to be his Pussy Galore for one night. Although I am aware a homely, slightly overweight woman, such as me, hasn't got a chance in hell.

'I'll help with the cooking this evening,' says Alex as the door closes on Bourey.

'You will?' I say stupidly.

'Unless you have some objections, do you?'

What possible objections could I have? I shake my head dumbly.

'Good, I'll meet you in the kitchen about five. Dress casual.' He smiles and wanders off.

Good Lord. I rush to my room to again rummage through my sparse collection of clothes. This is ridiculous, how on earth can I make a good impression? I spend all of an hour choosing something that I can wear that is both practical and glamorous. Let me tell you, this is almost impossible. Finally, after building up a sweat that even Alex would be proud of, I settle on a top with straps as thin as shoe laces, a short-sleeved cardigan and a flouncy skirt. I can think of a thousand reasons why I would not appeal to Alex Bryant in these clothes but choose not to. Instead, I try to muster up what small amount of confidence I have and continue to bash away at the keyboard in an effort to finish the article that Alex had asked me to write. Two hours later I head back to the kitchen where he is waiting.

'Reporting for duty ma'am,' he says saluting me. 'Where do you want me?'

What a question. I ask you. It is all I can to do to stop myself from replying with *Stand erect and follow me into the bedroom. We've got some undercover work to do.* Instead I blush furiously and clearly give away what is on my mind.

'Can I stand down ma'am?' he asks grinning.

Good heavens did he read my mind about the erectness. For goodness sake, I must pull myself together.

'As long as you follow protocol,' I say stiffly, and point to some onions.

'I've got a visual ma'am, shall I take them out?'

'Roger that.'

He grabs three onions and moves next to me at the kitchen table where he sees my folder with the articles inside.

'Have you finished them?'

I nod as I chop the chicken into quarters. I try not to look as he glances through the sheets of paper before slipping them back into the folder. We are both silent for a time and all that can be heard is our joint chopping and slicing. He washes and slices peppers while I chop a chilli. I am struggling to think of something to say but nothing comes to my mind.

'Toby is asking for me to be court-martialled,' he says breaking into my thoughts.

I freeze over the saucepan. How does he know this?

'What?' He surely is joking? Toby wouldn't be such a fool. I know he is stupid but surely not *that* stupid.

'But, that's mad. You're not in the forces any more and anyway why?'

He takes the wooden spoon from my hand and stirs the pan. I feel sure his hand lingers on mine longer than it should.

'For allegedly sexually interfering with you,' he says huskily.

I'm not sure if it is the huskiness in his voice or the words *sexually interfering* that produce the tingle in my loins, but produce it does. Sexually interfering with me? God, I should be so lucky.

'I feel sure I wouldn't have missed that,' I say without thinking. He turns sharply to look at me.

I'm sure I can feel the heat from his body, or is it mine? I swear I am on heat. Pussy Galore has nothing on me. If only Penelope was not on the scene I might have just found enough confidence to flirt with him. After all, Toby has let me down hugely and in the worst possible way. It has occurred to me over the past few days that I would be mad to forgive him. Who knows what he has been doing behind my back. The truth is that the whole Toby debacle has had a massive impact on my self-esteem. I honestly believe that no man could be attracted to me, let alone Alex Bryant. I'm not unattractive, I know that, but I just don't have the extra something that Penelope has. However, what I do have, that she most certainly does not have, is fresh chilli in my eye. God it is killing me. I attempt not to let Bryant see it but it seems like I am constantly winking at him and after his comment about sexually interfering with me, my winking seems highly inappropriate.

'Have you used your phone to speak to Toby?' he asks, barely looking at me and stirring the onions more than is necessary. I shake my head. I haven't turned my phone on and presumably neither has Alex, so how does he know Toby is asking for him to be court-martialled?

God, I can barely see. My eye is stinging so much. I fumble for a tissue and he turns to see why I have not answered and shakes his head despairingly at me.

'You haven't gone and chillied your eyes have you?'

'Well, I certainly didn't poke it,' I say miserably.

Trust me to use a word like poke after we had just been discussing his supposed sexually interfering of me.

'Come here,' he smiles, guiding me to the sink.

'If our phones are off, how do you know this about Toby?'

'I know everything,' he mumbles while looking at my eye.

He runs a cloth under the cold water tap and then lifting my head with one hand he uses the other to lay the cloth gently on my eye. Oh, bliss. I try not to swoon too heavily into his arms.

'How does that feel?' he asks. I find myself winking at him.

'Say no more,' he laughs.

I really daren't say anything more, unless I want to make a fool of myself. He turns to the pan that is sizzling and holds up the chicken.

'Shall I stick this in?'

Good Lord, why is it that everything he says seems to refer to something else and why do I find my eyes, or at least my good eye, wandering down to his crotch? It is all I can do to pull it back up. I force myself to nod and dab at my eye. I take the wooden spoon from him and he moves to the side so I can reach the pan. I turn and collide with him. Why is he standing so close? He is looking beyond me and out of the window. I see his shoulders tense. What now? What have I said for goodness sake? He is so close that his thigh is touching mine. My breath catches in my throat.

'We have visitors,' he says quietly.

My good eye darts around, while the other winks madly at him. Is this a mating call I have never heard of? Well it's better than *Hey babe, I wanna give u 12 inches,* I suppose.

'I'm going to lean forward and kiss you, so for God's sake don't pull away and slap me. I promise I am not making any attempt to sexually interfere with you.'

I try not to look too disappointed.

'I want to get a clearer idea of their positions and I don't want them to know I have spotted them,' he whispers, leaning closer.

Well, I've been strung some lines, but this one takes the biscuit. He leans forward slowly, his eyes so clearly focused on the window that I feel I should aim my lips for his. After all, I don't want him to miss now do I? All's fair in love and war so they say. I needn't have panicked, however, as his lips land expertly on mine. For a brief second my arms stay loosely at my sides but as the kiss deepens the overwhelming desire to bring one arm around his back and the other his neck is too much for me to resist. His lips are so warm and insistent. As I do so, his hand cups the back of my head and brings me nearer while the other arm is clasped around my waist. I feel my lower back being pushed gently against the cooker and have to hold onto him as I feel my legs go weak. His thigh feels hot against mine. If this is acting, what must the real thing be like? The kiss ends as quickly as it began and my lips feel bruised and numb. His head is slightly above mine and he looks into my eyes.

'I've got a visual. I need to get the alarm that is behind you so I can alert Lucky. Don't give anything away. I don't want them to know we've seen them.'

Good heavens, he was serious about the whole 'intel' thing. He wasn't giving me a line after all. He pulls me towards him again and covers my neck in gentle kisses and I feel myself shiver. This isn't real, I tell myself. You are like that hari currie woman, or whatever her name was. Mata Hari, that's it. But she looked like Marlene Dietrich, where I look more like Marlene Boyce out of *Only Fools and Horses*. Oh my goodness. I can barely think straight with his lips all over my neck and at one point, much to my shame, I feel sure I moan. His hand fumbles behind me as he tries to find the small square box. I reach behind and feel under the kitchen counter until my hand curls around the alarm.

'Quickly, Libby, before they realise I've got them in view.'

I pull it out of its casing and expertly slide it into his hand which strokes mine more seductively than it ought to. I can feel his heart beating against my chest and his breathing seems to have accelerated. He's a good actor I think, convinced he couldn't possibly have enjoyed kissing me. He fiddles with the alarm while keeping it hidden between our thighs and I feel his hand brush my leg several times. Apart from the simmering of the pot on the stove there is silence and the only sound is our breathing. Then I hear Lucky's voice coming through.

'I'll take him from the side,' Alex whispers into the box while looking into my eyes. I can't help noticing his lips are pink and shiver when I think he may be aroused.

'Do you need my bra?' I say through trembling lips. Well, there's no harm in asking is there?

His eyes seem to dart to my breasts and then up again.

'It can be quickly removed if I do,' he replies, and yes, there is a definite huskiness to his voice.

His eyes dart to the window again, and a few seconds later he gently pushes me to one side and runs through the main door. There is the sound of breaking glass and running footsteps. I grab the stove for support and realise I am trembling. I struggle to recover and sneak a look out of the window where Alex and Mr Navy are wrestling with someone while Lucky is waving a torch around. It is difficult for me to see what is going on but it looks as though Alex gets into animated discussion with the man before letting him go. I stare flabbergasted. Why would he do that? I pull a chair out and lower my trembling body into it. I feel quite emotionally battered. If just kissing Alex Bryant does this to me, what on earth would I be like if I had sex with him? I'd need a week off work. The three of them come roaring into the kitchen and Lucky sniffs hungrily at the pot on the stove. Alex smiles shyly at me but I find I can barely meet his eyes.

'What happened?' I ask while looking at Mr Navy.

'See you in a bit guys,' says Alex.

He waits for them to leave and then says,

'You're going to have to trust me. I'll tell you everything on a need-to-know basis.'

The soft voice has gone and the 'I know what's good for you' voice is back. Why does everyone treat me like an idiot? First Toby treating me like a fool in front of Serena and now Alex is talking to me like I'm aged seven.

'I'm past trusting men,' I scoff and for a second I am amazed it is me that has spoken.

A shadow passes across his face and his eyes narrow and then very quickly he is back to normal, attempting to smile.

'I'm not Toby you know. Talking of which, you might like to know he is here in Cambodia.'

Good grief. I am seriously amazed. In the space of one hour I have not only discovered that I actually can arouse the one and only Alex Bryant, the superhero of our times, but that my boyfriend actually does love me. Why else would he be here? The question is do I still love Toby? It is hard to reconcile the Alex Bryant of now to the one who had, only moments ago, kissed me at the kitchen window. He is behaving in a dismissive manner. Any suggestion of romance is pushed from my mind and I remind myself that men like Alex are used to improvising in moments of danger. He has probably kissed many a woman while trying to ascertain the movements of the enemy. He offers to prepare the starter while I change for dinner. I waltz to my room, my mind whirring. Why is Toby here? Surely this must mean he really does care for me. All I can think about is Alex's kiss. I can no longer deny that I find Alex Bryant very attractive and not only attractive but I also have feelings for him. It is seriously starting to bother me that he may well be in danger. I should try and talk him into flying home with me. Even as I think this I know it will be pointless to attempt as he is very much his own man and nothing I say will change any decisions he has made. I have to admit that his single-mindedness is quite exciting. If only I were more appealing in a 'Penelope' way. Surely, he could not possibly kiss like that without some feeling, could he? God I am missing old Orlando. I take my time changing, sensing he wanted to be alone for a while. I have no make-up so pinch my cheeks to redden them and spend a long time on my hair, pulling it up and releasing it until I get so hot that the only way is up. I finally emerge from my room wearing a flowery dress and a lace shawl that Issy had bought me last Christmas. It still smells slightly of Rive Gauche perfume and reminds me of home. The marbled floor is cool under my feet and feels lovely.

He looks up from preparing the table. His eyes linger on me and I feel myself blush. His eyes tell me I had not imagined his feelings for me when he kissed me. I am sure of it, and my heart does a little flutter. The room is wonderfully inviting. The table has been expertly laid for dinner and Alex had used all the best cutlery and wine glasses. Lucky has put decorations around the room. I feel quite moved to know they have done it so I wouldn't feel I was missing Christmas.

'I have something for you. I meant to give it to you earlier, but, well, things have been a bit busy haven't they?'
Good Lord, a bit busy is when you are slightly overwhelmed at the office isn't it? Not when you are kidnapped and rushed to a safe house. I rather think that is a bit more than busy, more like harassed I would say. He hands me a box and I look suspiciously at it.

'Don't tell me it's a brooch with a hidden camera, or a James Bond style homing device. You really shouldn't have,' I say, attempting to cover my embarrassment.

'I'm very aware that you gave up a family Christmas to come here. I hope they're to your taste.'
He must have showered while I was changing for he smells of soap. His hair is slightly damp and tousled. He has bought me a Christmas present and I have bought him sod all. Jamie might have hinted, he must have known, surely. I take the box hesitantly.

'I didn't buy you anything. In fact, I haven't bought anybody presents.'

'I didn't expect anything. Aren't you going to open that?' He nods at the box, obviously keen to for me to look inside.
I lift the lid to find two beautiful pearl stud earrings surrounded by diamonds. Not real diamonds of course, at least they surely can't be. I am about to speak when there is a light tap at the door and Mr Navy walks in. I'm beginning to wish I had a stun gun so I could quickly put Mr Navy out of action for a few minutes. Honestly, talk about bad timing. I mouth a 'thank you' and he nods, seemingly pleased. I toss my hair in the manner of Mata Hari and say I am just going to put them on and rush to my room to calm my beating heat and throw cold water on my loins. Honestly, this is getting out of my control. I shall be molesting him over the dinner table at this rate. I survey myself wearing the earrings in the small cracked mirror that hangs on my wall. After studying myself for several minutes, I return to the living area where Lucky is opening all the doors to let in the cool evening air. Bourey arrives with Samnang and they bow to us before handing me several dead chickens which Alex takes with a grateful bow.
I find it difficult to take my eyes off him throughout dinner. He has changed into a white shirt which contrasts beautifully with his tanned skin. His hair is still slightly messy from his earlier shower and his face seems to glow. I have to force my eyes from his lips

otherwise I find myself visualising the kiss over and over again until I feel faint. I force my mind back to the conversation in hand.

'Our main task is to promote the book. If that includes making it known internationally that the government here is corrupt so be it. Our position has been compromised but we can still do it with your help,' Alex says.

I look to the man on my left and shiver slightly. I cannot believe we have invited the head of The People's Army to our safe house. Samnang smiles at me.

'The food is very good, Lady Libby thank you.'

Mother would be very proud if she heard me being called 'Lady' and even more impressed if I showed her the earrings and told her about the kiss. I am beginning to think Issy was right. I need a good shag and preferably one from Alex Bryant. I quickly fan myself and begin to think I may well need smelling salts if I go on like this. On seeing me Alex turns up the fan and smiles, which of course notches up my internal heat even more. I am in danger of spontaneously self-combusting if this continues. I swallow the last of my starter and clear the table.

'Thank you, but Alex prepared this. I can only take responsibility for the main course and dessert.'

It is one of the few times I have said his name and it tastes seductive on my lips. It also seems to have an effect on him. Okay, I kid myself. He licks his lips but that's probably because they are dry.

'It is very good Alex, may I ask what we are eating?' asks Samnang, who sounds very gentle but I feel sure he would knife his enemy quicker than I could say Jack Bauer.

'It's cow's stomach,' responds Alex and I feel my own stomach somersault. Oh heavens, I must not throw up over the dinner table. It would most certainly be very unromantic and very unsexy. Jesus, what is he doing feeding us the stomach of a cow? Christ almighty, wasn't there enough chicken out the back?

'You have our help and our support Alex, but your protection is what I fear. Colonel Pong, as you know, does not wish you here and will continue to do his best to prevent any television appearances by you. My fear is that he will soil your name and I can do nothing to stop that.'

I place the bean chilli onto the table along with the curried potatoes and Alex leans across me to dish it up onto the plates. My breath catches in my throat and I cough slightly. I don't recall Toby ever having this effect on me, but then, it is impossible to compare Toby with Alex. The only similarity they share is that they both like my cakes.

'I need you to leak Libby's article onto the Internet. I can't risk it being traced back to us just yet.'

I hear myself gasp.

'You can't possibly do that. It needs at least two more drafts and editing and...' I begin protesting.

'It's perfect. I read it while you were in the shower,' says Alex firmly.

Oh Lord, what if Toby sees it. My life won't be worth living.

'We need to start blitzing the Internet,' says Alex handing the article to Samnang.

'Consider it done,' smiles Samnang.

'We are vigilant now,' says Mr Navy.

'I think you mean vigilante,' I correct.

'No, he means we must be vigilant. If Pong should discover that we are not prisoners of Mr Navy and Lucky, you can be sure he won't sit on that information for long. We all, and that includes you Libby, need to be very vigilant. Whatever he tries we need to be ready for him. Always remember, intelligence is the most powerful weapon.'

Any plans I had on eating dessert are well and truly quashed after hearing that little speech.

'Why don't we just go home?' I ask, thinking this a very sensible question.

'Because we care about the people here and the country, don't we?'

Everyone looks at me earnestly and of course I nod. But, do I care about the people here? Mr Navy pushes another plateful of rice at me with a wide smile while Alex looks keenly at me. I accept it with a grateful nod. I guess the truth is that I do care about the people here and I especially care what Alex thinks of me. I am finally beginning to realise that I may seriously be in danger and that Alex Bryant is my protector. What a lovely thought. Maybe I can tell him I feel nervous at night. Madam Zigana has well and truly surpassed herself. I only wish I could remember if she had said there would be two men in my life. Who would have thought it of me, Libby Holmes? I can't wait to tell Issy.

Issy

The Magnificent Seven we most certainly are not. I vow never to travel with Libby's parents ever again. Fenella insists on travelling Business Class and by that I mean she insists *we* travel Business Class. Jamie refuses very delicately, explaining his lover Philippe comes from a very poor background and would be quite uncomfortable travelling Business Class. Fenella is totally bewildered by this.

'But surely, darling, that is all the more reason he would like to travel comfortably. No one will hold it against him being gay and a Flipono if that's what you mean. In fact, everyone on board will probably think he is a nurse. After all, most Fliponos are aren't they? Especially the gay ones.'

I raise my eyebrows. What the hell is a Flipono when it's at home? It sounds like something I would wear on my head.

'I think you mean Filipino,' I say, in an effort to ease the confusion.

'Oh, I don't know what you call them dear, but I'm happy to pay the upgrade.'

'Well, maybe not Fluff,' chips in Libby's dad.

'The sooner they decide the better,' snaps Toby. 'I want to make sure my seat is a fair way from where they're sitting.'

'Why don't you book yourself on a homosexual-free flight,' I hiss.

'Can you do that?' asks Toby.

'Saints alive, I didn't know that. I say, how the world's changing, what?' says Libby's father.

'Don't be silly, Edmund, of course they don't have special flights for homosexuals. It's like saying we should have separate planes for coloured people, although that would be a jolly good idea. At least you could be sure of not catching anything,' sighs Fenella.

I never knew Fenella was such a keen racist.

'It's kind of illegal these days, to say that kind of thing, Fenella,' I whisper.

'What kind of thing dear?'

'You know. Things about coloured people and such like. It's kind of a crime to be racist now.'

She looks amazed.

'When did that happen?'

'About the same time they took the golliwog off the jam jar,' I say, edging her towards the check-in desk.

'I wondered what happened to that...'

'For Christ's sake,' snaps Toby.

'Does anybody know what time Penny left?' asks Jamie.

'Perhaps I should phone her. I don't imagine she will want to be seated near a pair of poofs,' quips Toby as he pulls out his phone. He has Penelope's phone number? What a sneaky bastard.

'What about that ATO man? Is he on the same flight as us? I think it is important to have some security with us,' says Jamie.

I couldn't agree more. In fact no one could be more excited than me that he is coming. I never for one moment imagined he would, and I can't help thinking this is the man Madam Zigana talked about. After all these are the most unusual circumstances ever. I wish Libs were here so I could tell her. Then again, it is because Libs isn't here that I met him in the first place.

If checking-in for the flight was not bad enough the flight was even worse. Penelope insisted on being moved from her Business Class seat because she didn't want to sit anywhere near the 'traitor's parents'. Although her confidence that Alex is okay and will be released shortly was reassuring for me and Lib's parents. Toby, meanwhile, seemed to invent every excuse possible to pop through to Business Class and it wasn't to see Fenella or Edmund.

'He's such a wanker,' complains Jamie. 'Why did he have to come?'

'Apparently, because he wants to propose to Libby, because he really loves her don't you know?' I say sarcastically.

I so wish Libs had more confidence. Then she would see Toby for the arse that he is.

The ATO's name is Jonathan and he really is a dream boat. I manage to swap seats so I can sit beside him. He is lovely and not married. At least he is not married any more having recently divorced. What a stroke of luck, or I should say fate. I wonder if Libs has met the man of her dreams as Madam Zigana predicted.

'We're so lucky to have you with us,' I say, truly meaning it.

'Indeed,' he responds.

I'm learning he is a man of few words. Oh well, who wants a man who talks all the time anyway?

'I do hope Libs is okay,' I say voicing my inner fears.

'If she's not safe with Ace Bryant, she won't be safe with anyone,' he says tersely. I feel comforted in an odd way.

The twelve-hour flight to Bangkok is tedious to say the least, and the fact that Jonathan barely speaks the whole journey adds to the tedium. We arrive at Bangkok and catch our connecting flight to Siem Reap. I am feeling quite exhausted. Fenella and Edmund have booked us all into the Shadow Angkor Hotel, which is way out of my league. Penelope has booked herself into a suite. After much probing, I ascertain that Jonathan is staying at the Shadow Angkor too, which sends a little thrill through me. Toby is a complete and total shit. He spent the entire journey flirting with the luscious Penelope, who spent the whole time rolling her eyes at everyone who didn't jump to her every whim. At one point, she got up to go to the loo during turbulence and when told to sit down, just swished her hair back in a manner that said 'Sod off' and headed to the loo anyway. What a prize bitch. What Alex Bryant sees in her I cannot imagine.

I got bloody cramp on the flight and do nothing but swallow bucket loads of quinine. I am sincerely hoping that the hotel is a decent one with proper loos and not bloody holes in the ground. I am all for adventure but not roughing it.

Finally, we land in Siem Reap and I try Lib's mobile again but get the bloody voicemail. Fenella and Edmund hire a taxi while I take a tuk-tuk. When in Rome and all that, and it's much more fun and Jonathan agrees and shares mine. Although it does mean we are somewhat cramped with our suitcases on our knees and our legs squashed. I swallow a couple more quinine tablets and attempt to enjoy the sights. The tuk-tuk driver spends a good ten minutes trying to talk us into visiting the temples the following day. We finally head off to the Shadow Angkor Hotel which he tells us he knows and which I fear he seriously does not. Toby, meanwhile, advises us all not to buy anything from a tuk-tuk driver.

'He might try to sell you heroin or opium. You can't be sure what these people have up their sleeves,' he says earnestly. 'And of course there is the white slave trade.'

It then emerges that the creep had hired a private investigator to try and find Libby and Alex.

'I would seriously impress on you not to attempt anything on your own if your chap should find something. You're not trained to deal with kidnappers,' says Jonathan in that lovely upper-crust voice of his which makes me feel like I am in a period drama film.

I so hope Libs is having a bit of an adventure with the lovely Ace. Jesus, she could be romping for England with him right this minute. I sincerely hope Toby's investigator doesn't barge in on that. I am finding it harder and harder to understand why Toby is even here. If he really cared for Libs then he would not flirt with every woman in sight. I just don't think he can bear to think that Libby might prefer someone else.

The hotel is quite idyllic and does have a proper bathroom and air conditioning. I fall onto the bed and think about Libs. I am knackered from the flight and am thinking I will make it an early night when Toby calls on the room phone. He says his investigator has found where Libs and Alex are being held and do I want to be there when he rescues Libby. The answer obviously is, 'of course'.

Chapter Twenty

I toss and turn for an hour. It is terribly humid and the fan doesn't seem to be helping at all. It is twelve-thirty and I am wide awake. If I'm not reliving Alex's kiss then I am thinking about Toby. So, he is here in Cambodia. If only I could turn my phone on and talk to him. I would at least have a better idea of what is going on in his head. Has he realised that he loves me after all? Is he truly sorry for what happened with Serena? How can I forgive him and do I really want to anyway? Then, of course, there was Alex's kiss. It was so real and passionate. Surely Alex couldn't have faked the warmness that emanated from him. What about the earrings? When had he bought those? What if he had bought them for Penelope? I quickly dismiss that idea. He isn't the type to give another woman's present to someone else. He is the strong and loyal type, someone you can trust. My stomach churns when I remember Penelope. I ask you, what is happening to me that I can forget Alex's fiancée? Blonde Blancmange, with legs up to her chin. Let's face it, he is an international celebrity while I am an international nobody. Alex, no doubt, is missing Penelope in more ways than one. It is unthinkable to imagine myself with Alex Bryant. The earrings were a nice gesture and I must see them for what they are. The poor man is most likely sex-starved. I suddenly feel very depressed. I have had an awful Christmas and in six days it will be New Year's Eve. The man I thought I loved, I realise I don't know that well at all. The man I think I could love doesn't even see me in a romantic way. My mind is racing so much that I feel I am going crazy. I throw on my nightie and a shawl and make my way to the kitchen for a cup of camomile tea. Mr Navy is on guard duty and he waves lazily at me from the veranda where he is smoking a cigarette. I walk into the kitchen where a sleepy Alex greets me. He sits at the table wearing shorts and a crumpled tee shirt and sips from a cup. I pull my shawl around me and wonder what my hair looks like. Honestly, I can't even get up for a cup of tea without him being there. Any hopes I had of appealing to him are now, well and truly dashed. He isn't going to ravish me in my granny nightie.

'You can't sleep either,' he says pulling out a chair for me. 'I'll make some tea.'

He points to the jug of palm-sap wine on the table.

'Do you want me to lace yours? It's the only way I am going to get some sleep.'

You can lace my drink anytime, I want to say, but of course I just nod and make a superhuman effort not to stare at his firm rippling thigh muscles. I feel myself flush and take some deep breaths.

'It's hot tonight,' he comments, pouring water into the cup.

God, it sure is and it's getting hotter. I feel my breasts suddenly tingle and fight the blush that overwhelms me. I sip from the tea, grateful for the warmth of the palm wine.

'I read your other article by the way and it's really brilliant. Why haven't you written more stuff?'

Because Toby always told me my writing was crap. I can't really say that.

'Toby always said my writing was rubbish.' It seems I can say it and just did.

He scoffs.

'What do you see in that loser anyway?' he says, while looking at me over his cup, his eyes twinkling.

I feel myself tense. What is it with me? Every time Alex criticises Toby my back goes up.

'He's not a loser,' I say defensively, and walk onto the veranda where it is cooler. I sit on one of the wicker chairs.

'And why do you always feel the need to defend him?' he asks, following me.

'I don't.'

The air is thick with the fragrant Jasmine that grows in the garden coupled with the aroma from Mr Navy's cigarette. The truth is, I do defend Toby and I don't have the foggiest idea why.

'Anyway, I don't know why you have such a bad opinion of him.'

'He's an idiot that's why.' He stands in front of me and leans against the metal railing of the veranda. I so wish he wouldn't do that.

'The way he treats you for a start...' He breaks off and looks uncomfortable.

I stand up and my shawl slips from my shoulders, revealing my thin granny nightie and even worse, my breasts. I see his eyes move down to them and hastily retrieve the shawl.

'Toby loves me,' I say shakily, wrapping the shawl tighter around me. 'That's why he has come all the way here. He wants to make sure I am all right. He must have known you would have put me in danger.'

'Are you saying you don't feel safe with me?'

Why does he always have to twist everything I say? And why can't I take my eyes off his shorts. I stand and turn to walk away but his hand on my arm stops me.

'Don't go,' he says softly and my whole body seems to tremble at his touch. I turn and find him standing very close to me. My hands grasp the shawl and I shiver involuntarily.

'Are you cold?' he asks, smiling.

'Freezing,' I whisper. My mind is screaming, 'take me take me before I change my mind.'

'It's thirty degrees tonight,' he says, his voice barely audible. His lips are close to my ears and his hand lightly touching my hip where he gently guides me back to my chair. I exhale and close my eyes. When I open them he is sitting opposite me.

'So, how long have you known Toby?' he asks. His voice now back to normal.

'How long have you known Penelope?'

He smiles and shrugs.

'I've known Penelope for what seems like forever.'

Oh Christ, what does that mean? I've known Penelope like forever and it feels like long enough, or I've known Penelope forever and we are so close that we are like one person. I am about to speak but hear shouting from outside at the front of the house. I can hear voices and they sound familiar.

'What the hell?' mumbles Alex as he rises from his chair.

Oh Jesus. Please don't tell me that Toby has come to rescue me? Couldn't he have waited until Alex had, so-called, sexually interfered with me? Alex pulls me into the house and locks the door.

'Don't be too concerned,' he says in a matter of fact voice to Mr Navy. Don't be too concerned? What does that mean? I watch wide-eyed as the veranda door is smashed and Toby and another man burst in brandishing baseball bats. I mean, seriously, what is he doing? I stare at them open-mouthed. Toby looks at me and then at Alex. He lifts the baseball bat higher.

'Libs, are you okay? Has there been any ill treatment? Has he or anyone else molested you?'

I stare at him. What the hell is he talking about? Molested me? Let's face it, Toby has put paid to that now. Well and truly. Don't you just hate do-gooders? Toby shakes his baseball bat as Mr Navy steps towards him.

'Don't even try it mate. My friend here knows karate and he'll take you apart.'

'Leave it, Mr Navy. He really isn't worth the effort,' says Alex with a smirk and sits back in his chair.

I look to the friend who is even weedier than Toby but I don't say anything.

'I do believe I had the pleasure of meeting your friend earlier this evening. I see you reported back very quickly,' grins Alex.

At that moment a sleepy Lucky comes into the room.

'Then you should have been expecting us,' quips Toby and swaggers towards me.

'Most civilised people knock you know, and wait to be invited in,' Alex says mockingly.

'What the hell are you doing Toby?' I ask quietly. Someone needs to be calm. It just isn't normally me.

'Charlie is an investigator. He found you. I don't know who the fuck is supposed to have been kidnapped here, you can explain it all later Libby. I'm going to report this and they will put him,' he points angrily to Alex, 'back on a bloody plane.'

'Charlie, huh,' says Alex mockingly.

I ignore him.

'Don't be stupid, Toby,' I say. I suppose I should be pleased that Toby seems to care so much.

This is terrible though. I am about to be rescued and Alex has not even made a pass at me, let alone sexually interfered with me. Issy steps through the broken door and I feel an overwhelming rush to hug her. She waves tentatively at me, looking a little uncomfortable.

'Libby, get your stuff, we're taking you home,' Toby orders.

I move forward but Alex gently pulls me back.

'She isn't going anywhere,' he says firmly, 'Most certainly not because you say so.'

'Libby, come on,' snaps Toby. 'And for Christ's sake put some clothes on.'

'Stay where you are,' orders Alex firmly.

I'm getting quite dizzy.

'Arrest that man,' declares Toby to the man named Charlie.

'For Christ's sake Toby this is not a bloody military operation. Don't get carried away,' yells Issy, pushing herself forward.

'Stay out of this Issy,' hisses Toby.

'Libby, get dressed, I'm taking you out of here. This guy is trouble. I read the article he leaked onto the web. He is supporting an uprising Libby and accusing the government of corruption. He's a warmonger. By the way Bryant, your article stinks.'

Hang on a minute. What article is he talking about?

'I'm calling Jonathan, this is getting ridiculous,' cries Issy.

Who the hell is Jonathan?

'Jonathan,' I mutter.

'Oh, he's lovely Libs, wait till you meet him,' she gushes.

'Toby, I think perhaps you and I should discuss this outside,' challenges Alex and at that moment I could have gladly killed him. Just what is he trying to prove? Issy looks horrified and shakes her head madly.

'Fine by me,' retorts Toby but I feel sure I hear a slight tremble in his voice.

'Don't you think you should put that baseball bat down before you injure yourself? Of course, if you feel you need it, I'd be happy to take you both on.'

Oh, this is just ridiculous.

'Libs you can't let them fight over you, someone may get hurt,' Issy pleads.

Of course, what she means is Toby may get hurt. We both know that Toby is unlikely to do much harm to Alex.

'After you,' Alex says, pointing to the broken door.

Toby walks outside and reluctantly puts the baseball bat down. Oh my God, this is terrible. I grab Alex by the arm. My hand on his warm naked flesh sends volts rushing through me.

'Alex, please don't hurt him,' I whisper.

He looks down at my hand and then into my eyes.

'Why aren't you pleading with him not to hurt me? Or don't you care if he hurts me?'

Why is he being so damn childish? I feel perspiration running down my back.

'We both know he won't hurt you. He doesn't know what he's doing...'

'He's an adult isn't he?' he snaps and walks outside.

Issy and I dash outside through the broken door with Issy talking madly on her mobile. Toby and Alex face each other like a couple of boxers and I wonder if I can bear to watch them. Lucky stands behind Alex while the investigator, who apparently knows karate, stands behind Toby.

'Your choice of weapon?' asks Alex.

'Don't be so ridiculous, Alex,' I shout.

'I can handle a fist fight,' replies Toby in a confident tone.

'Whose side are you on?' asks Issy excitedly.

'No one's of course. We have to try and stop this.'

'Yes, of course,' she says meekly. 'Jonathan is on his way. He knows Ace. I just hope he is not too late.'

Hearing Issy call him Ace takes my mind back to when I had first met Alex and how attractive I thought he was. Looking at him now I realise nothing has changed. The men circle each other and I wonder if I should close my eyes and ask Issy to tell me when it is all over.

Toby throws the first punch and Alex ducks to avoid it. Both men are sweating and I feel myself perspiring with them. Toby wobbles and before he can regain his balance Alex swings his arm towards him. Toby attempts to duck but is not fast enough and Alex's fist pounds his jaw. I hear a crack and wince. Toby sways but manages to stay upright and lunges at Alex. Alex puts his foot out and Toby stumbles but not before he lands a punch at Alex's groin. Alex moans and doubles over for a second. Issy gasps and I let out a small moan.

'Oh that was so out of order. Come on Alex,' Issy screams and I stare at her open-mouthed.

We watch with bated breath as Alex steadies himself. Toby throws himself at Alex but he sidesteps and Toby falls flat on his face. This is terrible. Toby grabs Alex's ankle and they both fall to the ground heaving and pummelling like wrestlers. I sense Alex is being gentle with Toby and thank God for that, but it still seems like he is beating the shit out of him. They finally part and I breathe a sigh of relief. Toby's left eyelid is beginning to swell and his lip is cut. Alex doesn't have a mark on him. Toby, what are you doing? Alex is so out of your league. Toby must really love me to do all this for me. I feel so wretched. Toby is panting heavily and I can't help wondering why Alex doesn't stop. Toby turns and grabs the baseball bat from the floor.

'Toby no,' I scream.

Alex looks to me and as he does so Toby charges at him with the bat. Issy screams while I am struck dumb. The bat is lifted high in the air and comes crashing down towards Alex's shoulder. I squeeze my eyes shut. The cracking sound I am expecting to hear doesn't happen. I snap my eyes open in time to see Alex sidestep Toby and yank the bat out of his hands.

'I should have known you would be a dirty fighter,' he growls. 'If dirty is what you want then that's fine by me.'

My stomach turns over when I realise Alex has no intention of being gentle any more. Issy and I watch horrified as he yanks Toby's arm painfully behind his back. Toby winces and yelps loudly as Alex throws him to the ground. I try to think of some way to stop the fight. Issy gasps as Toby's foot connects with Alex's groin again sending him moaning to the ground. I so wish Toby would stop doing that. I don't even understand what they are fighting about. It can't be over me. Men simply don't fight over me. It just doesn't happen. Alex's face is like thunder.

'Play fair, damn you,' he grunts and throws a punch which sends Toby crashing against the veranda railing. Blood trickles slowly down Toby's cheek and I stare at him horrified. Alex charges at him and throws another punch to his face. I can't bear it and before I know what I'm doing I have thrown myself between them.

'Libs, what are you doing?' Issy shouts.

I push my hand onto Alex's chest.

'That's enough. I can't stand here and let you do this. You are going to kill him.'

Toby moans behind me.

'I hadn't realised you cared that much for him,' he says angrily.

'I...'

'Or that you thought so badly of me. Do you really consider me a man with no control?'

'No, I...'

'Libby,' moans Toby. 'Let's get out of here.'

'Yes, why don't you and your trashy boyfriend get out of here?' says Alex, nastily.

I am so stunned, I cannot even reply. Issy looks miserably at me and then lays a hand on Alex's arm. He nods at her before storming off.

'I'll fetch your things,' she says softly.

How could he be so horrible to me? I was just trying to stop things getting out of control and all I've done is offend him. I sniff noisily and realise I am crying. Why do I always get everything wrong? Charlie helps Toby up.

'I'll have him fucking court-martialled. He'll be sorry. Let's get out of here Libs,' snarls Toby.

Issy hands me the few things she had retrieved and I reluctantly follow Toby to the car. I look back to see if Alex is by the window but there is no sign of him. I feel wretched and clasp Issy's hand. Why didn't I just leave things? I should have trusted Alex. I feel sure he won't give me a second chance. Someone please kill me.

Chapter Twenty-One

I am finding it impossible to concentrate on anything. It has been well over twenty-four hours since I left the safe house and I have hardly seen Toby. Penelope has a bad case of food poisoning, which Toby seems to have caught. He blames it on the 'merciless battering' that Alex gave him. I really couldn't care if he has dysentery. I have been reading Alex's book and feel stupidly embarrassed after discovering he has a black belt in martial arts. Toby should think himself lucky that Alex didn't slaughter him and squash him like a fly. What was I thinking of, breaking up the fight? It is not the first time he has improvised with underwear either. When his plane was shot down in Afghanistan he had used his co-pilots braces as a tourniquet. No wonder my father likes him

I am finding it very hard to feel anything for Toby at the moment. I have not heard a thing from Alex and don't expect to. I have no clear idea where the safe house is so I can't return to apologise. Not that I would mind you. I think he overreacted. Jamie thinks he will turn up for the TV interview. He then expects us all to fly home. Meanwhile, my mother is driving me mad. Why everyone and his dog had to come to Cambodia I will never know. The only good thing to come out of leaving the safe house is that I now have all my clothes again. In the space of three hours Issy and I have been dragged through every market known to man, forced to purchase bamboo sticks full of sticky rice and have each consumed a chocolate crepe from a street trader. At one point I thought we would never get out alive when one market stall owner pleaded with us to buy something and clung onto mother's arm so tightly that I thought the only way to escape would be to cut it off. Thankfully it didn't come to that. If that wasn't enough, we also did a tour of the local pagoda. Finally, with my feet aching, she agrees to a milkshake in the Blue Pumpkin café. We find a table outside and I sit down gratefully.

'I must text your father from the Blueberry,' she says excitedly, pulling out her new phone.

'Blackberry,' I correct.

I fan myself with the menu and smile at a tuk-tuk driver who winks at me. Issy flexes her feet and groans while trying to catch the eye of a passing waitress. I push two Ibuprofen out of a small foil pack and swallow them dry. I shudder at the bitter taste. I am missing Alex so much that it hurts. Issy's phone bleeps with a text and I check mine to see if there is anything from Alex, but there is nothing.

'Oh,' exclaims Issy as she pushes her feet back into her sandals.

'What's the matter, dear?' says mother, in that absent-minded way I know so well. She is concentrating hard on tapping in her text message.

'Come on, we have to go,' instructs Issy, grabbing me by the arm.

'But I haven't had a drink yet,' I protest, fanning myself madly with the menu.

'We have to go,' she says, waving over a tuk-tuk.

'But I'm not ready to go yet. Issy what is the matter with you?'
She sighs and falls back into her chair.

'Jonathan texted me and said I have to get you back. It's all over the news that there was a foiled kidnap plot to snatch you and Alex. They showed a picture of where you were both staying. Jonathan is worried you are in danger.'

I'm in danger? What about Alex?

'I'm going to try and find the safe house,' I say suddenly, surprising myself.

'What?' squeals Issy, 'but you can't possibly. You don't have any idea where it is.'

'I have a vague idea,' I reply, knowing full well that I have no idea whatsoever. I have an overwhelming desire to see Alex.

I wave over a tuk-tuk driver and ask if he knows where the nearest monastery is.

'I take you for five dollar. It take forty minutes maybe.'
Of course, I am quite aware it could be the wrong monastery but I agree, and we arrange for his friend to take mother and Issy back to the hotel. They are having none of it.

'I can't possibly let you go there alone. It might be dangerous,' argues mother.

'Quite,' agrees Issy with a tremor in her voice.

'Exactly and that is why I can't allow you to come,' I insist, pushing mother towards a waiting tuk-tuk.

'Where you want to go, you want see temples?' he asks.

'No, we don't need you. Please stop making such a nuisance of yourself. Here are two dollars for your time,' says mother sternly.

Oh God no, don't give him money. He looks at mother wide-eyed, takes the money and drives off. Suddenly, we are surrounded by a mass of tuk-tuk drivers. I am seriously tempted to sell my mother into slavery.

'You can't possibly come with me,' I exclaim loudly.

'Why can't I?'

I sigh. There are just so many reasons why not and nowhere near enough time to tell mother any of them. We are now overcome with a sea of tuk-tuk drivers and mother is getting irritated.

'No, I don't want the airport you silly man. I have only just got here.'

'I take you to temple, five dollar.'

'I take you to temple, four dollar,' offers another.

'You want to go museum?'

This is getting out of hand. I see mother giving money to a beggar and fight back a scream. If Mother continues giving people money, willy-nilly, everyone will want some. I pull her through the throng and into the restaurant.

'I don't know much about the politics here but if you and Alex are right about the government, then this Colonel Poo...' says Issy.

'Pong,' I correct.

'I don't care if it's Colonel Shit,' she snaps. 'It's dangerous for you to go alone. You should leave it to Jonathan. This Poo bloke...'

'Pong,' I correct again.

'What the fuck does it matter! It's bloody dangerous Libby.'

I feel my heart thumping in my chest at just the thought of Alex and Colonel Pong's henchmen finding him. My stomach has tied itself into knots. Alex is obviously in danger and the thought that he may get hurt makes me feel sick. I try his mobile but his phone is off. Why does he do that? Mother is looking at me expectantly and with that determined look on her face that I know so well.

'You're not coming,' I say firmly.

'You can't go alone and I insist on coming with you.'

'Me too,' echo's Issy. 'But I'm phoning Jonathan and getting him to meet us there.'

We are The Three Musketeers. When my mother is determined to do something there is not much I can do to stop her. I wave over the tuk-tuk driver.

'Just don't get us killed,' I snap, trying Alex's phone again.

The journey to the safe house is one of the longest of my life. I have no idea what I am going to do once I get there. Why was I so stupid to leave there in the first place? We fly past paddy fields and fishing villages and both mother and Issy hang on tightly as the tuk-tuk bumps along the dusty roads. Children on the front of their father's motorbike wave gleefully at us but we shoot by so fast that there is no time to wave back and we leave them engulfed in a trail of dust. I clasp my handbag close to my body while mother gasps every time when we go over a bump.

To my disappointment, the monastery he takes us to is not the safe house and I groan loudly.

'Can you take us to another one, please,' I ask.

Without delay we zoom off, mother's head jerking back as we do so.

'Could we ask him to slow down dear,' she asks breathlessly. 'Can't you remind him that we are British and that back home we have roads.'

I stifle my sigh.

'We don't have time to slow down. I did tell you to not to come.'

'Well, it is rather exciting. Wait till I tell your father. He will be so impressed with us,' she says clapping her hands excitedly.

I shake my head and moan as my hip bangs against the side of the tuk-tuk. To my relief I begin to recognise the countryside, I see the safe house in the distance and I feel my heart pound like a drum. By the time we reach the driveway to the monastery we are all windswept and just a little frazzled.

'I think we should walk from here,' I say attempting to hide the tremble in my voice.

'Wait here,' Issy instructs the driver.

'Aren't we going to wait for the others?' asks mother, mortified.

How I wish we could. But Alex would expect me to be brave. God, what am I doing? I'm a publisher's agent not the bloody bionic woman. I live in Fross for God's sake not planet Krypton. Everyone knows Alex Bryant and nobody knows me. I'm almost thirty and I would very much like to one day be forty.

'Would daddy wait for the others?' I say boldly, knowing full well he wouldn't.

'But your father is a military man, he is duty bound to go in. But, we are just women,' says mother in a shaky voice.

'Never think of yourself as *just* a woman, mother, you are so much more than that,' I say sounding like Emily Pankhurst.

'Yes, of course,' she replies, pulling her shoulders back.

I throw the camera strap over my head and push the camera safely behind my back.

'Come on,' I say sounding braver than I feel. I grab her hand and we slowly walk along the driveway.

'Ooh, I feel like I'm in a Tom Cruise film on a mission I've chosen to accept,' she whispers.

I give her a curious look.

'I feel like I'm in a horror film,' quakes Issy.

'Do we have a gun?' asks mother.

Do we have a gun... what is she on.

'A gun,' squeals Issy. 'When did you ever carry a gun?'

'Of course not,' I hiss back, wishing that I did.

'I've got my pepper spray,' declares mother.

I stop and glare at her.

'Why have you got pepper spray?'

'In case of rape, dear,'

'Oh my God,' moans Issy.

I don't like to tell mother that her chances of being raped are very unlikely. We slowly approach the bend that will soon bring the house into view. I feel my breath catch in my throat. What if they have got there before us? What if Alex is...? No, I mustn't think of things like that. We turn the bend and see a big black van parked near the house.

'Oh dear, do you think that is Mr Poo's?' asks mother, visibly shaking.

'His name is Pong, why does everyone call him Poo?' I snap.

'Issy told us it was Poo, don't shout at me.'

'I'm not shouting,' I hiss back.

'I don't see it matters what we call him, he's a shit anyway,' mumbles Issy under her breath.

'Bollocks, now look,' cries Issy.

I snap my head up.

'What is it?'

'I snapped two nails gripping that bloody tuk-tuk.'

'For God's sake Issy,' I groan.

'Sorry,' she mumbles.

Mother gasps and I look up to see four men bundling Alex, Lucky and Mr Navy out of the house. I push mother and Issy into the bushes and quickly follow. Alex's words materialise in front of my eyes, *Intelligence is the most powerful weapon. Always remember that.* Without a second thought I pull my Blackberry out and focus the camera lens onto Alex. I click the shutter several times and then try to get the other men into focus. My hands are shaking so much that I can barely hold the phone. Alex is pushed into the back of the van with Lucky and Mr Navy and two of the men climb into the front while the other two look around. I duck down and struggle to calm my beating heart. I can hear mother's rapid breathing and hope they cannot hear it too.

'Oh dear, dear me, we really should phone the others,' she whispers clenching and unclenching my hand.

'I'm sure Jonathan will be here soon,' Issy whispers comfortingly.

We watch as the van begins the slow turn to manoeuvre back out of the driveway. I shove mother further into the bushes and Issy and I dive in behind her. The van zooms past us. As soon as the van had turned the corner I grab mother's hand and run for all I am worth to the house. I skid to a halt at the sight of the motorbike which sits outside and recognise it as Bourey's. Mother starts to go into the house but I stop her. Issy and I stare at the bike.

'You can't Libs, you just can't. Please don't,' Issy begs.

'Go back to the bushes and wait for the others to come,' I say. I hand her my handbag and push my phone into my dress pocket before climbing onto the motorcycle.

Chapter Twenty-Two

Mother looks at me in horror.

'I'm going to follow them. I've got my Blackberry. Get Jamie to call me. I can tell you where they go.'

Before I can stop her she has shoved the handbag into the top box on the back of the bike along with her own. Don't tell me she is going to come with me.

'No way,' I snap lifting my leg over.

'I never knew you had it in you, Libby,' she says, while struggling in her pencil-line skirt to lift her leg over the bike.

'This is crazy, but fun,' cries Issy. 'I'll follow you in the tuk-tuk.'

God, we will be a bloody convoy. I watch with fascination as mother carefully removes a small pair of scissors from her Cath Kidston make-up bag.

'How did you get those through customs?' I gasp.

'There are ways dear. I have everything we need.'

She slices through the material and then cocks her leg over the bike.

'Hit it, let's rock and roll,' she cries.

'The Three Musketeers,' shouts Issy.

'Good heavens,' is all I can muster.

I turn the key in the ignition and experience a little buzz at the feel of the throbbing engine. Heavens, it's been a while since I had something so big and powerful between my legs. The last time I had ridden a motorcycle was aged twenty and I had driven my boyfriend's bike all around the village until mother got wind of it. I'm a bit rusty, however, and shoot off so fast that mother has to grab me tightly to stop from flying off the back.

'Don't lose us,' I call to Issy over my shoulder.

I zoom out of the driveway and after about five minutes I spot the van. I hear the roar of the tuk-tuk bike and pray that Issy can keep up.

'This is when we need a gun,' screams mother over the noise. 'We could shoot the tyres.'

My mother never ceases to amaze me. The free feeling I am getting from being on a bike again is wonderfully liberating. I really should do this more often. Not chase kidnappers in the heart of Cambodia, of course, but ride a bike again, most certainly. Since coming to Cambodia with Alex I have felt my confidence grow and I am beginning to think I can do anything. As we leave the countryside and enter the outskirts of the city I feel my stomach churn. How will I ever negotiate the bike amongst all those other motorbikes and tuk-tuks without causing an accident? I may well have to abort the mission if we go into the city. Fortunately, the van takes a turning before entering the city and we continue along the dusty dirt tracks. The road is so bumpy that I feel sure mother will bounce off the back of the bike. I slow down to negotiate the bumps and see the van disappear from view.

'Hold on tight, I'm going to have to speed up,' I shout.

I feel her squeeze my waist.

'And whatever you do, don't take your eyes off the van.'

'*Copy that,*' she squeals back.

'Bogie at three o'clock,' she squeals again.

'What, where?' I scream, swerving across the road.

'Not really dear, I've always wanted to say that and this seemed the perfect time. This is so exciting.'

I'm beginning to think my mother has been with my father too long. I feel my phone vibrating in my dress pocket and hesitantly remove one hand from the handlebars to retrieve it.

'Oh God, what are you doing?' she screams.

I lean behind and hand her the vibrating phone. I haven't considered what I am to do when the van stops. I follow it down a narrow track.

'I'll have to call you back Jamie, dear, we're in the middle of a mission and closing in on the enemy right now,' mother shouts into the phone.

My bum bangs up and down on the seat as we trundle along the track.

'Oh dear, I think my uterus ring just got dislodged,' groans mother.

I tactfully ignore her. We pass a group of water buffalo and race through a tiny village. I am beginning to feel confident on the bike and relax my neck muscles. The van slows and then stops. I skid into a clearing and almost hit a herd of water buffalo. The buffalo sit calmly studying us. Perspiration runs down my face and mother pulls several tissues from her Cath Kidston bag along with lip salve. She really is becoming a must-have accessory on an adventure trail. I am actually quite surprised she doesn't pull a gun from the bag. I look at the house ahead of us.

'Phone Jamie and give him the van registration. Jonathan may be able to do a trace,' I say, sounding like Jack Bauer on his way to CTU.

I think how proud Alex would be of me if he was talking to me of course. I turn to see the tuk-tuk pull up sharply and practically throw Issy out of it.

'Where is he?' she asks looking all flushed. It is stiflingly hot now.

'My Blueberry isn't working,' sighs mother.

I grab her phone and see there is no signal. Damn it.

'Come on, let's move,' I say like a battlefield commander.

We creep slowly through the bushes towards the old dilapidated house on stilts.

'That must be where they are holding him,' I gasp.

I feel so unattractive and am convinced Alex will think so too when he sees me. What was I thinking of wearing black today? I look like I am in mourning. What if he is still angry with me? Oh dear, maybe I really shouldn't be doing this. Toby, after all, has come all this way to be with me and all I have done so far is upset him too. I feel an overwhelming urge to cry and quickly pull myself together.

'Fenella is right, we should have weapons,' says Issy sitting on a log and fanning herself. I sit beside her and gently kick the coconuts beneath my feet. Mother suddenly jigs about excitedly in front of us.

'Coconuts,' she hisses, pointing at the ground, 'you are sitting under a coconut tree. They are so big and perfect for throwing at the enemy.'

Good heavens, she is quite right. I pick up two coconuts. Issy and mother do the same. It is very humid and my hair is sticking to my neck. I pull a scrunch from my bag and pull it back into a messy ponytail. Issy is looking horrified down at her feet.

'Shit and bollocks,' she cries loudly. 'Things are running over my feet, bugger, what the hell are they?'

We all look down, terrified at what we may see.

'There are bloody ants everywhere,' she yelps.

I look down to my feet and let out a little scream when I see hundreds of them crawling across my toes. It looks like one big black mass.

'This is when we need a gun,' repeats mother.

I look at her with raised eyebrows.

'Christ, they bite too,' yelps Issy, jumping up and down, resembling someone performing a war dance. It isn't long before I join her.

I can't help wondering if Alex Bryant is worth all this. Pulling a dancing and jiggling Issy behind me I continue walking down the bumpy dirt track as quickly as I can, shaking my feet as I go. There is silence all around us and not another soul to be seen. Issy clasps my hand so tightly that it starts to throb. Mother holds her coconuts to her chest like a body shield.

'What if they are poisonous?' Issy asks, voicing my own thoughts.

'I'm sure they're not,' I say, not feeling the least bit sure.

What if there are snakes here? Or God forbid, scorpions? There could be anything crawling around here and we wouldn't even know.

'Oh God, I just saw a lizard. Oh dear, oh dear,' mother shrieks. I kick out my foot but I'm not altogether sure why.

'Keep walking,' I order. I find myself wishing I was home in my little cottage in England, with the heating on full and surrounded by cake tins.

'What the hell are we doing?' shrieks Issy. 'Have we gone bloody mad?'

All that can be heard is a dog barking and Issy's rapid breathing. I feel like my breathing has stopped altogether. I wish I had a glass of that palm-sap wine, or two come to that. Instead of feeling hot I am actually quite shivery. I'm not going down with malaria or something, am I? What if I have caught something from those bloody ants? That's about right. I will save Alex, get him to somewhere safe, all the while sweating like a water buffalo and then, when we are safe, I shall collapse in the manner of Santine, out of Moulin Rouge, and dramatically die. Issy will be distraught but Alex will be inconsolable. They will arrange a beautiful funeral in the manner of Princess Diana. It will be in Cambodian style because Alex will say how much I loved the country and he will demand I am buried wearing the earrings he bought me and...

'Libs, what do we do now?' hisses Issy, breaking into my daydream. Her voice is shaky. I look down to our feet to see they are bright red.

I am plunged into the depths of danger again and my malaria is immediately forgotten when I realise we are very close to the house. Standing outside are two burly Cambodians, which we Three Musketeers are no match for. I freeze. What if they have guns? I hadn't thought about this before. Would Alex want me to risk being shot? I don't mind being a heroine and all that but not if it is too dangerous. Let's face it, one can't enjoy the accolade if they are dead, now can they?

'Libs, Libs, do we throw now,' says Issy attempting to stay calm, but her high-pitched voice gives her away.

'Yes, do we throw now?' echoes mother.

I turn and look behind wishing there was someone I could ask.

'Attack when you see the whites of their eyes,' I whisper, not knowing what the hell I am talking about but I read that somewhere.

'The whites of their eyes, Libs are you crazy?' whispers Issy.

'No, but I *am* in agony. My feet are itching like mad. At twenty-five yards, volley fire, present, aim fire!' I shout.

'Bloody hell, Libs, you're not Michael Caine and they are not sodding Zulus. We're in Asia not bloody Africa.'

'All the same it is jolly good fun isn't it? Your father will be livid to know he missed this,' giggles mother.

'Fire,' I shout and she immediately tosses her coconut and I follow suit with mine. We watch as they fly through the air like javelins, hitting the windows and doors of the house. The men scuttle like mad and start running towards us. Issy throws a coconut towards them knocking one man sideways.

'Good shot, Issy,' I yell excitedly and she punches the air in her excitement.

Suddenly, everything is bedlam. The other man races towards us shouting something that we don't understand. In my fear I lob another coconut which lands on his head knocking him to the ground.

'Is he okay?' I ask worriedly.

He is so still. I wish he would twitch or something. There is silence now and I wonder where the other two men are.

'I haven't a clue,' responds mother blankly.

'Do you think he needs CPR?' I ask, flexing my neck.

'Well, it wouldn't do any harm I suppose. Do you have some?'

'Have some what?'

'What you just said.'

'It's a manoeuvre, not a drug,' I snap.

'Oh God, what are we going to do?' asks Issy breathlessly.

'Life I imagine, if we don't get him breathing again,' I say unhelpfully.

A hand brushes my hip and I swing round. My mouth opens ready to scream when I see it is Alex behind me. Although I should say he could better be described as some kind of God. I only wish I looked like some kind of model but alas, I don't. His arms go around me and he whispers angrily in my ear.

'What are you doing?'

His breath on my neck makes me shiver.

'Rescuing you,' quivers Issy.

'Yes,' says mother, trying to suppress her swoon.

'Rescuing me from whom exactly?' His eyes are dark and flashing with anger, but oh, he looks gorgeous.

I open my mouth but nothing comes out.

'Oh dear,' moans mother.

'These men are protecting me,' he snaps angrily. 'You're lucky they didn't shoot you.'

'But we thought...' I say stupidly.

'I know what you thought.' His eyes bore into mine and I feel like I'm being hypnotised. He turns and looks beyond me to the motorbike.

'What do you think you're doing on that?' he asks, widening his eyes.

I pull back my shoulders. Surely he will be proud of me now.

'I know how to ride a motorcycle,' I reply timidly.

'Stupid woman, you could have killed yourself,' he responds dismissively.

Well, that's thanks for you. Why is he so angry? He should be pleased we came to rescue him. Okay, so he didn't need rescuing, but it's the thought that counts. Why is he being so horrible? More importantly, why doesn't he release me? As though reading my mind, he removes his hands and walks towards the man on the ground who is thankfully now moaning.

'I'd better check on the damage,' he says gruffly.

'I say,' whispers mother. 'He's a thousand times better looking in real life isn't he, but shorter than I imagined.'

I have to agree that he does indeed look gorgeous and not in the least short. I just want to wrap myself within the warmth of his body, although right now there is not much warmth being generated my way and I struggle to control my tears.

'Oh dear,' mumbles Issy. 'Perhaps we should go.'

A Mercedes roars along the dirt track and Alex groans. Jonathan leaps from the passenger side and runs towards us.

'What are you doing ladies?' he asks, but there is a good-natured smile on his face.

'Being dangerous heroines,' mumbles Alex helping the guard up. 'Take them to their hotel. I'll take care of the bike.'

Well, how ungrateful is that.

'We came here to help you and you could at least be a bit grateful. You're nothing but a stuck-up arrogant arse,' I throw at him angrily and proceed to climb into the car. Mother follows and Issy turns angrily on Jonathan.

'You might have said something,' she snaps. 'We may have been saved from making a fool of ourselves.'

'Alex asked me not to. I have to agree the less people that know the better. It's on a need-to-know basis. If you remember I said I was concerned about Libby. I never mentioned Alex.'

'Bloody need-to-know-basis,' I scoff.

'Oh dear,' mumbles mother again.

'Libby, Alex asked...' Jonathan begins.

'I'm really not interested in anything Alex has to say,' I snap.

Issy sighs.

'Oh dear,' repeats mother.

'Mother, please stop saying, *oh dear*.'

'Oh dear, I'm sorry, Libby.'

I sigh.

Chapter Twenty-Three

'Toby has severe commitment issues, Libs,' Issy crackles through my hotel room telephone. 'He has no idea about the emotional connection between the sexes, or the natural progression of a relationship. He is just a fuckdick without a dick. He is constantly flirting with other women, why don't you dump the little shit?'

Issy had only phoned to say Jamie had called an emergency meeting. The conversation had quickly progressed to her opinions on Toby. I can only seem to think of Alex who is a million miles from being a fuckdick and who I feel sure has a large one, a dick that is. Here I go getting all hot again.

'I wish I knew how I felt Issy. I used to get this churning in my stomach whenever I saw Toby and...'

'It was probably reflux. He has that effect on me.'

I ignore her.

'But I don't any more. I know I am still fond of him but that desperation I felt about getting engaged to him seems to have gone.'

'Toby is the vilest man I have ever met.'

'I don't know if I'd go that far. What about that man who exposes himself in our park every Friday?'

'Yuk, yes I agree he is quite vile, but he is probably providing a service. The old dears living in the home across the way don't seem to mind, but they have probably not seen a dick for like a hundred years. Okay, Toby is the second vilest man I have ever met. I would very much like to pop his head onto a platter and hand it to you at dinner.'

'What a lovely thought,' I gush.

'You're not thinking about Toby are you? I bet you haven't stopped fantasising about having filthy sex with Alex Bryant, am I right?'

I sigh.

'I've blown it with him. He is very cross with me. I really shouldn't have interfered. But I really don't know why he was *so* cross.'

'No, you shouldn't bloody interfere. If you had left well alone, Toby could now have been in hospital with concussion. What a shame. And you, no doubt, would have been summoned to the new safe house. Instead, we ruined everything.'

'Issy, you shouldn't wish things like that on anyone. Anyway, I don't believe Alex would have seriously hurt Toby. Did you know Alex has a black belt in martial arts?'

'Darling, I've read all his books. You're the one who seems to know nothing about your own client.'

'You shouldn't wish concussion on anyone, all the same.'

'Well, he is a wanker,' she mumbles. 'See you at Jamie's dinner meeting.'

I really can't disagree. In fact, should I have any doubts, I remind myself of just how Toby talks to me. I am not sure why he is here but it surely can't be because he truly loves me can it? Or maybe it is. After all, he hates countries like this but he came anyway. He also fought Alex for me. At least I think it was for me, but then again, if my memory serves me right, wasn't it Alex who called Toby out for a fight? Oh dear, I'm beginning to think I need psychotherapy or whoever it is you see when you can't sort your love life out. Mum bursts in on a cloud of 'Joy' perfume. She is wearing the Christian Dior suit that she bought for my cousin's wedding. A string of pearls dangle at her throat and long sparkly earrings hang from her earlobes.

'It's not an Oscar's dinner you know,' I mumble pulling off my towelling robe.

'I'm not having that Penelope woman think she is the only one who knows how to dress. Talking of which, what do you propose to wear.'

'Ah, actually...' I stammer.
She picks up the thin strapped dress I had lain on the bed and gives a disapproving tut.

'You'll never attract a man like Alex Bryant if you wear clothes from online catalogues,' she groans, picking it up with two fingers as though a cat had pissed on it.

'My married lover back home happens to adore that dress,' I say casually as I stroll into the bathroom.

She pops on her glasses and looks at me over them.

'Well both he and the dress will have to go. What about this?'

I pop my head round the bathroom door to see she is holding up a Laura Ashley print dress.

'Yes, fabulous, except the thing doesn't go over my hips and don't forget Alex Bryant will not be at this dinner but his lovely fiancée will be,' I say dryly and grab the catalogue dress which mother quickly snatches off me.

'Exactly, and that is why you have to look drop gorgeous.'

'Drop-*dead,* gorgeous,' I correct. 'And have you forgotten that Alex is livid with me?'

'I haven't forgotten how he couldn't keep his hands off you when he first saw you this afternoon, either.'

'I didn't really notice,' I say blushing.

'Oh yes you did.'

She winks at me. Good Lord, she is quite right of course.

'Yes, well this should do it. Try it on. I do believe you have shifted a few pounds. Your bum doesn't wobble like it used to.'

Well that's good news. I am quite surprised to discover she is quite right and the dress does indeed slip over my hips and I look quite amazing in it. If only Alex were going to be at the dinner.

'Perfect, now all you need is some make-up and your hair tied into a neat bun and you will actually look quite presentable.

'You don't have to sound so surprised.'

'I only wish Alex Bryant was going to be at dinner.'

I sigh heavily. So do I. I'm not relishing seeing Toby or Penelope but at least I feel a little more confident than I did earlier. Issy is already in the dining room and rushes to greet me, skidding to a stop when she sees my dress.

'Bloody hell Libs, you're looking fantastic.'

She looks past me and groans. I turn to see Toby. He gives me a lopsided smile. I attempt to smile back but it feels like my face has been botoxed.

'How are you feeling?' I ask kindly.

Issy smirks.

'Grateful I would think,' she scoffs. 'It could have been two black eyes couldn't it Toby?'

I nudge her in the ribs.

'You don't have aspirin by any chance? I don't trust the bloody pharmacies here. Their drugs are probably all spiked with heroin or something. This is a bloody awful country, Libby. I can't think why you wanted to come here. It's so hot too. I can barely breathe.'

'You could take your jacket and tie off for once,' I suggest.

'What?' he asks, like I've spoken in a foreign language.

'Keep your hair on Toby. She didn't ask you to remove your trousers. Even I couldn't stand that,' scoffs Issy. 'Who knows, you may actually grow to love it here. I can picture you adopting a baby and taking it home. One feels the compassion oozing from you,' she says mockingly while attempting to remove his jacket.

What is wrong with Issy tonight? I rack my brains to think of something intelligent to say and realise it would be totally lost on Toby.

'Do leave off. Are you sure you don't have any painkillers?' he grumbles.

The worst of it all is that my parents are totally ignoring him. In fact mother is making a very good job of looking right through him. I feel dead embarrassed.

'Sorry Toby, I never carry painkillers,' says Issy, not sounding in the least apologetic.

What a liar. Issy is one of those people who don't just carry a pack of pills, but a make-up bag full of them. She is the only person I know who takes two Paracetamol just in case she gets a headache and three Imodium in case she gets diarrhoea. Issy is, most certainly *a just in case* kind of girl. I imagine her bowels have totally clammed up. Knowing her she most likely swallowed enough Imodium to constipate an elephant before coming here, just in case. I don't imagine she will be shitting herself for some time.

'Fucking Bryant, I swear he has dislocated my shoulder and there are no decent bloody hospitals here,' moans Toby.

What a shame he didn't break your arrogant neck, I think. I give him a disparaging look and sit down. Penelope strolls in and his face lights up. Just what is he playing at? Jesus Christ, she looks like she has arrived for a sodding film premiere. She glances about and looks disappointed that there are no paparazzi. Although why she thinks there would be, I do not know. She strolls over, holding up her long ball gown. I ask you, a ball gown. As far as she is aware her fiancé is God knows where, with God knows who, and having God knows what done to him and she strolls in like fiancée of the year. Her face is plastered with make-up and it looks as if she has just had her hair professionally blow dried.

'No one told me there was a photo shoot after dinner,' says Issy. 'I would have popped my jewels on.'

'Oh hello,' says Penelope, greeting us. She gives a sideways glance to Toby and then flicks her blonde bob behind her ears in such a sensual way that I actually blush.

'Hi Tobe, how are you feeling?' she asks, glancing slyly at me.

'Surely she means toad?' whispers Issy.

'Shush,' I hiss.

Jonathan bounds into the restaurant and I see Issy tremble. Mother is walking about with a tray of sherry. Where on earth did she get that? She'll be coming round with pickled gherkins next. I grab a glass and throw it back gratefully. Toby pulls me by the hand and drags me into a corner.

'You're looking rather sexy tonight,' he growls huskily into my ear. His hand runs over my hip and travels round to my backside. Good heavens.

'I do?'

A small line of perspiration has appeared on his upper lip. He licks his lips and squeezes my buttock.

'It's been so long since we, well you know,' he says throatily, positioning himself in front of me. I gasp as I feel his hand sliding up my thigh. 'God Libby, I've missed you.'

I feel my breath catch in my throat. At that moment mother throws herself across the room like a rugby player and lands panting in the middle of us. I'm almost expecting her to tackle Toby to the ground.

'There you are, I've been looking everywhere for you,' she says with a smile while yanking Toby's hand roughly away from my thigh. I follow her gratefully to the table where Jonathan is greeting Penelope.

'Do you know why the press are not here?' she asks him.

'Probably because we have not informed them where we are,' he replies tersely and kisses me gently on the cheek.

'What on earth do you mean, you have not informed them?' She says, her voice rising.

'I've arranged a media blackout,' he responds, pulling out a chair for Issy.

Toby, who is now studying the menu, lets out a deep sigh.

'Jesus, isn't there anything a person can eat here that is safe?' He says slamming the menu onto the table.

'Do us all a favour dear and eat something that isn't safe,' responds mother.

Issy laughs. I give both her and mother a black look and throw back another glass of sherry, which tastes more like port, but never mind.

'A media blackout, what the hell for?' snaps Penelope walking around the table and brushing Toby's shoulder as she passes. I am stunned.

'Eat the rice honey, that's what I do.'

Christ almighty. I feel decidedly sick and look to Issy who fakes vomiting into her handbag.

'The blackout is to protect Ace, Penelope. That is what the hell for,' answers Jonathan pouring wine into a glass.

'*Alex* you mean. No one calls him Ace any more,' she says almost contemptuously.

'I do,' he snaps.

I want to snap that I do too, but it seems a bit childish to do so. Toby accepts a glass of cola and scoffs.

'I said *no ice*,' he snaps. 'Christ the bloody water here is lethal, why do they put bloody ice in the glasses. I swear I'll go home with some God-forsaken disease.'

He hands it back to the waiter. Jamie and Philippe wave as they arrive at the doorway. Toby jumps from his seat and moves to the empty one next to me. I blush.

'Hello, sexy,' he whispers.

Is this what happens when you lose a few pounds?

'Do you want a sherry?' I say leaning across the table to the tray.

'Good God, no,' he says and pinches my bum. I squeal and mother snaps her head round to look at us. I pull a face and sit back down. My eyes travel to Penelope and my heart sinks when I realise I am not a patch on her. I look at her wistfully. Obviously, this is not a good thing, but I just can't help myself. Her petite little breasts almost stand to attention and that dress fits her perfectly. I bet she has no wobbly bits to worry about.

Jamie holds up a hand and asks us all to be quiet.

'I've asked you to dinner because I think we should all be updated on what's going on. Jonathan, can I hand over to you?'

Issy looks at Jonathan and goes all glassy eyed. He stands up to address us.

'Thanks Jamie. Okay, we have ourselves quite a situation and from this point on I would request that no one speaks to the press. We need to protect Bryant...'

'That is every reason why we should speak to the press,' interrupts Penelope flicking back her hair and stroking her neck with her long pink fingernails.

'We have to agree to differ on this one and I would very much appreciate it if you would not speak with them.'

'Why the hell we are protecting that bloody bully is beyond me,' snaps Toby. 'Because a bully is what he is and you're all treating him like some hero.'

'Oh Toby,' purrs Penelope. 'Don't go upsetting yourself.'
What the hell? We all look wide-eyed at her. For a brief moment she looks slightly uncomfortable.

'Toby has been through a lot, haven't you Toby? He is only trying to help,' she says defensively and Toby nods emphatically.

'He isn't a bully,' I say louder than I had planned. 'Alex, I mean,' I add, just in case anyone thinks I am referring to Toby.

'I really don't think you know Alex well enough to comment,' sneers Penelope.
I pull the sherry tray towards me. I am getting slowly pissed.

'Don't do anything rash,' Issy hisses across the table.
Why does she always imagine I am going to do something rash? What is it she expects me to do? Surely something rash would be to have mad passionate sex on the dinner table. When have I ever done that? Blimey that would be the day.

'He is a bloody bully,' repeats Toby. 'Sherry is fattening, you know that don't you?'
I grit my teeth. How dare he make comments on what I eat or drink. We've broken up haven't we?

'Oh do shut up Toby, and I think you'll find I know Alex better than you think.'
Penelope raises her eyebrows and then appraises my Laura Ashley dress and finally gives me a scathing look.

'I love your earrings by the way, are they new?' pipes up Issy, attempting to change the subject.

'They were a Christmas present from Alex,' I say quietly.

'Ooh lovely,' she gushes. 'God, they're real diamonds aren't they?'

'Do what? What did you say?' asks Toby, his ears pricking up.

Penelope snaps her head round and glares at me.

'I hate to disillusion you, but Alex would never notice a size sixteen woman, who wears floral dresses from, Evans is it, that makes big clothes for women?'

Oh, she knows how to hit below the belt. What a bitch.

'Ooh very tart. The words obviously, not the speaker,' hisses Issy.

I blush and look at the floor. I'm not a size sixteen, what a cheek. Mother takes two glasses of sherry and puts one in front of my father and the other in front of Penelope before saying,

'Well, I am sure we would all like to see things your way dear, but I'm not sure if I can stick my head that far up my arse.'

Issy snorts and I bite my lip and think how nice it is that I can't always control my mother.

'What was that you just said, Fluff?' asks my father.

'How dare you,' gasps Penelope.

'Can we please move on,' snaps Jamie.

Penelope flicks back her hair angrily and gives mother a filthy look.

'Libby and her mother...' continues Jonathan.

'Fenella,' butts in mother.

'Yes, thank you. Libby, Fenella and Issy,' he stops and nods affectionately at Issy, 'under the impression that Alex was under forced guard, attempted a rescue attempt today. It is my fault entirely I'm afraid. Alex asked me not to reveal the plans until this evening. They were not to know he was in safe hands.'

'I said to Libby, if we'd only had a gun who knows what we could have achieved...' interrupts mother.

'Yes, quite so,' jumps in Jonathan.

'Of course we both have military backgrounds and Libby is quite capable and...'

'Why she is chasing after that fuckarse leaves one to wonder,' bellows Toby.

'When a woman finds a real man...' Issy begins.

I titter.

'Oh really,' complains Penelope.

'Oh shut the fuck up,' says Toby crossly.

'I beg your pardon,' says Penelope huffily.

'No, I meant her,' he says, flustered, pointing to Issy.

'Watch your mouth Mitchell,' snaps Jonathan angrily.

'You don't want another black eye now, do you?' says Issy, grinning at him.

'That wanker got off lightly. If Libby hadn't have stopped the fight I would have knocked his bloody perverted head off.'

'Tobes, please,' begs Penelope, feigning tears.

'Sorry, Pen. He brings out the worst in me. Him and homos.'
Pen? I look to Issy who just shrugs.

'I'm a fully qualified agony aunt and even I don't understand these two,' she says, quietly.

Jamie leaps from his chair and leans across the table to grab Toby. Christ, things just get worse and worse.

'Don't you bloody touch me, you poof. Who knows where your hands have been. You faggots make me sick.'

'You're a disgusting specimen of a man,' screams Jamie, walking around the table to get to him.

'Oh dear,' moans mother. 'Do something Edmund.'

'What, oh yes. At ease chaps,' mumbles my dad.

Toby's wine glass smashes to the floor and Penelope screams as her leg is sprayed with glass. To everyone's surprise Toby grabs two bread rolls from the table and throws them at Jamie.

'Don't come any closer, I'm bloody warning you,' snarls Toby.

I stare mesmerised. Has he gone totally mad? He is so focused on Jamie that he doesn't see Jonathan step behind him. Within seconds he is pushed back into his seat.

'Don't you think you have caused enough upset?' says Jonathan quietly but there is an undertone of threat in his voice.

'Yes,' adds Issy. 'You'd better put a condom on Toby. If you're going to act like a dick you need to dress like one.'
Toby gives us all an evil look while Penelope gently pats his arm. What the hell is going on with these two?

'From this point on, I don't want any of you to speak to anyone, or even look at anyone, without talking to me first,' instructs Jonathan. 'Bryant is currently being guarded and is safe from any kidnap plots. Your rescue attempts are to be admired, however,' he smiles at us and Issy goes all weak. 'Tomorrow, Alex will leave for the studio. It is carnival day which is useful for us. We are going to use a Buddha float to get him there. Pong wouldn't dare try to get to him at the carnival.'

'I need to see him, Jonathan, so please give me the address,' snaps Penelope.

Jonathan looks uncomfortable.

'Alex has requested that I do not reveal where he is. This is for everyone's safety. You will see him tomorrow Penelope, after the broadcast.'

She throws him a dirty look. Toby grunts and edges back in his seat.

'If you all seriously believe Bryant when he says the government is corrupt, you're bloody mad. That article he wrote was crap,' he scoffs loudly.

'I'm actually in touch with the person who leaked that for Alex...'

'Oh, I just love it, do tell us more,' squeals mother, who looks as if she may wet herself any minute.

'We really don't need to know about the article,' I say quietly

'I understand that you wrote that piece, am I right Libby?' he says, smiling at me.

I nod self-consciously. Thanks very much, Jonathan.

'Well done, Libs,' cries Issy.

'She's been brainwashed, you all bloody have. I'm getting room service. Sod this.' Toby stands up and storms from the room.

'He doesn't know what he's saying,' says Penelope softly. 'I'll just check he is okay.'

We all stare in disbelief as she follows him.

'He doesn't know what he is saying, my backside. If I had thirty pieces of silver for every time I've heard that, I'd be rich,' laughs Jamie.

Issy puts her arm around my shoulder.

'I'm going to find a dark quiet alley and snog Jonathan to death, you don't mind do you?'

I shake my head.

'I shall just finish off this sherry with a fish curry, don't worry about me.'

Oh no, don't worry about me. I'm only twenty-nine, single and slightly pissed and having dinner with my parents and two poofs. Yes, that's just about the story of my life.

Chapter Twenty-Four

The five small glasses of sherry, or port, or whatever has me quite senseless that all I can do on returning to my room is fall on the bed and practically die. I am woken by the bleeping of my Blackberry. I pull it towards me sleepily and then wake up instantly when I see it is a text from Alex.

'Good cycling, by the way did I mention that? Are you angry with me? If not, do you want to come over for a coffee? Bring your bra, one never knows. Can you also get me a shirt and tie from somewhere? Alex.'

He wants to see me. I feel a surge of excitement but decide I can't go. Let's face it, I am a complete disaster area. I really should tell Penelope and let her go for coffee. After all, she is his fiancée. I text him saying he should ask her. Another text comes winging back.

'Don't be silly, she doesn't have a Wonderbra. Besides I want you to come.'

I feel a strange flutter in my stomach and jump from the bed only to feel my head throb. A shirt, where can I get a shirt? Toby certainly won't be offering one. My father has some very nice shirts but they will be too big. Disaster, disaster, what do *I* wear for coffee with Alex? I break out in a cold sweat. Obviously it will need to be practical while at the same time appealing. I can't very well wear the Laura Ashley dress now can I? I don't want to be seen either. I imagine it will need to be something dark. I finally choose a brown silk shirt and some leggings topped with a black cardigan. God, I will roast. Hopefully it will be cooler this time of night. Oh, this is so exciting that I feel sick with nerves. I tap mother's mobile number into my Blackberry. After what feels like forever she sleepily answers.

'Fenella Holmes, currently in Cambodia, how can I help you?'

Currently in Cambodia, what is she on? Currently losing the plot more like.

'Mother it is I?'

'Who?' comes her puzzled response.

'Your daughter,' I sigh.

'Libby, it is almost ten o'clock. We've just got into bed and your father...'

I think it best to stop her there.

'Alex just texted me and...'

'I'll be there in two secs,' she says, fully alert now.

I had no sooner turned the phone off when mother bursts into the room. I scream and she screams back in return.

'Why are you screaming?' I cry.

'I don't know, because you did I think.'

'Alex has asked me to have coffee with him,' I say, as if making light conversation.

She jumps up and down excitedly, then gasps and claps her hand over her mouth.

'Do you think it will be dangerous travelling there at night, with all the drug barons and everything?'

Oh my God, I hadn't thought of that.

'No, I mean I don't think so.'

'We need a gun,' she says with a determined look on her face. What is it with my mother and guns?

'If only we were at home. You could have borrowed your father's shotgun.'

I stare at her amazed.

'I didn't know father had a shotgun. In fact, I didn't know he even went shooting.'

She seems to go all glassy eyed.

'Your father does a lot of things you don't know about,' she says with a wink.

Oh, how gross is that. Not the sort of thing you want to hear about your parents.

'I have to go soon.'

'I'll cover you.'

I shake my head. My mother seems to think she is in an episode of 24.

'Don't tell anyone.'

'Of course I won't. Is the *intel* reliable? Do you know for certain it is from Alex?'

I nod but she looks at me suspiciously.

'He mentioned my Wonderbra. He's had me remove it several times,' I say proudly without thinking.

Her mouth opens. She leans towards me and plonks a kiss on my cheek.

'Well done, Libby. I couldn't have wished for better. Now, when do you leave?'

'Soon, oh and I need a shirt and tie for Alex.'

There is a light knock at the door and we stare at each other in horror.

'Who's that?' asks mother.

'How do I know?'

'Libby, baby, are you awake?'

Oh God, it is Toby. This is all I need.

'Baby?' mouths my mother.

I shrug.

'What shall I do?'

Mother's eyes widen.

'Keep him talking, I can nip to his room and steal one of his shirts.'

I shake my head frantically.

'No, you can't. I'll take one of daddy's shirts.'

'They will be far too big. Toby's will be a better fit. Keep him occupied.'

Before I can object she has opened the door.

'Toby, do come in,' she says gaily and pushes him so forcefully into the room that he trips and collides with me.

'I'll be back in a sec,' smiles mother closing the door.

I gently push him away.

'You smell lovely,' he says huskily leaning towards me again. I quickly sidestep him and he lands on the bed. Classic or what?

'I thought your mother didn't like me,' he says running his fingers through his hair. 'I'm sorry about before, you know at dinner. I thought you and I could go for a drink or something. It's still early, not that there is anywhere safe to get a sodding drink but still...'

'Well, I...'

He lunges at me and this time I don't sidestep so well. In fact I do a sort of shuffle, lose my footing and fall back onto the bed with Toby on top of me. His hands roam over my body and I shiver. What is wrong with me, this is the man I want to be engaged to isn't it?

'God, you feel so good Libby. You and I are meant to be together aren't we? We're different to that prick Alex and his girlfriend Penny...'

We are? His warm wet lips are on my neck now and his tongue is softly winding its way down my throat towards...

'Toby,' I say firmly pushing him back. 'Mother will be back any minute.'

He pulls away and looks curiously at me.

'I'm sorry I snapped earlier, it's just this bloody country. It is driving me mad,' he says softly, winding my hair around his fingers.

His other hand is on my knee and I put my own hand on top of it to stop it rising up.

'Oh Libs, let's move in together when we get back. What do you say? Give up all this writing rubbish and I'll take care of you.'

What does he mean, give up the writing rubbish? I've only just started.

'This isn't us is it, Libby? Alex Bryant and his girlfriend are in a different league to us. All this political crap, I mean, who needs it? Let's get back to our simple life in simple Fross. You can start a little baking business. We'll get engaged, that's what you want isn't it?'

Simple life in simple Fross. Baking business? Good God, is he right? Perhaps he is. I am just a simple country girl after all. Alex Bryant is a well-known hero and award-winning journalist, not to mention highly acclaimed author. He appears on TV chat shows and radio broadcasts. He is every woman's dream and probably knows it. Oh heavens, what am I doing apart from making a total fool of myself? Isn't this what I have been wanting, for Toby to ask me to get engaged and move in with him?

'Oh, Toby... I...' I stammer.

Toby mistaking it for a plea of passion pushes me back onto the bed. His hand is on my breast, squeezing and caressing it like a piece of Play Dough.

'God, this heat Libs, makes me want you so much more,' he says into my ear, his voice thick with desire while reaching for the air-conditioning switch.

I jump at the sound of knocking and attempt to get up but Toby's lips latch onto mine and I am propelled back onto the bed by lip suction.

'You know you want it,' he breathes into my ear.

'Libs, what the fuck are you doing?' screams Issy in a voice so shocked that you would think she had caught me frolicking on the bed with one of the hotel staff.

'Kissing me if you must know,' snaps Toby sitting up. 'And if you hadn't have barged in we probably would have done more,' he says zipping up his jeans noisily.

Well, I'm not so sure about that. Mother then pushes past Issy and stares open-mouthed at us. Toby straightens his clothes and it all seems terribly sordid.

'Christ, what is this, a party?' Toby grumbles.

'Well, don't go getting any ideas that it's an orgy,' Issy snaps.

Toby scoffs loudly.

'As if,' he mutters. 'I'd rather walk on hot coals.'

I don't believe this is happening. God, I will never get to Alex at this rate. Toby looks from one to the other and then heads for the door.

'Buzz my room when you are finally alone and I'll pop back,' he winks seductively and walks out.

'Yuk, I feel sick,' mumbles Issy.

I exhale loudly. What is wrong with me? Just a few days ago I would have done anything for Toby to have made a pass at me like that. Honestly, it is just typical. The man I so desperately wanted to love me now seemingly does, and I think I love someone else. Mother pushes a shirt into my hands.

'I took it from his laundry in the end. It is waiting for him in reception. He'll never miss one.'

My mother doesn't know Toby and his shirts. Issy hops from one foot to another.

'Fenella told me. Alex is the kind of man you need. Go for it. Forget about that little shit Toby.'

Mother hands me two ties.

'These are your father's. I'm sure Alex will appreciate them.'

'Does dad know you have taken these?'

She waves a hand dismissively.

'His gout is playing up. He'll hardly notice. Besides once I tell him it is all in aid of you getting off with a military man, he will be more than happy.'

'I think you are forgetting he is engaged to Penelope and he's only invited me for coffee. He probably feels bad at the way he snapped at me.'

'You mean in the way she forgets that you and Toby are an item,' says Issy lowering her eyes at me in a stern manner.

'Exactly, and it seems that Toby and I are an item again and I shouldn't even be going for coffee. He should be inviting Penelope not me.'

'Yes, of course and we all know that Alex is the kind of man who needs you to tell him what to do. He has asked *you* for coffee, now bloody go.'

Issy pushes me towards the door with mother nodding earnestly. I suppose she has a point. I accept the tube of pepper spray which mother hands me and rush downstairs to get a tuk-tuk, scratching my toes as I go.

The journey there is slower this time and I remind myself that I had bombed it on the bike. I am so nervous that my body trembles and it isn't as cool as I thought it would be so I am also perspiring for England. Alex opens the door as soon as the tuk-tuk pulls up.

'I'm glad you came,' he smiles, pulling me inside. I can feel the heat from his body. Now I feel really guilty. It isn't like I am stealing Penelope's boyfriend is it? I mean, technically nothing is going on, apart from in my mind, of course, where just about everything is going on. And it is pretty indecent inside my head, I can tell you. Most of my thoughts consist of Alex Bryant ravishing me. I find I am looking at his crotch again and feign a yawn in an attempt to tactfully avert them. Heavens I feel quite odd. The two burly men I had seen earlier move aside so I can pass through but not before giving me a cautious look.

'I'm sorry about earlier,' I say, blushing as I walk past them.

'Great bike riding by the way,' Alex compliments me.

'That wasn't what you said earlier.'

He bites his lip and lifts his eyebrows. God, I've never been more aroused in my life.

'I was angry.'

'Isn't four bodyguards a bit extreme?' I say thinking aloud.

'It's to protect me from Toby,' he says. I turn sharply to look at him.

'No, obviously not, that was a joke,' he adds quickly as though embarrassed. 'I'm sure that Pong wouldn't risk anything extreme but I don't want him or his henchmen to sabotage my TV appearance tomorrow.'

He is wearing shorts and a white tee shirt and they somehow make him look young and innocent. I lick my lips and struggle to think of something to say. All I really want to say is *would you like to ravish me now or after coffee?* But, instead I say,

'I brought some sweet sticky rice. Would you like some? Mother bought so much today.'

Good God, I manage to say that in such a sultry voice that it sounds like I am offering him my breasts on a plate. He just smiles in that handsome way that he has and I swear my G spot trembles. He looks gorgeous and not all hot and bothered like me. His hair is a bit messy and it looks like he hasn't shaved but that somehow makes him look even sexier.

'I'll have some of that water you're holding.'

I pass it to him and his hand touches my own very lightly and I stifle a little gasp as my G spot does another little dance. I shall have to sedate my loins if I go on like this. We walk into the living area which basically is an open plan lounge-diner. Through a small gap in the door I see two other men sitting at the kitchen table playing cards. They nod at me before standing up and closing the door. Alex is silent for a while and I have not got a clue what to say. Finally he speaks and I am mortified at his words.

'How is Penelope? She is here isn't she along with everyone else?' Is that exasperation in his voice?

'She is fine,' I say quietly and then stupidly add, 'Worried about you and missing you, obviously.'

He turns to glance at me.

'And you, have you missed me?'

My mouth goes dry. My heart skips a beat and my loins do their usual tremble. Honestly you would think I hadn't had sex in years, not just weeks. Now, I must give the right answer to this question. Why is it whenever I am with Alex Bryant I always find myself answering some difficult question?

'Is there a right answer to this?' I ask, grimacing.

'Most certainly,' he replies with a smile in his voice.

Now comes the difficult part. Should I tell the truth and admit that yes, I have missed him and that I felt terrible about our stupid argument. Do I even go so far as to tell him that I actually have feelings for him? Whoa, slow down Libby. Don't forget he is engaged to Penelope and he did ask after her first. Yes, but Penelope is a bitch, right, and she is making eyes at my boyfriend isn't she? But hold on, is Toby still my boyfriend? Oh God, what a time to get all confused. I remind myself that Toby and I broke up. Yes, but then again, he did come all the way to Cambodia to rescue me, not that he has done a very good job of rescuing me but he did fight Alex for me, and he did say that he realised he loved me. So, why is he coming on to Penelope, or is she coming on to him? God, I'm getting a headache. I must not forget also, that I am really not the Alex Bryant type. I mean, let's face it, he is Ace, ex-SAS officer and British hero. Who am I? Libby Holmes, boring fat woman from the country whose only claim to fame is that she blew the national grid with her vibrator usage. That makes me look more like the national slut than national heroine. Oh dear, this is not going to work. Mother will be devastated.

'I may need to phone a friend,' I reply scratching madly at my feet and gasp when I see that they are red and swollen. He glances down at them and pushes me gently onto the couch. Great. Trust me to develop chilli red feet in the middle of a romantic interlude.

'Let me look at your foot.'
Not the most romantic come on I've heard. I lift my foot and he gently places it in his lap and, oh yes, there go the fireworks in my loins. Who would have thought feet were erogenous. After studying it for a few seconds he places my foot gently on the floor and reaches into his bag where he pulls out a first aid kit. Without a word he picks the foot up again and places it gently in his lap. I've never been more aroused.

'I'm going to clean it gently and then put some antiseptic on them. I think you should take an antihistamine when I've finished.'
I think I'll need a Valium when he's finished. However, I settle for an antihistamine and swallow it with the water he hands back to me. He sits beside me and I struggle to keep my breathing even.

'Well, did you miss me?' he asks again looking directly into my eyes.
I swallow and bite my lip.

'Yes, I did,' I say softly.

'Well, that's good,' he responds brightly and would you believe moves away from me, just as I am all ready to throw myself wantonly across the couch.

'By the way,' he continues casually, 'your face is covered in those bites too.'
Oh my God, no. Bugger and piss it.

'Oh no,' I cry. 'How could you let me sit here like this without saying something?'

'I just did,' he laughs.

I fumble in my handbag for a mirror.

'Come on, it's not that bad. I happen to find you very appealing with or without the rash.' He is smiling again and my stomach does a little flip.

'You do,' I say uncomprehendingly.

'I do.'

'But Penelope...'

'It's not working with Penelope,' he interrupts. 'We discussed our relationship weeks ago. Penny is too everything I'm not, too house-proud, too intense, too status dependent. Once we started living together I could see it wasn't going to work.'

Not working? Did he really say it was *not working* with Penelope? Surely I am dreaming. I fight an overwhelming urge to phone my mother. This is surely too good to be true. Someone like Ace Bryant with me, I mean cool or what?

'But I'm overweight and not in the least sophisticated...'

'You also sometimes talk a lot of rubbish. It's a shame about your temper and that silly tendency you have to defend Toby what's-his-name, but overall I have to admit to finding you great company and those articles you wrote were brilliant by the way and the way you rode that bike, well, classic I'd say, even if a bit wobbly.'

'You saw me?'

'I did. I was less impressed with the way you greeted my friends on your arrival though.'

I see he is smiling at me and I gape at him. Backhanded compliments or what? He leans towards me and I hold my breath.

'What about you and Toby?' he asks softly.

'Oh, Toby and I...' I stammer stupidly looking past him to the window and the bright full moon.

He continues looking at me.

'He has never committed to me and now I don't really want him to.'

'Right, well if that is the case then I'm sorry but I've just got to kiss you and this time I won't pretend it is for any other reason than I want to,' he says breathlessly, moving towards me.

My loins have gone insane now, and I can't blame them. I have lost my train of thought and all I am aware of is the smell of him, that all empowering smell of danger, urgency and manliness. My hand drops to his firm thigh as my body weakens. His gaze meets mine and I am engulfed by a tidal wave of emotion and longing. God, he feels so strong, so dangerous and so deliciously sexy that I feel almost faint. His hand strokes my neck and then he pulls my head gently towards him and I feel the undercurrent of his desire bubbling below the surface. His other hand cups my cheek. Beneath my own hand his thigh seems to be trembling. His lips seem so far from mine that I feel it will be forever before they come together. The only sound is his breathing, for mine has surely stopped. His hand has moved from my cheek and is gently stroking my back. My eyes close and the moon disappears and the only sensation is his warm lips on mine, urgent and demanding, while his strong arms hold me close. I'm in heaven and I'm in love. I feel I could stay in his capable arms forever, but he gently pushes me back.

'This really isn't the place is it?' he says softly and I hear the tremor of desire in his voice.

I try to breathe normally, but it is impossible. Alex Bryant has turned me into a quivering wreck. Good Lord, I am Libby Holmes, domestic goddess no longer. I have metamorphosed into a real sex goddess. Mother won't only be proud she will most likely, for the first time in her life, be speechless, as indeed am I.

I nod and try not to let my disappointment show. He walks to the window and draws the curtains. I am about to speak when he pulls me back into his arms. The smell of him again makes me feel faint. His lips hungrily devour mine and he urgently pushes me back onto the couch pressing his body against mine. I can feel the rapid beating of his heart and feel sure it matches my own.

'I so much want you to stay here with me,' he whispers into my ear, his deep voice drowning out the sound of our thumping hearts. His hand gently pushes down the front of my top and I grasp it with my own and hold it tightly. His head snaps up and he looks at me, the desire in his eyes so fierce that it takes my breath away.

'I'm sorry,' he says softly, removing his hand but still holding onto mine. 'I'm losing control, it's not like me.'

Oh, I don't mind. I try to breathe normally but my body is not having any of it.

'Libby, these past few days spent with you have been some of the best days of my life.'

I look around the room for some divine inspiration but nothing comes and all I can manage is a loud sniff for which he produces a tissue. God, I am feeling bloody traumatised.

'Are you free New Year's Eve, or do you have a date?' he asks with a smile.

'Well, I don't know. I've been inundated with offers for that night.'

He laughs and pulls an envelope from his bag.

'Here's a ticket for the Glass Dome party. I hope no one else is taking you because I would really like to be your date.'

Oh, mother will be so happy.

'The party will be...' he stops to check his watch. 'In just over thirty-six hours. After the broadcast I have to clarify a few things at the British Embassy and I may not see you before we fly home. Promise you'll meet me under the clock in the foyer at precisely 11.45, because I have something special to ask you.'

Don't faint, at least not at this precise moment. Libby Bryant, oh fuck a duck, it actually does have a perfect ring to it doesn't it? Mother will do her Dance of the Peacocks when she hears about this. Yes, well best not to think about that. Meet him under the clock. Ooh it sounds like something out of a 1940s film. I attempt to flick my hair back in the manner of Rita Hayworth but fail miserably as most of it is stuck to my neck. Let's face it, the hair, stuck to your neck and chin look, is most decidedly my own very unique style.

'Synchronise watches,' I say flippantly.

'Copy that,' he responds with a smile.

It is all I can do to stop myself from throwing my hot sweaty body on top of his. The muscles in his arms seem to ripple and I feel a shiver of desire run through me. He kisses me softly on the lips.

'You drive me crazy, Libby, you really do.'

Me, Libby Holmes, drives Alex-*slice-your-tongue-out*-Bryant crazy? Heavens, it must be something they put in that sticky rice. I've never driven anyone crazy in my life, apart from my mother of course.

'Promise to meet me under the clock?'

'I promise.'

Ooh, doesn't this sound a bit like we are exchanging wedding vows?

He turns his head as shouts from outside reach us. Oh no, why does this always happen to me? I jump from the couch and prick up my ears. I then hear a familiar voice and feel my stomach lurch. I close my eyes and sigh in exasperation. I know I wanted to be chased but this is now taking things too far. Talk about having romance backfire on you. I quickly straighten my clothes aware that Alex is looking intently at me.

'Did you tell him you were coming here?' he asks, almost accusingly.

'Of course not,' I say defensively.

Oh this is awful, why are we now acting so cross with each other?

'Libby, Libby, where are you?' calls Toby.

I look at Alex who is shaking his head.

'I don't believe this,' he says angrily, storming towards the door.

'Don't hurt him,' I hear myself say and regret the words immediately they are said. Why do I make the same mistake over and over again?

He glares at me and flings open the door. In the light of the moon I can see Toby struggling stupidly with one of the men while the other looks on.

'Toby, why are you here,' I say as forlornly as I feel.

'I should be asking you the same question,' he yells.

'She was invited. The question is, what are you doing here?' Alex barks. 'You're becoming an irritant to me.'

'Alex,' I gasp.

How can he be so horrible? He looks at me and shakes his head. The man holding Toby frees him and Toby falls to the floor with a moan. I run and help him up.

'Toby why did you come here,' I whisper softly.

Oh, this is just so awful and how could Alex be so loving one minute and then brutally angry the next? Perhaps this isn't the man for me after all. Toby rubs his back and then links his arm through mine.

'I thought you were coming to meet me. I was curious to see where you were going. I didn't think you were coming to see him. You surely don't want him do you Libby. He's just a know-it-all wanker? He's marrying Penny anyway...'

'No he isn't,' I respond quicker than I mean to.

'Well, Penny is pretty convinced he is. Anyway, I thought you loved me Libby. You and I go together, like... spotted dick and custard.'

'Spotted dickhead more like,' says Alex with a scoff.

Can it get any worse?

'Toby, I...'

'Earlier at the hotel you gave the impression you wanted me as much as I wanted you.' He sniffs and I see his nose is bleeding. This is terrible, what kind of people does Alex have guarding him?

'Did they hit you?' I ask, staring angrily at the men. 'Did you hit him?' I demand while Alex shakes his head in exasperation. How dare he do that and how dare he have his men beat up Toby.

'They are protecting me, Libby. What are they supposed to do?'

'They're bullies and so are you,' I say fiercely, while at the same time wanting to hug him. Oh this is just awful. What the hell am I saying? I love Alex, not Toby. What am I doing?

'So, you think I'm a bully do you? You seriously think I told my bodyguards to beat up your boyfriend?'

'I... I don't know,' I stammer, wishing I could just start all over again.

'It seems we are both under some misapprehension here. I'm sorry if I misunderstood.'

With that he slams the door shut. Oh no, now what do I do?

'I banged it Libs, in the tuk-tuk,' mumbles Toby. 'These dirt tracks are unbloodybelievable. Why don't they have decent sodding roads here?'

'What?' I cry. 'You banged your nose in the tuk-tuk, why didn't you say so?'

'I just did. Come on Libs, let's go back to the hotel and get a drink. I need one, I don't know about you. Leave him to sulk. He's an idiot. You don't seriously like him do you? He's getting married in a few weeks.'

Alex lied to me. How could he? He was using me just like Toby. I hate him. In fact I hate all men. I'm going to become a lesbian. Jamie will be able to advise me. Bugger everything. I wouldn't go out with him now if he were the last man on earth. Oh God, my love life is turning into an Austen novel with misunderstandings all over the place. Finally Toby has realised what he has in me and now I'm quite sure I don't want Toby. What irony.

***

I fly towards the mini bar like a demented woman. Not for the alcohol you understand. I know things are crappy in my life but they're not that bad. My face is itching like crazy and is so hot that I feel like it must be on fire. I pull out a bottle of Smirnoff and a can of lager.

'Christ Libby. We could have had a drink at the bar. Far more dignified,' says Toby standing in the doorway.

I slap the lager tin onto my hot itchy foot and sigh. The vodka bottle I hold against my cheek and flop onto the bed. Toby is beside me before I can say 'sticky rice'.

'Libs, I know I've been a fool with Serena and I promise you that's over,' he says prizing the bottle out of my hand and struggling with the top. He finally flips it off, spilling vodka onto the bedspread.

'I don't know what came over me. I think I temporarily lost...'

'Your sanity?' I mutter.

My room will smell like a bloody brewery. He pours the liquid into glasses.

'My perspective, that's what I lost,' he continues. 'I had shit going on. Anyway, you'll be pleased to know that you are much better at it than she is and...'

I jump from the bed.

'Oh, I'm thrilled Toby. Precisely what things am I better at?'

'No, what I mean... Oh, fuck it Libs,' he squirms. 'You're better than her in every way.'

I just want him to leave so I can close the door and dive under the covers. Why am I so stupid? What is wrong with me? For the second time I have blown things with Alex. He isn't going to give me another chance. He must think me so weak and silly. Damn it.

Toby is stroking my hand and it is just another unbearable sensation.

'You don't really like that prick do you? You and I are a million miles from them two. We don't mix in their world. We're simple people, you and I.'

Speak for yourself, Toby.

'I love you Libs. I've always loved you. I will make you really happy, just wait and see. Let's get engaged Libs. That's what you want isn't it?'

So, here I am. Everything going just the way I had planned. My boyfriend Toby is asking me to marry him. Everything is going swimmingly to plan. So, why do I feel like I am drowning?

Chapter Twenty-Five

Jonathan has called a meeting. I really couldn't care less. I just want to go home. What a fool I am. What was I thinking of, accusing Alex of having Toby beaten up? He could quite easily do that himself without asking heavies to do it. I can't believe I said it. Mother also can't believe I said it, and I expect Issy won't believe I said it either when I tell her. Someone kill me before I completely wreck my love life, such as it is. To make matters even direr, if that were at all possible, it seems Toby and I are now officially engaged. Why do these things happen to me? More importantly, *how* do these things happen to me? I never actually said yes to Toby's proposal, but if I did I certainly don't remember doing so. I spent most of last night with my head in the mini bar. Not drinking from it, you understand, but just to cool my face down. I was so hot and upset after Toby left, that the rash on my face and feet just went kind of insane. I order a coffee and sit miserably looking out of the window at the carnival preparations. Everyone is smiling. They must think me such a miserable cow. Issy bounces into the dining room, spots me and dives over.

'Hey, how did it go with Alex?'

I open my mouth to respond but she launches into an exuberant description of her evening with Jonathan. I sit quietly drinking my coffee feeling the tears well up. She stops and looks closely at me.

'Oh, no what happened? You didn't blow it?'

I nod miserably.

'Bollocks,' she exclaims.

'Toby came and caused a scene and I accused Alex of beating him up. He then said he was under some misapprehension about us and slammed the door and now I'm covered in this sodding rash and seemingly engaged to Toby. At least he thinks we're engaged.'

'Bloody hell Libs, I don't know how you do it. I really don't. I must say that rash looks rather awful.'

Terrific.

She follows my eyes to the door where Toby has just walked in.

'Fuck-a-luck-a-ding-dong, here is the very wanker himself,' she mumbles.

He grabs a passing waiter, talks to him in an agitated manner and then walks towards us.

'Ah, you're up,' he says to me and then to Issy. 'Whatever you do, don't eat the eggs, I've already complained about them this morning. I had room service last night and the pork chops I ordered must have been off. I had stomach pain all night. I swear they don't wash their hands here.'

He gestures to the waiter.

'Have you looked into it yet?' he snaps.

'We are looking into it now sir,' he answers in clear English.

'They've only bloody stolen my shirt. I tell you, these people. Bloody thieves the lot of them.'

I lower my eyes. At that moment my parents walk in followed by Jamie. Mother wafts over to me in a mist of 'Joy' perfume.

'Libby, darling, I just knocked on your door.'

She kisses me on the cheek and whispers in my ear.

'There's been uproar over Toby's shirt and Jonathan has called a meeting.'

She's got to be joking.

'We're having a meeting because Toby's shirt has gone missing, for God's sake,' says Issy.

'I'll have you know that was a Ralph Lauren shirt and one of my best,' snaps Toby.

Jonathan walks in and I swear Issy goes as soft as the runny egg that has just been placed in front of her. She looks at Jonathan hungrily.

'You're mad if you eat that,' remarks Toby.

'It looks very appetising to me,' she says, unable to take her eyes off Jonathan.

'Hello,' he says as he takes the seat opposite her.

Once Penelope arrives Jonathan begins the meeting. To my relief the meeting has nothing whatsoever to do with Toby's shirt. He informs us that Alex is fine and that the television interview will take place later today. He has arranged for us to watch the interview in the television lounge at the studio. Toby is not at all happy about this.

'I hope you're going to arrest the bugger after all this is over. I would like it known here and now that I am not happy in how he has behaved towards my fiancée,' Toby bellows.

'Toby,' I shriek.

'Fiancée?' echoes mother in a high-pitched voice.

'Saints alive,' says my stunned father.

'And when did this engagement take place?' Issy asks.

'She's simply doing her job,' chips in Jamie.

'Part of her job is becoming engaged to Toby? Well, I must say, I don't approve of that,' says mother sternly.

'I, of course, meant that spending time with Alex was part of her job. Who she gets engaged to is entirely her own business,' sighs Jamie.

'I am here you know,' I say in a 'sing-song' voice, but everyone ignores me.

'We're getting engaged as soon as we return home if you must know,' Toby addresses everyone.

We are? Shouldn't I be delighted? Wasn't this what I wanted? So, why am I wishing my name was not Libby?

'I love Libby. I know I've made some mistakes but I know she wants to start again.'

I shrink into my chair.

'Libby is this right?' asks mother.

'Well, I...'

'Of course it's right, why are you asking her when I just told you?' snaps Toby.

Not the way to get on my mother's good side.

'Toby, I think we should...' I begin but Penelope interrupts.

'Do you know Toby has had a Ralph Lauren shirt taken from his room?' she announces.

And one wonders why she should be so worried about that.

'I don't think there is anyone who doesn't know that,' Jamie replies sarcastically.

'It wasn't taken from his room,' I say defensively and get a kick in the shin from mother.

'Surely, it wasn't was it? Was it taken from your room Toby?' I add, feigning innocence.

'Actually, it was stolen from my laundry,' corrects Toby. 'You can't trust the buggers in this place.'

Penelope gives me an odd look.

'It's bad enough they bloody poison you with their stinking food without stealing from you too,' Toby sulks.

'I think we should make something of a fuss,' says Penelope assuming control.

'Thanks Pen,' says Toby laying his hand on her arm.

'I'll look into it,' Jonathan offers. 'Meanwhile if you could all make arrangements to check out of the hotel tomorrow. We will fly home tomorrow afternoon, unless you have any objections. I really want to get Alex out of the country ASAP. Obviously if any of you want to stay, then that is entirely up to you.'

'It won't be a day too soon for me,' remarks Toby.

'We may stay on, isn't that right Edmund. We've just bought a three-day pass to see the temples you see,' says my mother.

'More fool you,' says Toby dryly.

'I'll be glad to get out of here too. I've barely eaten,' complains Penelope.

'You look good on it,' comments Toby looking at her admiringly. Isn't he engaged to me? She smiles at him sweetly and turns to Jamie.

'I wonder Jamie, do you think I should go on the television tonight, you know to put over our perspective. A kind of *what it's been like for the families*?'

She draws the heading in the air and smiles innocently. I raise my eyebrows to Jamie. Mother sniggers and whispers, 'I'm glad she's not part of *our* family, I'd have to put her up for adoption.'

Jamie looks uncomfortable.

'Well...'

'It's been very difficult for some of us not knowing...' she stops to do a little hiccup and dabs at her eyes.

'Quite,' agrees Toby.

'It's not been easy. The food for a start, and I've really struggled in the heat and the malaria tablets have made me feel very unwell and it is very difficult to find the right clothes when you have to keep your shoulders covered. It's not an easy country to be in, but it is because our loved ones are in difficulty...'

'Quite,' repeats Toby.

God, I wish I had a violin, or even better, a sick bag.

'Why are you taking malaria tablets?' Issy asks popping the final piece of egg into her mouth to the disgust of Toby.

'Yes, I was wondering that,' agrees Jamie.

She looks appalled.

'Because we're in Cambodia of course.'

'Of course,' I say sarcastically. 'Except in this part of Cambodia, there is no malaria.'

'Don't be ridiculous, of course there is malaria,' asserts Toby.
Christ, whose side is he on?

'And I haven't really felt well since I've been here,' continues Penelope as though we'd never spoken. 'And of course, there are no proper doctors here. I do hope Jamie, that when we finally do get home, you assign Alex a different agent.'
Where did that come from? Is it my fault she hasn't felt well since being here? Jamie looks harassed, poor dear. Hopefully Philippe will be able to ease some of that tension a bit later.

'That will be for Alex to decide,' he replies wearily while answering his mobile.

'I assure you when I speak for Alex that is exactly what I do. I know what he needs. What he does not need is that Libby girl. If she hadn't have cried wolf at the beginning of this fiasco we wouldn't be having any of this. Poor Alex feels obligated to look after her and, let's face it, that's a full-time job.'
What a prize bitch.

'I'm going to sort out my bloody shirt,' Toby says and stomps off. Penelope stands up.

'I should go and pack,' she says innocently. 'I also have loads of emails to write. Wedding preparations and such like,' she adds, throwing a glance at me.
So, Toby was right. They are getting married. Alex Bryant is nothing but a lying toad. He used me. How could I have been such a fool?

'That was the studio, they want you there too, Libby. Alex said it was you who wrote the article,' says Jamie, clicking off his phone.
Oh dear.

'Toby won't like this,' Issy grins.

'You can travel with Alex, it will be safer,' mumbles Jonathan as he taps into his phone.
Issy is quite right. Toby won't like this at all.

Issy

'What the fuck?' says Toby.

We stare fascinated as the Buddha travels towards us. It is pulled through the streets of Siem Reap by an elephant. People have surrounded it, walking at the side and behind. I can't help wondering if they are aware that Alex and Libby are inside. Toby is looking rather dapper if I do say so myself, shame his language doesn't match his neat demeanour. He looks rather like an upper-crust British gentleman. Except, of course he isn't a gentleman and not upper-crust. We are standing outside the studio and finally get a glimpse of what we have been waiting for. The smell of Cambodian fare wafts past and my stomach rumbles. I glance at Penelope who stands next to Toby, her eyes riveted on the Buddha. The street traders have left their wares and stand with us, their eyes focused on the colourful floats travelling towards us. Giant brightly coloured lanterns pass by. It is a day of colour, smiles and enchanting magic and for a few minutes it is easy to forget about the corrupt government and why Alex is giving his interview. I clap my hands loudly in appreciation of the beautiful puppets and throw coins into the bags that are being held out to us. Many of the motorcyclists have stopped and dozens of the tuk-tuk drivers are following the elephant and Buddha to help it travel safely to its destination. Penelope's eyes are locked on the parade and I think I see her hand tremble as she gently twirls the parasol she is holding. She certainly looks remarkable in a silk shirt over a pair of casual, but very expensive, slacks. A string of pearls stroke her throat and a collection of bangles adorn her slim wrists. She is certainly the perfect showpiece for Alex to carry on his arm. Earlier she had been talking earnestly on her phone and I could only guess it was Alex. Standing next to Toby, I can't help thinking what a pair they make. They look like a couple of aristocrats. They only look it, mind you, as Toby has a hell of a way to go before he ever reaches that status. Jonathan's hand slips into mine and I feel a warm glow.

'Hopefully this broadcast will clarify everything and we can go home,' he whispers into my ear and I shudder. I know what I am going to have for my dessert this evening.

The crowd are surging towards the Buddha and Fenella gasps. Two policemen approach the elephant and I point them out to Fenella.

'It's okay,' I tell her. 'The police are here.'

But they walk straight past the elephant and the surging crowds and head toward us.

'Sir, excuse me?' one asks Toby. Penelope turns and knocks his hat off with her parasol.

'What have you been up to then darling?' Jamie asks with a snigger.

'Shut it arse licker,' Toby snaps. All images of an upper-crust British aristocrat are shattered. 'Where's your perverted little Filipino then? You're sure it isn't him that's in trouble.'

'What's going on?' asks Fenella as though everyone around her is speaking a foreign language.

I shake my head.

'Is it about the shirt? I bloody hope so. Have you found the bugger who nicked it?' asks Toby.

'Been harassing men have you Toby?' tuts Jamie. 'Shame on you dear.'

There is a great deal of noise as the Buddha gets closer to the television studio.

'We need to ask you some questions,' one policeman says firmly while the other is removing handcuffs from his pocket. Good God, what is going on?

'Oh my,' cries Fenella on seeing the handcuffs. She steps back and is grabbed by one of the policeman.

'No one leaves,' he growls.

Bollocks. What the hell is going on?

'Now hold on a minute,' I shout above the noise.

Jonathan puts a protective arm around my shoulders and with the other gently removes the policeman's hand from Fenella's arm.

'We're here for the broadcast. We are all here with Alex Bryant.'

I stare open-mouthed. I thought the broadcast was top secret, that no one knew about the Buddha only us. What is he doing? I pull myself from his comforting arm and turn to face him angrily.

'What are you doing? I thought Alex said we were not to tell anyone he was going to broadcast.'

'Alex announced it to a British national newspaper himself, about ten minutes ago. He knows what he's doing.'

I look hungrily at the comforting arm I had just shrugged off. He smiles indulgently at me and wraps it back around me. Suddenly there is uproar and we all look in horror as the Buddha seems to wobble. People are pushing towards it. They are attempting to touch it or kiss it. The elephant seems to stumble. There is so much noise that I cannot hear myself think. I spy Libs through a gap in the curtain of the Buddha and go to wave but I am ushered inside.

'Quick, come in,' shouts a voice from the door of the studio.

Jonathan guides me through the doorway where I collide with Toby in his rush to get inside. Jonathan roughly pushes him to one side and gestures for Fenella, me and Penelope to hurry through. We are followed by Jamie and Edmund. Toby finally follows us. The doors are locked and bolted as soon as we are all inside.

'Thank God for that,' says Toby breathing heavily.

'They'll come back,' advises Jonathan. 'What was all that about anyway?'

Toby shrugs.

'No idea.'

Penelope is demanding a jug of water.

'Not from the tap either. Bring me bottled water *and no ice*.'

We are directed to a stiflingly hot and stuffy lounge. Penelope demands air conditioning and fans herself with a small silk fan.

'I feel quite faint,' she tells Toby.

In front of us are glass panels which look straight into the studio. There are three chairs and three microphones. A short Cambodian man is seated in one chair and is testing the equipment.

'It's so terribly exciting isn't it?' squeals Fenella fanning herself with Edmund's handkerchief.

'I sense trouble afoot,' Edmund says dryly to Jonathan, while cocking his head towards the door.

'I fear you may be right,' agrees Jonathan.

Toby has removed his hat and looks more relaxed. Penelope leans across to say something to him and he laughs loudly, throwing his head back. My phone bleeps. It's a text from Libs.

'*Marjorie Proops, I need you.*'

I dash from the overpoweringly hot room and ask where the loo is. The dingy little room I am shown to is so dark I can barely see the small hole in the ground. I lock the door and phone Libs.

'Oh Issy, I don't know what to do,' she cries.

'What is it what's wrong?'

She hiccups loudly and I move the phone from my ear.

'I'm in love with Alex. He hasn't said one word to me. How can I tell if he wants me? Toby has asked me to marry him and I just don't know what to do. No one has ever asked me to marry them before. What shall I do? I'm not sure I love Toby any more. Oh God it is a mess.'

I go to sit on the toilet seat forgetting there isn't one and fall straight to the floor with a thump.

'Bollocks.'

Why does everyone ask me what they should do? How the hell do I know? Anyone would think I was Marjorie Proops. I'm probably the worst agony aunt on earth.

'When did he...' I begin and then realise she has been cut off.

Chapter Twenty-Six

The big Buddha we are travelling in has an odd smell that I can't quite define. It is musty with an oriental fragrance. It reminds me of the herb garden back at the monastery. I find myself craving to be back there. It was so lovely then and Alex was attentive. Why did I have to spoil everything? I clutch my bag tightly to me and take a deep breath to try and calm my racing heart. I think I know how Princess Diana felt when she was bombarded by a mass of fans and photographers. If I only I looked just a little like Princess Diana, then I wouldn't mind climbing out of the Buddha. Knowing that I look like Worzel Gummidge, however, makes the prospect of alighting a rather daunting one. Alex has not spoken the whole journey and the silence has been unbearable. I so wish he would say something. I lift my eyes to look at him and see he is tense and pensive. I find the noise and the banging on the outside of the Buddha rather alarming. We are supposed to be being transported in secret. Colonel Pong has roadblocks all around Siem Reap but not even Pong would stop a Buddha on a cart. It is the 'wanted man's vehicle of choice' Jonathan had said. Several times it has rocked and tipped sideways as the cart negotiated the uneven roads. I look anxiously at Alex but he is lost in thought. I blow a stream of air into my fringe to help cool my flushed face. It must be thirty-five degrees in the Buddha. I feel like I am in a sauna and my thin cotton dress is not keeping me cool. My hair sticks to my neck and perspiration runs between my breasts. This is just marvellous isn't it? Especially, as everyone is waiting at the studio for us. How typical, that when I have at last lost some weight and finally have a chance to be something of a celebrity, I have to step out of my chariot looking like I've stepped out of a sauna. I peek through the back curtain to see the mass of hysteria just feet away. It is one massive blur of people, tuk-tuks hooting like crazy and families huddled close on motorbikes. Good God, is that a pig, surely not? I pull the curtains and look at Alex who is on his phone. I retrieve mine from my handbag and text Issy. I try to get her advice on how to talk to Alex but my phone cuts out as soon as we start talking. I feel slightly sick, partly from the heat and also with fear. The Buddha seems to be wobbling so much that I am having difficulty keeping my bum on the small bench.

'I will talk to you later, Pen,' Alex is saying loudly. 'We have a lot to discuss but I'm not prepared to do it now.'

What is he planning to talk to her about? Will he talk to her about me? Is he going to tell her that it is over between them? It won't be because of me. I'm quite sure of that. He has barely looked at me and the only words that have passed his lips were 'Hello' when I arrived at the house. He has said nothing to me since. I feel so wretched. Penelope will no doubt look fabulous and greet us in the manner of Grace Kelly. Any hopes I had of alighting from this thing in the manner of Victoria Beckham have been well and truly dashed. What if there are photographers? Good Lord, I need to do something. If only I could pour myself a glass of Chardonnay, or even polish off a bottle. I never actually had dreams of appearing in *Hello* magazine but if I am going to I would much prefer to look sloshed than like a drowned rat. It is considered altogether rather cool to be photographed while sloshed when being a celebrity isn't it? I swallow the next best thing, half the contents of a bottle of water. The Buddha rocks and I'm thrown off the bench. I give a little strangled cry and land at Alex's feet. Was this what Madam Zigana had predicted? The front of my dress is now soaked from the water. It could only happen to me. His strong arms pull me up and plonk me beside him.

'Almost there,' he says gently.

'I look like I've wet myself,' I say miserably.

He gives me a weak smile.

'Toby has asked me to marry him,' I say. God knows why I say that.

He scoffs.

'I hope you will both be very happy. A romantic proposal was it?'

Why is he so hateful? I pull a hairbrush from my bag.

'At least it was one,' I say stiffly, throwing the brush back irritably when I realise my hair is too damp to brush.

I retrieve my perfume and spray myself with Rive Gauche, the familiar fragrance calming me.

215

'I love that smell,' he says softly and edges his hot body closer. I feel my heart dance, while my mind reels. Why doesn't he reassure me that everything is okay with us? Why doesn't he ask me not to marry Toby? Doesn't he care? I feel inclined to become celibate when I get home. I shall lose even more weight and get my hair cut into one of those shaggy wild styles like Meg Ryan. I'll go to the gym every day, well maybe every other day, and I'll exfoliate so much that my skin will glow. I shall then just use men and discard them like old shoes. I'll drive them mad sexually until they beg for release and...

'Libby?'

I am pulled from my daydream. The Buddha has stopped and the noise from outside is deafening. People are shouting and bells are ringing. He looks deeply into my eyes, and if it wasn't for the perspiration dripping into mine, I may have been able to have looked into his. I feel myself sway with the heat and my head is now thumping.

'Look at me,' I cry. 'I look terrible and I am so scared.'

'I have been assured that everything is safe. And as far as I am concerned you look fabulous,' he says wiping the tears from my cheeks.

'But...'

'We should go.'

There is a knock and the Buddha shakes as the curtains are pulled aside. I feel myself tremble. Alex runs his fingers through his hair and stretches. It is all I can do to stop myself from throwing my hot sweaty body on top of his. The muscles in his arms seem to ripple and I feel a shiver of desire run through me.

'Don't be afraid. I won't let anyone hurt you and whatever anyone else tells you, always remember, your writing is superb,' he whispers.

'Alex,' I begin, but the noise of the crowd drowns out my voice. The sudden brightness dazzles us. The cool air on my face is so wonderful that I almost cry with relief. The people are going crazy, waving, cheering and surging towards us. The strong smell of sizzling pork reaches my nostrils and I feel myself sway slightly with overwhelming nausea.

'Aleeeeex, Aleeeex,' they are shouting and I shake my head in disbelief. The man truly is a hero. After climbing from the Buddha he reaches out a hand to grasp mine. Samnang is waiting to greet us and I am happy to see a friendly face.

'The news went live about fifteen minutes ago,' he informs us. 'People have been going crazy ever since.'

People reach out to touch Alex. He climbs on a platform where a mike is handed to him. A loud screech emanates from it.

'Come with me,' shouts Samnang. 'You have less than ten minutes.'

I tear my eyes from Alex and allow myself to be directed to a small washroom where I am able to straighten my hair. The crowd are silent and all I can hear is Alex's commanding voice. I look at myself in the dirty cracked mirror of the equally dirty washroom and think what a 'fantabulous' place Cambodia is. I hurry back to Samnang who guides me to the studio. Alex joins us after a few minutes. Through a glass window I can see my mother with Toby, Penelope, Jamie and Jonathan. Toby looks worked up about something with his finger pointing at Alex. I turn my chair away from Toby and look at Alex fiddling with his headphones. I then realise what Toby is flapping about. I had totally forgotten all about the shirt. Oh dear.

Issy

Toby looks like he is about to have a fit. He seems unable to speak and everything that comes out of his mouth is garbled gibberish. He points at Alex with a shaking finger. Jesus, I just hope he doesn't start another fight here in the studio. Libs' pheromones must be in overdrive these days. Toby fights to find his voice and finally shrieks,

'He's wearing my shirt. The bastard nicked my shirt.'

We stare at Toby's shirt which is straining against Alex's firm muscular chest. It looks to me as if the buttons are about to pop off.

'He has more muscle than you though doesn't he Toby,' I hear myself say. I bite my lip realising the last thing we need is for Toby to go into a real frenzy.

'Where, I mean, who? What the...' he stutters and we wait with bated breath.

'How the fuck did he get my shirt?' he whines. 'Who the fuck does he think he is? First he tries to steal my girlfriend and then my bloody shirt. Christ, he'll be stealing my fucking identity next.'

I don't think so, Toby boy.

'I'm quite sure he's not trying to steal your girlfriend,' says Penelope stiffly. To prove her point she blows a sickly kiss to Alex through the glass.

Toby paces up and down like a tiger, giving Alex an occasional two finger salute.

'Oh, do grow up Toby,' snaps Fenella.

He continues to glare at Alex.

'I want him arrested when all this is over.'

A light goes on to tell us to be quiet. We all stare mesmerised as Alex is given his cue and the interview begins. Just as it does, the two men we had escaped from earlier enter the room and sit quietly at the back. Fenella grasps my hand tightly.   .

'Oh dear,' she mutters.

Libby on the other side of the glass looks equally concerned. The only person riveted by the interview and grinning from ear to ear is Jamie. The crowd outside are cheering. Alex is certainly the hero of the day.

'The book will sell like wildfire now. I'll need to set up more TV appearances when we get home. I might even see if I can get a book out with both Libby and Alex's perspective on the Cambodian trip,' Jamie gushes.

Meanwhile Penelope is giving Libs daggers. God, I will be so relieved to get home. As Alex's interview finishes, the two men move menacingly towards us. Fenella waves frantically to Libby as though pleading for help but Libs has gone. What follows is like something out of a nightmare. I try to be calm but there is so much shouting and jabbering that I think I will go mad. More police arrive and everything goes crazy. Libs bursts in and demands to know what is happening. Someone mentions drugs. Oh bollocks. What if this is like Bangkok? Jesus, we will all get the death sentence. Fenella is shouting how this is frightful and that she will contact her MP when she gets home. Shit, how will we get lawyers here? Jonathan stands on a chair and shouts there has been a terrible mistake as I am dragged away. I wonder if I will ever see him again. We are handcuffed and thrown into the back of a van. Jonathan shouts that all will be okay but I don't feel very confident. Libby is shell-shocked and nothing I say helps. Toby wraps her in his arms and she doesn't push him away. Where the hell is Alex Bryant? Madam Zigana never mentioned this, and if she did it was bloody cryptic. I only hope I get home to tell her she spun us a load of bollocks.

Chapter Twenty-Seven

I don't think my Wonderbra is going to be much use in this situation. Talking of which, where the hell is Alex?

'This is disgraceful,' cries mother, rattling her handcuffs madly at the little hatch between us and the driver.

'Do you hear me?' she shouts. 'Disgraceful! Just wait until my MP hears about this.'

Her coiffured hair is plastered to her face, and her foundation has streaked down onto her neck making her look like an Apache Indian. Oh dear. I hand her a Kleenex and point to her neck. She groans in despair and dabs at it.

'That's if you ever get out of here to write to your MP,' wails Issy.

'Kilimanjaro was never like this was it dear? They don't have politics there.'

Father nods. Penelope sobs silently and Toby puts a comforting arm around her. Charming, shouldn't he be comforting me? Although I have to say he was very comforting amidst that hideous uproar of earlier.

'My wrists are swelling up, look, they are all puffy,' sobs Penelope. 'It's these handcuffs. I don't do cheap metal, I'm allergic to cheap. Anything cheap brings me out in a rash.'

'I'd demand the nine-carat, diamond-encrusted ones if I were you,' scoffs Issy. 'I'm sure they have a pair for celebrities and stuck-up bitches.'

I cringe.

'Oh dear,' mumbles mother.

'Chin up, Fluff,' cheers my father who is obviously in denial.

'But drugs, I mean, holy shit,' wails Issy. I wonder if I should slap her. I'm only hoping that Penelope doesn't get hysterical and I'll have to slap her too. If I slap her there is a good chance a cat fight may ensue and that would be all we need. I am seriously having doubts about Alex-*won't-let-anyone-hurt-you*-Bryant. Where the hell is he?

'Will you shut up Issy,' hisses Jamie.

'Is it like Bangkok here?' she asks in a trembling voice. 'Will they shoot us?'

Penelope shudders.

'They need proof that we are involved in drugs and they don't have any do they?' I say sounding more confident than I feel.

'I want to know where that poofy little boyfriend of yours has got to,' growls Toby.

Jamie hangs his head.

'Do you think he is involved in something?' Issy asks.

'I haven't seen him since yesterday afternoon. He went to visit a friend in the city.'

'Sodding shirt-lifter, he is probably going to get us life,' yells Toby.

'Jesus,' I mumble.

'It will be okay Libs, I'm sure it will,' Toby says while moving from Penelope and putting a comforting arm around me.

I feel myself lean into him, although I am desperately missing Alex. Where did he go? More importantly *why* did he go? He must have seen what happened to us. If he's been arrested too then there is no hope for us. There is absolutely no one to help us.

If I thought the van was bad, prison is even worse. We have our personal belongings taken from us and are frisked down by a mean-looking guard before being herded like cattle into our tiny cells. It's nearly as bad as a flight with EasyJet. I swear there are cockroaches in our cells. Issy is thrown into a cell with my mother while Jamie, Toby and my father are thrown into another and, disaster of disasters I am thrown into one with Penelope who makes claim to the top bunk without even asking me.

'I'll have you all fired, do you hear me? Do you have any idea who I am?' Penelope yells while shaking the prison bars.

'Shit, shit, my nail,' she sobs, flapping her hand around.

'I don't imagine nail files are essential in here,' shouts Issy. 'Although I'm sure once they realise who you are, they will send a manicurist in.'

Penelope flops onto the hard mattress.

'Oh God, did you see things moving on there,' she screams while pointing at my mattress.

I find myself staring at her enviously. How does she manage to look so good? Here we all are in some flea-infested pit and even my mother is looking the worse for wear but Penelope just seems to come up smelling of roses. Now I come to think about it, isn't that a bit like Alex? No matter what the situation he always manages to look fabulous. I always manage to look like I have just dragged myself out of bed the morning after a wild night of partying. Toby is quite right. They are in a completely different league to us

'I'm sure we won't be in here too long,' says Penelope, seeming calmer. 'After all, Jonathan will contact the British Embassy and they will have us out in no time.'

She couldn't have been more wrong. Hours pass and what small amount of light there was coming through the tiny window quickly diminishes. Dim lights illuminate our new home. Our cells are next to each other, in a line off a corridor like carriages in an old-fashioned train. It is quiet, apart from a dripping noise and although we can't see the other cells we can hear each other as clear as anything.

'We're going to die in here,' Issy sobs.

We all go silent at the sound of rattling keys and slow footsteps. A guard pushes two bowls of rice and some very suspicious looking meat into our cell. But most appealing of all are the bottles of water.

'Don't eat it,' yells Toby as if the food has been laced with arsenic. 'And whatever you do, don't drink the fucking water.'

'I've been bitten,' moans Jamie.

A bang from outside makes me jump, sending the rice flying off my plate into Penelope's lap.

'You did that on purpose,' she hisses.

'I did not.'

'Oh my God, was that a firing squad. Oh Jesus, they are going to shoot us. They do that to drug dealers don't they?' groans Issy.

'It came from the street outside. I don't think they have public executions any more,' says Toby, who I imagine is gagging at the sight of the rice.

'How do you know?' hisses Issy. 'They are probably going to make an example of us. The whole world will watch our execution.'

'Do you think?' asks Penelope suddenly brightening up.

I stare at her. Jesus, is she bizarre or what? She'll be asking for a hair stylist next.

'It was probably a car backfiring,' says Toby.

'Are you sure?' squeals Issy.

Good God. I don't know how much more I can take. In fact, much more of this and I will shoot Issy myself.

'This food has been poisoned, I'm sure of it,' whines Toby.

'I read a book once about a prison in Asia and how they got people to confess to smuggling drugs. It was…' begins mother, in a haunting voice.

'Don't tell us, please don't tell us,' pleads Issy.

'I'm going to drink the water,' I announce. I am unable to control my thirst any longer.

'No,' shouts Toby. 'Don't drink that.'

I gulp down half the contents of the bottle.

'Shit, Libby, do you have a death wish or something?' mumbles Jamie.

'You can shut your homosexual mouth,' Toby shouts.

God, I hope I die soon if things are going to continue like this.

'You're so attractive when you're angry,' purrs Jamie.

'You bloody keep away from me, you fucking pervert,' Toby screams.

Penelope slides down from her bunk and onto mine, sending the rest of the water down the front of my dress. Damn, that's all I need. At least I can't drink any more I suppose. Maybe in a kind of warped way she has saved my life.

'Did you see that? Did you? There is definitely something alive in my bed. Christ, I have never been so degraded.' She trembles in front of me. No sign of an apology I notice.

'Well, you have now, sweetie,' calls Issy.

'Will you shut up,' Penelope screams.

I actually find myself feeling sorry for her. I flop onto my bed, not caring if there are snakes, spiders or cockroaches in it. It feels late. I can hear my father snoring and mother's gentle breathing. A surge of guilt overwhelms me when I realise it is because of me that everyone is here. I may well be the cause of them facing a firing squad. God, it doesn't bear thinking about.

'Alex would be appalled if he could see me like this,' Penelope moans while fidgeting on my bed.

'Never mind Alex,' Issy titters. *'We're* appalled at having to be with you like this.'

I fight back my giggle but she hears me.

'You do realise that you will never work with Alex again. One thing he can't stand is disorganisation and let's face it you're not exactly *Miss Organised* are you?'

I flap a mosquito from my face and wave it in her direction. After all, the least I can do is share.

'He happens to be the last person on earth I would agree to work with after this,' I mumble.

I'm rather pleased to see she is looking quite drab now. Her make-up is beginning to fade and her skin is drying out from the heat. She looks ordinary for a change. Not as ordinary as me, you understand but ordinary enough. She fiddles with her broken nail and looks about to cry.

'Are you feeling okay Libs,' calls Toby. 'That water isn't making you feel funny is it?'

'I'm fine.'

'I love you Libby. I'll get us out of here.'

'And what will you do?' asks mother sleepily in a scathing voice. 'Bombard them with swear words.'

'You may scoff. But when Libby and I are married I'll show you what kind of man I am.'

'Oh, won't that be revealing, Fenella,' laughs Issy.

'And you can shut the fuck up. Don't for one minute think you're getting a bloody invite.'

If only I could go for a walk.

'You think I don't know that you have been making eyes at my fiancé.' Penelope mutters under her breath.

Now what?

'I have not,' I protest, but my blush gives me away.

She laughs and slaps her cheek as the mosquito lands on it. I wriggle uncomfortably in my wet dress. I really am not in the mood for a confrontation with her.

'Alex would never look at someone your size in a million years...'

'I'm not that fat,' I say defensively, while hating myself for doing so.

She runs her fingers through her hair like a comb.

'Can I tell you something Libby? By the way, is that short for a proper name? Only I always thought *Libby* was the make of some kind of milk,' she says condescendingly.

'Elizabeth,' calls my mother, who obviously has bionic ears. 'Rather that than a name of a 1960s Thunderbirds puppet.'

Penelope gasps.

'Let me just advise you, Libby. Alex leads a very high-profile life and he needs a high-profile woman to go with that. When I say *high profile*, I mean someone that can cope with high maintenance and someone who oozes confidence.'

She gives me a cursory but critical look.

'Just look at you,' she hisses viciously. 'You look like something the cat dragged in.'

I fidget under her stare. Did I actually feel sorry for her a little while ago? I cannot think of anything to say. The worst part is that I happen to agree with her. I am just so rubbish and why I ever thought I could be a match for Alex is beyond me.

'Alex has strange ideas about relationships. He doesn't realise that if it hadn't been for me he wouldn't be where he is now. I'm the one the press want to photograph. It's important who he has on his arm. Very important,' she says raising her voice on the last two words.

Issy lets out a loud tut.

'If that's right, why didn't he invite you to the safe house?' I whisper.

She scoffs.

'What makes you think he didn't? Don't be so naïve, Elizabeth. Let's face it darling, I'm premier league, while you're barely third division.'

I'm struck dumb.

'He needs a successful woman on his arm darling, not someone who can't even meet the challenge of a diet.'

Oh, that was below the belt wasn't it? She climbs back onto her bed and I find myself hoping she may get bitten by a cockroach. Yes, I truly believe at this very moment I could gladly watch her eaten alive. What does that say about me? Of course, she is absolutely right. I was stupid to even consider that Alex and I could be a couple. Finally I find Mr Right and I'm all wrong.

'Are you still feeling okay, Libs?' calls Toby.

No, I feel bloody suicidal.

'I'm fine,' I answer, while wishing the water would hurry up and poison me.

Jamie rattles the bars of his cell making us all jump.

'I want a lawyer,' he screams.

'For Christ's sake, Jamie,' shushes Issy.

'We're entitled to a fucking lawyer,' he repeats.

He is quite right, of course.

'Let's hope your boyfriend has arranged one,' says Toby nastily.

'God, what I wouldn't do for a shower,' moans Issy.

'You don't know it was Philippe,' barks Jamie.

'Of course it bloody was,' snaps Toby. 'Else he would be banged up with the rest of us. You can't trust fags.'

'Toby, stop it,' I yell.

'At ease chaps, frayed tempers and all that,' pipes up my dad and everyone goes silent.

That's the thing with not speaking very often. When you do, everyone stops and waits with bated breath for the next words of wisdom. Except in my father's case they don't come. I sigh.

Don't you just hate mistakes? I mean, I don't mind when they are small mistakes but honestly when they are life or death ones it really is not good enough is it. Obviously this is one big mistake. I came to Cambodia to launch a book for goodness sake, and now I'm languishing in some hell hole of a prison. It will be New Year's Eve soon and I feel sure that entertainment will be sparse here in prison. I am dying for the loo. I must not think about the toilet. Not that I imagine they actually have one in here as such. A rattling of keys breaks into my thoughts.

'Your lawyer,' announces the guard and a short, chubby, sweating man walks towards us.

We look wide-eyed at him. His Panama hat sits lopsidedly on his head and there are stains on his shirt. My heart sinks. He takes us all in with one quick glance.

'Monty Snograss at your disposal as it were. Pleased to meet you. You all look very dandy, treating you well are they?'

We all look dandy? He obviously needs glasses. It is late in the day and he is half cut. A born-again alcoholic, just what we don't need.

'For fuck's sake,' moans Toby.

'Monty Snograss?' echoes Issy. 'Dear God, please tell me someone is playing a joke on us?'

'Are you drunk, young man?' asks mother.

Young man, has mother suddenly lost her sight as well?

'Mother put on your glasses,' I say wearily.

'It's the heat,' he explains stumbling towards her. 'You have to keep drinking, so to speak.'

He removes his hat to reveal a shiny bald head.

'Preferably water,' I say

'And not from the sodding tap,' adds Toby.

Monty Snograss whips a flask from his hip pocket and flops onto a chair in the corridor.

'I have excellent news,' he says taking a swig from the flask.

'Thank God. When can we go home?' asks Issy with a relieved sigh.

The thought of a cold English winter is suddenly the most wonderful prospect. I just want to get out of this hot and humid country and back into my lovely cold cottage and soft cosy bed.

'Home, good God, I'm not that good as it were. However, I am brilliant if I say so myself. I pulled you fifteen years. They were all for shooting you so to speak.'

What! Oh my God. But they're sodding Buddhists aren't they?

'Oh fuck,' cries Issy and I hear a thump.

'Is she okay?' I call.

'She's fainted,' replies mother who promptly bursts into tears.

Penelope grabs me roughly by the shoulders and shakes me like a rag doll.

'This is entirely your fault. Do something and get us out of here.'

The shaking has a bad effect on my bladder. I push her more violently than I planned and she lands with a crash onto my bed.

'I can't stay here for fifteen fucking years,' screams Jamie.

'Bad show,' mumbles my father.

'I'll have this country annihilated,' shouts Toby.

'Shoot us? What the hell do you mean *fifteen years*? We can't stay here for fifteen years. I'm almost thirty... Oh God, you have to get us a lawyer,' I whimper.

'I am a lawyer, so to speak.'

What is that supposed to mean?

'But we haven't had a trial yet,' says mother.

I slump onto the bed.

'Ah, trial was denied. Drugs and helping the rebels, you see. Tricky one is that, so to speak.'

Snograss hesitates and then adds solemnly, 'As it were.' I'm beginning to wonder if 'So to speak' and 'as it were' are some kind of code.

'But I wasn't helping them, she was,' Penelope snivels while pointing at me.

'Don't blame all this on my daughter,' yells mother.

Snograss pushes a tissue through the bars.

'I'm afraid sentencing has been made, best to make the best of a bad job as it were.'

'But we're not criminals,' says Jamie.

'No, of course not,' he says with a smirk.

'What the fuck does that mean?' asks Toby.

God, it comes to something when your own solicitor doesn't believe you.

'They surely can't deny us a trial,' I say.

'You can appeal but I've never heard anyone succeeding with that as it were.'

'But what about Alex Bryant, he can tell you I wasn't helping the rebels?'

He shakes his head and swallows more liquid from the flask.

'Ah, yes, couldn't trace him. He flew the nest so to speak. It's not unusual.'

'He wouldn't do that,' says Penelope.

'Seems he has,' snaps Toby.

I really don't believe Alex has flown the nest. He wouldn't just abandon us. If I don't agree with anything else Penelope says, I do agree with that.

'Things could be worse,' sniffs Snograss and sneezes into a tissue.

'Worse,' I cry, 'how could it be worse?'

'Firing squad, that's what he means. I told you they would shoot us. I can't stay here for fifteen years. We will all leave looking like old hags,' sobs Issy.

'Speak for yourself darling,' calls Penelope.

'Now, look here Snograss, there must be something you can do,' says my reasonable father.

Snograss stands up, wobbles and falls back down again. I try to hold back my tears.

'I've done my damnedest, old chap.'

I start to cry.

'Chin up, old girl. The time will fly by. Do you need anything? Malaria tablets, loo roll, ciggies, Gideon's Bible?'

I want to die.

'Oh God,' moans Issy.

'Bible it is then.'

How the hell did I get here? Seriously I am just a girl who likes making cakes and who struggles with her weight.

'We're doomed,' sobs Issy.

My bladder screams at me and I slide down the wall. We are doomed indeed. Just when I seriously thought things couldn't get any worse.

'Jonathan will get us out. He is probably...' begins Issy.

'Oh, he's being held by the army authorities. Didn't you know?' says Snograss calmly. 'I'll pop back in a few hours with essentials. I may have some news on old Johnnie for you then. In the meantime, keep your pecker up.'

He sways to the door and is gone.

'Don't even think of getting your pecker up,' Toby snaps at Jamie.

It looks like we're done for.

Alex

The air is full of smoke. The air-con has broken and I feel like I am banging my head against a wall.

'There is nothing we can do to help you Mr Bryant. The best suggestion I can make is that you leave the country as soon as possible.'

'There is no way I am leaving the country while my friends wallow in one of your prisons. Now, I suggest we find ways to sort this out.'

I'm tired, hot and extremely fed up. The head of police lights another cigarette and I look at Samnang who is getting more uncomfortable by the minute.

'It really is not sensible for you to stay in the city, Alex.'

Don't these fools understand anything I say? I'm speaking in Khmer for God's sake.

'After all, this has nothing to do with you,' asserts the police officer.

'You've arrested my colleagues without any evidence and one of the women you have in custody happens to be someone I am very close to and you say this has nothing to do with me?' I snap more angrily than I intended.

'Won't you please sit down, Mr Bryant. It's extremely hot in here I know. I apologise for the lack of air conditioning. I hope you are not finding it too uncomfortable. Our facilities are not as good as the TV studio I'm afraid.'

Samnang coughs nervously.

'We should get you to the airport, Alex, or a hotel at least. It really isn't sensible for you to stay in the city,' he says again.

'I've got a book conference to attend.'

I have no intention of attending the book conference. But I don't want these corrupt bastard police to know that.

'Safer if you cancel that, Alex. You've achieved a lot with the broadcast. It is best to fly home. Jonathan has just been released. I'm sure once you have made arrangements to go home, everyone else will be freed as well. It's the best thing to do Alex.'

'A very wise decision,' agrees the police officer with a smirk that I fight hard not to wipe off his face. 'I suggest you take Mr Samnang with you before I arrest him. Consider this my favour.'

'If you think I am leaving the country while you have...'

'We're aware that your fiancée has been detained. I understand there is some circumstantial evidence of drug trafficking...'

I bang my hand down onto the table, my self-control evaporating.

'You have no evidence, circumstantial or otherwise, damn you. And you know it. This is some kind of set-up.'

Samnang leans across to me.

'Don't push them, Alex, it really...' he whispers.

'I'll push them as far as I damn well please,' I say fiercely but I know he is right.

Samnang bites his lip and I put my hand on his shoulder.

'I'm sorry. I'm getting a bit irritated with it all.'

Irritated is the understatement of the year. I've had enough of all of it now. What was that idiot Philippe thinking of, buying drugs here? It gave them just the excuse they needed to arrest everyone.

'You know this is a set-up Samnang. They can't touch me after that broadcast so they've gone for the next best thing.'

'Philippe has been deported. I'm sure that is what will happen to Penelope and the others,' Samnang tries to assure me. 'It's just a matter of time.'

'Why don't you take the advice being given, Mr Bryant, and get on the next flight home? I'm sure your friends and fiancée will soon follow. Of course, while you are still here, it will just delay things.'
What the hell? He's damn well threatening me. I fight an overwhelming urge to punch the head of police into tomorrow. I lean across the table and grab his shirt collar.

'Alex, no,' shouts Samnang.

'Are you threatening me, you bastard?' I bark.
Samnang pulls me off. I watch angrily as the police officer brushes down his shirt and rearranges his collar.

'Let's just say your presence here is not helping your friends. Hopefully, they will learn a little lesson about buying drugs in Cambodia.'

'They didn't buy drugs here, you nasty little man and you know that. You've already deported the one that did. If you're trying to manipulate me to leave the country...'

'Now, why do you imagine that we would want you out of the country?'
I bang my fist angrily on the table and pick up my bag.

'Damn you,' I snap and follow Samnang from the room.

'I'll book you on the next flight out,' he says, calling over a tuk-tuk.
I climb in reluctantly.

'We will get them released as soon as you're airborne. I'll let you know.'

'You'd better, and if they don't release them I'll be straight back.'
I grit my teeth and debate whether to text Libby but decide there is not much point. She has chosen that idiot, and there is no way I am going to make a fool of myself over a woman. What on earth she sees in that moron is beyond me. If that's what she wants for her future, so be it. Women, I'll never understand them in a million years. And Libby is more changeable than the weather. I text Penny and hope she has her phone. What will Libby think when she hears I have flown home without even trying to help? She will be judge and jury and decide I am an unfeeling bastard, if she doesn't already think that. It seems she doesn't have a good word for me. If she wants to spend the rest of her life with that idiot, that's up to her. I'm not going to stop her.

Chapter Twenty-Eight

Jamie is a little delirious. He is telling us how we can survive by eating the cockroaches.

'Don't be bloody stupid, the things are poisonous,' says Toby.

'According to you everything is sodding poisonous,' snaps Issy.

'Better to eat the cockroaches than die of starvation,' responds Jamie, in a weird calm voice.

'But we won't starve, stop frightening us,' cries Penelope.

'You don't believe they will keep bringing us food do you? Oh, no,' says Jamie. 'Starvation is the way they do it. That way we may well slaughter each other, you see. You hear about cannibalism all the time in flea-infested prisons like these.'

'Shut the fuck up,' screams Issy. 'You're making me feel ill.'

'Don't worry, I wouldn't eat you if you were the last bugger here, not even if they offered you up covered in tomato ketchup,' scoffs Toby.

'You will, when you're desperate...' Jamie laughs evilly.

'Jamie, do shut up, there is no way we are going to eat each other. Christ almighty,' I say, horrified.

I hear Toby blow me a kiss.

'Maybe not in here, but when we get home, huh baby.'

'Now I do feel ill,' groans Issy.

At that moment the guard unlocks each of our cells and Jonathan strolls into the corridor. We all stare silently at him for a few seconds and I wonder if he is a mirage, if one can see mirages other than in the desert, of course. Issy all but faints at the sight of him and I have to admit to coming quite close to that myself. We have been locked up for hours. The heat is unbearable and our tempers frayed. Even Toby has succumbed to drinking the water. Mother has stated she will never ever travel abroad again and Penelope is going to sue everyone and everything in sight.

Snograss tumbles in behind Jonathan, swaying unsteadily as he does so.

'Everyone, it seems you have been reprieved. Old Johnnie is here to get you out,' he says, gleefully rubbing his hands together.

'It's Jonathan, actually, not Johnnie,' says Jonathan quietly.

'Yes, yes, quite,' replies Snograss.

Issy is frantically fiddling with her hair. Penelope bursts into tears which, for the first time ever, appear to be real ones.

'Oh, thank God, thank God,' she repeats before looking anxiously behind Snograss.

'Isn't Alex with you?'

I hold my breath. I half want him to be here while the other half doesn't. If he sees me now, that really will be the finish. I can't imagine how awful I must look. My dress, now dry, is creased to buggery. My feet are red and dirty and I don't even want to think what the rash looks like on my face.

'Alex is on a flight home...'

'Bloody typical, what a coward,' bellows Toby.

'There is a good reason,' continues Jonathan.

'Yeah, he was bloody scared, that's the reason.'

Issy stumbles from her cell and straight into Jonathan's arms which he opens in readiness. I feel deep envy.

'He has texted you, Penelope.'

Her face lights up while mine must have visibly dropped.

'They took our phones,' moans Penelope.

'Ah, yes, let me get that organised,' trills Snograss.

Penelope shoves her way past me and out of the cell.

'I want to make an official complaint about all this.' She flaps her hand at the guard.

'I think we all do, am I agreed?' echoes Toby. We all ignore him.

Snograss hands me my phone and I hurriedly check my text messages. There isn't one from Alex. I attempt not to let my disappointment show. Penelope jumps on me instantly.

'You were surely not expecting a text from Alex were you? I mean...'

'Of course not,' I snap back and walk hurriedly from the room. I almost collapse as the air conditioning from the outer room hits me. I fall onto a bench as my legs give way. I hadn't realised how traumatic the whole experience had been. Toby joins me and wraps his jacket around me.

'Good job I brought this wasn't it?' he says kindly.

His kindness makes me want to cry. How could Alex just ignore me like this? Didn't our kisses mean anything to him? I know I never imagined his feelings for me. Surely he can't just switch them off. Or had he always felt more for Penelope and was just having some fun with me? Penelope waltzes past with Snograss hurrying behind.

'Get the press on the phone,' she yells over her shoulder.

'If you would just give me five minutes...' he stutters while rushing to keep up.

'You're lucky I'm giving you the time of day,' she snaps, bursting out of the building into the cool night air.

Snograss plonks his hat onto his head and follows her.

'What a prima donna,' mumbles mother as she stumbles into the air-conditioned room. I make space for her on the bench.

Toby pulls me closer and wraps his jacket even tighter.

'How are you feeling?' he asks softly while gazing at mother. Don't tell me he is trying to make a good impression.

'I imagine she is feeling sick to the stomach,' retorts Issy.

'God, I feel weird,' she says leaning against Jonathan.

She winks at me.

Well, this is just great isn't it? I left home to escape my mad parents and my atrocious love life, only to have the lot of them follow me to Cambodia. I'm about to fly home and everyone's life is sorted except mine. Toby has decided he does love me and now wants to marry me. Issy has found her Mr Right and in the most unusual circumstances just as Madam Zigana had predicted. Mother is having her adventure even if it isn't in Kilimanjaro and as for Jamie...

'Ooh, I have a text from Philippe,' he cries.

Yes, well that is about right.

'He's really sorry. He had no idea buying a few ounces of pot would cause so much hassle.'

'No, of course not, what the fuck idea did he have?' scoffs Toby. 'As soon as we're married Libby I will expect you to stop working for that wanker,' Toby instructs, pointing to Jamie.

Penelope wafts back in from outside and gives us a filthy look.

'There is absolutely nothing out there. How are we supposed to get back?'

'I've arranged for transport,' smiles Jonathan. 'It should be here any minute.'

She storms out again.

'Come on Libs, let's go,' says Toby, taking my hand.

I pull it away sharply.

'What's the matter, baby?' he asks.

Can you believe this? I mean, can you believe me, in fact? This guy calls himself 'my boyfriend' and then boldly puts it about with another woman. He then dumps her, at least I presume he has dumped her, to follow me to Cambodia. I'm not even sure he followed me or whether he got coerced into coming because everyone else came. Does this sound like a man I really need in my life? Does this even sound like me? I'm not normally so hard on people. This impassive perspective could have something to do with the fact that I am dying for a pee, have been locked up in a cell without any air conditioning for hours and had to consider eating my mother to survive. I have also discovered that Alex Bryant, a man I really do want in my life, has no interest in me whatsoever. I also think I may be having another period. Only I could start a period whilst incarcerated in a Cambodian prison. If they are not big on toilet paper I don't imagine they will have a Tampax machine in the loo. I stand up.

'I need the loo desperately,' I whisper to Issy. 'I've got the curse I think.'

Mother groans.

'Did you say you had the red rose?'

'Who gave her a red rose?' asks Toby angrily.

'I'm not due for two weeks,' I groan as the cramps overwhelm me.

'It's probably wind then,' says mother knowingly.

'The anxiety and everything,' agrees Issy.

'More likely the fucking water, although I still don't understand what a rose has got to do with anything,' contributes Toby.

'You were a windy child,' continues mother, oblivious to my black looks. 'But that probably had a lot to do with the way you went at my breast. My nipples...'

'Mother,' I snap.

Someone kill me, kill me now.

'You need a loo?' says my father.

I nod and frantically look around. Jonathan points to a door and I fly through it to find myself in a tiny cubicle with a steep step. At the top of the step is a bowl. This is the toilet. I clasp my cramping stomach and turn to bolt the door, except there isn't a bolt. I can hear men's voices and quickly re-contract the muscles I had just released. Now what am I supposed to do? I clamber up onto the loo and practice sitting while holding the door closed with my foot. Great, I can reach. Christ, how is a woman supposed to remove her knickers, pee and insert a tampon while she has one leg up supporting the loo door? I drop my foot and hold the door with one hand while I struggle to remove my panties with the other. A pee should never have to be this difficult. Finally, seated comfortably on the loo, if you can call having one leg cocked against the door as 'comfortable', I finally relax my muscles and sigh with relief. If a woman can cope with this, a woman can cope with anything. I am never going to complain about public loos again. In fact, I am never going to complain again, period, if you excuse the pun. In fact, from this point onwards I am only going to do in life what I want to do. So, that was the moment, right then, right there, sitting on a Cambodian loo, that I decided I was not going to settle for anything less than the best in future. It is amazing what positive power a public loo can have on you when suffering with extreme wind. There is a light tapping on the door and my foot slips dangerously.

'Hold on,' I shout nearly falling off the bowl in my haste to re-establish the foot.

'Darling, it is I, your mother.'

Good heavens, why is she speaking in her posh telephone voice?

'I'll be out in two ticks.'

'Something has happened?'

I remove my foot and quickly throw my hand forward. What does she mean, *something has happened*? I've only been gone five minutes.

'Is it something nice? Like has Penelope thrown herself out of a window?'

'I can't think what has come over you dear. It isn't like you to be so rude.'

I fumble with my knickers and feel the perspiration running down my back. Trying to pull up your underwear with just one hand has to be an achievement worthy of a medal. I hear a sigh from mother and it dawns on me that she probably needs the loo.

'I'm almost done. You won't moan about the loos in Debenhams after you have used this one. You're not wearing your girdle are you?' I giggle.

I open the door and come face to face with my mother and...

'Alex,' I squeal reeling round to head back into the loo.

This is awful I don't want him to see me like this. Mother is bustling around behind me and I turn to her irritably.

'Stop it.'

She frowns and continues pulling at my dress. I slap her hand.

'What are you doing?'

'Your dress is tucked into your knickers,' she whispers breathlessly. 'Not the best impression to make.'

'I look terrible,' I whisper back. 'Don't let him see me like this.'

'But he already has.'

Sod it. I turn to face him, thinking it better he should see my face than my arse. Although on reflection, with the rash all over my face, my backside is probably more appealing.

'I always seem to be bumping into you outside a loo,' he smiles.

'I thought, they said, you had flown the nest and everything.'

Why do I always sound demented when in his company? I can't stop staring at him, and feel sure I must be dribbling. He looks tired but still gorgeous. I wonder if Penelope has seen him and feel my heart flutter at the thought that perhaps he sought me out first.

'You always think the worst of me,' he says abruptly.

I walk back to the rest of the group.

'I'm sure she doesn't. You don't do you, always think the worst of Alex?' says mother, running behind me.

I fumble for something to say but nothing comes to mind. Whatever I say it will come out wrong.

'I assure you, she does. I just wanted to apologise to you, I never meant for you to have an adventure in Cambodia, and to say that I hope you and Toby will be very happy.'

I stop walking and mother bangs into me. He still thinks I am marrying Toby?

'But...'

'I really can't believe you would think that I would abandon everyone.'

'No, she didn't think...' breaks in mother.

'Mother, please keep quiet.'

'I couldn't fly home without knowing, you, well, everyone was safe.'

Christ, am I ever going to get a word in?

'I...'

Why is it I can't construct a sentence now?

'There he is,' roars Toby. 'Have you been molesting my fiancée?'

And that was it. The one moment I had to put everything right with Alex was gone in a flash. You know that feeling, the one where you want the floor to open up and swallow you? I seem to spend my whole life experiencing it. I really don't understand why Toby would think some other man would want to molest me when up until now Toby has had little interest in molesting me.

'Alex,' shrieks Penelope. She charges towards him like a bull. Mother and I step out of the way. She flies into his arms and covers him with kisses. I bow my head and attempt to avert my eyes but he is looking at me.

'I knew you wouldn't leave us,' Penelope squeals excitedly.

'Oh, I'd forgotten all about her,' groans mother.

I wish I could.

Toby flings an arm round my shoulder and I can't somehow find it in me to pull it off. I watch as Alex very gently moves Penelope away from him. She clasps his hand tightly and gives me an evil smile. It seems the premier league team wins again.

Chapter Twenty-Nine

Did I really say I couldn't wait to get back to my lovely cosy cottage in cold England? It is freezing. The olive oil in the cupboard is a frozen block. I have icicles inside the cottage and my pipes have frozen, the pipes in my cottage that is. Even the plumber had a good laugh at that one.

'I bet they're nice and firm then,' he had joked. Don't you just hate smutty plumbers?

Even with the heating on full blast I can't get warm. I wrap myself in my long Marks and Spencer shawl, tuck my legs underneath me and settle back onto the couch with a glass of Chardonnay and a packet of marshmallows. I turn on the TV to watch a New Year's Eve omnibus edition of *EastEnders*. I don't normally watch *EastEnders* but I figure if anything is going to add to my misery then this will. I am going to wallow in my misery. I cannot recall a time when I have been more miserable. Even the butcher thought I looked a bit peaky and threw in half a dozen duck eggs to build me up.

'Have them with your bacon. That will bring the colour back to your cheeks.'

I never thought I would see the day when the butcher thought I needed building up. Every cloud has a silver lining I suppose. Duck eggs are fabulous in sponges. I decide to make one tomorrow. After all, what else will I be doing on New Year's Day? I certainly won't have my head down the loo like everyone else. I've been home for just over twenty-four hours and I am beginning to know just how Jack Bauer feels at the end of his twenty-four. I'm jet-lagged, weary, and still very single. Toby was lovely throughout the whole of the flight but I just don't love him any more. I didn't quite find the courage to tell him this until the taxi had stopped outside my cottage and he was all geared up to come in with me.

'I really want to be alone,' I had said, shivering at the front door.

He stood there, his nose running and unable to do anything because he was holding both of my suitcases. The temptation to wipe his nose had been overwhelming but I fought the urge.

'Now what's up, Libs?' he had asked between sniffs. 'I thought we were getting on really well.'

I had stepped aside so he could plonk the suitcases in the porch.

'Thanks Toby, I really appreciate everything you have done...'

He then plonked his wet lips and snotty nose onto my face and if I had any doubts about breaking up with him they all went in that moment. I stepped back and fell over the suitcases and landed with a crash onto the floor taking Toby with me. At that moment, my neighbour popped by to welcome me home with a Battenberg cake and a pint of milk.

'I saw you pull up,' he said brightly, watching Toby and I struggle to our feet. 'This is all we have I'm afraid, apart from a jar of beetroot.'

'This is great,' I said, taking the milk and Battenberg.

'I hate bloody beetroot,' commented Toby.

'You're not bloody getting any,' I almost said but managed to stop myself in time.

He had followed me, the Battenberg and milk into the kitchen and had filled the kettle for all the world like he lived there. I had taken a deep breath and then launched into my 'it's all over' speech.

'Toby, I really feel we have come to the end.'

'The end of what?' he had asked while popping the milk into the fridge and sniffing a tub of yogurt.

'Our relationship, I think it's time to call it a day.'

'This is off,' he had responded pointing to the yogurt.

'That is exactly what I'm saying. We are off, finished, kaput, over. I don't want to go out with you any more Toby.'

I finally said it.

'Is this because of that Alex Bryant?' he asked while returning the yogurt to the fridge.

'No, it's because of Serena Lambert and because you make comments about my weight and because I don't love you.'

For a moment I thought he was going to storm out, but he put his arm around me and pulled me gently into the living room and sat me down on the sofa.

'Shall I make you a nice cup of tea or something? Have a chocolate biscuit if you like. I promise I won't say anything.'

'I will have a chocolate biscuit if I want one but as it happens I don't. I don't have to ask your permission,' I snapped, jumping up and opening the front door to which he had very swiftly walked through.

'Let me know when you feel better,' he had quipped and I had slammed the door with a scream.

So here I am. Five hours before a New Year, with Chardonnay and a packet of marshmallows for company, and an omnibus edition of *EastEnders*. What more could a girl ask for?

The phone rings and I try to ignore it. It rings incessantly. It has to be my mother.

'Hello.'

'Oh, darling, you're there. I thought you would be out.'

'If you thought I'd be out why did you phone?'

'Well, one never knows. Good heavens, is that your neighbour screaming?'

I turn the volume down.

'It's *EastEnders*.'

She sighs.

'Oh dear, you must be feeling depressed. Why don't you come over? Daddy and I are going to the vicar's for New Year, why don't you come? They're having a monks and nuns party. You would make a fabulous nun.'

She's not wrong about that.

'I wouldn't enjoy it,' I say shuddering at the very thought of it.

'Your father said the same thing. But he's coming. I talked him into it.'

More fool him.

'I don't think he would make a fabulous nun.'

'Don't be silly darling. He's going as a monk. You can't sit at home moping.'

'Yes I can,' I say, reaching for another marshmallow.

After all, I might as well enjoy the New Year as best I can, and then I can start my diet once the celebrations are over.

Mother huffs.

'Are you absolutely sure he is going to marry that Penelope woman?'

I take a large gulp of wine.

241

'She announced it to *The Times*, didn't you see it? It was big enough. You usually read the wedding announcements,' I say eventually.

It had been Jane who had alerted me to the notice.

'What a wonderful way to start a New Year,' she had squealed.

I had only been back at work one day and felt more depressed than ever.

'I only read the wedding announcements in the *Jewish Chronicle*,' says mother.

'But we're not Jewish.'

'I know that dear, but they always seem more interesting as do their dead people.'

Christ almighty, I really should get my mother some counselling.

'How can dead people be interesting?'

'Anyway, I didn't phone you to talk about Jewish people.'

I pop two more marshmallows.

'You mentioned them, I didn't. I don't even read the *Jewish Chronicle*.'

'So, what did it say?'

I sniff loudly.

'I don't remember,' I say, opening *The Times* newspaper.

'Here it is. The engagement is announced between Major Alex Michael Bryant, son of Mr and Mrs Ian Bryant of Derbyshire, and Penelope Katherine Vistor, youngest daughter of Mr Stephen Vistor CBE of Hertfordshire and Mrs Leoni Ann Vistor of Cambridge.' I say with a hiccup.

'I didn't know he was a major and how could they do it so quickly. They've only been home a few hours?' I say, reaching for a tissue.

'Your father thought he was high ranking.'

'And her father has a CBE. I can't ever compete with that. Daddy won't get a CBE will he?'

'Well, he could try dear. Do you want me to ask him?'

Oh dear. I suppose she means well.

'It doesn't matter,' I say, feeling tears well up.

'Well, we could try and get a fake one off the Internet.'

Oh God. I tuck the phone under my chin and unscrew the top off some blackberry juice.

'Promise you'll come round if you change your mind. We're not leaving for another hour. I hope you're not drinking too much?'

'I'm drinking wine and blackberry juice.'

'Oh dear, you'll make yourself ill doing things like that.'

'Doing things like what? I'm drinking wine and blackberry juice, not shooting up cocaine.'

'Oh dear,' she groans. 'Promise you'll come if you change your mind,'

I promise to think about it and put the phone down.

Chapter Thirty

After the omnibus edition of *EastEnders* and what feels like a marathon session of *Strictly Come Dancing* repeats I feel quite exhausted. I check the time and am despondent to see it is only seven o'clock. God, I have another five hours to go yet. I turn the heating on in the bathroom and pour myself another glass of wine and wallow in the bath for forty-five minutes with a Mills and Boon. This just leaves me more depressed. I wander back into the lounge, dripping onto the carpet and flop miserably back onto the couch and glance at the TV where *Bridget Jones's Diary* is now on and Renée Zellwegger is kicking her leg high to 'All By Myself,' which is just what I don't need. My Blackberry trills and I answer the call from Issy.

'I've just spoken to your mother. You cannot stay home on New Year's Eve. That is bloody ridiculous and I'm not having it,' she screeches down the phone before I even have time to say hello.

'I'm quite happy,' I lie.

'Get your glad rags on and some lippy. We'll be there in about forty minutes.'

Oh no.

'No, I don't want to go out,' I whine.

'I don't give a shit what you want. Make yourself glam, you never know who you might meet,' she says chirpily, ignoring my objections.

'I don't want to meet anyone.'

'Not even Bradley Cooper?'

'Oh yeah, right.'

'Be ready. We're going to the Glass Dome. You've always wanted to go there. Jonathan has tickets.'

She hangs up and I am left listening to the dialling tone.

'I already have a ticket,' I whisper to no one.

The Glass Dome. I can't possibly go there. What if Alex is there with Penelope? I will die of embarrassment. I just couldn't bear to see him with her. I look at Bridget Jones who is now flirting unmercifully with Hugh Grant. I switch it off. I drag my heavy body into the bedroom and heave myself into a Christian Dior dress that mother bought me last Christmas and which, until today, I had not been able to squeeze over my breasts. I then lazily blow-dry my hair and drag it up into a messy bun before applying some lipstick and blusher. I spend some time looking at the earrings Alex gave me and finally put them on. I flop back down on the bed and sigh. I really don't want to go to the Glass Dome. I don't believe this. A few weeks ago I would have given anything to be invited to the Glass Dome for the New Year's Eve party. Only three weeks ago I was desperate to go with Toby. I even had high hopes I would be engaged to him by New Year. Thirty minutes later, Issy bursts in with Jonathan and within moments my bedroom looks like a bomb has hit it as Issy empties my wardrobe.

'Are you mad?' she reprimands. 'You can't go in that. You look like an old frump. Are you out of your mind?'

'I really can't go Issy, what if Alex is...'

She gives me a cold look.

'How will you meet anyone new if you're frightened to go places?'

I pout.

'Where's your Wonderbra?' she asks and I feel tears welling up again.

'Don't talk about my Wonderbra. It reminds me of Alex,' I whimper.

She gives me an odd look.

'What about these?' she says hopefully, holding up a two piece.

'No, the top is too low and my tits fall out.'

'You'd be surprised the number of men that go for that,' she laughs.

I give her a cross look and pull out the Jigsaw dress I had bought for the Christmas dinner.

'Perfect,' she smiles.

She hands me a bra, which thankfully is not my Wonderbra. I turn and step into the dress.

'Has Jonathan seen Alex?' I ask, turning for her to zip it up.

'No, I don't think Alex has been in contact with anyone since we got back. He's been busy announcing his wedding, don't forget.'

I wince.

'Don't remind me,' I sigh.

245

'Have you been drinking?'

I titter.

'Ooh yes, and I've been mixing my drinks. I've been drinking wine and black all evening.'

'Is that sensible?' she tuts.

God, she sounds like my mother.

'Issy, it's wine and blackcurrant juice, not an A class drug,' I say with a sense of déjà vu.

She drags me into the living room. I am grateful to get away from the hellish sight of my bedroom.

'Hello,' says Jonathan, looking slightly uncomfortable, fiddling with his tie and unbuttoning his shirt. It is uncomfortably warm in the cottage. No, actually, it is bloody boiling in the cottage. I have had the heating on high for the past eight hours and it's like a sauna. I throw back the last of my wine and allow Issy to drag me outside, where the cold air hits me with such force that I reel. Issy guides me by the arm to the waiting taxi. I feel the effects of the wine and realise I am a little drunk.

'I've got duck eggs,' I announce.

'How lovely,' responds Issy.

'I didn't know Alex was a major, did you know that?' I think I am shouting as Issy backs away slightly.

She shakes her head and pushes me into the taxi.

'Her father's got a BCG, did you know that? I mean how snotty is that?'

'Snooty,' she corrects.

'I think she means a CBE,' says Jonathan.

What does he mean, she? Excuse me, I am here, you don't need to talk over me. Then, to make matters doubly worse, they get all romantic in the back seat. Issy snuggles up close to him and all I can hear are lip-smacking noises. I make a determined effort not to look. Hearing it is enough, seeing it as well will just have me throwing up into my handbag. Don't you just hate smug loving couples? Even worse, don't you just hate smug loving couples on New Year's Eve? It feels to me like the whole world is full of smug loving couples and they are all going to the Glass Dome for New Year's Eve. Hundreds of couples, all holding hands and sidling up close to each other push into the overdecorated building. I predict I will be the only one not getting shagged tonight. I must be the only singleton here.

'Everyone is with someone,' I whisper to Issy, thinking how that sounds like a song title.

'Don't be silly, there are loads of single people here,' she says unconvincingly.

Oh God, to think I've got to be here for another three and a half hours. I would much rather be at home watching *New Year with Julian Clary*. Maybe I can get stuck in a lift or something. Anything would be preferable to standing around with lots of smug, drunk couples who can't keep their hands off each other. I feel quite nauseous.

'Who's that?' whispers Issy, as I trip up the steps and grab the back of Jonathan's trousers for support.

I look to where her blood-red painted fingernail is pointing. A tall handsome man is looking over at us and I recognise him as the man who had been in Dirty Doug's with Alex.

'Keep moving,' I hiss pushing Jonathan roughly from behind. 'I don't want him to see me.'

After what feels like an endless flight of stairs, we push our way through the throng of smug loving couples and find ourselves in the 'Princeton' room where the New Year's party is in full swing with couples smooching on the dance floor to Jimmy Durante's 'As Time Goes By.' I grab a glass of champagne from a passing tray and knock it back in one fell swoop. Issy and Jonathan disappear onto the dance floor and I am left alone. God, I've only been here five minutes and I'm a wallflower. I look around nervously for any sign of Alex and premier league Penelope. There doesn't seem to be any sign of them and I gratefully sway towards a chair. I plonk myself down and place my champagne glass carefully on the nearby table which is piled high with wedding magazines.

'Great idea isn't it?' yells a woman who has placed herself in front of me.

Bloody stupid idea if you ask me.

'Yes, brilliant.'

'I'm having my wedding dress made. I want lots of lace and pearls,' she says smiling widely and showing me lots of gum.

'Lovely,' I say, attempting to gush but it sounds more like a tiny retch. Why I am feeling so horrid? It isn't her fault I have chucked my boyfriend and lost the man I love to the daughter of a CBE.

'I'm having a joint wedding with my twin,' she tells me.

God, how dysfunctional is that. A tray of drinks floats by and I quickly grab another glass and take a long gulp, immediately sneezing as the bubbles get up my nose. She gapes at me and then takes a small sip of her own. I feel mortally ashamed. At least she is getting married, joint or otherwise. That's more than I'm doing.

'I'm not having a wedding of any kind, joint or otherwise,' I say hearing my words slur.

She sits beside me and gently takes my hand in hers. I shall be blubbering into my champagne next.

'Oh poor you, did you get chucked?'

'Yes,' I blubber, 'I kind of chucked and got chucked all at the same time, although I didn't mean to chuck...'

'Honestly men, they can be such bastards.'

I feel myself nodding so emphatically that my head starts to thump.

'Yes, I mean, the one I chucked, or didn't really chuck used me as a plaything, and then he goes and plans his wedding to his socialite girlfriend who...'

'What a pig,' she says waving her fist in the air and sending a tray of savouries flying. One lands on my lap and I pop it into my mouth.

'Yes, he would slice your tongue out with a pencil, he's that mean.'

She gulps. That sounded all wrong. It isn't a pencil is it? I know it's pen something. I finish the wine in the hope it will help me think.

'And her father is CPW, whereas mine is...'

I struggle to remember. This is awful. I can't remember what my father is. She claps a hand over her mouth.

'Charles, Prince of Wales?' she gasps.

'No, my father isn't the Prince of Wales.'

She shakes my hand.

'No, you said her father was.'

'Was what?'

God, it's enough that I can't remember what my father is without her questioning me on everyone else's.

'The socialite, you said her father was CPW.'

Oh God.

'Oh, no he isn't that grand, at least I don't think he is. I've never actually met him.'

Can we please get off the subject of Penelope? I see Toby walking towards us and grab a copy of *Brides* magazine. I sit staring at little net underskirts for bridesmaids when he says.

'Hello Jasmine, how are you?'

Christ, has he forgotten my name already? I lower the magazine to see him kissing the woman on her cheek. He gives me a lopsided grin.

'Looking at more brides' dresses, Libby?'

Jasmine stares at me in wonder.

'Oh Toby, is this your girlfriend, Libby?' she asks, looking all intimidated and star truck. I attempt to stand up in manner of celebrity but my head spins and I fall back down. Toby coughs nervously and smiles at me.

'Libby, this is Jasmine. She works on the paper.'

'Only the letters page,' she says apologetically. 'You're an agent aren't you for Randal and Hobson. I didn't realise you and Toby... Oh God, I'm so sorry. Have you made up?'

She lets out a tiny sob and I put a comforting hand on her arm. The DJ is yelling for everyone to take the dance floor for the next romantic smooch and I see her glancing around for her fiancé.

'Oh,' she swoons, 'this is our song.'

I feel myself go all maudlin when I realise I don't have a song with anyone. How pathetic is that?

'Would you like to dance?' asks Toby, removing the drink from my hand. 'Or are you here with someone?'

I'm about to ask him the same question when I spot Serena glaring at me from the opposite side of the room. He swings me onto the dance floor and straight into his arms. We sway slowly around the room and I struggle to find somewhere for my arms rather than around his neck but there is no way out it seems. If I let my hands dangle at my sides they brush his hips, which seems much worse than winding them around his neck.

'You look terrific,' he whispers with one eye peering at Serena. 'The sexiest woman in the room is dancing with me.'

I step on his foot and he winces.

'And the clumsiest,' I giggle, feeling I have had enough to drink but wishing I could get just one more glass. From the corner of my eye I see Issy shaking her head. It's all very well for her to shake her head. She has a partner for the evening. There is nothing worse than being a wallflower.

'You didn't really mean those things you said yesterday did you? Who will you watch Woody Allen films with now?' he says softly into my ear, while trying to nibble at it. I shudder at his kisses and feel my arms wrap tighter around his neck as the music and atmosphere overtake me.

'You still want me, you know you do. I'll do whatever you want Libs. I won't nag about diets any more. If you stay the way you are, you will be perfect anyway.'

'Toby, I don't know what to say.'

The truth is I not only don't know what to say, I actually seem incapable of saying anything. In fact, if I don't eat something soon I shall be incapable of walking.

'Just say you will give me another chance?'

'Well, I...'

I'm beginning to think giving Toby another chance isn't such a bad idea. I could work hard at staying on my diet and things could be just the way they used to be. We can put the whole Cambodia trip to the back of our minds and in years to come when Alex is on television talking about his books and his activism I can point to him and tell my children how I once knew him and had an adventure. I could help Toby with his writing. It could all be really cosy and loving and I start picturing our marriage like a scene from a movie. Toby tapping away at a typewriter (okay a bit old fashioned but this is how it looks in my drunken daydream) while I'm towelling down our youngest. We smile at each other and Toby asks my advice on the article he is writing and I give a very insightful reply. Toby's lips are softly brushing my cheek now and I sway slightly as my daydream overtakes me.

'We've still got to give each other Christmas presents haven't we?' he whispers huskily. 'God, I know what I want to give you.'

Good heavens and I can feel it too as it presses firmly against my thigh. He turns my head so I am looking into his eyes. His lips hover above mine for just a second and then gently they touch. His hand pushes on my buttocks and I gasp. At that moment Serena lunges towards me and takes me down in some kind of rugby tackle. It is at moments like these that I think being a wallflower is maybe not so bad after all.

'You scheming, conniving little bitch,' she screams into my ear. Her alcohol-fumed breath almost knocks me sideways.

What a bloody cheek. He was my boyfriend first after all. Her fingernails are clawing at my dress and slowly making their way towards my face. My God, she is demented. Her hands grab my head and she attempts to bang it to the floor. There are gasps and lots of oohs and ahs but no bugger attempts to rescue me. I slap her hard across the face sending her reeling back and while she recovers I jump up. Not bad for someone half pissed.

'Let's get one thing straight,' I cry angrily. 'I'm not the scheming, conniving little bitch. You are. You were seeing my boyfriend when he was still with me.'

The music stops and a small crowd have gathered. I frankly couldn't care less any more. I'm sick and tired of everyone taking advantage of me. Serena is leaning on Toby for support, and Toby is looking wide-eyed and open-mouthed at me. Serena's cheek is quite red and I feel rather guilty for hitting her so hard. I look past her to the array of sparkling baubles that hang from the ceiling. I have to blink several times to get them into focus.

'A bit of excitement on the dance floor I see,' bellows the DJ. 'That's the way, let it all out and free your soul for the New Year.'

Christ, what is he on? We all turn to stare at him as he wriggles and jigs underneath the huge 'Happy New Year' banner. Oh, don't you just hate New Year's Eve?

'How dare you,' hisses Serena. 'What's your problem Libby?' she spits, struggling to get up. 'Is it that you can't bear it that Toby is in love with me? He has been waiting for the right time to break it to you and finally dumped you yesterday. Which bit did you not understand?'

Jasmine plonks herself in front of me and points an aggressive finger at Serena.

'How dare *you,*' she fumes. 'Stealing other women's boyfriends. You should be ashamed of yourself. Just because your father is a CPW, it doesn't mean you can walk all over people. Poor Libby has been distraught at losing Toby.'

Well, I wouldn't go that far. A bit upset maybe.

'It's okay...' I begin.

'And it takes a lot of courage to come to a party on your own and be reminded that you're all alone and won't be getting married. It's not easy coming to terms with being on the shelf you know, and all thanks to someone like you.'

Christ, no need to rub it in.

'And she is a famous publisher's agent with famous clients.'
She's getting carried away now.

'And who the fuck are you?' responds Serena poking Jasmine in the chest.

Jasmines face drops and for one awful moment I think she is going to burst into tears. Toby groans.

'Let's get those wriggling bums back on the dance floor girls,' shouts the DJ in a shaky voice.

'It's Raining Men' blares out at us and people begin to slowly drift back to the middle of the hall.

I take Jasmine's arm and turn to Toby who gives me a shrug.

'Well, Toby, it's New Year's Eve, you make the choice.'

Jasmine squeezes my arm while Toby looks decidedly uncomfortable. Serena meanwhile takes a step closer and pushes her face in front of mine and for one frightening moment she comes so close that I actually fear she is going to kiss me.

'He finished with you, don't you get it?' she hisses. Jasmine squeezes my arm even tighter.

'Oh really, is that what he told you?'
I look at the shamefaced Toby.

'Well, you know what? I've finished with him for the third time. Here's hoping third time lucky.'

I pull Jasmine away and head for the ladies, where there is, of course, a queue. Everyone pities me and allows me to the front where Jasmine and I dive into side-by-side cubicles.

'I thought you were great,' calls Jasmine through the wall.

'So did I,' calls another voice.

'Me too,' shouts someone else.

Oh great, I have become an icon for women. This kind of fame I do not desire. I sit on the loo and stare at my knickers.

'Thanks for your support Jasmine,' I call back.

'Oh that's okay. Toby can't help it, you know, he just lacks confidence.'

He lacks something that's for sure.

'Libby, what sodding loo are you in?' yells Issy.
I unbolt the door and swing it open.

'Christ, I disappear to the buffet for ten minutes and you end up in a ballroom brawl.'

We spend five minutes hogging the mirror and complimenting each other before heading back to the ballroom. I stop to check my

Blackberry in the vain hope that Alex may have texted me to wish me Happy New Year, but there is nothing. The time is ten-twenty and I stupidly wonder if he will be under the clock, as he said, at eleven forty-five. Now I am being stupid. The man's engaged isn't he? It was announced today in *The Times* for goodness sake. The New Year will hold many changes for me. I can't possibly go back to work at Randal and Hobson, or if I do, I can't continue to be Alex's agent. I decide to go to the clock anyway, after all, there's no harm in just going there is there? On the other hand, I will just get all upset and maudlin and start the New Year in a miserable state. I spend the next hour avoiding the champagne and the buffet and just allow myself a few peanuts. I closet myself in a corner where I can clearly see everyone, and that includes Alex's old friend. Toby makes several half-hearted attempts to approach me, but Serena puts a stop to each one by either pulling him onto the dance floor, or into her arms for a long smooch. I do not feel in the slightest bit jealous, she's welcome to him. After an hour of this I decide it's probably best to go home and dive under the covers before the clock strikes twelve.

'I'm going home,' I announce.

'Before midnight?' says a surprised Jasmine.

'I'd much rather.'

'I'll get Jonathan to call you a cab,' says Issy giving me a hug.

I walk out of the ballroom, turn left, and glance nervously at the clock. A lone waiter clears some glasses that sit at its base. He gives me a hurried smile and rushes away. The distant sound of music and people shouting reaches my ears. The clock says eleven-thirty and of course, there is no sign of Alex. Why am I so stupid to think he would be here? The music gets louder as Issy exits the hall leaving the door open.

'Taxis are very busy tonight, but one should be here soon.'

'I'll wait downstairs, get some air. Thanks Issy.'

'I'll see you in the morning, well more like the afternoon probably,' Issy says while giving me a long hug.

I force a laugh and with one hand clutching the banister and the other my shawl I make my way down the stairs to the exit passing smug loving couples. I pull the shawl tighter and begin walking to the taxi rank. It is a full five minutes before I realise that I don't have my handbag.

Chapter Thirty-One

Harry leaves the ballroom at the same moment that Libby realises she no longer has her handbag. He is hot and tired and wishing that midnight would hurry up so he can go home. The coolness of the foyer helps a little and he pulls a handkerchief from his pocket to wipe his forehead. A passing woman gives him an admiring look and, not wanting to miss any opportunity, he reciprocates with a warm inviting smile. Harry had decided a long time ago that he was not going to settle down with just one woman, not when there were so many to enjoy. He takes a quick glance at the clock to see how much longer before it strikes midnight. Only twenty-five minutes, and that will pass quickly. His eyes alight on something sitting on the base and he walks a few paces closer to see what it is. He picks up the small sequinned clutch bag and stares at it for a moment trying to decide if it would be impolite to open it. Finally, he clips open the clasp and looks inside. He pulls out a lipstick, a small mirror and some tissues before retrieving what he really wants, a Blackberry. He scrolls to owner and smiles.

'Libby Holmes, well I never, and just where are you?'

He strolls back into the hall and looks around. The place is packed and it is almost impossible to spot anyone. He wanders to the bar, but she isn't there. He sees Issy and approaches her.

'Hi, how are you doing?'

Issy smiles while looking at him warily.

'Hello,' she says cautiously. 'Have we met?'

He looks vaguely familiar but she can't for the life of her think where she has seen him before.

'Sorry, we haven't actually met but I saw you with your friend Libby in Dirty Doug's a few weeks ago. You were talking with Ace.'

Recognition sparks in her eyes and he holds out Libby's bag.

'She left this by the clock.'

Issy groans.

'She was outside waiting for a taxi,' she says. He hears the despair in her voice. She grabs a shawl from the back of one of the bar stools but Harry immediately puts a hand on her arm.

'It's freezing out there; you'll catch your death. I'll go and see if she is still waiting and if I don't find her I'll come back with the bag.'

He sees the relief on her face. He grabs his jacket and runs down the stairs to the exit. In his haste he crashes into a woman who is coming in and knocks her handbag from her hand sending the contents sprawling into the street. After helping her retrieve them he turns to the taxi rank and hurries in the direction of the woman who is walking towards him.

Alex

Alex didn't know what the hell he was doing. It wasn't like him to be indecisive but he really couldn't make a decision, at least, not one that he felt was the right one. It had been a hellish day and his hopes that it may now improve seemed unlikely. What a way to begin a New Year. He'd always liked things in his life to be clear cut. He hated loose ends and right now there were far too many. At least tonight he would be able to clear up quite a few with Penny's parents. Not quite how he had hoped to spend his New Year's Eve. He checked his watch and was pleased to see he was on time. Penelope Vistor opened the door and on seeing Alex smiled widely.

'Oh honey, as always, you are dead on time.'

'I'm never late.' It was almost a growl and she leaned forward hesitantly to kiss him.

'Mummy and daddy are waiting.'

He exhaled and followed her into the lounge where Penelope's parents greeted him warmly.

'Right, old chap, let's get this wedding organised,' bellowed her father.

Chapter Thirty-Two

How could I have been so stupid? Who leaves their handbag behind? I try to recall when I had put it down. Of course, I had laid it on the clock base when I had put my shawl around me. That means I have to go back in and then I will probably miss my cab, and that means I will be stuck at the Dome for New Year with all those smug loving couples. I could kill myself. God, I'm heading towards becoming another statistic. Several drunks lurch towards me and I quickly sidestep them. What am I doing walking the streets in the middle of winter. I'll be mistaken for a call girl next. Actually, there's a thought. I mean, how hard can it be? And of course, there is plenty of money in it. Obviously, I wouldn't go in for that sado-masochism stuff. I'm not into pain or perversion. Shoving a tampon up my fanny is about as masochistic as I'll ever be.

'Hey, how are you doing?'

Good Lord, I've pulled already, nothing like starting the New Year with a bang. Heavens, did I really just think that? I look up to see it is Alex's friend, whose name I can't for the life of me remember.

'Oh hello,' I say pointing to the Dome. 'I'm just going back.'

'For this,' he says holding out my handbag.

'Oh.'

'You left it under the clock.'

'Along with my brain it seems.'

He laughs.

'How are you? I heard you went to Cambodia with Ace.'

Oh and where did you hear that? I wonder. My teeth are chattering and my toes, I swear, must have turned blue. I point to the small café on the corner by the taxi rank.

'I really must go in,' I say trying to stop my teeth from murdering each other.

'Oh God. Yes of course.'

He opens the door and ushers me inside.

'It is a bit cold,' he says draping his jacket around me. I quickly push my frozen hands into the pockets.

'How is Alex?' I ask haltingly.

No, no don't tell me. I really don't know why I asked. I really don't want to hear any more about the wedding.

'A bit pissed actually, haven't you spoken to him?'

Not for several days actually. I shake my head. Best to take the Fifth Amendment here I think.

'Did you see the wedding announcement that Penelope's parents put in the papers?'

Now I'm nodding. It's like someone slit my throat and pulled my puppet strings.

'Talk about *Fatal Attraction*,' he mumbles. 'Do you want a coffee, or hot chocolate?'

'What do you mean?'

'I mean do you want a hot drink, something to warm you up.'

'You said Fatal Attraction, what did you mean?' I repeat.

'Penelope's insane behaviour, don't you agree?'

That she is insane? Oh yes, indeed. I nod, but I have no idea what we're talking about.

'I thought he'd be at the party tonight, he had tickets...' he continues.

I stand up.

'I expect he's preparing for his wedding. I should look for my cab.'

'What wedding?'

For goodness sake.

'His wedding to Penelope, of course.'

'He's not marrying her.'

'What?'

'Didn't you know?'

'Know what?'

'He called it off. She just couldn't accept it.'

Oh my God.

'What's the time?' I scream.

And then it all comes rushing back to me. Madam Zigana's cryptic warning. What was it she had said?

'A few minutes can change the path of your destiny. A few minutes can make all the difference. '

Please don't tell me I have left it too late. Of course, the dashing man, whose initial begins with B, is Alex Bryant. Why did it take me so long to realise?

'Quarter to twelve, why don't you come back for the celebrations.'

'I've got to go,' I say sounding like Cinderella and just to prove it I lose my shoe in the run back to the Glass Dome.

'Look to the clock dearie. Don't forget that. A few minutes can change the path of your destiny. A few minutes can make all the difference.'

Alex, please, please be there.

Chapter Thirty-Three

'There isn't going to be any wedding,' says Alex, firmly.

Penelope gasps and clasps her mother's hand.

'Alex,' she exclaims.

'Penny, we discussed all this weeks ago. I don't understand what you're doing.'

Alex looks at Penelope's parents sympathetically. He realises that the poor buggers have no idea what is going on.

'I don't understand,' says her father, deliberating whether he should hand Alex a drink or not.

'It's simple. There should not have been a wedding announcement. Penny and I discussed the future some weeks ago. Since moving in together it has just not been working for us and...'

'Not working for you,' says Penny softly. 'I was happy.'

'I told you I wasn't ready to take the big step towards marriage and you said you understood. The next thing I know there is a wedding announcement in *The Times*.'

'We didn't know, otherwise we wouldn't have... Oh dear, Penelope, you should have told us,' says her mother falling into a chair.

Penelope glares angrily at Alex.

'I flew all the way to Cambodia to be with you and this is how you treat me.'

'I never asked you to go to Cambodia.'

'Do you know how much the flights cost me?'

Alex sighs heavily. Thank God he saw this side of her before they did marry.

'Well, if you flew Business Class, a hell of a lot I would imagine.'

She squints at him and if he didn't know better he could be convinced she was casting a spell.

'Don't worry, I'll reimburse you,' he snaps.

'I suppose we will have to ask for a retraction on the announcement,' says her mother thoughtfully.

'Tell them the truth, that he broke it off at the last minute,' says Penelope in a pained voice.

'That's not strictly the truth but frankly I don't care what you say.'

'This is a great start to the New Year, that's all I can say Major Alex Bryant,' says her father sarcastically.

Penny, realising she has her father on side, runs into his arms in tears. Alex turns to the small bar in the corner and pours himself a whisky, after all no one is going to offer him one.

'Nobody calls me major, Stephen, and you know it,' he says taking a long pull of the whisky.

'I've told all our friends,' sighs Penelope's mother.

Alex throws back the last of the whisky. He really can't stand any more of this. He had been honest with Penelope. It's not like he had strung her along.

'Tell people what you like. Tell them I'm the biggest bastard that ever lived if you like but just get this mess cleared up.'

He throws his jacket on and wraps his scarf loosely around his neck before walking to the door.

'So I'm a mess now am I?' cries Penelope.

He turns, exasperation written across his face.

'Grow up Penny. It wouldn't have worked. We stifled each other. You don't love me, you love what I stand for and that's not a basis for marriage.'

'Oh, I hate you,' she sobs.

'There are plenty more fish in the sea and better ones,' says her father pointing to the door.

Alex nods.

'Happy New Year to you,' he says on leaving. He means exactly what he says but knows they will see it as sarcasm and cannot be bothered to correct the misunderstanding. There have been far too many misunderstandings in the past few weeks that he is past caring. He checks his watch and climbs into the waiting taxi. Thank God, he had asked him to wait. At this time of the evening it is nearly impossible to get a cab.

'Where to mate?'

'The Glass Dome. Can you put your foot down? I need to be there for 11.45.'

'I'll do me best mate but we're cutting it a bit fine and this snow isn't helping. Meeting someone are you?'

He would like to hope so but he doesn't imagine that she will be there, but it's worth a try.

Alex

I swear there are more people outside the building than there are inside.

'Thanks,' I say, paying the driver and giving him the expected New Year tip.

'Happy New Year mate.'

I push my way through the crowd outside that are happily smoking and shivering. I almost fall over a man who is crouched down helping a woman retrieve the contents of her handbag. I consider stopping to help but know that I don't really have the time. I hand over my ticket as the heat hits me. I whip off my scarf before bounding up the stairs. I look around for Libby but there is no sign of her. My heart sinks. I reach the clock and exhale. I had been holding my breath. She isn't here. What a fool. What was I thinking? She is obviously with that idiot Toby. I check my watch. There are still five minutes. The raucous shouting and laughing from the hall reaches my ears and the temptation to go in for a drink is overwhelming. I've never been so nervous in my life. Surely if she was coming she would have been here by now. Looking at the clock I see it is almost 11.45. I throw the scarf down in irritation. What does she see in him? I look hopefully to the stairs but all I see are drunken couples waiting excitedly for the clock to strike and welcome in another year. A lone balloon floats towards me and I kick it absentmindedly. My stomach grumbles and I realise I have not eaten since lunch time and the smell of food is tempting me. Libby where are you? Buttoning up my jacket I begin the slow descent to the foyer and the exit doors where an overexcited crowd have gathered in the snow. Some are even throwing tiny snowballs. There are no cabs and I begin walking in the vain hope that I may find an empty café where I can get some food and drown my sorrows. Tomorrow I shall tell Jamie that I'm flying back to the States and ask if he could release me from our contract. That will be another business no doubt. Better that than loose ends.

Chapter Thirty-Four

'Bollocks and shit.'

The ice cuts into my bare foot and I want to cry. I hesitate for just a second and look back at my shoe. I debate returning for it but know that I don't have the time. Christ, it would have to be sodding snowing wouldn't it? My perfectly coiffured bun is very much a messy bun now. Tendrils of loose straggly hair hang down my face and my feet are blue, one is a kind of mauve blue colour, in fact. Christ, I feel certain I have got frostbite, which will no doubt turn to gangrene or something worse. That will teach me to run barefoot in the snow. I give the shoe one last lingering look and seriously consider returning for it when Madam Zigana's words reverberate in my head, *A few minutes can change your destiny.* I continue running. I skid into two men wearing dinner suits and they steady me.

'You've dropped your shoe, love.'

I attempt a smile and continue running.

'I can't stop,' I call back. 'The man I love is waiting at the clock for me. I have to get there on time.'

They laugh.

'Good luck, darling.'

'He's a lucky bugger.'

'Thank you.'

Another man who is walking towards me sidesteps into the road and beckons me onward.

'Happy New Year and good luck,' he says saluting me.

'Thank you,' I call back over my shoulder.

My heart sinks at the sight of an overflowing crowd. New Year revellers are spilling out of a nearby pub, congesting the pathway ahead of me. Oh no, this is all I need.

'Excuse me, excuse me,' I shout trying to weave in and out of them.

'What's the rush, pretty lady,' asks a very tipsy man in a white shirt and bow tie. 'Let's buy you a New Year drink.'

'The man I love is waiting for me under the clock at the Dome, if I don't get there on time my whole destiny will be changed.'

'Blimey O'Riley, come on chaps let the lady through. Her destiny depends on it.'

The crowd parts and I cross through in manner of Moses at the Red Sea.

'Thank you,' I shout again, thinking how nice people are.

I don't have time to check my Blackberry. Any hopes I had of bursting into the Dome and skidding to a halt at the clock, in the manner of Cheryl Cole, have all been dashed. It's all I can do to hang onto my shawl. The snow is beginning to fall heavily now and I have to keep blinking it from my lashes. I attempt to hail down three passing cabs but they just drive by. At least running is keeping me warm. The Dome seems so far away. I was sure I hadn't walked for that long. Please let him be there, please, please, God. I'll be a bit pissed if he isn't, especially if they have to chop off my gangrene foot. It would make a lovely romantic story for the papers though wouldn't it? *Book agent and budding journalist loses foot in race to meet fiancé. Frozen conditions cause gangrene for devoted Libby.* Oh yes, fiancé. I think I must be a bit delirious thinking things like this. It's what comes of exposing oneself to bracing arctic conditions.

I arrive at the entrance and skid to a halt as my one shoe slips on the wet slush. I feel my leg go beneath me and then I am flying through the air like an ungainly duck, landing with a thud onto my backside. I now have a purple foot and no doubt a purple arse to match. Wonderful.

'Are you okay?'

I look up to see a young man offering his hand and smiling at me. I take the hand and feel my foot throb as I put pressure onto it.

'You've lost your shoe.'

I've lost just about everything including the feeling in my backside.

'I have to get to the clock,' I say, my throat dry from running.

'You've got time, just under ten minutes now.'

Oh no. I push rudely past him and hobble up the stairs, pass the smug loving couples and attempt to tidy my hair as I go.

I reach the top and pant heavily. He isn't there. He isn't coming for me after all. I slide down the wall and sit staring at the clock which says 11.55. I slowly stand up and hobble to the base where I fall down and study my blue foot. I grab a cashmere scarf that sits on the base and hope the owner doesn't mind but my foot is in dire need of warmth. Before I can stop myself the tears start running down my cheeks. I sit alone with the minutes ticking by and heading slowly towards the New Year and all I want to do is flee but my aching bum and swollen foot won't let me move. Soon the clock will strike and I will enter a New Year alone. It isn't fair. The atmosphere in the hall is electric. Someone hands me a party popper and I wonder if I swallow it, will it blow me up. There are only so many ways you can kill yourself on New Year's Eve and using a party popper isn't one of them. The crowd is getting excited and I lift my eyes to watch the celebrations.

Alex is standing at the top of the staircase. For a split second I think it must be a mirage and that I am seriously delirious. He speaks and all I can think is how terrible I must look. My hair is an absolute mess and my face must be blotchy from crying, not to mention the state of my feet. If he ever did fancy me, he certainly won't any more, not now he's seen me like this.

'You're wearing the earrings,' he says softly.

'Yes.'

'I left my scarf,' he says looking at my foot.

The scarf is his.

'I lost my shoe,' I say stupidly.

The DJ is yelling a countdown and I look up at the clock. One minute to twelve. He doesn't move but continues looking at me.

'Where's your boyfriend?' he asks while slowly moving towards me. My heart starts thumping.

'He isn't my boyfriend. Where's your fiancée?'

'She isn't my fiancée.'

Everyone begins to shout the countdown with the DJ five, four, three, two, one and the clock chimes midnight. There is a loud chorus of *Happy New Year* and an explosion of party poppers. I pop my solitary one and smile at Alex.

'Happy New year,' I say attempting to stand up. His strong arms pull me up and hold me away from him.

'I wonder if you would like to go into the New Year as my girlfriend,' he asks gently placing the shawl around my shoulders.

Am I hearing this? Alex Bryant isn't marrying Penelope at all and he wants me to be his girlfriend.

'Even while a little bit chubby?' I ask.

'Even while a little bit chubby, yes,' he smiles.

'I will diet.'

'Why don't you start the diet tomorrow,' he laughs.

I fling my arms around his neck.

'Happy New Year,' he whispers before his hot lips crush mine.

Just wait till I tell mother that daddy doesn't have to get a CBE, or a BCG for that matter, after all. She'll be so pleased.